INITIUM

IN THE BEGINNING
WAS THE ROMAN ARMY

T W ANDERSON

Matador
9 Priory Business Park,
Wistow Road, Kibworth Beauchamp,
Leicestershire. LE8 0RX
Tel: 0116 279 2299
Email: books@troubador.co.uk
Web: www.troubador.co.uk/matador
Twitter: @matadorbooks

ISBN 978 1838593 636

British Library Cataloguing in Publication Data.
A catalogue record for this book is available from the British Library.

Printed and bound in the UK by TJ International, Padstow, Cornwall
Typeset in 11pt Adobe Jenson Pro by Troubador Publishing Ltd, Leicester, UK

Matador is an imprint of Troubador Publishing Ltd

CONTENTS

THE HILL		1
THE WORD		15
THE OATH		24
THE CHARGE		50
THE AUDIENCE		69
THE VISIT		101
THE DEED		111
THE DREAM		113
THE DUTY		119
THE AFTERMATH		143
THE DELIBERATION – I		235
	II	238
	III	275
	IV	291
	V	329
	VI	333
EPILOGUE		337

Postscript

THE HILL

There was a gully at the bottom where they could rest.

Fatigue, which slowed the reflexes and weighed you down to the dust on which you hardly knew how to sink your aching limbs, had to be resisted. Easier for him than most: he had other things to think about. This was his burden. There could be no let-up. If you weren't alert to every risk and possibility then you weren't doing your job. Keep with it, concentrate, no matter how tired and dehydrated you are. They could be close now, watching, and they'd know how to lie low, to evade if they could, how to fight if cornered. The main band of them had to be somewhere in this maze. Or away, miles away already, slipped through again. Ten to one this would be another wasted effort, designed by demons to sap their energies and morale interminably, until the next time, when they would have to do it all over again. Still it was what they did and what they were paid for, so if you had any sense you accepted and got on with it.

There were worse things in life. And you never knew, one day their luck might be in. There'd be a scrap, rewards of bounty, renown and recognition, even some leave for the luckiest. There was always that chance, and you had to play on it, stress the positive, make sure they didn't ease off. After weeks of tedium in the field, that's when leadership came to the fore, not the routine variety but something deeper. Especially with seasoned soldiers. If you wanted keenness then stick to the green, the greener the better. The older lags knew too well how to get by doing the minimum, to hold back from anything involving extra effort if they could get away with it. At some point with most of them you could get the best of both, that blend of experience and enthusiasm before they got too stuck in their ways.

The building-block which made all things possible was the dependable, self-contained individual who wasn't going to get very far up the promotion ladder, such as it was, but was quietly confident in his abilities, and on whom you knew you could always count. You wanted as many of those as you could get. Still it took all sorts, and you had to work with what you'd got. None in this backwater had ever seen proper action, but he had no doubt they'd perform well if the test came. He'd rather have this lot than battle-hardened veterans, who'd either be over-confident or more likely been around too long and gone the other way, and come to see risk in terms of fairness and survival, which was known often to have been a problem in the great wars of the past. There was a limit to the well of courage for all men.

Yet these particular ones, his own command that he'd trained and brought on and whose interests and futures he'd always tried to further, whether they realized it or not, were his responsibility and his alone. How they'd perform would be a reflection on him. He'd have liked to have been sure, but the fact was that few had experienced real danger. They hadn't seen mass casualties and possibly never would. Their forefathers had fought each other, and knew what it was to be on the wrong end of a ruthless killing machine, when the fortunes of battle went not for you but remorselessly against. They, he too, were lucky, a generation spawned by the great peace which had followed the civil wars. As he looked at them now, each with their own thoughts and waiting for their own next step into the unknown, he recognized the emotion edging into his own: feelings of pride, admiration, identification, and an empathy that could become disconcerting if it wasn't controlled.

Stay with it. Too easy to let the body relax, too easy to lose alertness. You might go through the routine more times than you could remember, march all day, lie in wait all night, patrol, always patrol, then when you least expected it the moment would be on you, the call to action when all would depend on instinct and speed and you hoped you would have enough of whatever it took – quick thinking, courage, stamina …

Stop drifting. What if the intelligence were accurate? Could this, here and now, just for once, just possibly, be the place and the time? Now they'd been out so long, worn out and worn down once more? To be teased then tested by Fortuna in this state – was this to be their lot? And why shouldn't it be? That's how it usually went, didn't it? Not when you were fresh and ready, but when you weren't. Less moaning, it could be worse, everything could always be worse. Yes there was luck, but also the skill of war. You made your own, both. Surprise was the winning tactic, to be sought and maximized on the largest scale down to the least, by them, by you. You looked for it in every conceivable situation, and you assumed they were always trying to spring it equally on you. So you took precautions, and you were a fool if you thought you couldn't be caught napping. Well not on his watch. Not with his command.

Very soon they'd be on the move again, able to expand their field of vision against the heat-haze, clearing the ground for a purpose, carrying out the mission. And if the chances of contact were to prove low after all, so what? It was another day, another sweep. They were professionals if not all volunteers, thorough, patient, ready to keep going time after time. And with no illusions. If they did find these bandits they'd be in for a hard slog, inevitably uphill, a long approach with the danger of snares and ambush at any moment, attack by missiles of all descriptions, stones of all sizes hurled and slung from the heights by determined, resourceful, well-rested opponents. Likely there'd only be a handful, and likely they'd be quickly away again, too quick to bring to battle, up and away to vanish completely ... or lure them on to another ambush...

Surely now they must know the force was in the general area, probably have a good idea of their dispositions and intentions? Could the cordon have been compromised? Could there be any chance of surprise left at all after their labours of the morning, when their movements must have been abundantly clear? And what was Century I up to? They'd been waiting too long for them now, for the signal that hadn't come for so long that it didn't seem likely now it ever would. Had something gone wrong? Was it his own company that was in the wrong place? Had he misjudged the country, where one hill looked very much like another and distances were deceptive? Could Century I have lost their way among the many spurs and re-entrants over on that flank, and borne too far off, out of earshot? Suppose even now they'd made contact, well out of sight, able to crow in the mess hall afterwards that it was they alone who had earned the glory, whilst everybody else had been pissing about and catching up on their beauty sleep. And suppose at that very moment they were fighting for their lives, against a concentration of the enemy way beyond what the intelligence reports had indicated, cursing their comrades for abandoning them in their crisis ...

He was squinting into the glare, up towards the short horizon, when the call came – off to the right, faint but distinct. At last! Recumbent figures were up and crouching against the bank, pulses quickening, fatigue forgotten, alert, expectant. No time to waste. He stood back to better his view against the broad bend of the gully, waiting for the last men to look in before the signal, then in one smooth movement they were up in a muted jangle of armour and weaponry, a shifting of weight to steady the poise ready for the move, and with another short wave of his sword-arm they were clambering over with javelin-butt and shield-base and shaking out silently into skirmishing formation. It was good to be off.

Very soon it was a matter of steady going against the gradient, not too fast, controlling the breathing, keeping an eye on the line as they moved up the long incline, accommodating the obstacles, maintaining the dressing, keeping the momentum going, needing no orders. This was the advance-to-contact, straightforward tactically if tense. They were covering as wide a front as he thought prudent, dwarfed by the scale of the landscape, the flanks wide open. You'd need half a legion to be sure of catching anyone who needed catching in country like this. There were never enough men to do anything properly, everyone knew that. You just had to get on with the task in hand with what you had. And be prepared for anything. So think dammit, think, and keep thinking. If the enemy appeared to one side, right now, how was he going to deal with it? Or directly in front ...?

The enemy! Where were they on this vast primeval slab of hillside? Where might the ground offer them a particular advantage? And where it did, what then? What should he be doing about it? What could he do about it, anyway? And what about the rest of the force? Would the back-stop be in place by now, in the right place, where they needed to be? Would it be strong enough to do its job? Would the enemy concentrate or disperse, fight or try and filter out? And what if they were more numerous than they'd been told? Never mind the usual handful from the briefings – could there be rather more about these hills than they might expect, concentrated, enough to take them on and check them, even push them back down the hill, perhaps to win those vital moments of delay which would allow the bulk of them to breakaway to the rear? So was he over-extended? How was he going to close his line up if they did become closely engaged, with control lost in the ensuing confusion? What if it were the main body they were facing, about to come right for them with a wild headlong charge down the slope, straight through his scanty ranks to effect a break-out, to their freedom and his lasting disgrace? That was the trouble with lightly-armoured garrison troops in foreign parts – fine for a bit of rock-scrambling in low-intensity operations, but always vulnerable to a serious encounter with a capable opposition. Where could he fall back to if they had to re-muster? What would …?

Such were his jostling preoccupations as he worked increasingly hard to keep up, trying through sweat-soaked brow to scan the slope ahead, concerned about the extremities beyond his line-of-sight, willing the NCOs to keep in eye-contact, stumbling over dislodged stones and scratched about with thorns. He was fit and lean enough for his age, but this was becoming a real effort, and he was conscious of some consternation in having to admit it to himself. Soon he was having to draw on all his reserves to keep up. What good boys these were, doggedly making their way up to the objective, ready for anything the enemy could throw at them. Good soldiers all – dregs from the city slums, artisans from the small towns of Latium, labourers from its farms and estates, used to few comforts, and now to monotonous rations, harsh discipline and the hostility of an unforgiving people in an unforgiving land. He told himself he knew them better than their mothers, knew they respected him for a fair officer behind a detached and bluff exterior, that he wasn't going to get them all killed through vainglory or total incompetence. And what of that? Was he flattering himself? Was he really good enough, worthy of them, despite his experience and for all his half-hidden concern for them? What experience, apart from Gaul? Wasn't it the truth that all those early years on the cold barbarian border after Germanicus' time had been almost completely, boringly, uneventful? … Concentrate. Control your breathing. Time it with the step. Left foot up, right foot up, left foot, right …, breathe in …'

They were aware, some quicker than others, of part of the hillside detaching itself, gathering pace towards them with an unfamiliar clattering which quickly became an ominous rumble, the spectacle surreal, as though all senses had to be momentarily frozen and nullified before the course of the object, an enormous boulder big enough to flatten a man, could be fully ascertained and natural reactions kick-in. In the event those nearest had ample time to dodge aside as it thundered on past and down the slope in a cloud of dust and debris. Crude and ineffective, he thought, but an unmistakable statement of intent nonetheless. There was no doubt at all now, they were properly engaged. The enemy wasn't just in evidence – they'd obviously got the measure of their pursuers. Strung out, almost lost against the immensity of the steep hillside, and with any surprise they might have hoped for now completely gone. Ahead it was all unknown.

Three or four darting figures had gone to ground, slightly left. Rock-pushers. Meaning what? – an outlier for a main position? If so the perpetrators might be avoiding falling back towards it, and it could be anywhere up there, but perhaps if anything more off to the right where the ground looked as though it might rise a little further, beyond their view. The plan had been for the main force to approach the feature from the north, but the spurs he'd seen at a distance earlier would certainly have slowed them. Could they have been forced to make a detour, taking themselves further out and beyond tactical reach, too distant to be any help? No matter. He couldn't let the others' situation concern him now. All he could do was keep his own company going, keep going at best speed and hope they'd have enough left in them for the fight ahead.

A little later they were over the main convexity of the slope and able to get a better sense of their situation. Far below, in the scanty shade of a ruined olive grove, he could make out the command and support echelon with its troop of Samarian cavalry; but of Century III anywhere on that south-west side, even allowing for the limited view there was not a sign. What if they hadn't heard the signal? Of course, the breeze! The slight breeze must have backed during the afternoon. The orders had been one call only unless there was an emergency – but what was this if not an emergency? There was no point in any attempt at stealth any more, he had to get Festus up somehow to secure the left flank whilst pushing on himself and maintaining the momentum of the advance. It was vital to close his part of the noose even though he couldn't be sure the other centuries were anywhere near. He might be on his own but it was a risk that had to be taken.

Wherever the others were, for Century V it meant closing with the enemy as quickly as possible now. He warned the trumpeter off and pointed the direction for the man's efforts with his sword. A chortled blast rang down the hillside, barely to parade ground standard but it would have to do. Damn! He should have done that the moment they had been discovered, but better late than never and the delay shouldn't make that much difference. Festus would respond in accordance with the co-ordinating instruction – wouldn't he? Though would he have heard at that distance? No time to worry about that. Press on, press on.

The great hillside was opening up before them now, the broad summit ahead and slightly right, the tops of the broken spurs just visible before they fell away on that side. If the enemy were on the crest, or lying low this side of it, surely there would be some sign of them by now, a head or two, even the smallest movement? If they had a clear line of escape they might be off already, making best speed along the ridge that ran away to the west, into the endless hills beyond and the safety of the coming night. But there were no visible defensive positions, and no obvious cover which would allow the enemy's retreat over the summit without being seen, yet with the sun still blazing in their eyes and casting dark shadows before them he couldn't be sure … and where had that boulder-party got to? He thought he'd marked the ground, but now further up the slope he'd lost it...

It didn't matter. The only thing that mattered was the enemy's main body, because there certainly would be one and it couldn't be far away now. For safety's sake he ought to be closing up, at least down to javelin's length, but with still no sign of the foe he couldn't do it yet ... he had to locate them before they could be fixed and engaged...

Where were they, for the Gods' sakes? Would they stand and fight? If they'd bolted, and if Festus had managed to warn the command group as planned, there was still a chance of maintaining contact if the cavalry could cover enough of the defiles on that front, but no enemy would venture into the plain beyond unless forced. He'd hide-up in the numerous caves and bolt-holes which riddled these hills, and as they knew only too well, trying to search everywhere with limited manpower was well-nigh impossible. If only the whole Cohort were here! They might then have had a chance of sorting these bastards out once and for all ... and where the hell was Century I?

And then ... at less than a hundred double-paces, heads and shoulders started to bob up and down over the crest-line and the first arrows came, blurs of shaft and feather from out of the sun, whooshing past the ear, thudding into shields, striking the rocks around and behind them. It was useless trying to pick the sight-lines up, and if you did it was only luck if you were able to move your shield up in time to stop an arrow in the face. Even more disobliging were the slingshot which rattled invisibly against them and of which there seemed an inexhaustible supply.

... To close the line up, or not? Not yet. He had to be sure of the full extent of the enemy position. No choice. They had to keep climbing and take it, there was no other way. A man dropped on his right, another on the left, spinning round and crying out with the agony of an arrow through the shin. On, on, keep on! Whatever happened they had to keep going steadily now, don't try and go any quicker up the gradient, just keep going, keep going, steady, ignore the casualties around you, hope it won't be you, close with the fiends that are taunting you with such impunity, in full view now, brandishing their weapons, screaming and hollering, rising to the challenge, taking you on, almost in range, almost there...

The trumpeter was totally blown. Nothing for it but somehow to find breath himself, find it from somewhere, make the superhuman effort. 'HAAAAALT', the loudest he could manage. Then: 'Prepare to assault'.

Across the ragged line men knelt, sheltering behind their shields, sticking to the drills for their lives now, grasping the javelin for the throw, waiting for the command. He held as long as he dared, for breath and strength, conscious all the while of their predicament and the mounting casualties, knowing he had to wait as long as they possibly could if they were to achieve any effect. Longer, just a little longer, more time for breath, a little longer ... He looked at Cornelius, no need for words, this would be a fight to the death, it was all or nothing.

The enemy were more numerous now, grown from nowhere, sixty or seventy at least, bursting with action, closed-up, well-armed and very definitely with the tactical advantage. At least he now knew where they were. And now was the moment, but they would have to reform quickly, on difficult ground within missile range and with an enemy quite capable of coming for them at any instant, with any sign of retreat on their part liable to invite the break-out – which if it came would be impossible to stop. He couldn't stay in extended line any longer. He had to get the flanks in. And press forward with the charge, if such description could be applied to the laboured movement they'd have to make up this never-ending slope. Just get the flanks in soonest and keep going. The only option.

Orders were shouted down the line against the din, acknowledged, the last long pause for breath, chest pounding, mouth bone dry, tongue cleaved to palate.

On the command the centre sections rose, ten paces up at the best attempt weary limbs and spent lungs could manage for the double, with super-human effort the loosing of the volley, ragged but effective, enemy falling or throwing down their shields transfixed and useless, the flanking sections coming in behind, another ten paces, another volley. Hold it. Rear ranks forming, passing through, taking so long, so long, men falling, the last sections in place now, all the while wild shouts from the furious enemy as the gasping but grimly silent century, now compact in two close-order ranks with shields nearly locked, the cheer on the advance, the abandon of battle as they began to close, the battle cry as they rushed the last few yards, strength and breath drawn from resources beyond mortal endurance, swords now, a wild hullaballoo of yelling and shouting as every man faced a desperate life-or-death encounter of sword and spear on shield, sword on sword, shield on shield. He was through to the front, parrying, thrusting, killing, conscious of a man going down next to him, a flash of steel as the heavy spearhead lunged towards him, a bearded face contorted and screaming, the killing thrust from nowhere, both arms so leaden they seemed incapable of function, Cornelius up with him, the wild visage tossed upwards and away in shock, another hirsute savage, huge stone raised behind his head, struck down before the full force of release, bodies tumbling in confusion, all order gone, just kill, dodge, parry, kill, in a frenzied time-lost flailing melee. Then gradually a semblance of order, the closing of ranks again as they stepped over the dead and dying, the discipline of the short stabbing thrusts that none but the best could withstand, the sense of forward progress. And then, and then, by all the Gods – a cheer somewhere ahead, and the helms of Longinus' double-century appearing above the rabble, beautiful, strong, orderly – their salvation. Never in their lives had they seen anything so wonderful. Gasping torsos found new strength, the certainty of victory spurring them on, the two disciplined bodies converging now, the enemy trying to escape, more cut down, then as if all had been pulled by a string, everywhere arms and legs slowing, the great whirring body becoming isolated actions, finally becoming almost still.

The tumult had subsided.

He rose to his feet, barely able to stand through weakness and exhaustion, trying to staunch the blood with a grimy neckerchief. With one last effort he managed a final hoarse command.

'Don't kill him!....'. For he knew his soldiers in this state would certainly do so if they weren't checked quickly. The battle wasn't entirely done yet: the last handful of their enemies stood cornered and blown, wild, proud, brave, dangerous, likely to take their own lives at any moment rather than be taken alive.

For what came next he had to give Longinus credit, though he must have rehearsed it. But then that was why Longinus Sdapeze was their Senior Centurion – worldly-wise, cynical, cunning, organized, well-heeled, always the winner – their veritable Dacian Odysseus, capable beyond his absurd youth, marked out for a golden future. He had had the foresight to practise it, and when the moment came his men pulled it off superbly. True they still had plenty of puff, but it was as slick as anything he'd seen in peace or war. One moment the cornered and desperate remnant was screaming animal defiance, weapons at the ready. The next a section advanced and loosed away devastatingly at short range, while another quickly closed in with nets and yet another went in with the sword as gladiators on wild animals, dispatching individuals as ordered. And it was all done, but for one still alive, the identified one, writhing and roaring like an enraged beast whilst his captors pinned him down.

It was finally over.

For a time it seemed the world had stopped. Everywhere men had sunk to their knees or lay prone in exhaustion. As limbs came back to life and they rose and began to move about, knots and clusters began to form and mingle, and then as if by some mysterious command and as one body both companies began to cheer, beating their swords on their shields in triumph of victory – savage, bloody, atavistic victory. They had won, after weeks of effort and danger in this god-forsaken wilderness; they had persevered, stuck it out, and eventually run their foes down. In open battle they had been severely disadvantaged – or at least Century V had been – yet had prevailed. They and their leaders had done it together, but chiefly it was they themselves, the soldiers, who had achieved it, by their training, by their devotion to duty, by their own courage and prowess. It was their moment, and they would celebrate it, that short glorious moment in all their lives. Then as the demonstration gradually subsided so the leaders started to move among them, with quiet words, hands on shoulders, rank put aside, the brotherhood sealed, the code upheld, honour and glory won. They had proved themselves, and their pride would now be forever justified. The wider world didn't matter. Not the Emperor, not the Eternal City, not even the Cohort or their century, though these last came close, very close. They had done it for each other, as soldiers and as only soldiers could ever know. It was something beyond description, more meaningful to them than any words could describe, and more profound than any of them could possibly have explained, or wanted to.

Sergeant-majors' commands brought them back from that short suspension of reality. The hierarchy re-asserted itself. And they started to function as two units again, tending the wounded, recovering weapons, sweeping the area for any enemy who might have escaped. They took note of the cunning way they had used the slight hollow of dead ground to their advantage, gave grudging respect for the fight they had put up, viewed with satisfaction the bloodied bodies which lay like stock felled in a butcher's yard, took the scene in so they could remember it to their children should they ever be fortunate enough to live a normal life one day. And thanked the Gods for their preservation and deliverance.

It would take some clearing up. The Century had been lucky – they could have had many more casualties. But too many had been killed or wounded, one of whom they'd had to put out of his misery, and some would not be soldiering again. It had been the biggest fight of anyone's experience and the biggest action for the Cohort in nearly thirty years. Longinus of course had done well as befitted his station and reputation, and had sealed the day in style, but everyone knew it was Century V which had borne the brunt and earned the principal honour. As for Festus, there had been much ironic cheering as his men eventually made the scene. They had caught and killed the rock-pushers, who had almost run straight into them, but he was furious for missing the main action, and had to be content with stretchering casualties down the hill and disposing of the bodies. Such were the fortunes of war.

It took a little while in his daze for him to realize from which particular part of the action the mangled gash to his upper arm had come, how the simple leather braid had probably saved him. Now in the aftermath it hurt more than anything he could ever have imagined, and would not stop bleeding badly unless he held it up, which soon became impossible. But they made him eat honey until he gagged on it, and dressed his wound tightly with it too, and told him he would live.

*   *   *   *

Desperately tired, shaky on his feet and with the pain throbbing unbearably, he picked his way slowly among the camp fires under the ancient olives he had looked down on a few hours before. The Prefect had been cock-a-hoop and most complimentary. The mission had been amply achieved, the Cohort had done exceedingly well and the message of success long since sent off to HQ.

He had been occupying himself punctiliously in passing these congratulations on to the other casualties, which was the only useful thing he could do. With the Century under Cornelius' capable command for the duration, the care and morale of his fellow-injured would be his pre-occupation now. Every one of his men had fully justified his confidence, and he would repay the compliment now. Truly they were a band of brothers, and in their shared condition the casualties would soldier on together in their own way. He had something else to do first however, something that had to be done before he could allow himself to succumb to the pain-filled night which awaited.

*   *   *   *

He stood the guard easy. In the near-darkness the net stirred. Its occupant could get to its knees but no further, tethered, spitting with rage. Were it not for the savagery of the fight and the blunting of all emotion, he might have had to confess to being a little unnerved when confronted by such enmity and brute menace in close proximity. For the victor, elation despoiled by loss and anger did not make for much magnanimity. The creature appalled him.

'So you're bar Abbas', he said, bending close to meet the white-eyed stare head on. Then slowly, deliberately, he said: 'I ought to kill you now – and save everyone the trouble'.

He wished he could have drawn his sword though he barely had the strength, and it would not have been a moral victory to unsheath and not use it. The spoken threat had been barely credible, but he'd had to say it regardless. The loathsome object crouched at his feet had to

13

know some fear. He stood there for a moment imagining the moonlit glint of the silent blade disappearing slowly to the hilt, the grunt and exhalation and expiry, the satisfaction as the job was done. Instead he had to content himself with all the contempt he could muster.

And walked away.

And he truly wished he could have done – killed him that is, for his dead soldiers' sake, though he knew his words had been but show and that the object of his disgust knew it too. If there was any justice the matter would have been settled very quickly – the sword-thrust through that vile and hateful body, the savouring of its dying moments as justice and revenge took their retribution. The man was a disgusting fanatic, an extremist renegade who had placed himself beyond any appeal to reason. His compatriots could keep their own ways, that was alright, but those who offered armed resistance to civilizing power had to be treated as the scum they were. Their own rulers recognized this. Why couldn't these maniacs see how pointless it all was, how futile the bloodshed they were prepared to inflict, not just on the keepers of the peace but on their own people too? Their claim to patriotism was false. Whatever they thought they were fighting for they were also cowardly robbers and murderers who wouldn't come out and fight like men, outlaws who forfeited any right to life. The only sensible solution was to kill them at every opportunity, though affairs of state had a habit of overriding the unsullied simplicities of military solutions. Prisoners could be useful for intelligence or hostage purposes, but on the whole there was only one way of dealing with those who sought to maim and kill and then run and hide. Orders however were to be carried out without question, and if the chain of command had reason to want this man kept alive then that was what had to be done.

*　　*　　*　　*

For the rest of his life he was to wonder whether he shouldn't have carried out his threat, that night in the desert hills west of the great salt sea – and to hell with the consequences.

THE WORD

'Yes, it's true. All of it.'

He went on: 'You know my man Matthias – in his fifties now and been with me and Sabena since we got here, through thick and thin. You couldn't ask for anyone better, in fact they've both been superb. He's one of those fellows – you know, really loyal and supportive, not just because it's his job. If our fates had been reversed in some drawn-out Saturnalia I don't think it would be any different. He'd do anything for us.'

'As a good slave should! That's the deal. Don't come back as one in your next life, that's all.'

'You'll never change – Senior Centurion … Sir. You'd go to the ends of the earth for the least of your soldiers if you thought they were worth it.'

'You'd better remember the pecking order round here. Good job I tolerate my inferiors – when we're not on duty. Go on, you're dying to tell me anyway. I may as well get it from the horse's mouth. Your arm's looking good.'

'My imperial award. I doubt there'll be any other.'

'You're probably right there. Well go on …'

'It was a few months after we'd got back to barracks. I was on the mend, life was almost back to normal. Largely down to my loyal household and the man who kept it running behind the scenes. It kept us all going during a difficult few months. Anyway he went down with some peculiar illness, though it wasn't a fever or anything like that. Overnight, he just seemed to be paralyzed – couldn't move, hardly speak even. So there we were, all his own family and everybody, all fussing

15

round trying to do our best, but to no avail. Naturally I had the camp medic look at him, but of course he isn't much more than an orderly and he couldn't do anything, so I sent for the local quack, who bumbled about and gave him some concoction or other, but it was all useless.

'This went on for several weeks, with old Matthias getting weaker and weaker by the day, everyone upset and starting to feel resigned to losing him. We did the best we could with the practical stuff and to support his family, but knowing he couldn't be with us much longer. He really did seem a gonner. Then one day I was in the lines and intelligence came of a group of locals coming down from the north, led by a preacher or suchlike, with a reputation for casting out bad spirits, healing the sick and all that sort of thing – you know how these people like their ascetics and preachers. He'd been drawing crowds in the hills for some time by all accounts, with quite a following and the whole countryside flocking to hear him. I'd already heard about it, so when the news came that he was actually nearing the town I thought "What have we got to lose? I'll go and see him, I owe it to my servant in his hour of need." So I did. I took a couple of men from the guard and headed for the market place straightaway.

'They couldn't have been there long but already there was quite a large crowd. It quickly gave way before the sight of us, of course, and before I knew it there he was – I knew immediately it was him. As tall as me, plain dressed, calm, with a presence that really struck you, detached in some odd way, with a composure I've never quite seen in anyone before. He showed absolutely no surprise to be confronted by Roman soldiers, or indeed by what I was about to say.'

'And what did you say?'

'I addressed him by name – Yeshua. You could hear a pin drop. He just stood there, listening. I said I'd come to see if he could help, that my servant, a good man and dear to me, lay desperately ill, unable to move and in great suffering. He asked where Matthias was, and I said he was in my quarters, then he said he'd go and help him, and made as if to start walking there and then, and I said "No!" That would have been unthinkable, especially with that crowd about him.'

'Too right. In company with an occupier? There'd have been a riot.'

'It wasn't like that.'

'They'd have turned in the blink of an eye.'

'So I said I didn't expect him to enter my house, but that he didn't need to, all he had to do was say the word, since I too was used to giving orders, and that as a man of authority also his word alone was sufficient.'

'Did you have to be so damned obsequious?'

'Respectful, I think. You couldn't do any other. He had such an aura of calm and dignity about him, as though he was with us in person yet somehow not confined to just that moment or those surroundings. I don't know why I said it – I'd had a sort of intuition, I suppose, but it just came out. All I know is that when it did, I really meant it, all that mattered right then was Matthias, and that I myself and everything I represented were completely incidental. He looked directly at me and said "Go, it will be done as you have believed". His very words. You can imagine the intake of breath, the sense of shock and total astonishment from everyone around.'

'Not surprising. Firstly you go and abase yourself to a Jew, then you dive headfirst into the thick of their religion, in public. Not to mention putting your escort in danger.'

'I didn't abase myself. I just treated him respectfully, man to man. It was all so quick and spontaneous, there was nothing contrived, no hostility from anyone. They weren't interested in me. Have you ever heard of these people behaving like that?'

'Like what?'

'Listening to all this without any kind of hostility towards me, or to him for that matter for passing the time of day with me. There was no chanting, intoning, banging heads against walls. It was just curious, normal people, excited to be caught up in something new and very special, and that they were being witness to it. It was a moment of expectation, even goodwill.'

'They were Galileans, weren't they? Not the hardliners we get down here. Anyway, you went home and there was old Matthias dancing around his bed.'

'Yes. I mean no, he wasn't, but he was up, he was talking, asking for water, clasping his loved ones to his bosom just like you or I would. He was cured!'

'OK, so your old servant who'd been a bit krank clearly staged a good recovery. Good news. But it was a coincidence. It happens all the time. People get sick, they recover. Even with serious illnesses people often seem to get some sort of respite. Whenever anything goes well, especially when it's clearly beyond our own control, we think it's this or that God that's smiled on us, and we thank them for our good fortune. And when anything goes wrong we see it as punishment and retribution and wonder what we've done to incur the Gods' displeasure. But anyone with the slightest sense knows there's no point trying to find any logic in it. Things either go well or they don't, no matter what we ask. When you had that conversation with the Galilean it was what you wanted to hear, so when you found your man alive and kicking of course it made you wonder a bit, especially in the charged atmosphere you experienced. But your servant was obviously going to get better anyway whether you'd gone off in search of this prophet or not – or been a hundred miles away and completely unaware. It was a coincidence, that's all.'

'But Matthias spoke and asked for water, and then got up, at the very moment I was with the preacher! I worked it out. The very time. Yes you're right about staying rational, but that is the fact. That's all I can do – tell it how it happened. I know that something made me seek him out that day and convinced me it was Matthias' only chance – and I had this insistent feeling that all would be well if only I could get a few moments in this man's presence – to hand him the burden, as it were, which was certainly beyond me. And then when I was actually there everything seemed to fall into place. There was an immediate sense of relief and calm, that all would be well. I only had to let go of my doubts and inhibitions, and ask. And with him standing there before me it all seemed so obvious, so natural and unpremeditated. I don't know what made me suddenly get it into my head that I had to do this – I just knew I had to do it. Do it, and believe. I had to believe that Matthias would recover, or there'd be no point in asking. Or else what did draw me – what was I doing there?'

'Don't we all have to believe? In Jupiter and Juno and the rest, if they are to show us their favour?'

'You just said "no", unless I'm much mistaken.'

'No I didn't. What do you mean?'

'First you talk of the gods, then in the next breath that it's all rationality and luck, and coincidence.'

'I suppose it's a matter of which Gods – and when reason becomes faith and faith reason.'

'That's gibberish.'

'We all have to believe in something Favonius, or else how do we cope with this big bad world? We need something we can all believe in together, to unite us and keep everything in its place. How do you think Rome, the Army, the State, civilization itself, could ever operate without the festivals and the temples and the great panoply of state religion if nobody believed in anything? And why not? Why shouldn't we? We might just as well put our faith in the Gods of our ancestors and what we were taught as in anything else.'

'Even if they're not entirely true?'

'Who are we to say they're not true? Wiser men than us have believed since time immemorial. It's a foolhardy man in this life who casts off divine protection.'

'Maybe. But then you can't believe in divinity on the one hand and rationalism on the other at the same time, can you? Not if you really think about it.'

'I don't see why not. Are you saying the just don't deserve to be heard, or that the bad shouldn't get their just desserts? We need to know the Gods are on our side, Favonius. You mustn't allow a man to perjure his soul, when he might be making the mistake that will not just bring catastrophe down on his own head but, if he's important enough, damn his whole tribe to the torments of Tartarus.'

'No, but you can try and reason with him. And what were the gods up to when our forefathers were suffering war and pestilence? Yes we kept winning through eventually, but did the civil wars have to last so long? Did so many innocent people have to suffer? And why didn't Jupiter save the Greeks from Roman arms when he was their mighty Zeus – or doesn't it count when it's an enemy we're talking about?'

'Because without the Gods things would have been so much worse! Favonius, we're born into this world and we accept the way it is – because that is the way it is. And we have faith because we have to believe in something, or else we're alone, like lost children, unable to see what's in our best interests and incapable of the necessary actions. It's only human to believe the Gods are on your side, that things will work for the best just so long as we give them their due. If it's reason you're looking for, this is enough. Didn't the victories of the past all come from some degree of tribulation? Didn't right prevail all through those times, which meant the suffering was worth it in the end if only men stayed strong and believed? And if you're a Greek, don't you have to take the longer view and submit to superior power as part of the divine will? – much the better for civilization if your own *genius* can be adopted and spread to new spheres of influence by those best able to do it? Didn't we have to take up the Hellenic mantle if Rome's great destiny was to be fulfilled? Anyway the Greeks asked for it by destroying Troy, and letting Aeneas free to start something bigger than any Greek could possibly have imagined. The Gods enjoy a good joke. Better ask what they haven't done for us, I'd say, rather than what they have.'

'Even though it's all a matter of luck?'

'But it wasn't. We're here now because one by one our enemies have been overcome by the vision and fortitude of our ancestors, but ultimately by the favour of the Gods. Look, it's a matter of recognizing the reality which all men believe, which is that life revolves around the fates and how dutiful we are to the Gods in seeking their protection and guidance. Nobody can explain it, or tell you how or why. It's just the way it is, and probably the only truth that matters. What you've just described to me about this Galilean vagrant is just another manifestation, isn't it? You want to question the existence of the Gods, yet are quite happy to accept another version of the divine which happens to suit you.'

'It's not a question of suiting me. It's just something of which I have first-hand personal experience – that's why I'm affected by it the way I am. It's been involuntary, the evidence before my eyes. I can't just walk away from that.'

'Believe what you want, but don't mock your ancestors, who won sufficient favour to beget you and send you out to go and do the same and pass the baton down to your own descendants. My advice is just let it ride – there's safety in crowds, and usually wisdom. Do what everyone else does, give the Gods their due, hear what this man from Galilee has to say if you really must, but don't get carried away, and be very careful who you talk to. There are times when it doesn't pay to think too deeply, or you'll end up going mad. Navel-gazing's an over-rated indulgence – it doesn't get anybody anywhere.'

'You can't experience anything like that without being forced to think a bit. I would challenge anybody who experienced what I did not to feel as I do.'

'How is everything in the Facilis household now, anyway? Is the old boy enjoying his new lease of life?'

'Matthias is fine. He'll have my roof over his head as long as he wants it. It's brought us all even closer together, and of course we wanted to find out more. We got to hear more of what Yeshua had been teaching about – how to live our lives to the full by caring for others, even our enemies, then later about the other astounding things he'd done around Capernaum before the crowds got so big and he was forced to take boat to get away.'

'Such as?'

'He cured his best man's mother-in-law of fever, and made some head-cases suddenly become normal. And ....'

'Yes?'

'And how whilst crossing the sea with his closest followers they were caught in a storm and he walked on the sea to calm the waves. And did many other astonishing things, making the blind see and the deaf hear, even raising people from the dead, and much, much more ...'

'Then you really are mad. This is delusional nonsense, Favonius. Here you are, pouring scorn on the Gods of our fathers yet being taken in with nonsense like this? Walking on water and caring for your enemies indeed! Have you lost all sense and reason? Are you really so naive to think these people are telling the truth, that they're not all suffering from mass hysteria, or high on some concoction, or out to start an insurrection led by their miracle-worker ... their messiah? And how long do you think the native authorities will let them carry on with gross blasphemy against the mighty Yahweh, the one true god – who rules them with a rod of iron?'

'I shouldn't have told you. I know how it sounds, but I also know what I experienced, and that I'll never forget it. It wasn't you that was there that day, it was me. How could I not be completely stupefied, and want to find out more, and understand what he's telling us? And he's not against us, by the way – he says we're all part of the kingdom of God, that everyone should acknowledge those things which are subject to human authority but also those that are rightly God's. So that's what I'm doing – trying to find out more and to follow his example as best I can. It's for you and me, your loved ones back home, for Sabena and my children, for Matthias and his family, everyone. Imagine how we could make everyone's lives so much better if we all just tried to live as he says.'

'So it really is Yeshua and his god for you then, is it? Well you'd better listen to me now, Favonius. If this gets out you'll be throwing everything away, do you realize that? You know what they'll say, we can't have officers and men spreading foreign cults and undermining our customs and beliefs, especially with wish-washy ones like this – we've got enough problems already. There's a duty on every one of us who hold Caesar's commission to uphold standards and morals, to show some solidarity, especially to subject peoples abroad, and not go around undermining the natural order. Because that's what it will amount to. If you challenge the system your feet won't touch the ground.'

'I know, I know. I'm not going to shout from the rooftops and jeopardize my career and my family's welfare. But you can't see and hear as I've done without wanting to share it with others, people who are prepared to listen, so all men of goodwill can come together and make the world with all its present cruelties a better place. That's where I stand just now, trying to understand what it all means and where I should be going – to do my bit. Where it's taking me I don't know, but I can't see why it should make me any less worthy of service to my country, and I can't just walk away from it. I know I won't be able to look at anything in quite the same way ever again.'

'You've had an experience, that's clear. With a touch of contrariness, if you ask me. You'd tear the Gods down in your search for truth and yet you're quite happy to suspend all sense and reason because of one particular incident you happened to be involved with, and, apparently, rumours of a good many more from this Yeshua which stretch credulity beyond any claim our own Gods ever make – yet if anyone takes comfort in their legitimate demands and our ancestral traditions, you go and impugn their integrity. It's a good job Uncle Longinus is a kindly old soul, isn't it? You were just doing your best for your servant, like any officer, any decent employer would. Fortunately there was a happy ending and you've allowed what was merely a coincidence to assume proportions which aren't just over the top, they're dangerous and, frankly Favonius, stupid. What you should be doing is looking out for your career – you can't have many promotion chances left now, can you? And guarding that lovely wife of yours.'

'That's rich. You'd be the only uncle I know younger than his nephew.'

'It's the wise head on young shoulders that counts.'

'And don't make the argument any more complicated than it needs to be, I suppose.'

'Simplicity is a virtue.'

'And duty, conscience?'

'There's no hope for you. Just don't forget to call me "Sir" on parade.'

'It's alright for you. No family responsibilities. Just a mercurial career to manage.'

'Poor Favonius. I don't suppose it was like this in the Twentieth, was it? No native prophets to complicate everything. Come on, let's go and have a drink. After a good bath we've earned it. It's a big day tomorrow.'

THE OATH

The apparent lack of any official recognition for the Hill of Luz, as last year's action soon came to be known, had been something of a disappointment, but one which had to be borne in private. It would not have been seemly to show anything but a becoming modesty on his part, or by extension Century V's, though as it happened such scruples sat well enough with his nature. He had the quiet satisfaction of the respect of the whole Cohort, and especially of his own men with their pride and morale both high; and he knew that wider recognition, while within his due, was not a matter for the indulgence of expectation. It was part and parcel with the ethos.

Not only was it not in his character to exploit the reputation he seemed to have gained within their immediate community, there was something very new and much more important in his life which militated against such worldly thinking. The higher perspective showed how narrow were the old confines: careers, advancement, material comforts, even health, were all mere trappings compared to the real prizes to be obtained by those who sought them out. Opportunity was given to see this, and the wise took it. The new way offered understanding, abiding love, true happiness, eternal life. The good things of the material world were blessings, not justification, a sign of grace, not reward. You still had to ask, and submit every little part of your being, as with the old gods, but instead of mechanistic subservience and capricious dispensation there was now constancy, loving-kindness and the gentle encouragement of the Holy Spirit. Breathing the same air and walking the same ground as himself were fellow men and women, family, friends and strangers, his soldiers, all of whom had precious souls with the potential to do good to each other, to spread the good news and further the kingdom. If you had heard the Word and understood it, then how you conducted yourself in life and everyday relationships had to be in keeping with it. It was all-embracing and applied to all endeavours, all situations. Nobody could say it would ever be easy.

Even for those who might be united in belief there would still be copious room for difference of opinion on the day-to-day practicalities of life, for all the usual clashes of interest, conflicts of loyalty and conscience, some perhaps of great difficulty, which would not, could not, magically disappear. That would be to expect too much. The new way gave a template for principle and conduct, though it couldn't be so fixed it became counter-productive. The reed couldn't be so rigid that it broke in the first gust of wind – could it? There had to be some flexibility, some scope for context and interpretation, or else the best outcome prove elusive, the chosen path mistaken, the divine will escape discernment altogether – surely? The business of living was complicated enough without having a whole new layer of concerns superimposed which taken to extreme could only end in failure and self-destruction. Mortals would be forgiven if they were tempted to quietly put to one side the possibility of trial; that time would come soon enough without having to be anticipated, and pray God for guidance when it did. The unthinkable was best left unthought. What mattered was the full life so freely given, which would always be infinitely more fulfilling than the worldling's pre-occupation with self. It meant more than a clean conscience and doing what was right. It meant rejoicing in the Father's goodness and abundance. It meant reaching out, in service to Him through service to others, and spreading the good news so that the kingdom might reign over all the earth.

The clarity was fleeting. Was there a conclusion of any use to be drawn from these ramblings? Where were the hard and fast anchor points in all this, the real so-what questions and answers which might distinguish between the ideal and existential reality? The prospect of absolute truth and perfect conscience receded alarmingly quickly when put to the test. Why was it so difficult for the divine will to be brought to fruition in the affairs of men? If it were all-powerful why couldn't it overcome their blindness and obduracy? Where was the certainty, when compromise with all its retreats often seemed the only recourse if the reed were not to break? New shoots might come forth, but they would be the next generation. For the current the consequences of breaking were unlikely to be pleasant, or fortuitous, or, very possibly, even in keeping with the divine will. But that was the point, again and again. What exactly was the divine will? And why was he burdening himself trying to find answers to the mysteries of salvation and the reconciling of the ways of God and men? No wonder the seers and ascetics of this land took themselves off to live in caves, away from the distractions. He could never be a philosopher, but perhaps as so often amid complexity there was a simple, unifying theme which had to be sought out and won. Had He not said: 'I am come to make all things new'? Mankind had been sinful in countless ways, but was now being offered a better understanding, a better life. That was the real and simple point. And he, a simple soldier, didn't have to tie himself in knots trying to explain the disparities, and nor should he worry about the snares and thorns which beset all who journeyed on this path. Faith was not dependent on entire understanding but on the reaching for it, which would come with knowledge and familiarity. The believer would be granted these things on his journey and made strong to face whatever might befall.

In the end faith was simple trust. It was also about commitment, and yes, cost, which he'd accepted, which was another reason it was so personal. Wasn't it clear that somehow through God's will he and his family had been called to faith through their personal experience, with their servant's travails and the meeting that day of blessed memory, that good had sprung from bad through the working of the Holy Spirit? Why else had the patrol rushed back with news of the arrival from the north country, to lead to that unlikely encounter in that obscure little place where nothing ever happened, where his world had collided with the truth and everything had changed, one life beyond all doubt saved physically, and another, his own, spiritually? Longinus could talk about coincidence as much as he liked. Too much good had come out of that day in Capernaum for anything of the sort, surely? What were the chances of it all being down to ... mere chance? What impulse had made him of all people determine to go out and meet Him and cross his soul with the Creator of the Universe? There had to be a guiding hand, and it was mysterious but immensely humbling and encouraging that it had sought him out, and did not disown him or his calling. It was a mystery. Faith must grow with understanding then, but understanding was also predicated on faith.

If to follow the Word was difficult at the best of times, in a hierarchical organization in which you did what you were told it would be more so. Applying the principles and remembering the spirit was not always going to be compatible with the carrying out of military orders. If he'd had to instruct his soldiers on the subject he might have said that, faced with a difficult choice, one could only hope the new calling would be in sufficient harmony with duty and conscience to guide them in all matters, however daunting the situation. And they'd say: 'Are you sure, Sir?' And in their doubt they would probably be right. They were men who understood the fundamentals of existence very well. What use was all this hand-wringing in the end? And he'd say: 'Didn't the prayer say "And deliver us from the time of trial", and that they wouldn't be tested more than they could stand?' And they'd shrug their shoulders, 'Yes Sir, if you say so, Sir'; except they'd never dare utter any such impertinence. And the thing would get done.

He couldn't blame them. They were realists, cogs in a great machine which swallowed you up and spat you out at will, and there could be no illusions. The Army used you entirely for its own purposes. Its ways had much to commend them, but orders were always and always sacrosanct, punishments harsh, advancement an uphill struggle; especially for officers the promotion game was ruthless. If you made a mistake or had the misfortune to be blamed for some problem or other, or if you were foolhardy enough to challenge authority in any way or cross someone who might then or perhaps later have any power over you, or were simply surplus to requirements, then it would be rid of you without compunction. No-one was indispensable, and there was no room for failure. Behind the ideals of the military ethos what mattered above all else was the mission of Rome, executed by senior officers who moved almost entirely within their own circles and who had little to do with the likes of him. How best then to stand up for yourself in the pursuit of merit and justice, or allow this new-found hand, which seemed to entail weakness and risk as much as any spiritual comfort, to guide you on your way? – that remained the nagging question. Any worthy principle was a fine thing and had a habit of not coming cheap, even if it could be clearly identified amid confusion. To follow the divine will would be harder still. If pushed the average man was unlikely to be enthusiastic. Such considerations were supine, unmanly, unnecessary and yes, counter-productive, and shouldn't be allowed to arise. That was part of the problem.

He had to admit his men would be united on that. Why should they have any time for niceties when the hard facts of their own existence were very clear? Who did he think he was to allow himself to be thinking like this, just because he knew more than them? Your soldiers deserved your best attention without any self-imposed impediments: just be grateful for your own blessings and don't make too many presumptions. Even the strongest comradeship born of the battlefield couldn't entirely bridge the gulf between officers and men. To them, deep down, he would always be a symbol of the privilege of the ruling classes who thoroughly controlled their lives and kept them firmly in their place.

Which was why it was up to the officer corps to earn their respect through the quiet demonstration of competence and just-dealing. If a little could be done to improve the general welfare and further the promotion chances of the most deserving, without in any way seeking popular favour, then that was the least one should be aspiring to achieve. There could be no profession of arms without loyalty, though it might not be easy for the more senior officers to engage in a sense of comradeship with the lowest ranks when their careers took them beyond daily contact, and familiarity at any level was unthinkable. It was regimental officers who bore the immediate duty and had the means to lead through example. This at any rate was the ideal to which all but the most egotistical would claim some ambition, an unstated assumption and something of which to be quietly proud. To serve in the Army was an honourable accomplishment for any man; to command soldiers a great privilege; to participate in victorious action glorious; to render personal service in battle noble, and worthy of acknowledgment among all ranks. So it was fitting that it was the Governor himself who would take the parade, and entirely appropriate that it was the Cohort, the centre of their professional lives and embodiment of their pride and fighting spirit, which was now finally, splendidly, to be officially honoured. The salt of the Army; faithful, dependable, unassuming, unsung, deservedly now the centre of attention; a stalwart representative of the many like it which policed the Empire ...

*   *   *   *

He had to bring himself to the here and now. Standing motionless on the cramped and stifling parade ground was draining, though nothing could detract from their sense of ownership of the place now given over to their honour, every window and balcony crowded with on-lookers and the wide miscellany of hangers-on which always appeared from nowhere on occasions like this. For today was the Cohort's day, no-one else's, and now the long wait under a broiling sun was nearly over.

There was a stir at the far end of the ground. The trumpets were sounding, the Commander-in-Chief arriving at last. He took the salute; inspected them; addressed them; and now after another flurry of commands they were stood ready to receive the newly-embellished Standard. He recalled the comments in the Mess following the rehearsal, how he'd had to rebuke one over-forward young man for mildly questioning the protocol of it. You certainly didn't criticize other officers and you didn't find fault with superior authorities, not in earshot of a field officer at any rate. But the young man had been right, and everyone knew it. And now it was happening before their eyes, and there was nothing anyone could do about it.

As Macula stepped forward to take the Standard with its new emblem aloft from the Governor, the full irony struck home and the anger welled. This was not right. It was a parody, an insult. For an outsider to intrude on their moment of glory was outrageous. It was their cohort which had done the work, their cohort for which they had fought and died, their cohort which was the repository of its own hard-won battle honours and every collective sense of duty and honour that mattered to them. This Cohort was theirs, not Macula's. He didn't belong to it: by fortune they did. An independent cohort was a rare thing; the great majority of men went off to a legion, which had its own set of loyalties however distant its cohorts might be spread. It was their special fortune to be in a unit reserved, like few abroad, for the sons of Rome. Its centuries were the smallest grouping of any tactical significance, and within them were the sections where men lived and trained and fought together. You identified with section, company, cohort because they each in their way identified you. Throughout any province you were known for your cohort, but within that for your century, and if you happened to command either then you cared for it not just as your own but as yourself, nurturing it, grooming it, tending to its every need, exhorting, reproving, defending it, since it was the best, just as any parent unit was the best, and whatever the internal rivalries you sank them in overriding loyalty to the greater, which was how you took your place in the Army. The Cohort, The Regiment: their home, and the reason for their existence.

Which made it all the worse, it seemed to him. They were being treated pretty shabbily, from a great height by people who obviously didn't care very much about how they might feel. No-one questioned rank having its privilege; that wasn't a problem. Patrician officers had always been a traditional feature of military life, and the Cohort had to be seen to meet the usual expectations in hosting the select few on occasion, on rarer ones over the years having a minor name within its own ranks too. The men were used to it and would accept it as normal, even something to welcome though they wouldn't be likely to admit it sober. The system was a convenient vehicle for aristocratic ambition, one of those facts of life which had to be tolerated. It was the way of things.

But an outsider? And Macula? Just because he'd shared their Mess for a while, here only to prepare the arrangements for the Governor's Progress and whose own little entourage of Augustans were mere spectators to the parade – Macula, taking their symbol of honour from the Commander-in-Chief and showing it off – to them? Of course he had no objection to his own victorious Century V being at the rear of the parade as a junior company, and no-one would have expected parade precedence to be broken; it was their rightful place. It was the man himself who was the problem. The man who had only the flimsiest connection with them, being from another regiment altogether, one known for its airs and graces and spending its time idling by the sea rather than sweating it out in the interior like the rest of them. The man who had the connection, the imperial touch, the personal fortune, which were clearly all the qualifications needed to receive such an honour. It was enough to make the most avid pillar of the establishment question the propriety. What purpose could there be in extending such preferment to an impostor, play-acting over real soldiers in this way? Or was it just him, this centurion, who felt obliged to react? The others would agree, he was sure, though on reflection perhaps he'd have to admit they wouldn't be taking it quite so personally. Nor perhaps should he. No! – they should be balking and bridling too. He bet those true champions of Rome, the Gracchi brothers, if they could have come back to this feckless age, would be making their objections loud and clear …

All the Governor had to do was hand the thing to the Cohort's *signifer* in the normal way, but it looked as if even he had to accommodate the politics of it – better obviously a few muted comments among junior officers than upset someone with Macula's connections, and forgo the chance to curry favour. So the gall was on display right in front of them. The brazen nonchalance of the man, affecting to converse so easily amid all the parade ground formality before the Governor's arrival, that's what had stuck in his craw. Macula, who seemed to think he could act like a broad-stripe senatorial tribune to some illustrious legion, lording it about the place and name-dropping at every opportunity, whom they all hated instinctively but to whom they had to mind their p's and q's as though they were small fry paying respects to the school bully – and who had seemed to take more of a sneering dislike to him than to anyone else.

You had to be very careful of this man. There was no telling the damage he could do if he took against you. And it looked as if he'd done just that, for some reason he hadn't been able to fathom …

*   *   *   *

As the Standard approached to be trooped before his lines he had some difficulty dispelling the mental image of punching the poncy little whipper-snapper on his poncy little nose. The whole thing was outrageous.

And then the Standard Party with its patrician bearer in his spotless white cloak was marching off back to the head of the parade, with the Governor about to order the imperial salute to bring the occasion to an end. It all transpired very quickly. With time to think he might have done differently, and forestalled the consequences, but that is not how it happened. As six hundred sword blades flashed in the sun and the loyal oath was loudly proclaimed from resolute lips, no-one could have said with any confidence that behind the burnished mask of his parade helmet this officer's was not among them.

Unnoticed, his unpremeditated hesitancy changed nothing at that point. The Rubicon was yet to be crossed. He had however taken the first step towards disaster, since for all men the mind works by increments, and one thing leads to another.

*   *   *   *

The reception which the Cohort put on that evening was a grand affair by their standards, with the Governor's staff, officers of the garrison and, most unusually, their ladies. It was rare to be gathered together in such numbers, rarer to be accompanied, and for the Cohort an event unique in recent memory.

*   *   *   *

When it came to recognizing the military contribution to the harmony of the Province their principal guest could not have been accused of favouritism, being by reputation equally aloof and dour to all, though it had to be said it was based more on scant impression and hearsay than certain knowledge. In any case it would be asking too much to expect much interest in the detail of Army matters, let alone of its individual members, which was depressingly typical for one who had been through the system himself, worn the uniform and known something of the soldier's life but then gone on to higher things, by which time the military had served its purpose. And now the man was at the top, burdened no doubt by cares of state they could only guess at, and far beyond any relationship which could be seen as in any sense reciprocal. The Army was the Army, its absolute loyalty and efficiency to be taken for granted. It was an instrument of government, not a partner, and from the exalted there was no place for any pretence at empathy.

Likewise you too had to impress yourself upon your own subordinates in every way possible. They had to know who was in charge. Orders were impersonal matters, and you weren't expected to interface below one rank down, except perhaps in a crisis when additional demands might break the bonds of convention. The Army was a constant, always on hand, immutable, its resources figures in uniform ready for the instant carrying out of orders in absolutely any situation. Soldiers might have thoughts and feelings of their own but these were of no concern to anyone else, least of all to important men on important business. It was pleasing therefore to be able to show themselves off this evening as this ever-reliable face, this unassuming unit with no great history or connections but which had shown itself quite capable of meritorious service – and for it to be acknowledged. It was interesting too what a little military success could do for those outside their ranks who would bask in reflected glory, but they weren't going to let that get in the way of their own sense of reward, they who had truly earned it. It would be for the officers of the Cohort, supported by their wives, to make the point.

The Old Palace, resplendent with light, beckoned them in with pipe and lyre.

*   *   *   *

Sabena stuck close to him, and she and the others naturally let Honoria the Prefect's wife, who had a great deal more experience in these things, take her rightful place in what for many was the challenge that lay ahead. As the hubbub subsided and they all waited in the nervous hush, there were few who were not conscious of the perils that lurked to ensnare the gauche and unwary, of the need to address the great people with enough spirit and character to show you were entirely relaxed but also lively and attentive and worth talking to, without undue risk of embarrassment, and never to be too forward in initiating conversation unless you were very sure of yourself and your subject. For the self-conscious, especially the younger women, it was a vision of terror; even for the majority a little nervousness amid the general excitement was only to be taken as normal.

For those in the outstations the annual progress was almost the only chance they had to get together, to meet their kind, see the city and enjoy some luxury shopping. Any event which broke the tedium of garrison life was on no account to be missed; and this one in particular was appropriate due for their endurance and loyalty, both to their husbands and the Army, a rare opportunity to sample something of the privileged life for themselves, while being always aware they could at such times be both a considerable help or a considerable hindrance to their husband and his career. Those to whom a formal dinner did not come easy could reflect that anyone could make a hash of it, or have excruciating memories revived, unameliorated by the apparent ease with which others never seemed to have any difficulty with these trials. Naturally it helped if you were passably presentable, though more important was a certain extroversion of character. If the timorous could only have known the true feelings of the happy accomplished ones, and even those of their illustrious guests, who in their time and in their own circles had experienced blunders of their own but learnt to shrug or laugh them off, they might not have been so worried. Fortunately as the VIP party now made its way further into the room and more and more people were introduced, the noise level, though suitably respectful, rose pleasingly enough to mask the tensions, and if there were to be some exquisite calamity or other then at least fewer would see or hear it. Wives had their husbands to shelter against, and their husbands the soldiers' bond with the Governor, and it wasn't going to be so bad. Sabena was nevertheless glad she had been sparing with the refreshment.

In fact the Governor and his Lady were as properly gracious and faultlessly impressive as anyone could have supposed, and the great man had been well briefed. He knew all about the Hill of Luz and listened attentively and joked with him, spending considerably longer than might have been expected before allowing the Prefect to move him on, the Governor's wife the while chatting to Sabena, remarking how proud she must feel of her husband, enquiring after his injury, of her children, and how she must have been enjoying the delights of the city after the privations of a small provincial garrison.

And then she turned to him. He was as amenable to glamour as any man there, even the plainer matronly sort – the expensive scent, the face soft and homely, auburn hair thick and drawn-up, the little crows' feet that played at the corner of dark lively eyes, and as they met his he had to suppress the little flash of excitement which momentarily if involuntarily entered his consciousness. The concern for his injury expressed so publicly he inevitably found embarrassing, but there was what seemed to him real empathy in the womanly admiration, and he could not deny he found it rather pleasing. He appreciated the undivided attention, the intelligence and the warmth, the sureness of touch quite equal to her husband's, the swish of her gown, her impeccable manners, the faultless poise.

Then it was over, and as the imperial couple moved on he felt what he imagined everyone felt in their turn – relief, pride, quiet satisfaction, and, as had no doubt been intended, an inordinate sense of identity with the great ones, who had throughout seemed genuine, engaging, listening more than talking, asking the right questions, raising polite laughter, conversing with everybody they were introduced to far longer, and thus delaying their banquet, than anyone could have expected. Some of the senior officers would have had some contact with the Commander-in-Chief before, perhaps one or two with his consort, but now the magic had been well and fully cast upon the whole assembled gathering, and the bond, however slight, cemented. They were clearly in safe hands; Rome's mission, to rule well this land among so many others and grow in prosperity and continuity at home, was being consolidated; and they, the Cohort, the whole Army, were part of this destiny and could be relied upon to do their duty, just as the Governor himself could be relied upon to do his. It was good to be thus united, and, duly flattered, they could now enjoy their evening. There would possibly be an opportunity to mix with the guests after the meal, but the aim for the next few hours was to relax on their couches and savour good food and good company as their just desserts.

It did cross his mind that Sabena was deserving too, not least of some special attention from him. She hadn't had much chance to enjoy herself in recent months, having to bear the brunt of his convalescence and house-leave so long, the lack of conjugal relations in the first weeks when all he wanted to do was sleep, more lately his devotions in prayer and reading and his long conversations with her on the faith. It was understandable these usually seemed to turn out rather more one-sided than he would have preferred, despite his best efforts. Everyone was different, and she hadn't met Him herself, had she? He couldn't hold that against her. It would all come good in time. Anyway he ought to show how much he appreciated her, that she certainly didn't have anything to worry about in the Governor's Lady or any other woman. Silly idea! It was his Sabena who was the cleverest and easily the most attractive in the room, still young, still spirited. When heads turned it was for her, not her hero husband, and he knew how very fortunate he was to have her and be loved by her. And she seemed to be having an enjoyable time with their house-hosts Vergilia and Brutus.

Towards the end of the feast the Prefect of the Cohort got to his feet and began a formal speech of welcome. Tribune Veranius was of the type much valued by the military establishment – a safe pair of hands, adept at employing the minimum of effort when he could get away with it, but equally capable of great exertion when necessary, favoured too with the sure sign of a 'lucky' officer which didn't fail to get noticed in the right places and was more or less guaranteed to take him far. Perhaps in truth his record was largely unknown, but he was clearly not without some experience. He certainly knew the value of a cheerful disposition in raising morale, how to give the impression of competence through the avoidance of detail or conspicuous commitment to any cause which might seem remotely controversial. His ambition could be taken for granted despite the studied casualness bordering on the languor so characteristic of his class: the more demanding the need, the more consummate the performance. A classical education, underpinned by judicious breeding and the accumulation of a respectable if relative degree of wealth, had ensured self-belief was felicitously apparent in all endeavours. Confidence would know no bounds. In company as august as this he naturally excelled, imparting to his remarks that confirmation of his abilities, careful flattery of the distinguished guests, understated pride in the cohort of which he had the honour to command, the touch of levity to please all, the satisfaction of the desired effect. It was what a commanding tribune was supposed to do, to bring the team together and front up for it – well, off the field of battle, anyway; and he was in his element. How well the evening was going, with the principal guests obviously enjoying his hospitality, and reputations being enhanced most satisfactorily.

Shortly it was the Governor's turn, and they realized at once they were witnessing something few had come across before, the assured tones of the accomplished statesman at the height of his powers, who could bring them the word of Caesar himself whilst still speaking of things to which they and their own experience could relate. He flattered them openly and comprehensively, and they in turn quietly flattered themselves that this was perfectly normal, almost an everyday occurrence, and not just for the dinner and the finery and all. Here he was, in the flesh among them, talking as though they were colleagues whose personal support he valued, whose help he needed in giving the Province the good government it deserved. And there was no better way to achieve the Roman Peace than through the fine old, time-honoured Roman ways of honour, of austerity, frugality, dignity, duty, valour, loyalty to family, loyalty to the State and its living embodiment the Emperor, loyalty to the Gods who continued to bring them greatness and prosperity.

To Favonius mention of the *mores* of the old Republic had strong appeal, though in truth they belonged more closely to an age everyone knew had long gone. If only, he thought, the ideals of those days were indeed still universal among their countrymen and their leaders.

Politicians liked to talk about these things, but it seemed to him such invocation of the glories of the past now had more to do with justifying the ordering of society for the benefit of its more comfortable elements than genuine concern for those who made it work and defended it.   It was still the rich who took the pleasure and the poor who took the blame, and probably always would.   In taking the obvious line of self-identification with such an audience, however, the Governor was being predictability safe;   whether it entirely accorded with the reality was another matter.   Favonius was pondering on this in an unfocussed sort of way, only half-alert to what might be coming next, when he heard:

'... so it is my very great pleasure, as Prefect of Judea, Samaria and Idumea, to commend to you one such in our midst, who has shown he has these qualities of our countrymen in superb degree, and who deserves every possible admiration and praise.   For *Cohors Secunda Italica Civium Romanorum* clearly has such a hero, and we ought to honour him now.   I call on Marcus Favonius Facilis to come forward and receive this Imperial Medal for Valour'.

And after a pause and numerous 'hear hears' from the assembled diners, 'Come, Facilis, where are you?'

He was taken completely unawares.   He'd been so strict with himself in dismissing any such idea, even with the impending parade and the heightened sense of government at work which the Governor's Progress always brought, that any idea of singling him out for recognition would prove to be a genuine surprise.   Nobody had said a thing;   no tip-off, not a hint.   Now it was very suddenly happening, and he'd better liven up. All eyes on him now, with Sabena's touch on his arm and her soft 'go on, go up' in his ear, he rose, in surroundings that seemed very different to the scene in which he had been only a relaxed spectator a few moments before, approached the VIP couches as naturally as he could contrive, and took his prize, the Governor addressing him conversationally and hanging the heavy silver medallion around his neck as he leant forward.

To great applause he turned to go, but the cries of 'Speech! Speech!' were breaking out and quickly becoming too much;   with so many expectant faces all turned his way there was no chance of escape.   His oft-practised preference for the honesty and immediacy of spontaneity in such matters suddenly didn't seem very sensible. Addressing soldiers was nothing compared to this, yet as he stood there with his mind whirring a voice of calm told him to recover his presence of mind, that he was a man of experience who'd had to handle a lot worse than speaking in public, that all he had to do was keep it short and straightforward and everything would be fine. He was among friends, after all.

'Your Excellency, you do me a great honour, more than I can say. For as everyone of us here knows, I was only carrying out that duty of which you have just so eloquently reminded us. Anyone of us here would have done the same, and stepped in to take my place. As it was, the honour fell to Century I and Century V, and by our soldiers' efforts and bravery we carried the day. It was by their noble sacrifice that Rome's enemies were defeated and the cause of civilization advanced. I thank you, Your Excellency, I thank my brother officers and soldiers of the Cohort for all their support. I accept this honour on behalf of them all, and shall of course treasure it as long as I live.'

And with that he returned to his place, at once bashful at the banality of his little speech, relieved at its reception by the prolonged applause and shouts of 'Facilis! Facilis!', and trying not to break into too wide a smile as they patted his back and shook his hand. His oratorical efforts hadn't been very adventurous but he had told them what they wanted to hear. You didn't need to reach for the heights of rhetoric on occasions like this: people evidently just wanted to follow convention and hear the obvious spoken out loud, however banal, as though it was the mere saying of it rather than any attempt at originality which somehow satisfied the common need. Now in that room with its warm candlelight and obvious comradeship it seemed to satisfy their sense of order and mutual obligation too. It allowed everyone to move on naturally and for the rhythm of the occasion to resume. And it was rather good to be popular.

Veranius approved. He had always respected his centurion, knowing there was more here than met the eye: quieter than the incomparable Longinus, though probably as reliable; certainly more personable than Brutus, who needed no help and liked everyone to know it; sharper than dull Cogitus, less outspoken than Festus, equally capable as Petronius despite his relative lack of seniority. This officer had no apparent side; he was proving a fine ambassador for the Cohort tonight; and to his enormous satisfaction he could see the Governor was impressed. When this year's promotion roll came around he'd have to see what he could do; a gallantry award such as this would do him no harm at all. He'd be a loss to the team, but he was a deserving case and there was no doubt now his suitability for advancement should be recognized. He hadn't been the one who had actually taken bar Abbas, but it was very plain by whose efforts the deed had been made possible. 'One medal', the word had come down from Caesarea, to represent the whole Cohort, and it hadn't been a difficult choice to make. Longinus was a first-rate officer already destined for greater things, and didn't need further distinction at this juncture, whereas Facilis also ran a good company and his promotion would be popular with the men, who all knew exactly what had happened on the hill, and had their own ideas about who deserved what for services rendered on the battlefield. It would be arranged.

And, thought his prefect, it would do no harm regarding his own standing with the Governor either, which was never an idle consideration. With the top man on board and his own credibility safe-guarded, any objections from interfering types like Macula would be effectively side-lined. Not that there was any good reason why there should be any objections, but you never knew: officer promotion could be a fraught and haphazard business, and everyone knew strings got pulled from time to time. It was a pity the ambitious young tribune from First Augustans and his man didn't seem to get on, though it was no secret the interloper wasn't the most popular, and he could understand why. He hoped there wouldn't be any need for any sort of collision, but he wasn't going to have one of his officers disadvantaged, least of all by an outsider, no matter who he was. And he might have his own career to consider but he wasn't to be seen failing on one of the principal responsibilities, moral obligation towards one's subordinates. Honour, almost as important as one's name, existed to be upheld.

*　　*　　*　　*

The hero had scarcely sat down to the acclamation of all present when the next step on his fateful journey was taken. The ghost of a fore-thought had been subsumed without conscious articulation. Putting that off had been the easy option, and now with the heady atmosphere of the evening and distractions all around it had been completely overlooked. Had he forced himself to think about it properly, however, he would still have convinced himself it wasn't going to happen. Why should it? There'd be the loyal toast, of course, but that would be all, nothing more, none of that stuff about dead emperors ... they hardly ever did that, there was no reason to do so now. No point in worrying about something that wasn't going to happen. No point in contingency thinking, too difficult. No point worrying about the worst possible case. It shouldn't, wouldn't come to that. No-one would notice anyway, not on a night of high spirits with the wine flowing freely. If by some chance the worse came to the worse he would do the only thing he could – put himself in the hands of Him who guided in all things, and meet the moment when it came. It could be put out of mind, so he would.

The gavel was banged down somewhere in a corner, so hard it made the ladies flinch.

'All stand, please.'

'To Tiberius Caesar, Imperator.'

'To Tiberius Caesar, Imperator!', they responded, the men with right arm across chest, then cup to lip, seats and conversations resumed in respectful time. It was going to be alright. He could relax.

And then:

'All stand', and they all rose again, expecting a toast to their guests or to The Cohort or some such, listening intently to catch the wording.

'In the seventy-fifth anniversary year of the great victory at Philippi – to Augustus Caesar, Imperator, The Deified One.'

There was no time to think.

'To Augustus Caesar, Imperator, The Deified One!' came the loud rejoinder.

Like the rest he saluted, Sabena by his side. His lips moved, he started saying it, but didn't finish; and the cup, though raised, did not pass them. They took their seats. All seemed normal. He'd done what he'd had to and it was gone.

Presently however he was aware of something that he couldn't quite put his finger on, something which immediately disturbed him even before he could be sure what it was. And then he was, very sure. It was a snake eyeing its prey, boring through him across the room, fixed on delivering its venom, and freezing the blood in his veins: the malevolent gaze of Licinius Macula. He avoided it, but it was Macula alright. Of course it was him, though it had not been his voice calling the toast; it had been the Mess President's. It had to be him, Macula, Junior Tribune of the First Augustans, serpent in a room full of mice. It was probably him behind the wretched toast, too, who was supposed to be their guest but wasn't acting like one, obviously determined to make his superior breeding clear to these provincial plodders, how they all had to honour the great emperor whose name was borne by his own superb regiment, and with whom he was slightly connected by some distant and nefarious means, quite sufficiently to keep their own commanding officer, a mere knight, in his place – hence all the strutting about in the morning. Because he was a tribune of the First, because that was what you did if you were a distant relative of the great man-god himself. It was enough to make a proper soldier weep. The god-defying brass cheek of it.

He should have felt more anger, not fear; but fear cold and overwhelming had him in vice-like grip. He was the timorous prey, cornered, powerless with panic, awaiting the strike which would bring extinction. As he turned away in contrived conversation he felt sick to the pit of his stomach, his mouth drying up as he tried to carry on talking and affecting to hear what his neighbours were saying. Gone in an instant were the satisfaction and pride he had been enjoying so undeservedly, replaced by very different emotions. He strove desperately not to show it, but for him the evening could not end soon enough now, all conversation seeming distant and meaningless, the smiles hollow, the mouthings incomprehensible as the discomfiture within wore on for what seemed interminable hours of desperate horror. He emptied his goblet, called for more, tried to remember to act normally. He was glad his wife was by his side, as diverting as usual, though for the first time ever in her presence an uncomfortable, insidious little feeling surfaced through the chaos before vanishing again. He had to blot it out and reach for safety.

His darling wife – how he needed her now. She wasn't one to let anything go to her head, but he didn't need to be reminded she wasn't averse to enjoying the effects of her charms. He'd never reproved her before and he was in no position to do so now. There had been an instance or two when other men's interest had been a little too obvious, which afterwards they would joke about quite happily, and for all he knew there might have been others he wasn't aware of, but it had never bothered him. Their love had always been rock-solid, her loyalty ever assured, their special union secure from the beginning and blest with the gift of children, and to this citadel there had been added the wonderful discovery of the new life of faith, which gave fresh insight into the preciousness of life in all its fullness and hope for the future.

It didn't matter that she wasn't as enthusiastic about the faith as him; not yet. Even among those who heard the Word and took it in the response would be varied. Everyone was different, and everyone grew in their own way. What mattered was the whole, the direction, the good heart on which the Holy Spirit could work and cast out reluctance and doubt. It seemed women were as likely to receive and believe as men, probably more so. The followers they knew about most were men, but then religion everywhere was men's preserve and prerogative in terms of holy priesthoods and household headship, because like everything else in every society it was men who were the deciders and the actors, and nobody ever thought it should be any different. There could be no revolution there. Yet women were undoubtedly open to the word of God. They might not be among His closest disciples and seemed to be largely absent from the lives of those companions, but that wasn't surprising; His men were the agents through whom the world would be changed, which needed action and courage. That didn't stop Him having women friends or respecting the half of the human race which bore its lot in acceptance and forbearance; stories of His compassion for them abounded. They might stay behind the scenes but they were more than capable of understanding, of being instruments of the Almighty in their own right, of responding to the gentleness of the Holy Spirit in the battle against the carapace of masculine indifference.

The good thing was that Sabena had heard the Word, and had received it in her own way. She was in the right place, and in the fullness of time it would grow and make her complete, and in so doing further strengthen the bonds of their little family. Their children were a happy consequence of a greater glory, a sign of God's providence to be received thankfully, given so that united together they could face anything, and live their lives as He would wish. Of that there could be no doubt. It was good to see her enjoying herself, and being herself.

The happy diversion was fleeting. The present danger was still there, pitiless, immovable, grown even more menacing. Not even his wife's close presence, not even the inchoate scraps of comfort which had raced through his mind these last few moments, could suppress the dread which would not go, the helpless abandon, the sickening fear. He was being weak, when he should have been resolute, but it wasn't a matter of simple courage, or concern for himself alone. The terror was an image of exposure, humiliation, of everything he loved put in jeopardy, total ruin, all in free-fall into the unknown, towering toward him like a gigantic wave which would sweep away everything that was good and true. The Father might be on the throne of heaven and his Son in life with all His power and certainty less than a mile hence, but now both were beyond reach, as distant as if they never were. He the man of authority too was proven only weak flesh and bone, so frightened he had no answer to this panic which had finally brimmed over to leave him pole-axed and helpless. Because ... because ...

He had realized. Because his mortal soul had realized he had just made the biggest mistake of his life. Of course he had. And with that blinding realization had come immediately the bitter foretaste of loss and disaster looming unstoppable out of nowhere, as though to say 'now see what you've done, serve you right for all your arrogance and conceit.'

The scene, the atmosphere, the noise: was this hell? Sabena's obvious enjoyment, the grotesque caricatures of faces in every contortion, the raucus laughter, the demented strains of the orchestra, all made for an unbearable torture threatening at any moment to bring the final apocalypse. He avoided looking toward the top couches: wherever he might be able to let his eyes rest for a moment, it certainly wasn't there. In his imagination he could make out Macula whispering in people's ears, brows furrowing, heads turning, all eyes on him now; hear the ear-splitting call to report outside to the Adjutant, the sudden hush, the snide low-spoken comments; or the deadly word delivered by a brother officer in his ear to prevent a scene.

He spent the rest of the evening numbed with the enormity of what had happened, scarcely able to think or utter a coherent sentence. What had he done? The loose thoughts that had come into his head on the morning's parade had crystalized with a vengeance, though he could not possibly contemplate trying to marshal them into any sense now. He didn't need to: the situation was starkly obvious in its all wine-filled clarity. In hubris he had rolled the die, and any idea of being able to right it now, of regaining any sort of restitution, was out of the question. He was going to pieces. Nemesis had his name, and he only had himself to blame. It was his own making, his blunder would soon be revealed for all to see, and they'd all soon see too how he'd be reaping the inevitable consequences of his folly. What would Sabena say? Or Longinus? – not even his stalwart bulk was any help now. Cornelius? What would his loyal second-in-command, with whom there was such strong mutual respect, think of him now? Tonight perhaps no-one would notice anything amiss, but they soon would. The nightmare of this evening was bad enough: if he got through this there'd be more to come, much more. Deserted by now entirely of his wits, it was all he could do to maintain any semblance whatsoever of the Centurion of the Fifth.

*　　*　　*　　*

To his great relief nothing happened: no message, no bawled summons, nothing. In fact everything seemed to have continued quite normally. He allowed himself a little leeway. Could it be he was in the clear after all? Could they just hold out a little longer, he and Sabena, see it through just a little longer, then slip away as soon as it was safe? They had to, of course: hold out. Hold out. For as long as it took. Can't, mustn't run. Just grin and bear it. Keep drinking. Perform, like an actor. Do what you have to do. Survive.

The Governor's eventual departure made it no better. Veranius and Honoria were still there, no doubt feeling they could now fully relax with the remaining guests and savour the triumph of their day. The Daedalian agony would have to continue. In fact, he told himself with what presence of mind he could muster, now that there was no risk of embarrassment to the VIPs the danger was all the more. At any moment the barbed comment, the sarcastic remark aimed at him and him alone, would cut through the chatter and laughter, and it would be Macula's sneering tones behind it. He tried his best at good cheer with the rest but no amount of drink could shake him out of the numbness which obliterated all pleasure. On and on it went, that night of torture and turmoil. Getting away from it seemed all that mattered, but it was impossible to break mess etiquette without drawing attention. There was nothing for it but to sit it out and endure, endure.

At last with the Prefect and the dreadful Macula gone too, after an interval as brief as he thought safe, he managed to give their excuses and get Sabena away. They all protested of course. Everyone wanted Sabena to stay, as did she before merciful sense finally prevailed. It was the children who saved them. They really did have to get back to the children. The servants couldn't be expected to stay up all night.

*　　*　　*　　*

Back in their borrowed quarter in the barracks behind the Old Palace, with the immediacy of the ordeal over and his worst fears calmed, he allowed himself an attempt at some rationalization through the fog in his head. No-one but Macula had appeared to have seen what he'd done, or rather hadn't done, but why had the man singled him out that way? Why among so many people had that stare managed to find him so unerringly? It can't have been his imagination – at that stage he'd still been sober. And it was obviously deliberate, but why would he want to do it? Was it plain personal animosity, something he'd done to annoy the man? If so, what? Jealousy over the medal? He wouldn't have thought so. Macula hadn't been on The Hill, had no right to behave as though he had some sort of authority over him, wasn't even in the same cohort. Couldn't rule it out though, especially if there were some sort of regimental rivalry involved. Unlikely; you didn't let anything like that become personal, not unless you were seriously unhinged.

Sabena? Unthinkable. With all Macula's wealth he'd be able to get any woman he wanted – not that he could imagine any decent woman ever looking at him, but then status and money accounted for a great many things. But perhaps … And Macula was important enough and grand enough to think he had some sort of entitlement to her favours, husband or no. The fact the wretch couldn't have set eyes on his wife before this evening didn't come into it: he'd seen shameless predatory behaviour before, and the perpetrator get away with it. Power did that to men, and to the women on the receiving end of such attentions too for that matter. And he obviously had more than the Governor's ear, which made him unassailable. No, no, no. Sabena would never find him attractive. She just wouldn't. So jealousy? Sheer hatred? Why, for pity's sake? Hatred of course – how could there be such venom without it?

It went on, this fitful, prying, painful, unstoppable speculation. Calm it, think, use your head. Too much to take in, too many wild notions. The possibilities were definitely there though, weren't they? Perhaps it was the combination. The combination that had proved too much for someone like Macula, prompted him to cast propriety aside and embark on this vendetta. No again, he was reading too much into it. Why couldn't he simply take it at face value? Go back to the start. The man had just happened to be looking at him at the same time the toast was being taken, happened to notice his lips stopped moving on that last fateful word, barely noticeable, not noteworthy to any normal person, but the attention still drawn, the intuition confirmed by the lack of obvious swallowing, the conclusion drawn, the rage. Yes, that was it. Understandable if you're a fanatical worshipper of dead Caesars. Did it change anything? No. It didn't change the fact. He'd done what he had, failed to respond to the toast, and been seen to have failed.

But it did. It changed everything, and there was no chance involved. You'd have to be very consciously looking at someone before the precise moment to notice anything like that, especially in that sort of light and at that distance – you would, it was impossible otherwise. Macula would have had to have been looking hard, but people didn't do that when toasts were being taken. You always looked up, or through, as though the act were some kind of exercise in philosophical detachment, which in a way it was. So the man must have deliberately chosen to have looked him out, and having done so had all his suspicions rewarded by that fluke, of seeing exactly what happened, following which the prolonged stare with all its fury had come as the involuntary response. How could anyone, least of all a commissioned officer, dare to insult the great Augustus, founder and father of Imperial Rome? So there it was. Simple. It was pique. And probably ordinary dislike, probably something he'd said on the two or three times they'd actually spoken. He could almost relax. He had the answer.

Are you quite sure? Does anyone behave like that, even with others they don't get on with? Sure there couldn't be something else?

Oh no. Surely not. No, please. Not Yeshua. Please God, Macula couldn't know that. He couldn't possibly know that. But the wine told him it was so.

The cold logic froze him to the marrow, worse even than the other terror-filling moments of the evening. He could now see where he was in this desolate plain of horror. Duty, destiny, truth, life, death were all here. He seemed to have been sucked into a black hole from which there was no escape, no going back; only confusion, disaster and destruction. Was there nothing of any hope in the desolation? Why was he being led to this wilderness where everything good was turning to dust? Was he just a hapless man on his own like any other, bereft of God, a free but half-blind agent blundering about and getting everything very wrong indeed? Were those idle musings of the morning which had gone through his mind like wisps of vapour any use to him now? Where were the purpose and certainty which had led his convictions so unequivocally until now? Where was all this leading? What on earth did he think he was doing, getting into a mess like this? Why was he, a reasonably successful career officer, taking risks like this with his career, never mind his family? In one short evening he had managed to turn a life of privilege and achievement into one of difficulty and danger. You had to be very careless, or very stupid, or both, to have brought such a calamity on your own head. And what would Yeshua have to say to him? Or for Himself? Right now.

Blow it, he was a Roman Army officer, a man of standing. And he had every right to think and behave as he saw fit. *In vino veritas*, indeed.

* * * *

Sabena clearly was not best pleased they'd left. She'd get over it. She wasn't insensitive, and she was after all the best of mothers. They'd had to leave the party at some stage, and it was late. She must have realized there was something wrong, so she wouldn't hold it against him anyway. He'd tell her all about it when the time was right.

As he finally gave himself to her arms his rational self told him quietly, matter-of-factly, that this could be the last time. The last time, tonight. Tonight however, no matter the hollow fear that would not go away and would still be there in the morning, there should be some pleasure. Tonight, or for what was left of it, he was still the luckiest of men.

THE CHARGE

It was not good form to be late for morning parade after a heavy night; he had to hurry. He recalled earlier days when he'd simply a sore head to contend with, and for better reasons than this, not this burden of fate which now dogged him so heavily as he made his way through the barracks. It was probably already too late. The order would be there, waiting for him in clear writing. 'Report to HQ immediately, Adjt', it would say. Every hope and ambition, everything he held dear would be blown away in an instant if he made a mistake now, or faced a direct accusation he couldn't refute. He had nevertheless to be seen to be acting as though all were normal. There was no alternative, and no point in doing anything other. He reminded himself that no-one around him knew about this yet – no-one in his immediate circles anyway. His best bet was to accept the challenge as an inevitability but downplay it, as though this were another day, and carry on.

There was no message, and thankfully a good deal to do. The fort was bursting at the seams, the usual complement swollen with troops brought in from outlying garrisons for the Progress, his own company among them. It had been generous of Brutus to share his family accommodation, though they would be glad to get back to the spaciousness of Capernaum and their own routine. You had to be a certain type to enjoy city duties, with the hierarchy of thrusters all out to impress, the constant ceremonial mounting of guards, the ever-present tension outside in the streets, where you didn't venture alone. The Century was next in line to do a tour here, but it wasn't something that he looked forward to; better by far to be away where life was agreeably quieter and you were left largely to run your own show.

The muster over, and fighting off sluggishness of body and mind, he immersed himself in the usual routine, keeping well away from Cohort HQ. It was good to engage with his soldiers and their myriad problems, usually petty but which to them could assume enormous proportions and often took an inordinate time to sort out. The good centurion was a father-figure as well as disciplinarian, and if you had a reputation for fairness and consistency it could do you no harm. Loyalty worked both ways, as everyone knew. Everyone also knew whose needs always came first, and it wasn't theirs: it was the Army's, the insatiable machine, the restless behemoth ever constant in its demands. Discipline in all situations was to be rigorously maintained at all times, orders obeyed instantly and punctiliously, from the lowest to the highest on pain of the severest punishment. Once you accepted the system you realized its impartiality, that it gave a kind of freedom. Everyone knew exactly where they stood, whatever their rank. The practice of it might be rough-and-ready, not to say brutal at times, but how else could an army work? There was no place for questioning in the face of the foe; indiscipline meant inefficiency, and men getting killed unnecessarily. Training had to be hard and tough, obedience instilled and assumed as a matter of course, and fear certainly came into it. Men had to fear the lash more than they feared any enemy.

But it wasn't the only consideration. The good commander had also to be respected if he aspired to get the best out of his command. You did have to let everyone know you wouldn't put up with any nonsense, but you didn't have to be a monster. The key was consistency and even-handedness, which instilled confidence, which itself was always a prime battle-winning factor; the good soldier would then go beyond the normal limits of duty, even unto death, for his friends, for you. And you led by example, which meant being as proficient as your men and sharing danger and privation. The system would leave its mark on you, something no-one who had not been subjected to it could fully appreciate, but few who experienced it regretted their service, and those who went through campaign service, and especially the trauma of battle, would carry the experience for life. You identified with your fellow soldiers, the more so once the common bonds of mutual respect and selflessness had been cemented. There was nothing quite like true comradeship; only after it was proven could there be any relaxation in the more overt aspects of discipline, since there was then less need.

Men came to depend on these ways, often to the extent of having problems adjusting to civilian life after discharge, when in reaction their self-discipline could also break down, but that could be no concern of the Army. Self-discipline was essential to group discipline, and both entailed the rigorous maintenance of standards: relax the standards and both they and discipline suffered. And standards were indivisible, always an essential feature of an organization which might be rigidly hierarchical but was also one large team, which depended completely on everyone doing their job and doing it well. Give way on one area, give way in time on all; once any aspect of conduct or performance was diluted, even for the most plausible of reasons, then others would be affected and probably weakened too, until eventually essential cohesion would be lost. The only way to guard against that was to stay the best; and the only way to do that was through discipline and obedience.

Perhaps that particular maxim was best not dwelt on further. He might be about to test its application.

*   *   *   *

Once he had eaten something at the mid-day break he began to feel brighter, and managed to find some time for himself. The situation had to be confronted rationally. The sensible approach was to bring as strong a sense of detachment and objectivity to it as he could find. It was true he could very well be in deep trouble from which there was no going back, that his immediate future was full of uncertainty and danger, more unnerving than anything he had ever encountered on the battlefield. Whatever he did he had to stay cool. He wouldn't be able to stop allegations being made, or any other unwelcome development, and neither could he dare allow himself the possibility of escape, that he'd got this whole thing out of all proportion. But at the very least he now had a good idea of what he might be up against, and the morning had passed and nothing had happened. His position was by no means hopeless. He had his integrity and reputation, and he still had his wits. He didn't have to roll over meekly; there would be every scope for an effective defence if he kept his head and used his common sense.

Which was about as far as he got before the doubts started crowding in.

Lie, you mean.

He could. He could simply deny it, maintain that his likely one and only accuser must have been mistaken. It was very unlikely anyone else had searched him out at dinner from the many assembled faces there present. That would have required pre-planning and concerted effort, and why would anyone in the Cohort want to go along with that? They were his brother officers, weren't they? What about from the wider garrison then? He didn't have any enemies he could think of – at least none that would hold so strong a grudge to get involved in something like this. Anyway how would they have known what to look for, when he'd scarcely had time to think himself? He'd acted spontaneously. Alright, it was also unlikely Macula just happened to be looking at him when the toast was proposed. So he'd been waiting … and – of course!

No more doubt – quite certainly Macula had been behind its calling in the first place. How else could you explain such an exhortation to remembrance of an historical event, which wasn't totally obscure but of which nothing had been said in any garrison order or any conversation he'd heard, and certainly wasn't referred to in common parlance from one year to the next? Hang on. It wouldn't be obscure to the First Regiment of Augustus, that was also very sure. He seemed to recall from his school history that the proclaimed anniversary was a bit premature in regard to the precise month of the great battle, where Octavius and his fellow conspirators finally consolidated their power-driven, unconstitutional stranglehold on what little remained of the old Republic, but what was a month or two if it allowed young Macula to impose on his rustic inferiors? The man may not have placed much store on trapping him on the off-chance of finding his loyalties wanting, but the chance had come off better than he could have dreamt. He could easily have got someone else to observe too, just in case this centurion of the Second Italians fell for it, or with all his patrician riches arrange for a less truthful witness after the event. He had to be ready for anything, therefore, and in any case get his line straight. All he had to say was that he really couldn't remember, but if there had been some sort of hiatus in his response to the toast, well he must have had a frog in his throat. Or he'd had toothache. Anything to answer the question. If it ever came up.

One more thing was certain: he'd be well advised to avoid a confrontation. Telling someone like Macula that he must have been mistaken would be fraught with risk. Some sort of explanation was clearly desirable, and any which so much as hinted at admission to the accusation had to be avoided at all costs. On all the possible relative advantages and disadvantages of the courses open, however, admission or outright denial, he was having difficulty thinking through. And there was something else pressing.

What about the next time? If Macula was going to be around much longer he merely had to arrange some sort of repeat performance, and this time there'd be witnesses a-plenty. When was the man's attachment up? Presumably he'd be leaving with the Governor on his return to Caesarea, but as with his earlier arrival so perhaps with his leaving; it could be later, therefore, but you'd have to be on the gilded staff to be party to information like that. Even after his departure what was to stop him putting pressure on Veranius, perhaps through the Governor himself, to ensure another toast to Augustus at some suitable occasion when he really would be watched for any repetition? Veranius wouldn't be happy but he might have no choice. In this year of the great Caesar god he'd have no choice at all.

Where were fine principles now?

For there was a more fundamental problem which had lurked unbidden but which had been rising relentlessly to the fore in these pre-occupations, and could no longer be suppressed. As in every good military appreciation the problem was not to be left to instinct and assumption: it had to be spelt out and thought through. Was he going to stand up for his faith, or was he going to deny it? That was, as he at last forced himself to confront it, the central question. If he admitted the offence, pleaded some problem or other and gave the requisite assurance it wouldn't be happening again, then he might get away with it, probably with a reprimand delivered in the severest of terms but with no official record and little blemish to his reputation. It raised the question whether he'd be merely putting off the evil day when it might happen all over again, with all its predictable consequences, but importantly it would let him off the hook that threatened immediate danger. It would also give him time, time to consider further, time perhaps for Macula to disappear out of theatre and the whole thing to blow over with the least possible damage. Someone had to know mercy and fortune – why not him? Was he so underserving?

And if he were to make so base an admission or ask so false a question, what sort of man then would he be? There was one material fact he wouldn't be able to deny: he'd failed to respond to the toast, which was a reasonable and lawful command. He could apologize, explain, with luck talk his way out of it for now. But there was another inconvenient fact, was there not? – the reason, the real reason: the true explanation for what he'd done. That was the only thing that really counted, and it was that which he could admit, or that which he could deny. And if he had a shred of integrity he'd have some admitting to do, not only on the material facts of any accusation but, God save him, the Word. The Word in all its detail, the Word with all its power to shock, to inspire – and to enrage, because it would all have to come out. How else could he justify his actions, but for the simplest, most beautiful fact of all, the Word of the Very God himself? And if he once confessed it, how could he not tell the whole truth? A casual admission hoping to play the whole thing down surely couldn't succeed. The questions would keep coming until he was quickly and thoroughly exposed. Wouldn't they?

So the only right and honourable course was to admit everything, the whole truth, because it would be dragged out whatever he did, and better to volunteer it from the start. That's what speaking the truth meant, the whole truth and nothing but the truth. That's what being a follower meant. So then, he must fight with the sword of truth. It had only been a dinner toast, during a social occasion with ladies present, a symbolic gesture in good cheer, not an oath solemnly made on parade or at a formal libation to the gods. So what was all the fuss about?

But then ... it would be Macula's hand behind it when the onslaught came, and a man with his vindictiveness wouldn't be letting up. He'd press it with maximum force, he had the influence to see it through without let or mercy, and once in motion nobody would stop it, much less defend him. There could be no doubts about the outcome. People might want to carry on respecting him personally, but not what he represented, which they'd see as gross misjudgment, disloyalty and betrayal. And for what – fable and folly? Did he really have to go so far? Why did he have to stake everything on this? Wasn't there a middle way, that didn't involve telling a falsehood or being inexorably drawn to a point from which there was no return whichever way he turned? Or would it be better to admit everything from the start and simply tell the truth, no matter its dire implications?

And what good did he think could possibly come from that? Who was he to claim he didn't engage in falsehoods, anyway? Everyone knew there were times in life when you had to be economical with the truth. There was a greater good, and if it meant a little dissimulation to avoid pointless harm and unpleasantness, that was acceptable. No-one went round the forum proclaiming their inner secrets, or blurting out things people didn't need to know, or telling people gratuitous home-truths which wouldn't help anyone. If you were in a hole, stop digging. Better then to deny it. Say what you need to say to stop things getting any worse. That's what Sabena would do, and what she would want him to do now.

That's what they'd all do. 'What's the purpose that needs to be achieved here? What's the greater good in this instance?' they'd say. 'Honesty can't always be the best policy. It certainly isn't in war against an enemy. Come on, you're a soldier, you know that. In fact it's your positive duty to lie in such circumstances. And don't tell me this isn't a kind of war, when there are the likes of Macula around, or that he isn't the enemy. First principle of soldiers' law – deny everything. They can't touch you if they don't have a confession. Be strong, don't deviate, don't give room for any doubt.'

The inner voice broke off and he almost laughed to himself – the number of times soldiers had stood before him on orders and denied they had anything to do with this or that, when their guilt was obvious. It was part of the game, what everyone expected. Yes, sometimes. But then on other occasions a miscreant would exhibit some honesty, perhaps even some remorse, and you'd have to seriously think about the wider perspective, taking all things into account, about the man's future, about tempering the award, perhaps even the verdict. Regulations had to be upheld, justice done, breaches punished, example maintained, authority justified, but you also had to take account of character, and reliability, and the consequences which might apply if you were too harsh. Every case on its merits but also within principle, he supposed, even if that meant a little loosening around the edges. Insight and foresight would find the right outcome.

But of his own situation there could be no such clarity. So much was unknown, unpredictable. Veranius was a reasonable man but probably not the most reliable under pressure; he'd put a case up to a point, and then bend. No-one was safe from the reptile who'd turned up among them. Loyalty was the unit's glue, but now the serpent was loose in their midst and undermining the bonds which held them all together. If trust was so important how could he not admit the truth to his commanding officer, whatever the consequences? On the other hand you didn't burden your superior with a dilemma of his own if you could possibly avoid it. It was an unspoken aspect of command, a powerful one in the military fabric, and the senior you were the more it applied; nobody would thank you for elevating a problem when it was your responsibility to contain and resolve it yourself, by your own initiative and whatever means you thought appropriate. Don't create difficulties, solve them. If you had a problem then you kept it to yourself and overcame it yourself, the more so if others might otherwise be dragged in.

At least he was alone in that nobody else was involved; he hoped. But what about Sabena and the children? They were his overriding duty, not his career and not the Army. They were his inspiration. They were his life. And it was undoubtedly on that fundamental simplicity alone that he would have based his decision had he only been his former self – to say nothing, do nothing, nothing whatsoever which could ever remotely be to their detriment in any way. But that wasn't quite how it was now, was it? They were still as precious as ever, that went without saying. But now there was something else. Much more, in fact, which he just couldn't ignore: the truth, the force, the reality which when finally he was faced with the choice of denial had to be professed for its own sake. His faith. If it was goodness and loving-kindness which led him now in his new life, how could ill become of it? Having experienced revelation, didn't he see there was a new way to follow, and hadn't they been assured of guidance in what to do and say in the hour of need, that all things would work out for the best? Out of chaos there would be calm, in his life and in his mind.

*   *   *   *

It was a relief to be brought back to the present by the fussing of the company clerk. He could almost allow himself the hint of a possibility that the day might end as routinely as it had started. The front seemed to be working. He was doing his job, the Century was being administered, the afternoon was drawing on, everything was normal, there might even be grounds for some cautious optimism. He could begin to look forward to knocking off and finding release in the bosom of his family.

The sergeant-major admitted the runner. His nerves immediately tautened. It was a routine occurrence, part of everyday administration, but he knew before the man could open his mouth what he was going to say.

'Adjutant's compliments, Sir. You are to report to the Prefect, Sir. Now, Sir.'

*   *   *   *

So this was it. Suddenly there could be no hiding in the mundane, no relief, no escape. Just dry numbness and the unreal walk across the parade ground, the tightrope he must follow to safety or perdition, so help him God. God, or all the gods? – an ironical question, he thought. Funny how the essence of great matters could often be caught in a few pithy words. Very well, he knew what he had to say. He might keep his life if he was lucky; but it would mean court-martial, dismissal with disgrace, no pension, no privileges, possibly imprisonment, probably alienation from his wife and family, certainly destitution. It was so easy to fall into despond. All his thoughts on strength and ideals had evaporated as the morning dew. 'Steady' he told himself. He wouldn't be alone. He had the best Friend anyone could ever have, and he had to follow and be brave like a good soldier. He wasn't going to tell a falsehood, even if it would cause difficulties for his commanding officer and untold problems for the future. He had to tell the truth, and he hung on to that thought as he waited to be called in. For there was no chance the summons could have been for anything else.

*　　*　　*　　*

He saluted, and his heart sank as he saw Macula standing at the back, a tactful distance behind the CO's desk. The Adjutant wasn't there. Perhaps the proceedings were to be informal, if that signified anything.

'Stand easy, OC V. I'll come straight to the point. Tribune Macula tells me he saw you fail to give the toast to Augustus last night. Can this be true?'

'Sir, I did make the toast to the Emperor, and I also saluted Augustus Caesar.'

'I'm not talking about the toast to Tiberius Caesar. I'm talking about the second toast, to Augustus. The deified Augustus. You didn't respond to the proposal from the mess president. You didn't drink the divine health.'

'That is correct, yes, Sir.'

'Why not, Facilis? I assume you had an impediment of some kind, a sudden inability to swallow, or something like that, eh? Nothing wrong with that, it can happen to anybody. Tell me that is so.'

'I cannot say that was the case, Sir. I ... I just found I couldn't say it.'

'Couldn't say it? Why not, pray?'

'I felt I couldn't, against my conscience, Sir'.

'Your conscience? What on earth do you mean?'

'Sir, I have no problem giving my loyalty to the Emperor, or to his predecessor. But I cannot give him – or any other mortal – my loyalty as a god.'

'Why ever not? Is Augustus not indeed a god – deified by the express wish of the Senate and Roman People, whose servants we are? As soldiers we've always pledged our loyalty to him as Caesar the Deified One, and, when the occasion demands, drink to his immortal memory and present divinity, don't we?'

'Yes, Sir. I'm sorry, I had no intention to be disrespectful. And I did salute him, and started the first part of the response. And I have no difficulty drinking to the immortal memory. It's his divinity I cannot recognize, Sir.'

'It is not for us to pick and choose in these matters, Facilis. "Deified" was part of the toast. In fact it was very much integral to it. The loyal toast might be in the mess, taken with wine, but it's also in practice a solemn oath of allegiance to the supreme commander, a god himself. It's quite straightforward, just like anything else we have to do, and we do it properly, because it's perfectly clear it's a matter of duty, of complying with a lawful command and established custom and practice. So please tell me you will do so the next time we drink to Caesar Augustus Deified. It is, you must realize, an entirely reasonable request, is it not?'

Macula moved forward. 'Sir, I do believe Centurion Facilis needs to prove his loyalty to the great Augustus Deified by making the oath now, while he stands before us.'

Veranius spoke over his shoulder. 'Thank you, Tribune. I am the commander of this cohort in barracks. When I require your advice I shall ask for it.'

'But this is beyond your powers as a commanding officer. A centurion's too senior. It's got to go up the chain of command.'

'The chain of command!?' Veranius half-turned, speaking sharply. 'This is entirely an internal disciplinary matter, being dealt with by interview. My subordinates report to me, through the chain of command in this unit of which I am the senior tribune and commanding officer. I will deal with this officer as I see fit, including referring to superior authority if that is my judgment. This is not a summary hearing, and these are not orders. There's no charge, and let us hope there won't be one.'

The Prefect contemplated his fingernails, addressing the next remark to his subordinate.

'It's a good job Tiberius Caesar hasn't been deified too, isn't it? — despite the rather bizarre attempts of his obsequious Greek subjects down the coast to do so even while he's alive. Because if he was and you refused that oath you know what would happen then, don't you? We have to know exactly where you stand. You cannot as a commissioned officer withhold your oath of allegiance, either to the living Caesar or the deified Augustus, who still holds the authority of Imperator over us as he did in his life on earth, and always will. Assure me now, you do accept that?'

'Sir, of course I pledge my loyalty to Tiberius Caesar, who is our lawful Emperor and Commander. And I can swear loyalty to the memory of his predecessor, though he has been dead for nearly twenty years, as your reference to "as he did in life" correctly describes his mortality. But I cannot pretend that Augustus Caesar is a god.'

'You do understand the difference between *deus* and *divus*, don't you? All we're doing is commemorating the recognition of his *numen*, his divine spirit, not as a god with power in the nature of gods, and not to be confused with the *genius* or divine presence or guardianship in all of us, our families and the places and things around us, including every unit and camp in the Army. The *numen* acknowledges our recognition from the beginning, the apotheosis, and through it Augustus lives on with us to help protect Rome and its people. We honour him because of the divinity thus conferred upon him, as well as the virtues of his *genius*. What's so difficult about that, eh?'

'It was commented on at the time and didn't meet universal approval, I believe, Sir.'

'Dammit man. Who are you to question the ordering of Rome? It's Augustus' memory that we're honouring here, instituted by great men who understood Rome's greatness and our eternal debt to its deliverer. Don't think Facilis, just do it.'

'I'm sorry, I can't, Sir.'

'There's no such word.'

'Honoring his memory as the founder of the Empire isn't the problem, Sir. Nor his accomplishments as Imperator.'

'What then?'

'The claim that he could have any sort of divinity, which I believe he rejected in his own lifetime. Sir.'

He knew he'd gone too far, but it was too late.

Macula moved as if to protest again, but Veranius raised his arm purposefully, without turning round. He rose, looked him in the eye for some time, exasperation slowly becoming resignation. He spoke quietly.

'Very well. You must realize this matter will have to be reported to my superiors and considered at the appropriate level. You know too I can well do without this now. We're about to be fully stretched on the streets out there, and I don't need one of my officers creating manning and disciplinary problems in the middle of it all. You are now to consider yourself under open arrest. You are to confine yourself to living-in accommodation in the Officers' Mess, where you are forbidden to discuss this or make contact with anyone until further notice. Anyone, do you hear? Think on it well, Facilis. Use this opportunity to do some serious reflecting on the nature of reality. Are you quite clear? I want your assurance that next time an oath of loyalty is required to Caesar Augustus, wherever and whenever that may be and in whatever form as prescribed by lawful authority, you will give it in full. If you can satisfy this direct order by tomorrow morning then we can forget this incident ever occurred. If not then I will have no choice but convene official proceedings and refer this matter upwards. Dismiss.'

'Sir.' And he caught a glimpse of Macula's furious face as he saluted and marched out.

The position could not have been plainer. The problem was out: the prelude, if he didn't retreat, to full and public exposure as a self-confessed enemy of the State.

*   *   *   *

As he adjusted to his surroundings he attempted anew to gather his thoughts. He had survived, and had a few hours to consider his position, of which more had been revealed, and more quickly, than he might have hoped. The allegation had been made, and he had admitted it. His fears had been well-founded; it hadn't been a fevered imagination that had run him ragged and brought him to this pass; his intuition had been borne out only too well; and when the crunch came, for better or for worse he'd been honest. Too honest. The material fact of his admission had not only been established, he'd allowed himself to make a foolish comment on controversial past national events which could be construed as sedition, and provide more evidence to be held against him. He'd been given an unambiguous order to rectify his misdemeanour which would effectively mean renouncing his faith. He hadn't yet been forced to admit either his full apostasy or his conversion, however, for which he had to be grateful, but that would be the next thing to be dragged out of him, no doubt, inexorably played out in a train of events he and he alone had initiated. The CO had been unusually short with him, and he'd had a right to be angry. More positively, he thought, his show of ire might have been a protective attempt to keep Macula at bay and the matter retained within his own powers, in a legal process which once launched would be likely to escalate beyond his control. All things considered he'd been lenient, given the incomprehensible behaviour with which he'd been presented by a respected lieutenant. Loyalty had been compromised, and in more ways than one. He could see that. Irritating your commanding officer was never a good idea.

So what had he, miscreant, expected? For everything to carry on as normal? Veranius could have gone a lot further, either by insisting on a fresh oath there and then or arranging for formal orders and likely referral to the garrison commander; he could also have pursued the matter of religion in earnest, which might have led anywhere, but nowhere very pleasant; instead he had seemed pointedly to have avoided it. He could imagine the discussion after he had left the room, the Prefect having to tread carefully with the arrogant young interloper,

who had so much power to damage anyone's career.   Of course he
regretted putting Veranius in this position: as supportive as he might
be, he couldn't be expected to protect him when the pressure was really
on. The only conclusion to be drawn was that nothing was certain. His
confession had not only deepened the trouble he'd created for himself, it
had also seriously risked alienating his superior officer, who would have
no choice but abandon him if he didn't give way. Macula's evidence, even
uncorroborated, was no longer the issue – it was his own testimony by
which he would be damned. But it had to have been that way. To allow
himself now to think otherwise was only to invite more doubt and self-
recrimination than he could cope with. At least he'd told the truth and
stuck to his principles. Hadn't he?

If this was the price of faith then the circumstances of its profession
seemed quite unreal. That men should argue over loyal toasts to dead
emperors might in sensible times be risible; in the reality of his situation
it was deadly serious. No-one in their right mind could fail to overlook
the prospect of court-martial and whatever dire retribution might lie
beyond. No-one in their right mind would put himself out on such
a precarious limb like this. It was a fact: hailing a dead emperor as
some sort of god was normal for a people who venerated their family
ancestors to the point of worship.   Good Romans had always done
it; his parents had done it, and brought him up to do it too. It was
unremarkable, normal, natural, traditional, seemly.

So what was wrong with the same idea applied to the father of the
nation? Octavius, great-nephew and adopted son of the first Caesar,
who could justifiably have claimed to have brought peace out of a
generation of internecine ruin, who had taken the Julian mantle and
imposed the new arrangement of state to endure in his own person
and issue, sealed with his own re-naming. Rome could only fulfil its
greatness if its deliverer stayed central to its identity, not as dictator
but as father to his people, with all their folk myths and attachment
to the Senate and their own self-image as The People, and everything
that made for unity and strength. What was more natural that those
same people should venerate his memory as they would their own
fathers'? What was fitter that the ancient gods, takers of human form

and guardians of every endeavour of men, should admit this one of superhuman achievement to their number? And what more seemly that the Army, direct heirs of his prowess in the field, now required his own unquestioning obedience in this matter, like every other man who had sworn allegiance to their Caesar when first they became a soldier, and every new year since?

Only to someone who faithfully tried to follow the man from Nazareth it must be impossible.

Very well then. He must face the consequences. Indeed the trial had already begun. He might have only one night to see whether he was worthy, whether he had the courage and the faith. There could be no illusion that once the train was set in motion, neither repute nor virtue nor any kind of justification could avert an outcome of utmost misery, and very likely death.

But fool! He only had himself to blame. This was just the down-payment of the price for his trouble. He'd acquired this insane idea from somewhere and now he was throwing everything away, all that he'd worked for and all that he loved. So he had it coming to him, as his soldiers would have said, and it would be poetic justice for his hubris and naivety to think that anything like this could ever end well, whether for those of genuine faith, weak faith or no faith at all. To contemplate otherwise was pure madness. The certainties of the spirit were all very well from a remove, not so convincing when you were actually in that black hole you'd dug for yourself and suddenly the sides were caving in.

Thus the threads of doubt and resolution pulled this way and that, until he could stand it no more. At last in the calm he was able better to think of Whom he was follower and servant, in Whose name they had been encountered and brought into the way. The Prince of Peace was with him. All would be well. There would yet be a path through the thorns and snares that had sprung up around him so quickly. Prayer would bring strength and guidance.

He would not be alone.

*　*　*　*

The men were told their officer commanding had been taken ill and was being kept in quarantine in single officers' accommodation. The word would soon be out from the Mess staff that the Centurion of the Fifth did not appear to have anything wrong with him, with some speculating freely on the real cause of his confinement, but for the time being no-one could possibly guess the truth behind this most unusual occurrence.

*   *   *   *

'You idiot!' Longinus exclaimed in exasperation.

'Thank you for coming.'

'Have your lost your mind, Favonius? Can't you see how ridiculous you're being? Get word to the CO now, tell him it was all a mistake, a thoughtless aberration when you didn't know what you were doing and that you'll rectify it now.'

'I can't do that.'

'Yes you can. Tell him you were drunk or something and that it won't happen again. Just say the words, you don't have to believe them. Can't you see, not everyone has an over-developed sense of honour like yours? If you're never prepared to give a little you'll be destroyed.'

'This isn't about honour.'

'Oh really? What then?'

'So has it got out?'

'Not yet, but it soon will. Come on, out with it. What's behind this?'

'I haven't told a soul. Thank you for letting Sabena know. How is she, and the children?'

'How do you think?'

'I wish I could have been able to explain to them. Will you do it for me?'

'Explain what, exactly? How you're letting down the woman most men would give their eye-teeth for? Surely you've discussed this nonsense with Sabena before now?'

'It's not nonsense, and yes, of course I have, but she doesn't have the … the faith, quite so strongly. She hasn't come to that stage yet.'

'If she ever does. What do you expect her to do – turn to a god that seems quite happy to destroy you all? You must see her tonight. You need some sense knocked into you somehow or other.'

'So you haven't told her why I'm here?'

'Of course I've told her. Your wife has a right to know her husband's as good as arrested. What passes between you after that is your business. But you'd better tell her straight. And listen to her.'

'I'm stuck here.'

'She'll be in to see you. I've seen to it.'

'Thanks, appreciated. And you, how much do you know?'

'I'm the Senior Centurion, Favonius. The CO's concerned. We're both concerned. We just want you to see sense. You should have spoken to me first.'

'How could I?'

'That's your problem. But soon won't be. It'll be out of your hands. But if you'd given it any real consideration and discussed it properly you'd have realized my answer would tell you all you needed. All for this god of yours. Pull yourself together.'

*   *   *   *

He was to be out of the reckoning for the next two days, the subject of numerous conversations on his future, though his present predicament was but a fragment in a story beyond the wildest imagination. Momentous events were afoot, and without any help from him the world would go its usual way regardless, pre-occupied and oblivious to what it would barely notice. The Cohort would continue its duties, maintaining the presence and keeping its corner of the Empire in order. In the city beyond his confines the climax of the season was now approaching, with the bustle of folk in from the countryside, noise and cooking smells all around, and everywhere, on every corner and from many a thousand courtyards, the bleatings of sheep, unsettled, unknowing.

Had he been free and not beset with his problems then events might possibly have turned out otherwise. Direct linkage might be only tenuous, yet who would be able to say from the tangle of moving pieces that the history of the world might not have been very different? Unwittingly he'd already had one chance to change it; unwittingly he could have another; his difficulties with the oath were part of this story of connection, though his field of vision was perforce limited. The state of his mind that late afternoon was an all-absorbing pre-occupation with his great dilemma, which to him directly concerned his loved ones above all, and a few others to lesser degree. Unbeknown was a far wider cast, none of whom could appreciate the import of the unfolding drama in which they too were players of some extent. His own survival was crucial. Ironically, notwithstanding his dire predicament, he was probably in the safest of places available.

If he had been at liberty there is no telling what might have happened.

THE AUDIENCE

Veranius knew he would have to move quickly. Naturally he hadn't been prepared to give that disagreeable young man the satisfaction of asking whether he had already been to the Governor. It would have been highly irregular if that had been the case, but he would not have put it past him to try. The political interest was strong, the situation exceptional, he had the social status and who-knew-what commission to interfere. This was no time to be pre-empted and defer, even to somebody as powerful as Macula. A wise officer would seize the initiative and get in first.

The Governor's diary for the day would be full but might squeeze in a principal officer of the garrison if he pleaded urgency. It was pushing his luck, but to have delayed could have been fatal. If he was to make an effort to save his centurion he had to get to the Governor before any preconceptions became fixed by a rival briefing which might not be entirely objective. He would rely on the unspoken code of the Army, and hope the Governor was still enough of a soldier to respond. It was a risk, of course, when his own reputation and credibility might be at stake, and exposure to the top man himself would only compound the risk several times over. First things first. A commanding officer's prerogative of access didn't normally extend beyond his immediate superior; the Province's unusual command set-up made it feasible, however; the garrison commander would be unlikely to refuse; it was fortuitous the Progress was on, with the Governor and his staff in residence, and when normal protocols might be loosened; and he did have that connection, which it was time to use.

Not that access was any guarantee of success; he was well aware of that. An individual's fate would count for little against the accepted norms, which in the Army were probably more rigidly maintained than anywhere else, but the Army also purported to be systematic, and capable of dealing with extenuating circumstances. These could always be elevated, if you were confident enough. The higher a matter was taken the wider the considerations likely to have to be taken into account, and in this case they'd be numerous. The downside was there would be others who would want to have their say too, with motives of their own and possibly not all related to the military dimension. Whilst he had no reason to doubt the Governor's judgment in this matter, neither would he care to predict his reaction. He couldn't claim to know him well, having met him properly only twice, for his initial interview and then last night, when he'd held back admirably, he thought, from overplaying the opportunity for ingratiation. Men of quality didn't need to indulge in anything so vulgar, but ought to conduct themselves in the same straightforward manner of relaxed formality as if they were in the superior's position. The cause of one's career called for nothing less.

That was the more subtle and proper way to make an impression, if not, he might concede, always the most effective. Not that style was likely to make much difference anyway; so far at any rate the Governor had shown little inclination to take him into his confidence. There had been only the merest hint of any recognition of their social affinity and shared region of origin, but then what did you expect with such an obvious disparity in age, seniority and wealth – indeed, from anyone in high authority with such an unflattering reputation? There was a distance about the man, a coolness which went beyond the usual aura of assumed dignity and reserve so often displayed by the great and the good; and everyone knew about the stubborn temper. Was he judging him too harshly? Rarefied status and near-absolute power made for an understandable detachment, and it took an exceptional incumbent to break the mould and treat their subordinates like fellow men. Perhaps it was different back on the coast, where life would be considerably more congenial and the garrison there more relaxed than in the tension-racked atmosphere of the city. There was no time now to cultivate the relationship as much as he would have liked, but at least there was one, of sorts, and the omens were good. Last night's reception must have been sent by the Gods. This was the moment. He had to do it.

For, whatever his personal feelings, the circumstances of the case did warrant attention at the highest level – not so much the business of the oath itself, which was manageable if unfortunate, but the strange involvement of Tribune Macula, and the distinct possibility of things being said in high places which might not altogether reflect well on his own position. The problem was the risk element in seeking the meeting. Either the great man would see at once it was something he ought to know about, and, with a bit of luck, wish to give some direction on; or he'd take the concern badly, as a troublesome trifle with which he categorically should not be bothered; an indication, furthermore, of some weakness and lack of judgment by the officer bringing it – a serious mistake on whose part, in fact. That was indeed the problem. He could only be guided by what he'd prefer if he'd been in the Governor's boots, and reckoned on the former possibility. You didn't get to the top, or stay there very long, without knowing everything that was going on. The Province might only be a minor prefecture but everyone realized how difficult it was to manage – a test for the most astute of statesmen. And knowledge was power – far better to be informed than not. The rock-bottom of it was that he'd only be carrying out what he considered to be his duty, and the Governor would understand that. Yes, he had to be told. He was the seat of final authority, with unquestionable power to make or break, to ordain life and death, and he'd been out here longer and knew the place better than any of them. He was the old hand, who'd know what had to be done.

He could thus almost congratulate himself that he was acting quickly and decisively to solve what threatened to be a considerable dilemma for the chain of command, while being rather less sure, if he were totally honest, about the realities of his own ability to find the right solution. To save an officer who didn't seem to want to save himself? He couldn't go through all that again; but how to assuage his own somewhat ruffled ego and retain any sort of influence on the process now? He must be guided by his better instincts, of honour and loyalty, and at least try his best.   All the same it would be prudent not to commit to a position which might prove indefensible.   He would have to test the water and see how things developed, always remembering how vital it was to keep his own credibility intact.   The first thing was to block the troublesome tribune before he could do irreparable damage.   Speaking up for his centurion was important, and so too was protecting his own interests and quashing this challenge to exercise command of his own unit as he saw fit, without any interference from a popinjay like Licinius Macula. The Governor would find different angles to come from, no doubt; that's what accomplished men did.   So yes there was considerable risk, but everything had a cost and everything a benefit, and a balance always had to be struck.   If only things could be left to the Army!   What was it that got into these soldier-politicians' heads the day they exchanged cuirass for toga?   Why couldn't they just carry on with the simple ways they'd all once been part of and enjoyed?

Because the ambitious top drawer weren't real soldiers, that's why. Not most of them.   The Army was a convenience, a means to an end, which was a public career with the riches and recognition that went with it, a seat in the Senate to live out their days in useless pontification and petty scheming.   Those who stayed in the military were often very good indeed, it had to be said, and they were all products of the same system. And who was he to say that, who had himself inherited privilege and a fortune of sorts?   It was the order of life: everyone had their place, someone had to do the dirty work, and someone had to supervise them. And he ought not to demean the politicians in one breath and turn to them for guidance the next.   Be grateful for the system, that you were part of it, that one day you too might be offered some agreeable sinecure and more favours from the Gods.   You might even stand for office yourself, pursuing advancement with the same vigour you seem to want to decry in others now.   Don't close doors that don't need closing, not yet.   It was after all the duty of the leaders of society to put their advantages in life at the service of the State.

Before that there was a military career to follow, and right now a little difficulty to resolve.   And as in most things which depended on the consent of others, success was more likely if the approach were relaxed, collegiate – the attitude the privileged few should always adopt in their relations with each other. Hadn't he just told himself so ...?

The runner was back. He would be seen at the eleventh hour.

*   *   *   *

By the time he reached the Camp Commandant's office on the upper floor of the Praetorium he felt more apprehension than his habitual appearance of effortless ease might have indicated to an observer. Even he, now off his own ground, couldn't entirely suppress it. There could be no certainty: one slip and his own career could be brought to a peremptory halt, more likely stifled behind the scenes without him even realizing it until future promotion lists started to confirm the unwelcome truth.

That notion had to be banished. Confidence was the word and confidence the method: all that was necessary was confidence, plus the light touch which went with it like a horse and carriage. So often with these things it was the fortuitous remark, the shared joke, the indefinable empathy which did the trick, more than any amount of hard work and meritorious achievement away from the limelight; then the Gods could show their favours continuing years hence. Such was the fraught business of furthering one's career, of which impressing one's superior was by far the most important ingredient; but it had to be treated like the game it was, and done with as little obvious self-regard as possible. Advantages of breeding and education ought to make that second nature, and so it must be now. There must be no hesitation, no self-doubt, no introspection. Important men had the power to break you on a whim, chance encounters and difficult situations the potential to daunt the bravest hearts; but nothing would intimidate the man of the world who knew how things should be done.

He did have to see the Governor alone, however. It wasn't Veterus the camp comedian who would be the problem; it wasn't him who was likely to question the need for confidentiality. It was the secretary-*cum*-personal assistant, Seneccio, who was sure to be about and who might see things very differently. He would have to play it as it came, but there was no doubt he had to make every effort to get the Governor by himself, or else at best what he had to say would be hostage to fortune, at worst spin off on unpredictable trajectories to possible disaster. If the secretary were to be in attendance the whole enterprise became immeasurably more problematic. Macula might just as well be there too, and the whole thing as good as over and done with. He hadn't thought of that being a serious possibility until now; with the moment of truth upon him it seemed to be little other. He remembered too how he'd agreed to Macula being present at his own interrogation of the errant centurion. How the wheel of irony would have its turning and inconvenient way! The notion of him turning up again had to be resisted. All challenges were to be faced and overcome. There was no alternative.

*   *   *   *

Veterus wasn't very helpful. It would be quite impossible without going through the Secretary – 'You know how things are.' He wasn't altogether surprised. The old soldier could be forgiven; he wasn't going to jeopardize his relations with the top man, not after years of hard soldiering and with a cushy retirement to look forward to. He was quite happy for a commanding officer to have a personal interview, but all appointments had to be vetted by the personal secretary and this was no exception. There was no point in arguing; Seneccio was clearly already party to the situation. The only thing for it was to put his request for privacy personally to the Governor directly they met.

It was well known commandant and secretary didn't get on, both seeing their prime task as defending their respective military and civil interests against the other, and the comical notion struck him that here was undisguised rivalry more suited to a couple of schoolboys. No doubt the old soldier would have liked to have sorted the skinny little freedman out in short order if he ever had the chance, but the man had been in post for years and, it had to be assumed, had the Governor's full confidence. The military were always being unreasonably jealous of their own affairs, he could hear Seneccio saying, but as gate-keeper he had the sole and exclusive right to be the one that took all business, and his own informed slant on the priorities therein, to his master – how else could the Governor's time be managed efficiently or the right decisions made, especially on civil affairs, of which he was principal adviser? The Army didn't exist in isolation. It had to comply with imperial policy covering every conceivable aspect of government. Which was fair enough, though he like every other commanding officer would have no doubts with whom they would rather deal. Politicians and their hold on power were a fact of life; their acolytes behind the scenes, career-seekers and assorted politicos with all sorts of personal agendas and influence of their own, were equally dangerous. None were to be trusted under any circumstances; that was the received opinion among his own profession, and he had no reason to disagree. If Macula had already got to the secretary you could be sure the Governor knew everything too, whereas the fewer who knew anything about this matter the better. Above all the determination of its outcome had to be kept out of the hands of people like this. The Army was straightforward, robust and honest, politicos invariably devious, weak and mendacious.

The three of them proceeded at pace down the corridor almost as though it were a race, with him, by far the youngest, politely bringing up the rear. None spoke. He could sense their thoughts, and they no doubt his.

They paused on the threshold, Seneccio triumphant and entering alone. Presently they heard a voice within, becoming louder as its owner approached in person.

'Ah, the Prefect of *Secunda Italica*. Come in, won't you? That will be all, thank you gentlemen. I expect my commanding officers to have the right of private interview.'

His relief was short-lived. As soon as they were alone the Governor said: 'Do take a seat. Thank you so much for last night. Such a convivial evening, we did enjoy it. And the Second looked superb on parade. A fine unit, Veranius, you can be very proud of them. Now, I imagine you've come to talk about Favonius Facilis.'

*   *   *   *

'Yes, Your Excellency, I asked to see you as soon as your commitments allowed', he said, doing his best to give the impression that the Governor's question had come as no surprise. Blast that snake Macula. He'd got in first after all. With that runt of a secretary too, no doubt. It didn't matter now.

'Well what's your view?'

View?! What did that mean? View of what, exactly, when there were some aspects probably best not volunteered? Not the punishment, surely? Not already. He couldn't jump to an answer on that, not so soon, not without some considered thought. He hadn't expected it, of course. Stupid of him: no contingency plan, no reserve, disaster. He tried to think, desperately, although this conversation after but a few moments was only going in one direction. Did the Governor really know everything, or could he be using shock tactics to unsettle him and force his hand prematurely? In the confused and instantaneous workings of his mind only one word loomed large, and it was that one again – irony. Hadn't he only just conducted his own interview with his centurion along very similar lines – the direct, disabling, disarming approach designed to achieve instant mastery? Very possibly. Effective tactics, scarcely surprising. Soldiers didn't beat about the bush. Evidently they weren't alone, but then the Governor had been a soldier too, once. The system had done its work, and honed the style with a hefty helping from the school of statecraft: the only way to respond was to be equally forthright. Don't be ridiculous! Play it safe. Accomplished military tribunes had nothing to learn when it came to oral warfare. Three things were certain. He had to assume that Macula had given his own version in full. It wasn't worth taking any more risks by being over-defensive, thus speedy recounting of the full position was clearly in order. And a direct answer to a direct question was definitely advisable. It had nonplussed him a little, but the reply was out in a couple of heart-beats.

'It's extremely unfortunate, Your Excellency. No-one saw him or complained, except apparently Tribune Macula. Although when he came before me and had the chance to deny it, he didn't.' Conscious that he could not leave it there, he added quickly: 'He is technically guilty of course, but it might be premature to condemn him.'

'He's been got at, don't you think?'

More confusion. Where was the Governor going now? Got at by whom? The frightful Macula? His peers? Himself? Anyone? He could only hope the cool exterior was still in place, but the best his flustering self could do was:

'Your Excellency?'

'Come, Veranius. Your loyalty to your subordinate does you credit. But your man has been captured – by those Galileans, hasn't he?'

In the seemingly endless pause that followed, all half-formed notions on the possible course of this discussion became as nought. There was no point in pretending to any sort of initiative now. He might still hope for an invitation to find a solution to this problem, as the junior of two wise and dispassionate men bringing their experience together to mull over the options, so that what might once have been intractable became with surprisingly little effort quite simple; but to reach that point it was looking ominously likely he was going to be put through his paces; and at this rate he wouldn't be getting very far. Faced with informed authority the only sensible course was complete candour. He knew about the prophet from Nazareth of course, but nothing about any contact with anyone in the Cohort, no. This was serious territory. To have had any inkling of a foreign cult affecting his command, and not to have reported it immediately, would always have been a highly questionable lapse on his part; to have failed on this score when the Governor himself seemed to know all about it – that would be an error of cardinal proportions. Admission of ignorance was the only way to safety, but before he could say anything, the Governor went on:

'And I understand you neglected to question him in that regard.'

'I … I'm sure you're right, yes, Your Excellency. And, no, I didn't know at all. I had no idea.'

'Well I'm led to believe that's the case, Veranius. I'm surprised you had no idea.'

'I'm afraid not, Your Excellency.'

'Never mind. It's well understood that a commanding officer has lots of things to worry about. On the other hand, the moral welfare of our troops is rather important. Especially if it involves potential disloyalty of any kind, don't you think?'

'Of course, Your Excellency.'

'It's incumbent on all commanding officers to be alert to such things, wouldn't you say?'

'Yes, Your Excellency. I'm sorry.'

'So tell me, what's to be done with Centurion Facilis, with his idiosyncratic views on religion and the deification of Caesars?'

'I'd hoped, after a suitable assurance of good conduct, you would be able to pardon him, Your Excellency.'

What was he doing? He didn't have to let his rapid defeat undo him as completely as this. Or had he just posted a lame signal of defiance, a forlorn rising to a challenge when all was undone and there was nothing left to lose?

'Pardon him? My dear Veranius, there's so much of interest in that pregnant little phrase. That would be quite a novel line to take. And rather open to interpretation, we might say.'

'I mean … I mean if he does the sensible thing and recants, of course Your Excellency.'

'Yes, I understand he's gone away to think about it. Not a bad move on your part, in fact quite pragmatic. Though not perhaps one that would meet with universal approval.'

Macula had done his job thoroughly. There could be no half-measures now: if he was going to take the little bounder on then caution had finally to be abandoned. It was all or nothing: it had to be a full-blown defence of the centurion. No point in prevarication. The gamble had already been entered; it now had to be followed through, however high the stakes were becoming. He must reach for what little guile he could find.

'Your Excellency, I am indebted to the diligence of Tribune Macula. If it hadn't been for him this wouldn't have come to light, and of course we have to know immediately if foreign cults have infiltrated the Army. But I'm sure you'll appreciate my concern. I don't want to lose a good officer. There must be a way of resolving this.'

'Ah yes, the Junior Tribune of *Prima Augusta*. An ambitious young man, very keen to live up to his birthright. Quite understandable.

As senior cohort they are my Guard, after all, and one does have to indulge them from time to time. That he'd want to make a point or two about pedigree and all that sort of thing, and no doubt make a name for himself – very understandable. We all know how young officers can get carried away with regimental rivalries. And what with the season of Augustan anniversaries almost upon us – only ten days to the First Victory and the Declaration of Imperator, if I'm not mistaken, and what a pity we won't be in the city to enjoy another round of oath-making – it would have been churlish to refuse a reasonable request about the trooping of your standard, don't you think? It's a pity for your man he's been smoked out a little earlier than might have been expected, but rest assured it would have come about sooner or later. Anyway, we can see how Tribune Macula might be a little sensitive on the subject of Augustus Deified, can't we? And I think you were quite right to take up his suggestion of the oath at your dinner.'

His discomfiture was sealed. He'd had no choice over either the form of the parade, with Macula's strutting up and down like a puffed-up juvenile cockerel, or the dinner oath; and the Governor knew it. The former event might have been unusual but the latter was entirely unexceptional, and you didn't raise objections over either if you had any regard for your own future. Besides, he could hardly have been expected to foresee the outcome of one individual's problem with the toast to Augustus and the difficulties it was causing. There was nothing for it. He was going to have to let Facilis go.

'Yes, Your Excellency. We are privileged to have such a distinguished young officer among us.'

'I'm pleased you see it that way, Veranius. You agreed because it seemed eminently reasonable and you didn't want Second Italians to appear disobliging. And I imagine your soldiers were delighted to get the chance to show their loyalty too, to be every bit as loyal in fact as those smart fellows by the sea. But this is all by and by. The important thing now is your man. You obviously think highly of him.'

That was a strange comment. You could almost think it offered a sliver of hope, but it would be forlorn. If his centurion really did have to be sacrificed, now that his own sympathies had been ruthlessly exposed and his position revealed as indefensible, the least he could do was put a good word in as mitigation. 'He's one of the best, Your Excellency. Brave, reliable, honourable. His men respect him, without great show but solidly enough, and would follow him anywhere.'

'And would you trust him yourself?'

'With my life, Your Excellency.'

'I see. And of course he is the Hero of the Hill.' And after a pause: 'If it had been anyone else in this ... situation ... it might have been so much easier. You said reliable, but the trouble is – is he? Now, this day, I mean, with this burden that he seems to have placed so neatly on himself? Is it at all plausible it's not going to follow him around and cause all sorts of inconvenience to others, all because we failed to grasp the nettle, when they would rightly have every expectation not to be encumbered with matters of this sort? Let us not forget he is a man of free will. If he insists on condemning himself by his own words, in the end there isn't much we can do about it. There's more to duty than the brotherhood of *Secunda Italica*, is there not?'

'Yes of course, Your Excellency. Military discipline must be maintained at all times. The chain of command has to be seen to uphold the demands of loyalty to the Emperor and the religion of Rome. Facilis was given a lawful command to pledge his allegiance to Augustus Caesar Deified in my presence, and he refused.' And he added: 'And my duty is to uphold that discipline and enforce the regulations.'

'Indeed so, Prefect. I'm much gratified for your confirmation of the facts of the case. And now, what is your recommendation?'

He had been kept firmly in his place, which is what he had deserved. 'Your Excellency, the situation demands that an example is made.'

'I'm gratified you should think so. Now we can proceed. So how is this to be done? You're his commanding officer.'

Had he to utter the very words of condemnation? Was this play-acting to be the sudden end of the deadly game he should have cautioned himself against from the outset – worse even, due to the abundantly clear risk now to his own career, than a pre-emptory decision in which there would have been no discussion whatsoever? He'd blown it, his prospects and family's fortunes thoroughly compromised, and all over one individual who in his stubbornness and foolishness was the cause of this ridiculous affair, who had effectively determined on his own destruction, and was now all but lost anyway. The Governor had played him along and was probably thoroughly enjoying his discomfiture. If Facilis' fate rested on his CO's wits then he had been failed badly, but it had been he himself who was the greater fool – for having anything to do with the man's obsessive delusion over a foreign god which wasn't going to help him, or anyone, ever.

An officer's judgment was so important. Whatever your other qualities, if you didn't use your head then things were bound to go wrong which really shouldn't, and the reputation from that kind of failing would soon follow you everywhere. This whole business was rapidly shaping up to be just such an example of unbounded folly, totally unnecessary, wanton, gratuitous, irresponsible in the extreme. What had he thought he was doing, taking the Governor on in a one-sided little contest which was always going to end in disaster? How could the Army be expected to put up with such loose judgment on his part as this, given the fundamental need for discernment and discretion in its leaders? What of the greater loyalties that underlay the soldier's ethos, or the primacy of the group over the individual when the group's cohesion was at stake – especially when they were being negated by such an elementary error? He should have known better. Bludgeoned and browbeaten, he could almost hear himself say the words: "I recommend due process of military law, Your Excellency, followed by immediate execution." But faced with the abyss he struck out on impulse. What he said was:

'I cannot betray him, Your Excellency. He should be allowed to go off to some backwater far from here where he can continue his career in obscurity and be less likely to upset anyone, at least until he's got this fixation out of his system.'

It had to be the end of his own career, obviously, and he would regret this for the rest of his days. Showing weakness was not a virtue deserving of leniency. It simply guaranteed everything would be lost, including, for good measure, the original object of his concern, his centurion. He would have plenty of time now to appreciate the virtues of the simple life back on his impoverished estate in the Samnian hill-country, a promising career casually tossed away, a scolding wife to remind him of his failure into a bitter old-age. It was not what he had sought this interview for.

*   *   *   *

The Governor rose. 'Let's go and have a look at the jewel of empire,' he said, moving over to the balcony. Veranius joined his leader in a survey of the great city, its day's-end sultriness rising up to meet them in the changing light.

'Impressive, don't you think? Built to rival our own. An asset, we must believe. On the other hand, perhaps we should rue the great Pompeius and his men ever coming here and leaving us this ... legacy. You've been honest with me, Veranius, and must excuse my little game. I was interested to see how far you would go.

'Whatever decisions we take in the course of our careers, we have to proceed from a basis of getting the facts straight first, don't you agree? The emphasis being on all the facts, all of them in their context and not just those to which we might be partial. Then it becomes a matter of judgment in deciding the important ones, discarding the less relevant, making reasonable allowance for what we don't or can't know, sifting the pros and cons, coming to the right conclusion, choosing the best course of action from a range of options based strictly on the possible – because there's always a choice – keeping in mind the broad scheme before us but not overlooking important detail, keeping everything as simple as possible, mindful of the likely side-effects, with half an eye for the unforeseen, and never failing to ask ourselves what we're trying to achieve and whether this really is the best way of doing it.

'All very logical and essentially simple we might think, but you'd be surprised how many apparently intelligent men never seem to get the basics right, and cabals and committees no better. They fall at the very first stage and run around with an incomplete picture, or make false assumptions, have unreasonable expectations, get distracted, get stuck down rabbit holes, then wonder when it's too late why the wrong decision got made. Or they have good intentions but don't think everything through, so we have the law of unintended consequences. Or they allow themselves to be swayed by vested interests, or wishful thinking, or downright emotion, or those with the loudest voices, or whoever speaks to them last. None of us are clairvoyants, no matter how well we think we trust the omens, and there's always the imp of misrule to contend with – if anything can go wrong, it will. And hindsight's a wonderful thing, but how often can we look back and see what should have been done, and force ourselves to admit that getting it right really shouldn't have been all that difficult?

'No wonder the history of mankind is so full of strife and failure – we will keep getting things plain wrong. It's as if the more blinkered our existence the better, as though reason is there to be denied, on any pretext which suits the agenda. It seems that's our distinguishing characteristic. And the further we advance from the natural state and become civilized – and I use the word in the ironical sense – the further removed we seem to be from reality and the more we turn ourselves on our heads with self-justification and unreason. Soldiers, farmers, medical men, the housewife with children to feed, in fact anyone who has to work to eat, or anyone who understands the basics of life and death – these are the realists, who know the priorities, what has to be done and how to do it, and can't afford to slip up lightly.

'All of which isn't to say we don't sometimes have to resort to being what some would call unreasonable when dealing with difficult people who would be an impediment – let them prevail and nothing gets done at all, because appeals to reason aren't always enough. Your task is the pursuit of reason tempered with realism and the will to implement it against opposition, Veranius. But you'd better be right. Well, you won't be every single time, of course. We all make mistakes. Success goes to him who makes the least. Wouldn't you agree?'

'Of course, Your Excellency.'

'And I'd say this, Veranius – as a rule there's no point in inflicting more pain in this world if we can possibly avoid it. If a commanding officer could find a way of dealing with a case of the type before us without prejudicing good order and military discipline, we would all hope he would follow it. So it shouldn't be beyond our wit to find a satisfactory arrangement in this instance, particularly when it's not yet common knowledge.

'Facilis' valour on the battlefield is neither here nor there – we expect all our officers and men to do their duty efficiently. The situation here, however, is of a brave man who's the braver for sticking to his belief and at great personal risk, and that's something with which we should have some empathy, even if it might require a little imagination on our part. On the other hand we can't overlook the disobeying of a lawful command, and the facts in that respect seem clear and unlikely to be disputed, in which case the only verdict a court could recommend would be a guilty one, with a suitably severe sentence for deterrent purposes. That would be the way of it. But what of the wider considerations here? – bearing in mind news of a court-martial, with its possibilities for scandal, would probably get out despite precautions, and there's also an argument too for going public anyway and letting everyone know the penalties for this sort of behaviour.

'It wouldn't be the first time the Roman Army has been influenced by foreign cults, and I doubt it'll be the last. Do we guard against every sort of contagion and disaffection, or just those we disapprove of most? What would be worse – the cult spreading through inaction, or the cult spreading through over-reaction? And that's before anything about bringing the civil affairs dimension into the equation. How might the local population and their leaders react, and how might that affect us? If the Nazarene's message were seen to be popular with the Roman oppressors, how would that impact on relations with the civil community, especially its leaders? It all needs weighing up, and invariably quicker than you'd like. It's radical analysis and radical solutions we're always after, plus expedition, and if you can wrong-foot the opposition while you're about it that would be a bonus – because the opposition is the constant factor, it's always out there somewhere. But, you ask as a simple military man, how does all this fit in with saving your centurion?'

By now his mental processes had come to a near-standstill. Was this some kind of subterfuge to complete his discomfiture and seal Facilis' fate beyond any further doubt? Was this the Governor simply clearing his own mind? Could he be about to offer a participatory decision, the end-point of that worldly-wise discussion he might have hoped for in the beginning? The bear was loose and dangerous. He had to summon his reserves, keep up, stay agile – and say something.

'Yes Your Excellency, but I confess this is so intractable I venture it would tax the Gods themselves. Perhaps that's the best answer – to defer the whole business to them. Isn't that why we take the auguries and seek the divine providence? If there's so much at issue then that seems reasonable to me, particularly as the immediate matter in hand concerns them – an oath to one who shares their divinity.'

The Governor raised an eyebrow. 'An interesting line, Veranius. And who do you suggest is best qualified to pour over the entrails in question, other than the Province's senior upholder of state religion – *id est* me? Another commanding officer? Old Veterus? As part of court-martial proceedings? In public, as prescribed for divine consultation? Or in secret – in which case where would be the validity? And how do you propose to get the right answer? And what, exactly, would be the question?'

'I don't know, Your Excellency. We can only fall back on the Gods to show us the way.'

'The gods again. Why ask them, who treat man with disdain and cast their misery about whether deserved or no, and seem to delight in rewarding the base and chastising the virtuous? You must know what Jupiter Best and Greatest would have to say in the case of Centurion Facilis, should we ever have the temerity to raise his case as just another disobedient mortal – stern retribution, of course, that anyone should dare question the divine order and contemplate false religions. Do we propose to unleash the divine wrath on ourselves too, in chastisement for our own failings in that department?'

There was a flicker of a smile. 'That is, of course, if the gods exist. Or anguries to be consulted.'

Perplexity, aroused and confirmed, was become astonishment complete. Had he heard correctly? Nothing he could have said would have been an adequate response to such surprising questions posed so deliberately. But that had been a little smile, no mistake. He was rooted to the spot, unable to respond.

The Governor continued. 'No sooner than the Augustan celebrations are over it's the Birthday of the Eternal City. And do you know what I've got to do when I get back to Caesarea, Veranius? I've got to go and kill a cow. A poor, garlanded, innocent cow, done to death personally on behalf of the Senate and Roman People by their principal representative in Judaea, who's more concerned to keep his toga clean, because that's what our forefathers in their rustic ignorance thought they had to do to survive. Pray tell me how on earth that's going to help anyone now?'

An answer was needed whether he liked it or not. In as calm a way as he could, he said: 'Real faith in the gods passes some men by, Your Excellency, but these are the ancestral gods of Rome, who made us great and the rulers of the known world – we must honour them if Rome, and our families, are to continue in their favour.'

'Oh don't be so conventional, Veranius. Men will believe as they're schooled, expected and commanded. The more so when the gods are enmeshed in the apparatus of the State, and we are all brought up to believe in the glory of Rome and its divine provenance and destiny. The gods gave hope and assurance, and, when men were organized into city-states, continuity and order, and strength and refuge in times of trouble, and now we're in the days of modern empire they continue to demand allegiance to its founder as the living embodiment of the political and social cohesion required for its future. It would have been anathema in the old Republic, which had a different view on hero-worship, but that's progress for you. Would ordinary people really believe in any of it, not just the man-god but the whole superstructure propping him up, if they just stopped to think what they're doing instead of accepting it all so blindly? Shouldn't we be turning to the natural philosophers to tell us about the real world, rather than persevering with the myths of our ancestors, who could know no better? And underlying the particular question of oath-taking, can any man of flesh and blood really become a god when his mortal life is over, able to influence the affairs of we who are still alive, and demand our never-ending obeisance?'

There was a safe response. 'But Augustus Caesar lives as that embodiment of the nation, Your Excellency. He may not have the full interventionist powers of the Gods but we believe his spirit guides and protects us, just as the ancestors of a household will watch over its present members, and that by his continuing leadership he is fully worthy of the reverence of his countrymen – without exception.'

The Governor returned to his panorama. 'The Senate was tactful enough to wait till he was dead before conferring the ultimate accolade, Veranius – having lived so long with the ambiguity which the great man himself encouraged, going right back to his adoptive father. Though how anyone could contemplate enrolling Tiberius in his living days, when he's made it very clear he's against it, does seem a trifle sycophantic. Yes I know I had it put on that foundation stone in Caesarea – "To the divine Tiberius". But it's merely a mark of respect, a bit of flattery to keep the Greeks happy. The worship of his predecessors in their lifetimes was actively encouraged out here, but it's an accepted tradition and no surprise they keep raising statues all over the East. It's only a matter of time before craving for power gives us the fully alive man-god of flesh and blood who can do no wrong, whose every word must be obeyed, not by dint of wisdom, or justice, or military might, or even because it's the divine will as ordained through the auguries – but because the man is a god because he says so. It's insane, but I fear no-one's going to stop it.'

'Though who knows what our Caesar may achieve, Your Excellency? He could prove entirely deserving of divinity.'

'Tiberius? In self-exile on his island hide-away – though who could blame him his suspicions after what he's been through? I've tried to show support and keep him interested. I dedicated the aforesaid temple to him – not a word of thanks, mark you, though not particularly surprising when you never really knew who wore the purple. The only way I could get to Caesar was through my wife, and that wasn't easy either. How could I be frank when everything I did was caught between competing factions bent on power and influence, and anyone with any sense was trying to keep their head down? Yes, Aelius Sejanus, of whom one could speak so much. Anyway he's gone, but now we've got the equally dreadful Macro and it's becoming equally bad, believe me.

It's not hard to see how cares of state make people embittered, and how that soon corrodes trust and loyalty and percolates through the whole body politic. The worst of it is that by all accounts the scion Caligula's showing some unfortunate tendencies of his own. The living man-god may not be far away. Did we do well to replace the Republic, Veranius, for all its latter-day corruption? Sometimes I think the old guard had it right. We seem to have unleashed tyrannical ambition worse even than in our grandfathers' time, and not just among the governing class. Where's the common good, civic virtue, public honour?

'Oh dear, do I shock you?'

He was incapable of reply.

'So can you blame me for becoming a little weary, Veranius? How do you think it felt, to be offered the *cloaca* of empire? "Don't worry about the Jews, just manage them in the margins, leave them to their own ways but take no nonsense either, collect the taxes, consolidate the coastal cities, maintain the status quo, that's all that can be expected." Don't those people realize how different this place is? Can't they see the East is a bottomless pit, where our greatest men end up embroiled and too often corrupted and ruined? Not just Pompeius. Crassus, Antonius, even Julius Caesar and Augustus in his former self – they all had to come out here, one after the other, and they all ended up with nothing but trouble, usually fatal.

'We should long ago have settled for control of the coast, taken what trade we wanted and left them all to their own devices. These lands have entirely different ways of thinking from us. They've got more sects and deities than you can shake a stick at, which we'll never understand or overcome as long as the sun shines. And doesn't that tell us something about men and religion? For every new strange people we hear about so we hear too of yet more gods and goddesses, all jostling for men's attention. How can they possibly all be true? But anyway, "get yourself to Judaea, we need someone out there who knows something of the religion, expect to be there quite a time because it's a diplomatic quagmire and we need continuity, you'll only be a prefect not a proper governor, but don't worry, you'll come under the wing of the real version in Syria but that's just because he's from a leading senatorial family and needs a command the size of his ego, though actually he isn't there at all and you'll have to defer to his deputy, but he commands three legions and that's just a fact of life, and as a special privilege you can take your wife, but only because she's who she is.

'I'm sorry, Veranius, forgive my indulgence. You shouldn't be having to hear my problems.'

'Your Excellency'.

'So I did as I was told, determined to be fair but strong, and yes, to make my mark with Tiberius, with whom I got on well. Gratus had generally done a good job but he'd been allowed to stay on too long, and let a few things go. So when on my first progress I made a point of allowing the escort's standards to accompany me into the city, I knew very well what I was doing, despite what those know-alls in Rome thought. I had to start as I meant to go on, and show these people who was in charge, as any governor would in any province of the Empire, but especially here where we always seem to have to keep on reminding them.

'Naturally it was the First Augusta who were with me, and I'd already decided it was time they stayed for a tour of duty, so it was the first time they'd been in the city with their standards for years – and, as it turned out and very regrettably, the last. For all the fuss you'd think I'd fixed the things to the Temple wall rather than ensconced them in the Antonia. As for getting them into the city by night, what else were we expected to do if it was evening when we arrived after a long march? I confess even I was surprised by the reaction though. The whole male population was immediately up in arms – not literally, you understand – perhaps it would have been better if it were, because we could then have responded in kind. Petitioning me, demonstrating day after day over this violation by Augustus' image. Then blow me down when we left to return to Caesarea thousands of them trooped after us the whole way, and when they got there they set up camp in the stadium and carried on for five days and nights, shouting, praying, wailing, lying about beside themselves with grief and protestation, baring their necks and pleading to be killed rather than suffer any more torment. It was quite extraordinary, though I must say you couldn't help but be impressed by the fervour.

'This was the power of religion over a whole people, and no-one could doubt the sincerity or the passion. So I relented, told them the Augustans were anyway shortly to be withdrawn from the city for other duties, which wasn't strictly true but there has to be some dignity in this life, and duly did so. Which is why the First to this day haven't come anywhere near Jerusalem since. I still tell everyone that as my senior cohort their rightful place is guarding the seat of government back at the coast, so I suppose a degree of face has been maintained.

'It can't have been easy for you, Your Excellency.'

'Talking of graven images, I did care to make sure my coinage didn't have the like – just a harmless symbolic reference or two to libation, as you know. The experts told me we had to have something reflecting the *status quo*, so I agreed. There's still the odd bit of muttering about that now, though funnily enough no-one ever seems to have any qualms handling the more valuable examples of Caesar's currency, complete with his likeness – they're all glad enough to have some of that in their purse.

'Things could always be worse, I suppose. I hadn't ordered a bloodbath, which earned me some respect from the moderates. But it didn't help my relations with Caiaphas, who'd been around some time and tried to treat me like the new boy from the first, which of course I was at the time. But I'd always tried to show respect. We've never interfered with their religion or their internal affairs. We've only been interested in the *pax Romana* and promoting prosperity. Providing subject peoples keep the peace and don't use religion to subvert the State, they are free to pursue whatever belief they want, and the Jews are no exception.

'You know of course neither Pompeius nor Marcus Antonius in their time could resist entering the holy of holies? You'd have thought once was enough, but no, Antonius had to come and see for himself too. For us it's as if gods can't exist without something to show for their presence – who knows, perhaps the Jews are right about that. And as we know, the great mystery was only deepened further when the veil was torn aside to reveal – nothing. And every time there was a falling-out with the locals, reparations had to be made. These people's dedication to their faith and attachment to their land is impressive, we have to admit – but intransigence taken to impossible lengths can be something of a frustration. Rather an under-statement, one might say.'

The Governor turned to face him again. 'You weren't around when the aqueduct problem started. Twenty miles of engineering – no small feat, if it had come off.'

'Long before my time, Your Excellency.'

'What you may not know is the extent to which the project was riddled with corruption from the beginning. I don't mean the alleged misappropriation of Temple funds, of which it goes without saying I was roundly accused. I mean the systematic embezzling of donations in the hands of the Sanhedrin, which controls the receipt of all alms-giving in the Precinct. Work on the aqueduct had been started years before but come to a halt for lack of finance, and the Province's tax-take, once the centre had taken its share, wasn't enough to get it going again. I thought I was doing some good. The city needed it, more so with every passing year, and army engineers don't grow on trees, they had to be put to use when you had the chance. So I made a decision. I decided the Temple funds were a legitimate source of funding for this purpose. After all they were the people's money, from every cleansing bath, every sacrificial offering, every peace offering and all the rest, the modest donations of a poor but devout people. And by their own laws available for use towards their own good, whether in doles to the needy or for public works – and what greater need had the inhabitants of a thirsty city than good clean water? Of course it was me that was accused of siphoning funds – ironic term for an aquatic theme – which were both public and sacred, as well as undermining the local culture and insulting its religion, whereas in reality I had done no such thing nor ever had any such intention. I was even accused of being in league with Sejanus to milk this lucrative source between us, in a master plan to systematically grind Judaea and its people into the dust under the pretext of the standard exactions due from any other province. Anyway, no aqueduct, no progress, no peace.

'Why is it every time I come on the annual circuit there seems to be heightened unrest? Perhaps I'm being paranoid – it's not every year

– let's say one in two. Because the next episode was when I agreed to address a public meeting explaining a very necessary rise in the poll tax. I took the view that imperial policy needed to be explained to the people, and that the only honourable way to do that was to go and speak to them. That was, I soon came to see, a mistake. Angry people don't want rational explanations – they want their way, and if they can't get it, then it's open defiance and retaliation. I thought I was being quite brave at the time, but "foolhardy" would be a more accurate description. I'd taken the precaution of having a company of Samarians on hand in case it went wrong, which it did. My attempts to address the crowd were completely in vain, things got quickly out of control and soon the mob was surging forward and threatening to engulf the podium and the inadequate guard around it. Without any command from me the Samarians came charging out from around the corner, which was fortuitous, but then laying about with their swords, which probably wasn't – there's no love lost, as you well know. There was complete pandemonium and I was bundled away. I couldn't have done anything to stop it even if I'd tried. Considering what the Samarians are capable of, the casualties could have been very much worse but unfortunately the running fight got into the Temple Precinct and a few Galileans there for the Passover were killed inside, which compounded the crime even further. You can imagine the hysteria: "Roman troops defile Sanctuary and kill unarmed protestors" – which they were, I have to admit. And I was accused of dressing up the Samarians and hiding them in the crowd, when that would have been far too problematic – they were simply in reserve in case they were needed. No matter, I got the blame as usual.

'I had to double the garrison and protect the working parties on the aqueduct, but I was determined to carry on, and somehow we held the ring and things gradually got back to normal. Then yet again I was stopped by Rome, who wanted me to find some other source of funding for the work but still wouldn't reduce the province precept, so we were over-taxing on one hand and under-funding on another. In the end I told Caiaphas the engineers were being posted, which was actually true and outside my control, and that all work on the aqueduct would

shortly stop.   He couldn't help smiling, the old fox, and all I could do
was exhort him to use the Temple funds for the tangible benefit of the
people in future, since I could have no further legitimate use for them.
Poor relief was after all his business, not mine.'

'It was a genuine attempt to improve life for the city's inhabitants,
Your Excellency.'

'I almost managed to get my own back with those votive shields we
put up here in the Old Palace last year.   No graven images, but some did
have "son of god" on them, though considering they were in honour of
Caesar and his step-father Augustus, from various benefactors and out
of public view you'd have thought it no more than mildly controversial.
Cue the usual uproar, and once again I was forced to back down, this
time by Antipas and his sons writing to Tiberius direct, even though
this was well outside their legal and geographical remit.   Perhaps it was
more a case of frustrated nostalgia for his old palace, which suits us very
well, I don't know.   Anyhow I was required by the Emperor personally
to remove the things to the temple at Caesarea.   Considering it had
been me who had commissioned the temple and dedicated it to him
in the first place, it was an outcome not without the ubiquitous irony.
Personally I thought the shield scheme had struck the right balance,
by honouring our Head of State and his authority without undue
provocation of local sensitivities.   But clearly not.'

'Quite right, Your Excellency.'

'So I've done my best Veranius, I really have.   I've stuck it
out, for more years than I care to remember.   I've run the whole
course – enthusiasm, consternation, incredulity, frustration, anger,
disillusionment, resignation, though I'm not going anywhere in the
sense of actually resigning, oh no.   Not voluntarily, anyway.   I've had no
support from the centre whatsoever, not the least sign of gratitude for
keeping the Province in order, and now I can't wait to go, given the right
pretext – of my choosing, not theirs.   But I've kept the peace, which
is probably more than my successors will achieve.   And I have I think
come to see a little of the truth, about man and his gods.   We all think
we're so right, and it takes much time and effort to change minds, but
the inescapable conclusion is that many people are beyond reason and

never will be brought to see it. And not one of them is worth the life of a single one of our soldiers.'

'Indeed not, Your Excellency.'

'Now back to practicalities. The Passover is almost upon us. The city's heaving with people from far and wide and about to explode as the Nazarene fulfils his mission. The only good news is that for once they've got something to take their minds off us. And amidst all this you have an officer causing problems who needs to be dealt with.'

'Yes Your Excellency. I'm sorry, it's the worst possible time.'

'Perhaps. Perhaps not. We could see it as a little diversion from what might otherwise prove a very trying business. A distraction, but nothing that can't be put right. Your man has had the misfortune to cross Licinius Macula, who seems to be the only witness.'

'Yes, Your Excellency. We only have his word.'

'I doubt he invented it. Aristocrats of any shape or form have better things to do than get involved with lesser beings for no cause. It's beneath them and bad for their reputation. There's got to be an explanation. I'm afraid he may have had good reason to observe your man closely when the appropriate opportunity arose.'

'Your Excellency?'

'My dear Veranius, you don't suppose his posting here is a coincidence, do you? Macula's uncle is thick-as-thieves with Sutorius Macro. I'm being watched, Veranius. Forget the distractions – it's me they're interested in. The social climber finally risen above his station, never popular with the old guard, abandoned by his erstwhile patron Sejanus who unfortunately went increasingly astray and who's now left us anyway, friendless after being stuck out here so long, sitting on a hotbed of trouble he can't be trusted to handle, and signally unable to extract the fortune they still think is theirs by right of rapine. It's all about de-stabilization – causing trouble, any sort of trouble, in the hope something will crop up to cause another crisis and get me out so they can have a clear field.'

'Great Jupiter', Veranius said quietly.

'That's the backdrop. And the motive. Throw in zeal and it requires only opportunity and means to be complete. In the form of our young tribune of ill-repute we seem to have all the requirements in place. Overweening confidence in destiny and abilities, fanatical allegiance to the idea of a great god-emperor if not the present mortal incumbent, brazen promotion of same and self at every turn, ruthless obliteration of resistance should anyone be stupid enough to resist – all in one young man, though alas not uncommon for his class. Then your centurion appears with his convenient apostasy. Where there's one apostate there must be others, and with the populace in ferment and Sanhedrin furious over the spread of this new sect even to the army of occupation, the job's almost as good as done. With enough of this, what other mischief might befall? Another nice little problem for the Governor to make a mess of.'

'This is incredible, Your Excellency.'

'I wish it were. It is, I'm afraid, the reality. I had no choice but include Macula in my top team. That was made very clear from the beginning. So he gets to hear the intelligence at the highest level. He knows about the Nazarenes and their disaffecting activities. And he's aware of Facilis' dabbling in the margins.'

'It's been known for some time then, Your Excellency.'

'Of course.'

'But no-one told me, his commanding officer.'

'No. We had to see how far the contagion would go. Who else might succumb, so to speak. More important, as far as I was concerned – what a man believes is his business, as long as it doesn't affect anyone or anything else, and I was determined there'd be no intervention in native affairs. The sect had to be given its head and events allowed to run their course, with the Jewish authorities left to manage the situation. You would have been advised of your own little problem sooner or later, but there also had to be some sort of proof, evidence of apostasy, which when it materialized would be incontrovertible. Thanks to the alertness and public-spiritedness of our young colleague that has now been obtained, rather more quickly and easily than might have been expected – or, one must add, wished. One still has reservations on the method, and on the whole one regards the whole distasteful business as very unfortunate, but subordinates must be allowed some leeway, and one has to say the idea of the special toast was rather a clever one. Not even I remembered it was the seventy-fifth anniversary of Philippi coming up.'

It was becoming confusing and dangerous again. He was browbeaten into silence.

'Not to worry, Veranius. The Army's not about to go soft. Disaffection is not about to grip the land. The Zealots will always stay a threat but they're not strong enough to cause real trouble just yet. The native authorities will make short work of the Nazarenes, who are completely harmless. Rather to one's regret – it would have been interesting to see where all this proselytizing might have gone.'

'I'm sure everything will stay under control, Your Excellency.'

'And the Governor gets to keep his job. Providing of course nothing stupid happens over your centurion.'

He stayed silent.

'An interesting case. To be made an example, or a show of leniency? Is the aim achieved by recourse to the usual violent suppression, or by quietly managing the problem out of the way, even with a touch of tolerance? Do we best honour ...the gods ... through vengeance, or magnanimity? In either case – to reveal, or to cover up? How do we discourage anyone else thinking of taking up with this sect? And when we catch them, what do we do with them? Facilis is lucky to have you – he could have been under rather more persuasive treatment by now. It would certainly help if we could be certain about its spread.'

'Yes, Your Excellency. A dilemma. I can't believe it's anything but extremely isolated. There's only Cornelius with him at Capernaum and he's far too level-headed for that sort of thing. And you wouldn't think it had any appeal to the soldiers.'

'I hope you're right, Veranius, but the need is for caution.'

'Yes, Your Excellency. Then perhaps the best course is to smoke out any more there might be – which argues for avoiding any precipitate overt action. And ...'

'Go on.'

'A quiet posting-out, Your Excellency.'

The Governor looked him full in the face.

'My dear Veranius, how many of us *equites* are there out here?

Precisely three, counting Justus in Caesearea. Men of our class should stick together – especially we Samnites, don't you think? One day you may have a legion, and perhaps in time you'll find yourself with real authority, when problems like this will seem quite minor. Principles are fine things, but remember also there will be considerations of state which will seem infinitely more pressing, many of which will affect your own position, either directly or indirectly. It's the latter you've got to watch, since they're the ones which tend to creep up on you and bite you where it hurts. You have a duty to yourself to survive. Without power nothing can be accomplished, therefore one must acquire and keep it by all reasonable if not available means. If you're not prepared to be economical with your finer feelings then stay home, tend your vines and live quietly. Men of position have obligations. They have to know how to exercise discretion and how to live with themselves in doing what needs to be done. If they once admit weakness then nothing will get done. Your concern for your centurion is commendable, and you will I am sure find the right solution. It's up to us to uphold the glory and honour of Rome, relying on our own judgment and never the pedestrian laxity we see all around us. We are all to some extent prisoners of circumstance. The wise man may know how best to break free and contribute some improvement, but only the bold will do what's necessary to achieve it. We can't just wish for the right outcome – we have to make it so. You must find the Roman way. We are nothing if not a pragmatic people. Thank you for coming to see me.'

*   *   *   *

The walls of the old building still radiated the heat of the day as Veranius descended the steps in the twilight, returning the guards' salute and with his head spinning. He now had consciously to come to terms with what he had heard with his own ears. It had been flattering that the Governor had given him the better part of two hours of his time and taken him into his confidence, quite recklessly so, it seemed to him. Before he could begin to try and make any sense of it he had to give thanks: his great gamble had, it seemed, paid off. He hadn't been sacked on the spot, and there was no intimation his decision to raise the matter would be held against him; on the contrary, there had even been a hint of a promising career to look forward to. There had been some reference to that most awkward charge against any commanding officer, that he hadn't been fully aware of what was going on in his own unit. Nevertheless he'd been granted something of the collegiate and confidential discussion he had hoped for, if a somewhat one-sided version, and hadn't the Governor more or less alluded to the need for initiative in his final remarks? Yes, it appeared he'd done the right thing, and for a moment he allowed himself to speculate on what view might have been taken of him if he hadn't. With so much at stake he preferred not to ponder too long on an answer.

But why the confidence, and the confidences, gratifying as they were? What he'd just heard had been most unexpected, and might take a little while to sink in. With so many candid revelations it was difficult not to see the man in a different light. He'd known the bare facts of the Governor's time in province. There had been nothing new about his problems concerning the native administration, but the full extent of his ill-disguised disappointment with the government in Rome had been extraordinary in the extreme, his remarks about religion highly controversial. Why the apparent abandon? Why the trust in a relatively junior cohort commander, which if it were ever reported could only add greatly to his difficulties back home, where there'd be no shortage of willing ears? Was there any reason why he shouldn't take the Governor's confidence at face value? Where was this leading? Was he, his loyal lieutenant, being used, or was he merely superfluous?

He couldn't see that. Those in positions as rarefied as the Governor's had a lot more on their plate than people realized, and didn't he himself know something about the loneliness of command? It had been an expression of trust, an unburdening by a world-weary, rather solitary man to one of his own, if much removed in rank. The Governor was to be taken at face value. The underlying cause of the present trouble was Macula, the only man in province who socially outranked him, who was evidently here for purposes which were decidedly hostile, which must have been extremely awkward though good manners would always put on a show of civility.   For himself, the uninformed supplicant caught up in what was becoming an increasingly tangled web, there was a fresh perception.   His leader, man of enigma and aloofness, had no less sensibility than anyone else.   It seemed it took a crisis for some truths to see the light of day.

He'd gone to the Governor to get some cover for the Cohort and its commander, with the additional benefit of generally making his number; and received instead an object lesson in the actualities.   He had also received a privileged insight into affairs of state beyond his normal purview, however much he might persuade himself they were routine for men of class and ability.   The only qualifications necessary for success were birthright, judgment and boundless self-confidence. There would be problems along the way – how could it be otherwise when mind-sets were so strong, interests so opposed and fate so fickle? To counter that you had to keep the Gods' favour, but it was equally important to select and maintain the aim utterly single-mindedly.   It was a matter of perspective: as the Governor had remarked, you kept a clear and steady eye on the whole whilst dealing with the detail. Managing one obdurate officer in one unit in one small garrison no longer seemed quite so fraught with difficulty.   There might be no immediately obvious solution, but it would come.   He'd had the nod at the highest level to take a little time over it, including the posting option if he needed it, and that it would be more than acceptable in this situation to oppose the likes of Macula; so that's what he now had to go away with and work out.   If it did finally end the worse for his centurion then such an outcome, whilst unfortunate, had to be placed in its full context.   In fact, looked at objectively and in the round, it was quite an interesting test for a commanding officer.   Of course he was up to it.

Nevertheless, why couldn't the Governor, being so forthcoming, have been a bit clearer on the particular, insistent and still pressing question, of precisely what to do with his recalcitrant centurion? Perhaps he didn't know either, or care, but then he didn't need to.   It wasn't primarily his problem – at least, not yet.   It was the commanding officer's, and what would be would be.   Very well, it would be up to him. The Governor had been straightforward, and frank to a fault. He would be wise to repay him by showing his confidence was well placed. He had, thankfully, played it well enough so far. His luck had held.

But, as the Governor had said himself, he'd better get it right. That, he might have thought, could serve as a suitable postscript to this day of drama and revelation. The Nazarene wasn't the only one to have lived it dangerously. It was the luck of life: some won, some lost, whatever their just desserts; but using one's head was always essential.

THE VISIT

Brutus was less cautious than hitherto. He wasn't going to ask Sabena to disguise herself. A headscarf would have been sufficient before, but it wasn't necessary now. Brutus Bassus had his First Class in the bag and important things to attend to. The prize was as good as his. She would walk by his side, openly and proudly.

Recognition and reward were only his due. His reputation as something of a bull, which he'd never done anything to dispel, had seemed to have done him no harm; the key thing was to be very careful not to upset anyone who might have an influence on your career while simultaneously ensuring everybody else knew you weren't a man to be crossed. Finer feelings didn't come into it; the successful officer demanded respect, prided himself for being rock-solid reliable, and kept his name clean. Getting his way was simply the best means to efficiency, running his company on the tightest leash hand-in-hand with a growing authority beyond it. Those who were not prepared to ply their suit and compete would fall by the wayside, and rightly so. The Army existed for his sort, and he was happy to oblige. Ambition, controlled and contained, underpinned his whole being. He'd been a late starter but he was making his name now, and the future looked good. He looked forward to the fortunate cohort somewhere which had his name on it, and then he'd really fly.

The only fly in the ointment was his marriage, but it was not his fault that had now become a considerable problem. Vergilia had inevitably been left behind. It was unfortunate and he had no wish to hurt her, but she had become impossible. In hindsight he should never have married her. There were no children, thank the Gods;

with everything else going so well it was clear he had their blessing in that regard too. He couldn't really blame her. There'd been a spark once; they'd been young, with no family pre-arrangement, no catch or coercion, but without the right background and with few prospects it seemed a good move at the time to have her modest fortune and the respectability of the married state. He'd long concluded he must have been mad. Neither of them had appreciated how the increasing demands of his career might affect the relationship. She had not moved on or developed in step with his advancement, to the extent that she was now an embarrassment, capable of being both gauchely retiring and crassly outspoken for no good cause almost at the same time. She was not a wife suitable for a senior officer, and if he seriously aspired to become one then something would have to give. It would not be much of a loss: any trace of the allure she might once have offered had long gone, conjugal relations a painful memory from a distant past. It was all he could bear to be in her company, and the familiarity forced by the need to keep up social appearances had become intolerable – the more so of late as it looked as though she'd finally realized the bleak outlook for their continuing union. And how could she not, what with his increasingly cold demeanour and open exasperation at her attempts alternately to please him and stand up for herself? Without doubt she had become a liability, and he could not go on. It would be a high-risk move and might not come off, but if necessary he was quite prepared to forfeit his career. That would be a pity, now that his patience with the system was finally being rewarded and his prospects suddenly very bright indeed, but if push came to shove acceptable. For the real prize, the best prize of all, was worth any other ambition many times over: the loveliest woman any man could ever wish for, so different from pinched and peevish Vergilia. This one was beautiful, confident, socially secure, clever, not the most industrious but capable of great application, drily witty, biddable yet spirited, never tiresome, a loving if strict mother to her children and a popular figure in any circle. As an asset to anyone's career she was beyond compare to the poor creature with which he had inexplicably managed to saddle himself. And far too good for her husband.

With a bit of luck he would have both her and his career, but if in the end the Army pulled the plug it would matter little. For a woman like that a resourceful man was justified in going to any lengths; nothing but nothing could be allowed to get in the way of that which had clearly been ordained. Not only was she desirable: incredibly enough she was also available. Truly the Gods had conspired to light his path. The quartering arrangements for the Progress had finally sealed their love-match, and now she was there for the taking, her dolt of a husband getting it exactly wrong and now out of it, helpless as a chicken tied for slaughter. Luck like this could never come more than once: the opportunity had to be seized with both hands. He had the real prospect not only of career success but eternal happiness with the woman of his dreams before him, and he fully intended to have both. And if he couldn't, well – even if he were cashiered in the process it would be a price well worth paying. They would go off together and life would be fine. Concern would not be necessary. Success was assured. She was a jewel beyond compare; even her children seemed compliant and amiable. It had merely required the opportunity, which had surely now come. Just a little while longer, a little more effort, and she would be, delightfully, deservedly, eternally, his.

*   *   *   *

It would be long after supper in the Mess so there probably wouldn't be anybody about except a minion or two. The expedition in hand would once have been too risky to contemplate; in this state of mind any thought of risk now seemed trifling; he was following his destiny and no-one was going to stop him. No-one was likely to report anything odd about an officer accompanying a lady at an unusual time such as this when normal routine was disrupted, even if they knew she wasn't his wife, and once in the Antonia it was only a corridor and a staircase to reach the single officers' rooms. There would be no-one to worry about there; with luck most would be engaged in some entertainment or other. Anyway, if anyone had the impertinence to ask, hadn't the lady requested his services personally? And there was a fall-back: they'd probably know about the arrest – and what was more natural that a trusted friend of the family should have the honour of escorting her to see her beloved husband? And if the Senior Centurion, who lived in, thought that privilege should be reserved for him, he could buzz off too. This had nothing to do with the honour of the regiment and all that nonsense. Sabena and he would go where they pleased.

The protective pride and sense of ownership he felt as he put his arm around her waist gave him enormous satisfaction. At last they could step out side-by-side; though the darkness had come and there were few people about, they were walking out together in the world, and it was good. Before long it would be in the full light of public knowledge, and, in time, acceptance if not whole-hearted approval. The favoured lovers, joined in their single destiny – and he with promotion and prosperity to come. The Gods were smiling indeed, the happiness of the happy couple clearly meant to be. What could possibly go wrong? And now it was important her time with the husband should be brief. 'Half an hour', he told her. 'Too risky for any longer.'

*   *   *   *

'How are you, my friend?' he said, offering his hand as Favonius drew the curtain back. 'I've brought someone to see you. I'll be outside.'

Husband and wife rushed to embrace. 'I've been so worried', she said. 'Is everything alright? Are they feeding you?'

'Yes, yes of course. Very well. Yes, I'm fine. Not much fun being cooped up like this, but it makes for a comfortable cell.'

'What's happened? What have you done to deserve this? Can you move around? Can you talk to people?'

'Up to a point. I'm on my honour not to walk straight out, that's all. I'm supposed to be ill. Can't lie down all day and night, though.'

'So why are you under arrest? What on earth have you done? Tell me, exactly, Marcus.'

'Come and sit down. Would you like some wine?'

'We haven't got long. Brutus has been a brick but we shouldn't expect him to be taking risks.'

'That's true. I owe him one. Tell him from me.'

'Well, tell me. I want to know. This must be so serious, to do this to you.'

'I'm waiting to see if I'm to be charged or not.'

'Charged?! Charged with what?'

He hesitated. 'Treason, probably.'

Sabena gasped, her hand to her mouth in genuine shock. 'Oh no! Oh no! How can this be? Who would do this to you? Why, why have they done this?'

'It's complicated, Darling.'

'Then tell me, I want to know.'

'I didn't respond to the toast to Augustus last night.'

'What?! Of course you did, I was with you.'

'No, I stood and raised my arm, but I didn't say anything. Or to be precise—'

'Well I didn't raise my arm either, so that means I didn't do the oath properly either.'

'Not really', he gave a little chuckle. 'Wives don't do salutes.'

'You didn't say anything?'

'I got so far – but I couldn't say "deified."'

'Nor did I.'

'Didn't you?'

'I couldn't say it either. Perhaps they should arrest me too.'

'I can't drag you into this. This isn't women's business.'

'You mean a woman's word doesn't count.'

'I didn't say that.'

'But for goodness sake! How could anyone have noticed a little thing like that. They must have been watching you.'

'They were, I'm afraid. Well, our friend Macula actually.'

'That horrible man! Oh how could they? How could they let him do such a thing?'

'You know the sort he is.'

'Anyway that's not treason, not from someone who's just been awarded a medal for conspicuous gallantry. And who cares?! And who else could possibly have noticed anyway in a crowded room full of people who've had too much to drink?   I assume they're going to need a witness.'

'Macula's far too powerful to need that.'

'So what's he got against you, to accuse you of this?   I take it he is your accuser.'

'Yes.   I was expecting him to denounce me all last night.   I could think of nothing else.'

'I thought you'd gone a bit quiet.   You hid it well.'

'I didn't want to spoil the evening for you, Darling.'

'So what's happened?'

'This afternoon.   Veranius had me in, with Macula there too.'

'And you denied it.'

He paused.

'Marcus?'

'No, I didn't deny it.'

'Oh Marcus'.   Sabena sighed, and the sobs came quickly.   'No, no, no … how could you, how can this be?'

'I'm sorry.   I couldn't deny what was only true.'

'You could have done.   You could have done, Marcus.   Why didn't you?'

'I … I cannot break my word, Darling.'

'But you're quite prepared to break *us*.   To ruin us – us, the children, you and me, everything.   I've heard you say it – first rule of military law, never admit anything.   You could have said it, Marcus.   Like one of your soldiers.   You could have done it for us.   You could have said you had a problem with speaking … anything, anything just to give an answer.   Veranius would have let you off, you get on well and he thinks so much of you.'

'Yes.   But he can't help me.   I don't have a leg to stand on.'

'What do you mean?'

'The CO's ordered me to take the same oath, tomorrow morning. In his office.'

'And you'll do it.   Marcus, tell me you'll do it.'

He bowed his head.

'Oh no.   No!'   The tears flowed freely now as she stood distraught. He held her tight while she sobbed for some time, before finally fetching a towel and drying her face, still lovely despite her anguish and the remnants of her light mascara. It was her face that had first attracted him all those years ago – fresh and girlish, bright eyes smiling, hair soft and scented, perfect lips so kissable then; and still now, though he resisted. He used to tell her how she never needed to make herself beautiful; she just was, naturally, and that he must be the luckiest man in the …

He stood away. 'Macula and I never got on from the start. It wasn't just the arrogance. I think he knows about us. About Capernaum, I mean. About our faith. That's what's behind this.'

Sabena was quiet. After a while she said: 'Is it so bad to give Augustus Caesar his due?'

He paused, hesitant though not surprised. He would have to choose his words carefully. He wanted to be thoughtful and tender, but he had to say it though he knew she would object.

'Darling, when we decided to follow Him we had to leave the old ways behind. How can we follow His words and still recognise the old emperor as a god? That's what the toast was about. It wasn't about Augustus as a man, but as a god. And knowing what we do now doesn't make that possible, does it? We who witnessed what He did that day and heard Him speak, how can we doubt that the true God has revealed himself to us through his Son and thereby made all things new? And that being so, surely we have to live the life of truth, even though that means taking the rough with the smooth, and not just when it suits?'

She answered fitfully between gentle sobs. 'Since that day I have done my very best to understand and believe with you, to bring the children up in the faith, to say our prayers, to try and put others before ourselves, though heaven knows I've found it difficult. It's so hard to really believe, and we're just … human beings, with all our many weaknesses. And yes I've failed, because I am only human. I failed with the wretched toast last night. I didn't say it but I mouthed it, because I'm weak and I just didn't think it as important as you do. But it doesn't mean anything really, in fact nothing at all. It keeps everyone happy – well most, anyway – and what's the harm? Life's too short to get so fixated on things like this. We do what we can, but we have to know where to draw the line. I've supported you in this faith as best I can, and I've never tried to discourage you or argue about the rights and wrongs and all the other things I could have done. But what do you imagine he would tell us now if he was here, in this room? "Go ahead, test your faith to destruction, take the disgrace on your own head and have it hacked off, and let your wife and children be cast into penury"? Wouldn't he be much more likely to say "Do what's best for your family, take the wretched oath, so long as you remember the real God where it really matters, in your heart and mind, which nobody can take away from you?" Isn't that what he'd say, to us, now, if he could? Come to think of it, isn't that what Matthias would say too?'

And he was sorry, full of pity and doubt, fear and remorse.

And found himself saying: 'Sabena, you know how He talked of brother fighting brother for His sake. I pray that this trial might be taken from me, I pray for you and the children, for all of us in this situation, that some way might be found which spares us this torment. I can honour a dead emperor, but what I cannot do is acknowledge his so-called divinity and at the same time be true to Him who really is divine, because to do so wouldn't just prove my unworthiness, it would also be tantamount to denying Him. I'd be in a state of betrayal. I would have failed through the weakness and cowardice of one of my sex when it's manly strength that should be being shown. I never set out to find the real God, but I did – or rather, he found me; he found us. It was meant to happen, wasn't it? – that we should find the way to truth, and now we've found it we cannot turn back. We have to keep our hands to the plough, knowing it is the only way to salvation. If we renounce our faith then we are as before, only worse, since we had heard the Word but then eschewed it, to be cut off from our heavenly Father and lost in sin and darkness. Something happened to us in Capernaum. We would not have believed had we not seen with our own eyes. But we did see. And we have to stay with the truth and the light if we are to follow Him and all have everlasting life.'

'Well Husband, I still pray too. I too believe in what he says, not in the same way as you but in my own way and in my own heart, and before we can think about eternal life we have to care about the present and our family – our children, our own lives. That is our joint duty, yours and mine together, yet you seem to have forgotten yours. You should be asking why a loving god should ever want to put us in this position. If he's so loving and so powerful, why has he allowed this to happen? You should be putting the practicalities first, and the most pressing of those is keeping yourself alive, for all our sakes.

'It's quite obvious to me only two people can testify against you – Macula, and now Veranius. So I will have to do what has to be done. Like the she-wolf, Husband, if you won't fight – I will.'

'I know'. He held her by her shoulders. 'I know the faith hasn't been quite the same for you, Darling. That's only natural. We're all different, we all react in different ways and we all have our own ideas of what's best. And you never met Him, whereas I did. And you do have a mother's instinct to defend the children above all else, which is good and proper. And it's good that you're with Him in your own way, Sabena, even if your faith isn't quite the same as mine. Watch and pray and hope all will yet be well. I need your prayers. I need you to stay strong too. We can do this together, I promise. You know you and the children mean so much to me. You really are more than any man could ask for, and I love you so very much'.

He kissed her. 'Fight like a she-wolf?'

'God gave me intellect. It's up to me to use it.'

'You're going to flash your eyes at Veranius?'

'Well I don't think I could bring myself to look at the other one.'

'We always did joke about that, didn't we? I don't think Veranius would put up much resistance.'

'Is there a mirror?'

Sabena straightened her hair. 'I must go.'

'I'll do all I can to get us out of this, I promise.'

'That's better. It's your over-concern for the next world that worries me.'

'I'm still very much in this one, Darling. You know Yeshua's in the city, don't you? He's close, very close. Try and get word to Him if you get a chance. We need their prayers for guidance and blessing. And pray too, My Darling, as I will tonight.'

' Farewell, Husband.'

'Farewell My Dearest. I do love you. Say "thank you" to Brutus.'
'I love you too.'
And she was gone.

It was wonderful to have been together again for a little while. Together they'd see this through somehow.

*   *   *   *

So this, he thought, is what Yeshua had meant, about suffering for His sake. Yet the pain and the dilemma seemed less about the wrongs of commission and omission of half a life-time, or redemption, or salvation, but far more about innocents being drawn inexorably into the mire – his family, his beloved wife and children, friends too, all being dragged in because of him and him alone. Hard enough to understand in the abstract, beyond cruelty to face in the fact, nevertheless this was how the test was to be. He thought of them all in their grief and distress, and the unthinkable should it come to pass. His beloved wife, angry and perplexed; his dear children, too young to understand; and his dear old mother far away at home, who needed him so much. He could bear it no longer. He turned to a picture in his mind's eye of the Master and his disciples, close by somewhere in or near the city, living out the mission bravely amidst their enemies. He prayed, and tried every avenue of mental effort to analyze his predicament and how it might be solved, but hard as he might he could see no way out. If there really were a way then it would be through God's will and it would be revealed, but all he in his impotence could do was return again and again to the one thought, to commend himself and this great burden to Him who governed all things and whose way was the way of life and peace. He prayed, and prayed, and prayed, to the Father, to the Son, to the Holy Spirit, until his knees could take the hard stone no more and his mental energy was spent. With that he managed a little fitful sleep on the unfamiliar couch, until the first cockcrow, uncommonly long before the dawn.

His drowsiness gave a few moments of repose before the worries of the day were back upon him; urgent, intractable and inescapable.

THE DEED

The ungainly bundle hit the ground with a dull thud. There was no more to be done but leave as quickly as he had come.

On its return journey the conveyance rounded a corner too late to avoid running into a commotion. Numerous dark figures bearing torches were filling the narrow roadway and approaching quickly; the driver's only course was to carry on and brazen it out. He pulled his hood down but could make out the glint of weapons in the flickering light and hear the controlled voices of determined men; the uniforms weren't those of auxiliaries. One stopped the mule and another peered into the cart, said something before moving on hesitantly. Heads looked up to survey him, and then in their midst he caught sight of what they were doing. A man was being pulled along on a rope. Momentarily as they passed in the shadows there was the sense of a meeting of eyes. There was no obvious sense of panic or anguish, though the scene was dramatic. Then at some distance came two or three others following without lights, until they too were behind him and it was all quiet and dark again, as though it had been a disjointed episode from some night-terror. He kept on, thanking the Gods for getting away unscathed from an encounter which might have been very awkward indeed. If he'd been challenged there'd have been no certainty how it might have ended, though the party seemed to have been too intent on its purpose to bother much with him. In another time and place he might have been foolhardy enough to reveal his identity and challenge them, since they had to be either the King's or the Temple Guard and supposedly responsive to lawful authority, but there'd been no need and he'd had good reason to exercise caution. There was enough to think about without inviting complications. Stray encounters with armed men in the dead of night were best minimized.

With the danger gone the questions started to come. These were restless days for the city, but nevertheless why such unusual activity at such an hour?

By the time the cart was back at the fortress its driver was once again properly resplendent in full uniform. The gateguard suppressed their curiosity and saluted smartly before being detailed to return beast and cart to the stables whilst the driver went off to get his head down. He was confident it would not be long before the result of his handiwork was discovered. There would undoubtedly be much coming and going, with the Samarians having something useful to do for a change. He guessed it would only take a few hours into the morning for someone to be found who could make a positive identification of Gaius Licinius Macula.

He was right, of course, though it would take a little longer for the news to get out. Everyone was to be busy that day.

THE DREAM

Claudia's tresses, luxuriant on the soft silk pillows, shook violently as she woke with a start.

'Are you alright, My Dear?' Her husband was awake watching the first glimmer of light in the east.

'I've had a terrible dream.'

'It's alright, I'm here. Let me hold you.'

'A terrible dream.'

'What about?'

'The man from Nazareth.'

He tried to make light of it, murmuring in the restrained tones of the bedchamber. 'I can't get away from it, can I? Every meeting I go to ends up with one subject – Yeshua the Nazarene. Never mind the rest of native affairs, or customs and revenue, intelligence and security, manpower shortages – he's all they want to talk about, the name on every tongue. Even yours, My Dear. So of course he gets into the subconscious. You mustn't let it worry you, it's only a dream. Everyone has them. They don't mean anything. They're just little fragments of thought that get lost in our heads to pop out again in weird jumbled-up ways that never can make sense – because they're the product of an over-active imagination which we can't control when we're asleep, that's all.'

'It wasn't like that. I can't explain, I just know it was very clear and very real. You've got to keep away from him.'

'Keep away? What do you mean?'

'Don't have anything to do with him.'

'But I can't do that, My Dear. I'm the Governor. I have my

responsibilities.   If I didn't face up to all sorts of difficult people and situations almost daily, why, absolutely nothing whatsoever would ever get done.   Anyway, you approve of him, don't you?   It doesn't sound very consistent.'

'This man is trouble for you.   He doesn't intend to be – quite the contrary.   It was all so vivid, horrible beyond words.   But he's going to suffer unspeakably.   And … and … everyone's going to blame you.'

'Claudia My Dear, you must stop this at once.   It's just a nightmare you've had.   Everybody gets them.   I get them.   A little morning sunshine and they're all gone, out the window, disappeared in the light of day.   You really mustn't distress yourself like this.'

'Am I given to distress then?   Is that what you think, that I'm a silly nervous woman?'

'Of course not.   But nightmares can be very unsettling.'

'This wasn't any ordinary nightmare.   Everything was very calm and orderly at first, with all the sense of helplessness and inevitability you get in dreams, with no obvious violence anywhere, just the unnerving sense of it lurking under the surface.   Then he was being vilified, everyone was angry and you were in it too somehow, and soldiers, lots of soldiers, then it all became so transitory and incoherent and frightening, with earthquakes and great walls tumbling down and everywhere slaughter and terror and boots marching and choking black smoke and horrid sights and sounds in unending chaos till it seemed the end of the world had come only it wasn't the end just an infinity of hate and suffering for ever … I don't know what you were doing but afterwards there was this sort of pageant, of strange peoples in strange clothing speaking in languages I couldn't understand, all blackening your name, one after the other, until I couldn't bear it any longer.   That's when I woke up.'

'How interesting.   And was I being my usual self, or just pig-headed?'

'I'm frightened.   I wanted to help you but I couldn't.   I felt so helpless.   It was as though the whole world was against you.'

'Dear me.'

'I'm so afraid … so afraid that what I saw was … the future.   That Yeshua is going to die – be killed, very soon, today even, that this day of my dream will be the world in years to come, far, far into the future. All those people, all that disgust and condemnation. So different from any dream I've had before. It was terrifying.'

She shivered a deep shiver. 'Oh, this is so horrible. Can't you see? – Yeshua is innocent. If he dies at your hands it will be you who bears his blood for all time.'

He was holding her now as she cried uncontrollably on his shoulder. 'We should… never have come here … to this horrible place … with all its cruelty … where everyone hates us … so much. This land of so much … so much blood … and hatred.'

'It's all right, My Dear. I'm here, I'm with you. You're upset, very upset. But it can't be that bad. Nothing's happened yet. We have all the resources of Rome at our disposal – our justice, our army, our genius for handling disputes, all the centuries of experience in setting an example of civilization to people everywhere.'

'This isn't about that sort of power.'

'That's true. Yeshua of Nazareth isn't our problem. He's the concern of the native authorities. If he's been upsetting them then there isn't very much we can do directly. All we can really do is hope that justice prevails and an innocent man isn't punished.'

'But that's it. He's broken their laws, and he will be punished, horribly.'

'Then that's not going to be anything to do with me, My Dear. If for some reason he ever came before me because of some matter of law to be dealt with, then you know I shall ensure fairness and impartiality as far as it's in my power. I really can't see how anyone's going to blame me for that. If it's the Jewish law that's in question, that's for them to resolve; if it's a matter for Rome then I shall do my duty. We must be strong, and be seen to be strong. And keep things in proportion. It might be very briefly top of the agenda here now, but it'll soon blow over. None of this could ever be more than a local footnote, to be lost and forgotten almost as soon as your dream.'

'But they mean to kill him. He's undermining their authority.'

'I know.'

'But he's a good man.'

'Yes.'

'They'll accuse him of blasphemy.'

'They will.   And they can punish him with a fine or religious sanctions, but they can't imprison him.   And they certainly can't kill him.'

'Then they'll try and trick you so you have no choice. They'll accuse him of insurrection.   And what will you do then?'

'I shall find him not guilty, of course.   So you see, there's nothing to worry about.   Come on, it's going to be alright.   He's not going to come to any harm from us.'

She was drying her eyes now.   He tried to be tender.

'It would be so good to talk to him ... to see if he could be helped in any way.'

He looked close into her eyes. 'It's more than having nothing to do with him, isn't it?'

She didn't answer, and they lay back together for some time as her sniffles subsided, and watched the first streaks of the new dawn.   How much he had come to depend on her, he thought, since those early years.   Contrary to the predictable asides of his detractors he hadn't married her for her connections, undeniably useful they might have been in the beginning.   He'd needed a wife for his public career; she was available, and amiable, and over the years their affection had grown through comfortable familiarity.   Having a background like hers would understandably be a burden for anyone's state of mind, and allowances had to be made.   She had never known her real father, and mercifully she had been free of the failings of her mother and the more outrageous traits of so many of her relations.   So she could be forgiven her impulsiveness, and what woman wasn't emotional at times?   He valued her essential goodness, and increasingly over the years her constancy. To him she was still attractive, perhaps a little to other men too; and she had borne him their dear son, safely back in Caesarea with his nanny and tutors.   She was his good companion, and if she could sometimes be a little irksome with her foibles and opinions these were a small price for domestic harmony.   And if now she was telling him about an especially vivid dream which seemed to her to be pertinent to the latest events in the tension-racked city the least he could do was forbear to be overly-critical. Stay sympathetic, keep calm, dismiss the fanciful, be strong for her. But how to reassure, when it looked as though a difficult day lay ahead, and experience told him it might not end well – and when everything she had said had run shivers down his spine?

'Why do you say that? What harm could it do to speak to him?'

'Because the Governor's Lady doesn't make a habit of entering into a personal relationship with every eastern mystic that happens to come along. And she doesn't go antagonizing the local hierarchy just because she has an interest in comparative religion.'

And at length he added: 'How are you feeling now?'

'A bit better. Thank you.'

'Come on then, Mrs Governor. The day is here. We must be up and doing.'

And with that he was on his feet.

*　　*　　*　　*

It was as well they had risen early. They had barely begun their breakfast when the ADC was admitted.

'Your Excellency the night's reports are in and it's urgent' was the breathless announcement.

'Very well. What's the form?'

'There was a disturbance outside the city in the night Your Excellency and we think they've arrested Yeshua of Nazareth and put him on trial and they all seem to be coming this way right now Your Excellency.'

'Just a moment, young man. Take your time. Who is coming this way?'

'The Chief Priest, Your Excellency, with this Yeshua under escort and a sizeable entourage.'

'Where are they coming from?'

'The Chief Priest's House, Your Excellency.'

'Are you sure they're coming here?'

'No doubt about it, Your Excellency. Several score.'

'How long have I got?'

'Not long Your Excellency, they're nearly here.'

'Is the QRF ready?'

'They're deploying now, Your Excellency.'

'Thank you. You may return to your duties.'

'Your Excellency.'

The Governor returned his wife's worried gaze but there was no time for conversation. The sounds of a crowd were already audible.

'I shall do my best, My Dear', he said, and kissed her cheek. 'Don't worry, everything will be alright.'

THE DUTY

It was soon apparent this was not the start of an armed uprising; equally no-one could doubt that a serious event was underway which could easily get out of hand. The Chief Priest and his retinue had stridden purposefully to the outer court with their prisoner and hangers-on behind them, though it was still early morning. The last troops were hurriedly getting into place as the deputation came forward. The Governor emerged into view, whereupon there was a visible surge in the rapidly swelling crowd onto the open pavement where the priests could approach him. For a short time it was possible to catch a few words before the noise grew too much, rising and falling as those closest reacted to the leaders' oral encounter, punctuated by cheering and roars of assent, accompanied by ripples of movement among the onlookers trying to get their view, the throng growing all the while in numbers and turbulence as though a tempest at sea which must soon carry all before it. Then all of a sudden there seemed to be a breaking-up. Priests and guards had turned and were now threading their way back with their prisoner, the packed onlookers parting just enough to let them through and then follow on behind, the place soon left almost empty save the thin line of soldiers who had kept their ground. To those who could not have had a full idea of what was going on it must have seemed a strange episode, the sort that feeds on rumour and speculation, the general purpose the more confusing for lack of any attempt at an address from the authorities by way of explanation. One man had brought all these others out onto the streets in unaccountable fury; religion was involved, because the denizens of the Temple were also out in force; it was important enough to bring the Governor himself to the scene; and no sooner than any clarity seemed to have emerged it was all over.

But it was not. It was the lull before the storm.

It was not long before numbers began to grow again from every direction, gathering in knots, disputatious and garrulous. The whole city seemed in turmoil, taut and expectant, with crisis in the air and satisfaction clearly absent. The word had it Caiaphas had been sent off with a flea in his ear to the Hasmonean Palace, which had evidently been controversial. This was not a matter for a foreign potentate, and definitely not one whose adherence to the true God was skin-deep at best. Herod Antipas might be the heretic's nominal ruler but this was not Galilee; this was their land, their faith, their holy city that was being violated and they, the true believers, who would put an end to it. Antipas had better mind his own business, better still depart to where he belonged. The chosen people no longer had need of his kind. The priests would soon be back, empty-handed; and this time they would mean business.

The speculation was well-founded. Within the hour the whole process was being repeated, the original crowd now larger and spilling back until the whole space was jammed solid with shouting and gesticulating men, every nook and cranny full, all other movement near-impossible, the clamour rising all the while. The puppet ruler had spoken, but wouldn't take responsibility, it seemed. What did anyone expect? Who needed kings anyway? He was not theirs; God's elect did not need them. The true guardian of the nation, their High Priest – he would show them. This was their moment, which they were going to win. This was the people showing their resolve against the occupiers, determined to have their will and their ways given the primacy all decency demanded.

Caiaphas the High Priest approached as resolutely as before, the Nazarene now mockingly draped in expensive Hasmonean purple, almost hidden by the jostling helmets and spear points of the Temple Guard. It seemed every able-bodied man in the city was now venting his outrage at this upstart, this impostor, this traitor, the din rising in crescendo, making first normal speech impossible and then seeming to overwhelm all senses. The Roman cordon, reinforced now, stood shoulder-to-shoulder, struggling against the press. None among its number could have been immune in that cauldron of resentment to the open hostility confronting them; any moment their line might be swept away by sheer weight of numbers if the mob turned its fury to action. Two worlds were in collision, and the line, symbol of division, would have to hold. But there was a deeper hatred that day, and for once the occupiers were not its object.

A sudden hush fell. Again the Governor came down the steps to speak to the High Priest. From those in the crowd close enough to make out their conversation emanated choruses of approval and disapproval which rippled backwards and forwards until all was again seething confusion and anger, continuing even as the prisoner was handed over and taken in to the inner court. Tension grew, and grew again, and must surely burst soon. It seemed a long wait for a crowd so exercised, most of which was denied any sense of what might be going on within. In reality it was less time than it took to boil an egg.

There was a flurry of movement at the entrance. Governor and accused emerged to a great roar, then once again a hush descended as expectant faces strained intensely to try and catch what was going on. The Governor spoke briefly, and no sooner were his words out than another fury broke loose, more intimidating and defiant than anything before. It took the prolonged efforts of the priests to eventually restore sufficient calm for the two leaders to resume. Then again the rhythmic swell, the rising and falling of the rushing tempest as the crowd reacted to the theatre before them, and a new sound, a chant, barely discernible at first but quickly gaining in rhythm and volume against the din, an unmistakable call rising in crescendo: 'bar Abbas, bar Abbas, bar Abbas, bar Abbas'. On and on it grew until it had total dominion, a wall of sound against which no other could compete. Then another lull, short, eerie, ominous, and the final almighty roar, so deafening that even the stoutest heart must have flinched before the mighty noise, and straightaway at full volume: 'Crucify! ... Crucify! ... Crucify! ... Crucify! ...CRUCIFY!'

*　　*　　*　　*

In his makeshift cell, and in her dressing-room, Favonius Facilis and Claudia Procula made their respective devotions with all the concentration their troubled minds would allow, knowing with terrible certainty what the tumult meant. Much closer to the baying of the mob outside, the Governor's Lady knelt with eyes closed tight, trembling as she summoned every last vestige of conviction for her prayer to be heard. It was the only thing left, and who but she, frightened as she was, could pray so knowingly? Was she not His only friend among her own kind in this heartless, merciless place? Almost, not entirely. She remembered: Favonius would be praying too, wherever he was.

It was the centurion's only resort also. For him those distant sounds and the events they signalled could have been emanating from within the corners of his prison confines, so present and ominous were they. There was only one meaning. The time had come. The Son of Man was set to meet His fate.

In his great discomfiture he had wild visions of boyhood heroes and stirring action, of rushing out single-handed to mount a desperate rescue, of the moment he too should act for duty and honour and go down in glory for his Lord and Master; but nothing could change what was happening out there, not his own death or anyone else's. Death was come to Yeshua bar Joseph, alone of God, full prophesied and bitter. If he'd learnt anything it was of the Father's love and tenderness – and will. It was the divine will which had to be borne out, a great mystery beyond understanding which had to be obeyed. It was hard, so very hard, but it had to be done. Whatever was ordained had now to be endured. What difference could his own death make, the demise of a nameless foreign soldier, other than bring unwelcome certainty to his family's own fate, when there might still be a chance of a better outcome for them? He had to get a grip. Prayer was the only hope, that the consolation might be transmitted, that Yeshua might know He was not alone, that others were with Him in mind if not body, even if their own weak unworthy souls were all they had to offer at this dread hour.

*   *   *   *

Increasing alarm on the ground had brought the remainder of Century I down from the fort during the earlier lull. Longinus had joined the officers of the staff in a short line of their own astride the portico, and he'd caught most of what had been said outside, and then everything within the outer court of the Praetorium. He had seen first-hand the fury, the pent-up frustration of an outraged people who had finally found a legitimate outlet for their defiance of the oppressor on this, their special feast-tide. The protest had been impressive, but then that was what uncooperative peoples who harboured absurd notions of independence always did – turn any grouse into a pretext for outrage, the real target of which was the imperial power. The sensible thing was to accept the benefits of civilized government, not turn out baying and howling and getting worked up into a state of frenzy. Hatred and violence masquerading as righteous indignation – that's what it was; men at their worst, blind with rage and blood-lust. A flight of javelins or two would soon have dowsed their ardour, but there had never been much chance of that. They had to deal with reality, with what was happening and the limitations on their own ability to respond. And the most important reality was what was going on in the eye of the storm, not its wild periphery. The dialogue between the Governor and the High Priest, and then the Governor and the prisoner – that had been of the highest drama, as though wrought straight from Greek tragedy. Against the continuous torrent of noise, and having to worry how his soldiers were coping, it would have been easy to have missed it, but something made him concentrate hard on that above all. Little did he think then they would be words which would be etched in his memory for ever.

Off to one side of the courtyard now, though openly and deliberately visible to a large section of the crowd, his men had overdone the scourging. Pieces of lead and sharp sheep's bone braided into leather thongs were enough to reduce any man quickly to flayed meat, but you wanted the victim to be just able to stand and carry his burden, otherwise somebody else had to it, which usually meant one of them. The sergeant had got it wrong, and he'd have words with him later. Anyone could tell this man was over-beaten, already unsteady on his feet and near-insensible. He would have a chance to recover a little as they waited for the timbers to be brought from the fort, but they started to fool around in mockery of this king without a throne, fashioning a rough coronet of thorns and ramming it down on his head, sending scarlet rivulets down his face and neck. It was unnecessary but not the sort of behaviour which you would normally put a stop to. It was what soldiers did, playing to their own gallery and coarser instincts as well as the crowd's, oblivious to the gratuitous pain they were inflicting, an act of ownership and mocking indifference rather than deliberate malice. This was nothing to do with the Jews any more, though they were quite happy to let them watch. The man was in their charge now, and would die like any other serious criminal who didn't have the protection of Roman citizenship.

In the midst of that extraordinary scene, which indeed later seemed to so many of those who witnessed it to be strangely disembodied through all the cacophony, against the seething mass of mindlessly yelling contorted faces, the justified priests, the backs of the soldiers holding firm against the weight of numbers, the red of the senior staff with the toga'd figure of their leader, all caught in a moment of time that would come to be eternal – the man stood, bowed slightly but still with dignity, back and shoulders bloodied with weals, beard and hair matted with blood and sweat, arms weak by his side.

Somewhere from out of the building a servant appeared bearing a towel and approached tentatively, offering it the man. He managed to take it and weakly wipe his face, then handed it back, looking directly at the bearer for a moment as if in thanks, before the cloak was thrown back on him and the outfit made complete. Soldiers' sarcasm had been exercised, however primitive; and Longinus had watched it all, knowing that this was what they did and had to be allowed to do, and that the crowd had to see it too. And so the man was led out to their full view, in extirpation, gratification and satisfaction. 'Behold the man', the Governor said, and the crowd responded in another deafening roar, now of approval.

The execution party would comprise much of his own company, this being a serious event requiring a high level of security; and he would attend personally. No-one liked executions, especially like these; there was too much waiting around, and it was no way to see a man die. Thankfully they didn't come around too often; some of the younger ones hadn't seen it at all, so it would be good training for them. It was a duty that had to be done, and done well like any other; as with many things, it wouldn't get done by anybody else but soldiers. And it did need to be done. Law and order had to be maintained and example made. He might have wished that it hadn't fallen to him, but like most disagreeable jobs the best thing was to steel your mind and proceed almost as though it were not happening. Short of sleep and a decent breakfast, he wished he was anywhere but here, but it didn't do for a senior centurion to be thinking like that.

The stores arrived and the work section fell in. Two men took the cross-piece and held it up for the man on whom all eyes now rested, who without a word stooped, took the load and slowly straightened himself as far as he could under its great weight. Longinus nodded; the sergeant prodded the prisoner with the butt of his javelin; and the procession began on its way, the clamorous mob following on and ahead to mark its progress through the narrow streets. Longinus marched with his lead section, clearing the way through the crowd which surged around on all sides, still shouting and showing its fists but not interfering with the double file of soldiers that held the flanks, which had to close in where the way narrowed, regaining order when it allowed.

The heat of the day was already building. It was going to be another nice one, he thought; the sort when fluffy white clouds contrasted with a cerulean blue though the sun always seemed to be shining, when spring flowers danced and leaves rustled in a gentle breeze, birds sang, girls hummed at their chores and people went about their business and made their plans for the morrow; a day when life would go on for the vast majority of creatures that lived on earth and ate and drank its goodness, and for whom and for which that tomorrow would come; but not for this poor unfortunate nor the others who would shortly die with him on Golgotha, the place of the skull as these people called it. Could anyone not about to die at the hands of others ever understand – understand what it was like to know their life was really about to come to an end this day, without the slightest doubt, without the slightest hope of reprieve, but that life for everybody and everything else would carry on unchanged on the next, and the next after that, as if the snuffing out of this one meant nothing, almost as though it had never been?

For a soldier it was different. The cold fear that stalked the quiet before the action, the hollow void before the moment of battle when you realized the morn you'd just lived through might be your last, that the next might dawn without you – that was normal fare. Anyone who had ever fought in a serious campaign knew that feeling at some time or other, and most knew too how to live with it. At least an army could get its blood up and stir itself to action; if you had to die you would do so like a man with boots on and sword in hand. And there was always a let-out – you might survive, by your own efforts or good fortune. There were times in Gaul when it hadn't looked good, when the possibility of death and defeat had seriously to be faced, but there'd always been a fighting chance, that if you kept your head and behaved like a warrior your side would prevail even if you perished. You were just one part of a mighty machine, the overall purpose of which was beneficial and honourable; others would avenge you in time, and the Army would win in the end no matter how many good men might be lost in the fortunes of war. It was the lucky ones who saw their tomorrows, and who would come to write the history. And after the wars you re-joined the rest of humanity with its unnumbered, unrecorded tribulations which would always remain so, its countless minor acts of unsung courage against ill-health and adversity, and took what was coming, and went when it was finally your time – because there was no choice.

But for this man about to die there could be no chance of rescue or escape, no reprieve, no miraculous last-minute stroke of fortune, no tomorrow, no glory; nothing. Not for him any more of the simple sights and sounds, the commonplace experience of the life he had known on earth. For him that life was being taken away, not by want or disease or mishap, not in the heat of battle, but slowly and deliberately by the will of men, where there could be no resistance but only passivity in the face of torture and gratuitous cruelty. If that were also the will of the Gods, then who was he to question it? If it were not, because they had no interest, then it was settled in any case. It made no difference, because it was happening, now before his eyes, and nothing would change it. How tenuous was man's hold on life! The sun which gave warmth and light to all was now relentlessly blinding this poor wretch and the two others who awaited him in their torment. The body which it had nurtured and made strong was now to be the very means of its own agony, contrived by fiendish minds to eke out its longest, most tortuous death. And this man did not deserve it.

He checked behind, called to keep the pace down. The prisoner was stumbling on the uneven paving stones, finding it harder to put one step in front of another. It was less than a quarter of a mile now, but for someone already severely weakened by shock and pain, who could have had no sleep or sustenance, carrying his cross to his death, it was a physical ordeal even the very strongest might fail; it could be no surprise he was clearly already exhausted. Several times the column halted whilst the victim had to stop and rest, each time finding it more difficult to rise from his knees and take the enormous strain of the baulk across his bloodied shoulders.

The centurion returned to his thoughts on the transience of life, of how every step now was another step to oblivion – oblivion for a man whom, rather to his surprise, he had found himself seeing in a very different and unusual light. He couldn't have helped but be impressed by his dignity back at the Praetorium; now there was something else, and it was more than respect. It was sympathy, a sudden sense of sympathy which had rushed him and caught him unawares. Here was a man who was being put to a hideous death who patently didn't deserve it. Just suppose the fates had reversed their roles? How would he be coping if it was he that was trying to find the strength to carry a fearfully heavy beam to his end, amid people obviously enjoying every moment of it, who had clamoured instead for their murderous hero – the one he should have accidentally killed in a case of mistaken identity at the Hill of Luz? The ways of men were too often unsavoury; and so were the multitudinous weavings and windings of destiny. Could what was happening before them, by their own hand, really be the will of any kind of god?

*   *   *   *

He didn't realize what had happened until he heard the shouts come up the line. The man was down on one knee, blood dripping down his nose to spot the dusty ground, his hands still grasping the timber as though he needed it to support himself and there yet remained some willing purpose in this journey to oblivion; he was becoming unable to function, unable to get up, unable hardly to lift his head. And with no little consternation he knew that what he had been feeling was more than respect, more than sympathy: it was out-and-out compassion. First had come the imagination; then the empathy; and now the full-bloodied concern, with anger and revulsion not far off. It had come quickly and he couldn't stop it. True, he had to admit he had been impressed with the man's composure the moment he had first seen him, all through the mockery of a trial and the way he seemed to accept his fate before the screaming mob, without remonstration, one man it seemed against all the hatreds of mankind. But now to see what that enmity entailed on this inexorable path to pain and suffering, how it was killing a man who by his every demeanour was obviously blameless and very, very brave — how could anyone with any decency not be moved to see his plight?

There was another kerfuffle behind. He started to retrace his steps again, then realized there was no need. The sergeant had got the problem under control. Somebody, no doubt with a little military encouragement, had stepped in and was now taking the timber up. The man was brought to his feet once more and steadied; and they stepped off again up the steep alleyway, the man now behind and relieved of his burden, stumbling slowly on. 'Well done you.' 'Well done that man.' 'Well done all', he thought.

The place of the skull had already been secured by the time they got there, the uprights lying awaiting their charges, two other criminals stooping battered and cowed under guard of his men, the noise from the expectant crowd which had already gathered reaching a climax as the procession and its accompanying throng spilt out from the gate and made its way across the rubbish pits and up to the little eminence. Within a ring of steel the execution party set to without delay, ignoring the screams of pain as the two others went up first. He did not recognize them but there was no reason why he should. They were common criminals, probably brigands, no doubt fully deserving of their fate. There was no point drawing proceedings out any longer than necessary, and no point either in allowing his thoughts to distract any further when concentration was needed and no amount of any more philosophizing could change reality. The sooner it was all over the better.

It was the man's turn. They stripped him to his underwear, half led him, half carried him up the short slope, placed him down back-first, pressed his arms against the rough-hewn, mortise-secured wood that already bore his blood, and began the securing, gripping his limbs tightly as the thick iron nails were hammered in through the wrists and the agony of it made him writhe beneath them, then through the awkwardly crossed feet, in just the right place through the bone. One of them fixed the placard the Governor himself had ordered they brought with them, a command was given, and in one swift movement they hoisted the post up in its slot and secured the foot with stones, the whole structure in place quickly and without ceremony; and with barely a glance the men gathered the few tools of their handiwork and fell in for further orders. The sergeant let them draw lots for the bloodied coat of purple, still worth a penny or two, the only possession worth anything remaining from three men's lives. It was better than letting the locals get their hands on it, and it was how soldiers always made the best of their own deceased comrades' effects.

The mood of the crowd changed from fury to scorn, from outrage to justification and satiation. 'Save yourself', and 'If you can!', and hollow laughter became the refrain, but the crowd soon grew bored and presently started to thin, wagging their heads and muttering about the folly of unbelievers as they went. They had seen crucifixion before; it was alien and brutal, but effective and an accepted means of keeping society in order. Now justice had been done and the people's honour restored, and there was little point in seeing these criminals and blasphemers actually die, which would take too much of anyone's time.

*　*　*　*

And so it was, for the first time after all the tumults of that day, there could now be heard the sound of weeping. As the pressure on the cordon eased, Longinus gave the order to let the relatives through. They rushed to the cross and gathered at its foot, knelt in prayer or reached up with outstretched hands, crying and calling out in their native tongue. Not one, either of the women or the men among them, would leave that place until the end. Like the soldiers around them they had their duty, though surely it was as harrowing as human beings could stand. They became quieter as time went on, murmuring in prayer and comforting each other, the women quietly sobbing, the men mostly stood still or squatting, all through the long hours that followed. One or two of his men had better Aramaic, and gradually a degree of understanding impressed itself upon their consciousness. From the start, as they had held him down he had said 'Father, forgive them, for they know not what they do.' In all their harsh and simple lives they had never heard anybody say anything like that before, ever, to anyone. Unless you were a complete brute it was impossible not to be moved, though of course equally impossible to show it. This manner of death, vicious even by their standards, was the visitation of Roman power on slaves and foreign miscreants, lesser mortals to whom was reserved the least dignity and the most drawn-out pain possible. It was the ultimate deterrent against irredeemable elements for whom, dehumanized, there should be no mercy, and in ensuring obedience through salutary example it served the common good. What manner of man could this be though who was dying so quietly, stripped and battered for all to mock, yet dignified when all normal dignity was gone, deserted but for these few family and friends? He hoped he would be able to find the same courage if by some trick of the Gods it could ever be him that hung there.

*　*　*　*

Some of the things said that were roughly translated for him as the day wore on made little sense at first. 'Behold this day you will enter paradise' had clearly been a delusional little outpouring of false comfort, a figment of the imagination of someone with no way out of his predicament, a vainglorious statement of defiance against everything that was obvious. But why say it to a criminal? Because, as the corporal thought he'd heard, it was in answer to one of the two who had managed to say something, words of repentance, the other remaining defiant and deriding. Didn't everyone believe they were going to a better place than this hard life one day? Were they, sophisticated Romans, exemplars of civilization, watched over by the true Gods of benevolence, not themselves promised release from earthly cares and the gloomy shades of Pluto's realm? All could agree on that, and that those who deserved it would go to a better place. But hadn't the man also claimed there was only one god, just as the Jews believed, and that he himself was this god's son? Which was preposterous, even by the bizarre ideas of the East. It was manifestly dangerous to say anything like that, when benevolent Gods might become very jealous Gods indeed, and among men too: for the Jews with their unshakeable views of blasphemy and retribution it would be blaspheming madness, for which there was only one penalty. Would the self-respecting son of any real God allow himself to be treated in this way, with public disgrace and humiliating execution? What was so special about this man that he could make such a ridiculous claim, anyway? Fine, he was dying bravely in an appalling situation, but that didn't make you a God. You needed to have achieved unchallengeable greatness to begin to be eligible for so unimaginable a distinction – even the greatest men of Rome did not qualify, unless they had done something as epoch-making as founding the Empire, while the ancestors, who guarded the household and defended the nation, never for one moment aspired to number themselves among the greats of Olympus. No. It was moving, and different insofar as this was clearly a very unusual man, able to say profound and rather moving things to his very end, and clearly much loved by his family and followers. But he was still only a man, as evidenced by his dying. And this was a legal execution, and you had to do your duty and steel yourself for the job in hand. It was as simple as that.

*   *   *   *

When later however the man charged one of his followers to take his mother as his own, it brought the full pathos of the moment back again. And when one of the mourners brought a reed and a sedative in a jar, he allowed it to be offered up. It seemed the least he could do for someone who didn't deserve any of this, though the man refused it anyway, evidently preferring to hold on to what little consciousness he retained. He had spoken a few words to his followers in the first hours, and to the man at his side, whilst he still could; yet he had not once made the slightest sound of complaint. Only once later did they hear him whisper 'I thirst', and they would try again with wine, but by then he was no longer able to move his head or open his lips. The grip of death was closing in.

The Senior Centurion wished it would come quickly now. The drawn-out agony only served to encourage thoughts which demanded his unwilling attention, and were becoming increasingly persistent. For all his attempts at detachment, weren't there some questions to be answered? Weren't wanton cruelty and blind injustice winning here? Wasn't that the incontrovertible reality, and if so, why were these apparently so necessary? In fact – why had any of this come about at all? It was a thought too far. Not now. The horror was enough. Of all the ways men could meet their end this had to be the worst. If you were lucky you died in your sleep, or dropped dead after a fulfilled life; if not then you wasted away, or died in varying degrees of misery and squalor. If you were a woman you had to face the additional trials of childbirth; if a soldier the risk of capture and torture, injury and maimed impairment. If you were a slave then your life was barely your own anyway, your worth only an inventory value, and whether you lived or died generally of little consequence. Pain and suffering seemed to be the lot of everything that lived and had sentience, and to everything whether sentient or not came a final end. But no-one deserved to die like this. Only the most cruel and infernal minds could have devised such an inhuman punishment, alien actually to his homeland but readily adopted as the ultimate deterrent, something no-one with a shred of decency should inflict on mortal flesh, yet now visited upon men with casual acceptance as though it had been thus since the world began. Death the indifferent leveller brought everyone low in the end, yet here it was being drawn out in as deliberately a protracted manner as possible by men on their own kind, as though enough cruelty and suffering didn't already abound. You didn't have to look very far to see that merciless suppression by the immovable forces of established authority was the natural order everywhere, wreaking havoc on men and women who collectively comprised the human race, every single one of whom had hopes and aspirations, cares and needs, and were capable of going wrong in the ordinary course of their lives; and some of whom had to go and get themselves in additional trouble as if the day-to-day weren't enough. He thought of Favonius, grappling with that conscience of his and concern for his family, with the very real prospect of the direst consequences hanging over his head too; at least for him the end would be quick and honourable. Self-imposed difficulties carried no special moral defence, nor offered any better chance of deliverance.

And wasn't he now in that same boat? Being engaged with the duty company's business had been a welcome distraction. There had been no time to brood. The great Longinus didn't do brooding, they would all have said, but even he hadn't been in quite a situation like this. Did he really have to do as he had done? For now he thought of Macula's body lying on the table that morning, recovered by the Samarians before the day's trouble had begun. They had asked him to make the formal identification. 'Yes, that's him, Licinius Macula, Junior Tribune of the First Augusta. 'Looks like garotting', the Samarian centurion had said. 'Favourite method with the Zealots. No wonder we all thought we were in for a fight this morning. That'll teach him to be out on the streets at a time like this.' 'Yes', he had replied.

The ways of men were indeed strange, their devices and designs far too complicated ...

*   *   *   *

In the early afternoon the air started to become oppressively sultry, and the clouds, which had been steadily building for some time, began to darken and billow overhead, then gradually become motionless like a great pall hanging over the city. At first they had expected a thorough soaking on their forlorn scene, almost empty now except for the main cast and a few onlookers who appeared from time to time to stare and jabber. The stillness matched the figures on their crosses. All movement on those gaunt emblems had ceased now, all attempts by the victims to shift their weight abandoned to the crushing asphyxiation which was remorselessly overcoming them. The thief who had railed and cursed had fallen silent except for occasional groans. All that remained of feeble effort was barely perceptible exhalation, as chests and bodies sagged leaden and the pain had to be borne without respite, inexorable and almost soundless. He'd been concerned for one or two of his younger lads, but they were coping well enough with this soulless business; you didn't let any sort of weakness affect your bearing, no matter how appalling or harrowing the task. The end wasn't far off anyway, and he decided it was safe to withdraw half their number since the security threat had now all but gone. He would stay. He could have left somebody in charge, but in view of the occasion's high profile and the personal involvement of the Governor in the morning's proceedings it was appropriate he should report personally.

That was the ostensible reasoning, at any rate, but there was also an inner voice, and it was telling him to see it through – to see this wretched business through to the end. He wouldn't have cared to articulate it, much less rationalize it, but he positively wanted to stay, of his own volition, and not just because it was right to be with the last of his men until the job was finally done. Drawn by what force he could not tell, from its first seed it had now become pressingly insistent. This spectacle, this execution, wasn't just cruel and gratuitous: it was wicked. And there was more. This man needed him, however crazy that might have sounded. And, he realized with equally arresting clarity, he almost seemed to need the man, though his broken body must be close to the end now. Because he was setting them an example. Because he was showing how a man should die in the face of unspeakable indignity, with courage and dignity, so quiet yet so great, that all men who would ever be born should see and marvel as he did now, if only they would allow themselves to do so and though it could only ever be in their imagination. Because this man was innocent. Indeed he was innocence personified, as innocent as the thousands of lambs killed in the city this last day, sacrificed for his god and his people. And as the spirit left the body so all the goodness, and tenderness, and love, was shown overcoming all the miserable misdeeds of hateful, stupid, ignorant little men. Because this man was as defenceless and pitiable now as any man could ever be, and needed strong new arms and strong new voices to carry his message of hope and love for mankind. Was that, in his voicelessness, what this man was telling him, himself, this hard-bitten, conceited, over-assured, over-young officer with all his glittering prospects ahead of him, who had already seen men die and relinquish theirs without hope? It was a question too big for him, too big for anyone.

He must return to his rounds and spend time with his men, posted now in half-sections around the little crag. Crows were starting to gather in the gloom; and time, like the heavy air, stood still.

*　*　*　*

Two well-dressed men were asking to see him, and were let through.

'Good day, Centurion.'

'Is it? This'd better be important.'

'My name's Joseph, Centurion, and this is my friend from the Sanhedrin, Nicodemus. We have a letter from the Governor, authorizing me to take the body for burial.'

'Oh really? I don't think so.'

'It's true Centurion. Please, read this.'

He took the letter and scrutinized it. It seemed authentic at first sight, the message to him personally from the Camp Commandant and in the Governor's name. Try as he might he could find no fault with it; the bearers were obviously men of substance and clearly too had the approval of the mourners. He would comply. Apart from anything else it would save his men the bother of disposing of another body.

'Very well. You may have him when it's done. Where do you intend to bury him?'

'I have a tomb ready, around the northern wall beyond the far gate. It's new, just been made for me.'

'How will you get the body there?'

'With my beast.   And with the help of these good people, and Nicodemus here. We'll need time to prepare.'

'Very well, but he's to go straight there, mind.   No mumbling around for hours on end.'

'You wouldn't deny him the rites of his people, surely?'

'Keep it short then. My men will only be around long enough to bury the other two.'

'Thank you, Centurion.' And with that they withdrew and joined the other mourners; and he thought no more of it.

*   *   *   *

The afternoon dragged on.   Soldiers were changed around between stations to give relief from the boredom, otherwise there was little to vary the scene: his men, rigid, reliable; the followers, subdued, still faithful; remnants among the onlookers, victorious in their zeal; the sombre silhouettes of the crosses, gaunt against the lowering sky which was becoming so dark they all began to remark on it.   Daylight was being slowly expunged from horizon to horizon. It was like the ethereal gloom of an eclipse, which some were acquainted with, but the darkness seemed to emanate from the clouds themselves, and no-one had said anything about an eclipse being due.   The almanacs might have had it somewhere, but there had been no auguries consulted or libations made to his knowledge.   You did get dust storms and rainless storm clouds in these lands, but not like this, with no movement, all the dark of a thunderstorm with no thunder, no lightning and no rain, just ever-increasing gloom. They might as well get used to the dark as they'd be there all night anyway, one man quipped.

Some figures broke away from the priests' party, which had remained to see justice done long after most spectators had gone. He let them approach.

'We understand you've granted permission for the deceiver's body to be taken.'

'Yes. What of it?'

'"The Sabbath starts at sundown. We don't want these criminals out here till the last moment. We have a lot to do before then. And we certainly don't want bodies hanging here defiling our holy time.'

'If you can tell when sundown is in this fug you'll be doing well.'

'All the more reason to act soon.'

'Meaning?'

'Break their legs now. We want them dead.'

'When we're ready. Not before.'

'So you're prepared to violate our Sabbath?'

'I didn't say that. You'll have your Sabbath, and we'll do the breaking when it suits us. This is an official execution, not an act of public convenience.'

'And you'll be releasing the body to the High Priest.'

'Will I? On what grounds?'

'On the grounds that we are his official representatives, and it is his wish to take custody as his right.'

'I know of no such right. Anyway, you're too late. As you obviously know, those gentlemen there have permission to take it and bury it according to your custom.'

'What do you mean? On whose authority?'

'My Commander-in-Chief's. The Province Prefect, to you.'

'You mean the Prefect has personally ordered you.'

'Yes. Officially.'

'Show us. Show us the letter.'

'See for yourself.'

They took it, looked, and looked again, the reaction evident in their faces.

'Signed by a Roman to a centurion about a common criminal. We would hope he's got better things to do.'

'Signed by the Garrison Commander for the Commander-in-Chief. That's good enough for me. And you.'

'We have our own channels of authority, centurion. All members of the Council answer to the High Priest. Including your ... gentlemen.'

'So where is his letter?'

'You should do this, officer, and you should hand the body to us or incur the wrath of the High Priest and the whole people.'

'Possibly in half an hour – the breaking of legs, I mean. But no body. You're not having the body. It's going to a rock-tomb which will be properly secure.'

'So you, a mere centurion, would break the peace of the country – for a criminal and a blasphemer.'

'I don't know about blasphemy, priest, but the man's no criminal.' He felt an urge to draw his sword. 'There is no authority to take this body other than the one already given. Or do you wish to challenge *my* authority.'

'You haven't heard the last of this.' And with that, furious, they left for the city gate, leaving two men behind to continue observing.

There was a fleeting thought that he should place a guard on the tomb from the outset, tonight; but he dismissed it. There was no need. They'd done enough.

*　　*　　*　　*

He wasn't normally the sort for lengthy self-examination. He had approached the deeds of the day with his customary speed of analysis, and it was rare for his instinct to let him down. Besides, this was a trifle compared to that earlier business. Yes he would live on his wits, but he was up to it, and on a matter such as this he would decide for himself; nobody else. It was an attitude which had taken him thus far, and he wasn't about to change. In the unlikely event he had got the priests' demand wrong, the lack of any authoritative counter-order to the instruction he'd already received would give him all the defence he needed. And he could deal with angry protests if they materialized, and quickly call for reinforcements if necessary.

The unusual request of the man from Arimathea was interesting though. He'd had to accept it as authenticated, but who was this apparently modest man and why should he be trusted? And what might it signify that he was accompanied by an elder of the Sanhedrin?

Perhaps they both were councillors. There was no point in speculating about divisions among the Jews; evidently the general condemnation of the man from Galilee even in high places was not entirely unanimous, and there was concern over decent disposal of the body which was only fitting. Demeanour counted. The two were socially far removed from the other mourners, but seemed to genuinely share their sorrow, and there was none of the usual arrogance about them. Nevertheless he should be careful not to let this peculiar new-found feeling of affinity with these people gathered close-by affect his judgment, and he had to recognize there would be some explaining to do if the Sabbath wasn't properly respected, with all that could lead to; the Governor certainly wouldn't be very happy about any mistake like that. It came down to this Joseph again, but from what he'd seen there was no cause for alarm; everything was in order; the Sabbath wasn't going to be violated; and he'd probably have made the same decision on release of the body himself, without any cover from on high.

So the family would have their son, and they deserved what little comfort the gesture could bring them. Crucified corpses were rarely claimed, here or anywhere else. That was the Army's job, as usual. The custom here was to unceremoniously dump them in the gully which ran up to the western wall, cover them roughly with stones and rubbish, and return to barracks for tea; they weren't worth having his soldiers dig them graves in this rocky ground, that was sure. This time, for this man, it would be different, and good that someone was going to take care of his mortal remains. Whatever the priestly hierarchy were up to in trying to claim him, it was most unlikely to match the care and concern of these good folk in their loss, whose bearing in grief was touching him too disconcertingly now.

Yeshua had clearly evoked the very strongest loyalty and affection among his followers. What if he really had been innocent, interested only in spreading his message on his true god, which by all accounts was the same god of the Jews but which had got him executed for blasphemy? He didn't understand, and didn't think he ever would. But it had got to Favonius, hadn't it? – and he was no fool. Religion was a queer affair, when you looked at it. Men would decree death, and die themselves, for something which really, when you came to analyze it, didn't seem worth a candle, let alone dying for. Fortunately old Jove was a bit more easy-going: you paid your respects and thanked him for guiding your country, you and your own, and that was more or less it. A few might take it more seriously, but not pragmatists like him. Life was too short. But here, in this country – here religious observance dominated every aspect of existence, every detail of daily life. This man had outraged the authorities by transgressing the most deeply held tenets of the faith, and compounded his crime by exposing their hypocrisy. No wonder they wanted him dead. The vengeance of his own people was to be taken as read: the real question was for the hated Romans, who had the power. Had a great injustice been committed, to leave this blameless man hanging just a few feet in front of him? Had a great blunder been made which might perpetuate that injustice and sit badly with Roman arms for years to come?

He, man of action, had rather not think about it.

* * * *

The waiting continued. About mid-afternoon, or as close as they could judge in that stygian gloom, just after his followers managed to moisten his lips for the final time, the man from Nazareth in Galilee uttered his last, the silence broken by a cry of 'It is finished', everyone astounded by its volume and clarity after so long with no sound or movement; his chest, struggling almost imperceptibly for so long, still at last.

Weeping and groaning broke out in lamentation. The body above seemed no different than before, with the head down at the same angle and no discernable overall change. Was this really the end? It seemed mercifully soon compared to the norm. The man had been exhausted from the outset, so it was possible. Longinus picked his way up to the cross, and looked closely. With relief, he thought yes, he's gone – face slightly to one side, haggard but still handsome before the ghastly pallor of death could extend its embrace; eyes closed, peaceful; the chest completely still, sunk under drooping shoulders; lacerated arms outstretched, the wrists a torn and bloody mess. Standing and looking at those arms, they seemed to him to reach out for all the sufferings of mankind, its pain and woes without number, and for all the cruelty and ignorance which blighted its presence upon the earth. What had this man died for? Because he had believed he was the son of god? Yet hadn't he just said not one hour past: "My God, my God, why have you forsaken me"? What could it mean, if he himself had felt betrayed and deserted at the very end? How could that square with his god or his claim to be his son? Was he just another mad mystic in a land of mystics, if one with a very different message? Love god, whoever this one god was, love your neighbour, help the needy, keep the secular law, promote peace. Many could agree with all that, including the Jews themselves, who punctiliously tried to observe the moral code as well as the ritual minutiae; but as Favonius had told him, there was more to it than that, much more. It was about forgiveness and mercy, forgiving others as well as seeking personal redemption of one's own sins; gentleness and generosity of spirit; not doing good works to signal virtue but for their own sake; knowing the right and doing it; seeking the truth always and the will of this god; and coming to him by his grace through his son. How could anyone embrace this terrible end if they did not truly believe in what they were doing? But the man had proved mortal, like everybody else, and was now reduced to this, done to death on a hard wooden cross on a stony hillside beside a city wall, slaughtered so the sins of the world might be forgiven. Could this body hanging here possibly, really, be the son of god? The Son of the Almighty no less, who by his teaching and example had pointed the way to salvation for all men? Longinus looked up at the leaden sky and around the faces of his men, frozen at that moment looking on like him, then back to the broken body before him. He did not claim to be clever, for all his reputation. He did not claim to understand the world beyond his profession. He was certainly no philosopher. But he was moved to say, loud enough for them all to hear: 'Truly, this was a great man.'

He thought later he should have been bolder.

*   *   *   *

They broke the legs of the other two with the heavy hammer, and both quickly succumbed. On reaching the man the sergeant speared his side with a javelin thrust to make sure he really was dead; and the cross was lowered and dismantled in reverse order, the relatives still close by. As soon as the nails were out then the body was theirs. Hands reached out to reclaim their own, and for some time they all stayed there, cleaning the blood away, the women crying and hugging the prostrate form. There would be no rush to carry him away, Sabbath or no Sabbath; the spices and the cloths could wait; he would let them have as long as they needed. This was their moment of indescribable grief and passion, joined with relief it was over, of supreme tenderness and unity in love which would abide into their eternity.

Eventually, as they got ready for the journey around the city wall, a man came over and said 'Thank you, Centurion'; and then the mother, putting her hand out to place it on his arm. Her tear-stained eyes met his for an instant; he reciprocated the gesture; and then she was away to re-join the others.

Much to his disgust, as he gave the orders to pack up, he had to avert his eyes from those of his men. There could be no place for emotion.

THE AFTERMATH

The events of the morning had been dramatic, though in hindsight they could have ended much worse. That the Governor himself had been forced to exercise his own authority in what was essentially a scrappy little local matter, which in its execution had once again shown its limitations, had been regrettable; he had at least secured a conclusion, if not a particularly elegant one. The imperial interest could take some satisfaction that its representative had shown as much even-handedness as could have been expected, that a volatile situation had been contained and a serious outbreak of unrest averted. Pragmatic diplomacy had been employed without undue favour. The Zealots were happy; they had their leader back but remained nevertheless a small and essentially impotent minority. The native authority had stood up for its rights and its sway over the people, and could be said to have had a victory of sorts though, crucially, without getting its way on official endorsement of the condemnation. The man from Nazareth in Galilee whom they claimed was so heinous had gone off to his death and his cowed followers would be dispersed without trace, when only days before what had seemed a large proportion of the population had been cheering him on with mass disorder in the air. There had been no counter-demonstration at the climax, no attempt at rescuing their idol in his hour of need, and only a rump of what were presumably his family and closest followers had stood by to the end. There would be no more trouble at the Temple now from irresponsible social revolutionaries committing blasphemy and disturbing the peace, and the business of the whole city could return to the Passover commemoration and in due course normal routine. Peace would have its dividend for all, and for the priestly faction there was no doubt: the battle of wills had gone decisively in their favour, the object achieved by whatever means necessary, and with the added benefit of being seen to defend their religious rights from the occupying power when the opportunity had arisen.

In the Antonine and Praetorium there was tacit recognition that another milestone had been reached in this administration. Where views on its management of the affair might have been less than entirely supportive they were strictly confined to the most private of discussions. Authority was constituted for a purpose and not to be questioned, and there was little point wasting time and energy speculating on the rights and wrongs of what the high command had determined as the best course, especially when the pressure had been on for a speedy decision in what had effectively been an extemporary public trial.

For the more thoughtful however the episode had raised much to think about. If the Governor had managed to solve the problem with the minimum fuss possible in the circumstances, neither had he added much lustre to the imperial genius for government. No-one could deny the difficulties inherent in bringing good government to this people, which unlike any other in the Empire was so irritatingly and single-mindedly determined to keep its own distinctive identity. The Governor had managed to inflame and appease in equal measure, and there were no illusions his final offering would make its leaders any less recalcitrant. Was it simply misfortune which conspired to wrong-foot him every time a dispute brewed up, or did he have an innate personal flaw which somehow always contrived to make things worse? An innocent man had been condemned and duly taken off to execution, whilst another who was a known and violent enemy of the State had been released, and manifestly without any degree of recantation on his or his following's part. No-one needed reminding either that soldiers' lives had been lost to catch that firebrand in the first place, and would probably now have to be jeoparded again. It was high-risk to be seen to be yielding anything whatever to malcontents like this, who had no intention of co-operating and never would. The Zealot threat was in constant danger of increasing, and when it came to fundamentals there was little to choose between the overt hostility of the militants on the one hand and the self-interested, self-dignified pillars of the native establishment on the other, which were too careful and too clever to be involved in armed insurrection, though were just as implacably opposed to the usurpation of this land granted by ancient covenant; and were thus all the more dangerous.

The hotheads and the wisebeards – both detested each other as undermining the cause of liberation. For one it was about the immediacy of the present and the unacceptable outrage of the foreign yoke, for the other a question of patience and pragmatism. Things would change again as they always did in the longer term; as long as the people kept to their religion and followed their priests and stayed obedient then they would be saved. If that meant professing loyalty to Caesar in this generation then that would be done. It was good politics; it prevented bloodshed and destruction; it kept the people together; and, through their religious observance, it gave latitude and power to their true guardians. Rome could take its taxes and play at empire-building for the time being: the people of the Lord would meanwhile keep their way of life and raise their eyes to the hills whence had always come their help. Had he not made them and the whole of heaven and earth?

The settlement worked. Peace had been kept for a generation. The only problem was that it was an uneasy one. The extremists were always there, ready to pounce, and every so often something would come up which threatened to set the tinder-box alight. It needed cool heads to prevent disaster, but as long as the Lord was worshipped and obeyed and priests and people dutiful then the priority would have been met, and the people would be safe and prosper. Their land might remain occupied for the foreseeable future, but time was on their side. The Prefect's problems with Rome were well known; his weakness was to their advantage, and it would be self-defeating to bring about his replacement if that might mean getting a very different man in charge, perhaps with a mandate for serious repression. Insurrection would make that worse as night followed day, and Romans were not known for conspicuous self-constraint when putting down rebellions. Better therefore the man they knew than the one they didn't. The Zealots were difficult enough to handle; they presented a tightrope between collaboration with the occupier on one side and truck with revolutionaries on the other. The last thing needed was anything that might lead to mass rebellion, the outcome of which was unlikely to end happily. The long stand-off would have to continue, and there was no hurry. The Lord God was on their side. The people would have to wait for their salvation yet, which suited their guardians very well.

For the Romans it was the perennial question of how far to accommodate local sensitivities. Once more it seemed the religious establishment had aggressively defended what it claimed were its rights whilst simultaneously managing to profess loyalty to Caesar; and when the crisis came the priests had been rewarded with what some might have regarded, controversially perhaps, as unseemly haste. The Governor had taken the obvious way out, however. It had not been pretty but if he had not acted as he had the result, so the consensus went, would have been another protest to Rome, more civil disobedience, probably an increase in insurgent activity, probably a broader wave of resentment among the general population against the occupation, and certainly his person. The reaction would have been little better in Rome itself. He would have shown he wasn't up to the job, yet again; he had been there too long; his continued presence was inextricably linked to these endless disputes; the only way to get things back on track between Roman and Jew was to have a fresh start, with a new man.

But it had not been quite like that. The situation had been contained. The potential for serious civil unrest had been forestalled. The Zealots had made an unexpected gain, though they had also been shown these last few months to be no longer a pressing threat, in which case the release of their leader was containable. The priests had got their way, but their pre-occupation with the preservation of their own authority was of less consequence from the wider perspective. A point had been made on the assumption of innocence of the accused, notwithstanding that effectively it had then been rapidly conceded in a diplomatic gesture of cooperation; and possibly too there had been some success in avoiding being drawn too much into native affairs, not least in the dangerous matter of religion. Peace had been maintained at remarkably little cost, insofar as there had been no essential change to the status quo, and all in all the Governor had probably done the best that could have been achieved in difficult circumstances. Faced with far worse consequences than the sacrifice of an innocent man, who despite his apparent peacefulness seemed to have been posing an inordinate challenge to the good order of the Province, he had done the only sensible thing – given in as quickly and gracefully as possible. Was that not what statesmen and diplomats usually did when there was a bigger fish to fry? When the opportunity had arisen out of the blue to make the one-sided exchange for the Zealot, he had taken it. The prime aim remained intact, that these people should pay their taxes and give sufficient recognition to Caesar to satisfy his honour. And who had this man of no importance been anyway, with his strange message and obvious political weakness, who by entering the sacred city in provocative pomp and overturning money-tables was already as good as dead, and would soon be completely forgotten?

Some of the less cautious or career-minded junior officers would have liked to have seen more vigorous action taken, with the priests faced down and the man possibly exiled somewhere or otherwise managed. The details were of less concern than the palpable need to teach these people a lesson on the meaning of power. In the Army however power was very far from theirs; the prevailing view of their seniors was that the Governor had got it right. The preacher from Galilee had been no direct threat of course, but he had succeeded in putting the religious establishment into such an agitated state that it could easily have led to a major confrontation. 'King of the Jews' was what the execution party had mockingly called him. He might only have been a harmless holy man, his followers proven few on the day and genuinely peaceable; it was plain however the Jewish establishment had seen him as an existential threat to their authority, and that a serious challenge to them was in no-one's interests other than the Zealots'. Whether bar Abbas' release would favour the co-existence lobby or the would-be insurrectionists was yet to be seen, but once it had become the obvious option the Governor had surely acted sensibly. Given the clamour for the release of the rebel chief and the need to maintain public order there had been no real choice. It might have been a mistake to have kept bar Abbas alive in the first place, since the bargaining-counter had turned out to be of mixed value, but no-one could have foreseen that; so while some might have relished the chance both to crush the Zealots and put the priests in their place once and for all, wiser heads could see the merits of inaction. The main thing was to do what was necessary to keep the peace, and that had been done. As for the man from Nazareth, if it came to worrying about the fate of one innocent against the good of the Province, especially when the individual concerned was not a Roman citizen but simply at loggerheads with his own people on matters of their religion, there could be no contest. That was clear enough.

The Governor had not been outwitted, therefore, despite anything the High Priest and his friends might say. No law of Rome had been broken, and he had made the point by washing his hands of the matter for all to see. If he had defied them and released the man he might have weathered the storm but not without a great deal of aggravation, the undermining of his own position even further and the risk of a major revolt, this time backed by much of the populace. And it was the case that he would have had to explain it all in yet another difficult report, effectively offering himself to the whims of the embittered old tyrant of Capri who had never shown much confidence in him. After so many years of genuine attempts to get Judea on a better footing, and with little to show for the effort, why should he bother any more? Why persevere trying to convince Tiberius and his lackeys that governing this place was like no other, that no matter what anyone did it would always be an impossible task? They'd soon change their minds if they had to put up with the carping and the intransigence themselves. The higher ambitions of government simply could not apply here; this was a people that could never be won. His attempts to hold the line should be welcomed, not criticized from a thousand miles away where they had no idea of the realities. In fact he had done rather satisfactorily, a better job than his detractors in Rome would ever understand. Very well, they would have their report, suitably down-played; they would get to hear of these events anyway, and it was better to be open than secretive. Besides, it might provide a convenient distraction from another matter which demanded a full explanation.

*   *   *   *

Because for some there was something more immediate to consider. No sooner had the headquarters staff gone back inside the Praetorium on stand-down from the alarum than CO Second Italians was summoned to the Commandant's office. There he was informed of a certain discovery.

'So your senior centurion didn't tell you?'

'No, Camp Commandant. He wouldn't have had time.'

'Odd business. Not the most popular of officers, that one.'

'Shouldn't speak ill of the dead. We both know the type. Seemed to derive a peculiar satisfaction in rubbing everyone up the wrong way.'

'And exempting himself from standing orders, naturally. Well that's what garrison orders are for. Being out-of-bounds is a prevalent military offence at the best of times, let alone the Passover. New in theatre but he really should have known better.'

'Yes, and even newer to the city. The Boss should have kept him back at base.'

'I'm not sure he had much choice, Veranius. Any idea why he might have taken himself off to the city?'

'None whatsoever.'

'No suspicion of private needs having to be met?'

'Not that I know of. I'm not an expert on his personal habits. You'd have to ask Caesarea for a view on that.'

'Justus isn't going to be best pleased. You don't expect to send VIP officers off on a jolly to end up losing them.'

'The only thing we know for sure is the stain on his tunic wasn't blood. It was wine. Perhaps he'd just had a hard day, like the rest of us.'

'In fact he's going to be furious.'

'Well don't blame me. He was on my held strength for the duration, but that's about all. You can't seriously expect me to have confined a member of the aristocracy to barracks, can you?'

'You'd better try and convince his commanding officer of that. Macula was on your charge. No, Justus won't be pleased at all.'

'Poetic justice for canvassing to get him to First Augustans in the first place, if you ask me.'

'You're his acting commanding officer, Veranius – or rather were. Someone has to be held accountable, and it isn't going to be this headquarters. Oh yes, and I want a report from last night's guard on all comings and goings through the main gate.'

'Yes of course. But I can't do much until Century I gets back from the execution duty – last night's gate guard will be down there among them.'

'Right. You'd better get off and sort it out.'

Veranius was appreciative the compressed timeline had been fortunate; with so much going on there could have been no reasonable expectation of having to worry about guard reports. Without that small convenience he might have been caught floundering. The significance of such a potential source of evidence in determining how a high-profile individual had died was obvious, and a commanding officer should have been in a position to volunteer the information immediately rather than allow the garrison commander to take the initiative.

He could have been more robust in his responses just then, too, he thought. This might be the time when he'd have to start pulling some status on the old so-and-so; the small matter of class was always there to be subtly deployed if it proved judicious, and he now had, he thought, an understanding with the Governor on that score. Whatever was necessary to defend his own position would be done. On the other hand he'd always prided himself on punctilious respect for rank and office, and he wasn't going to upset Veterus without cause. The old campaigner was at the end of his career, and anyone with sufficient foresight to see their own future in a careworn figure like his could almost feel a modicum of empathy; he couldn't have much longer to go, and he'd no doubt done his bit for the Service, as well as his time. Just so long as he recognized there were limits to others' manners and patience and that he wasn't the only one with some weight to throw around.

On balance, gratification on that count was probably best delayed. The order concerning the guard report had been quite reasonable; it was what he would have done himself. And you had to smile a little, since it was all a bit of a silly game anyway. Life in a competitive organization was so much about appearances and petty acts of one-upmanship and domination, attempted or achieved, not so much between superiors and subordinates, who by and large didn't have need to hold each other in such relationship, but between peers and near-peers. That was where the tension could lie. It was about keeping a nose out in front, preferably in full view of everyone else. It was a comment on the pettiness of human nature, and you saw it all the time. By such means careers were helped and hindered, but if you didn't play then you'd lose by default. Annoying as he was, Veterus was just trying to hold his ground like everyone else. He wasn't likely to be very sympathetic to the likes of Macula, or to him either come to that, but at least he'd seemed straight. The imposition of high-born young men on the professionals of the Army had always been part of the greater system since ancient days; it gave the future leaders of society some military experience and helped fit them for a career of public service, and was just one of those facts of life that had to be put up with. Real respect might or might not ensue, but that was true for anybody. Rank had its privileges, as the saying went, and there was no point resenting those who enjoyed them. He only needed a little patience for his own rightful place in the real pecking order to receive its full and proper recognition …

And digressions like this didn't solve anything. There was no excuse for any commanding officer not knowing exactly what was going on in his own unit, in detail and at all times. The responsibility for that was his alone. Significant irregularities from last night's guard report were far more serious than any amount of trouble from an aggrieved populace, since they reflected on his unit and on him; and he had to get to the bottom of its potential for revelation quickly. He thought of recalling the Senior Centurion, or going down to the west wall himself to go and find him, but then of good reasons against. The execution was an important task which might still need an element of crowd control. It would be wrong to interfere whilst there was any risk of that going on; it wouldn't be all that long now; and anyway there was his dignity to consider. Officers of his rank didn't demean themselves by showing up at such tawdry events, nor would it do to be raising suspicion among the men of undue haste in the higher echelons, or lack of confidence in their own officers. He would wait, and comply with the order on the guard report in appropriate time.

He had another reason why he ought to go along with the garrison commander obligingly. The day's crisis, when they had thought there might be fighting in the streets and only his senior centurion between the mob and the Governor's own person, was over and behind them. The question of his other centurion was not. A lesser officer might have been feeling the pressure by now, he assured himself – two major problems to cope with simultaneously, both potential career-stoppers and both immediate reminders of the stakes involved. The less cautious would be the wiser for some essential prudence. He really shouldn't be gambling with his career on his tenuous relationship with the Governor, for all his initial sense of reassurance from their talk: social affinity only went so far, a morale-boosting chat one thing, resolute independent judgment another. Certainly command was a lonely affair, but then he was more than up to it; destiny was there to be fulfilled and he wasn't going to be deterred from pursuing it or fail a challenge, especially when there was a moral dimension – his duty to his centurion – to add justification. It was also necessary that appearances were maintained, and those with the right background and capabilities had no excuse for shirking them. If you did then you didn't deserve to get on. All he had to do was keep a cool head, exert his authority and act decisively when the time came. Wasn't that what he'd been doing?

The good thing was that Veterus had given no indication that he had any inkling of the oath business – surely he would have said if he had? The Secretary almost certainly knew, since it was inconceivable Macula in his political role hadn't told him, but as Seneccio wasn't in the Army chain of command there was still some chance of a breathing space. It couldn't be for long. Facilis' future would have to be decided very soon. If he once lost control it would be out of his hands and subject to rapid escalation in the military legal system, with all its potential for further revelations and predictable consequences for his centurion. If he acted now there was a good chance of getting him away and keeping knowledge of the whole affair limited to a very few, which would safeguard his own interests too. He would have to find a good pretext for a posting, but it could be done. The one thing he could not do was risk stating a falsehood himself, and there was always the fall-back if all else failed: if it became necessary he could ditch his scruples, behave like any other career officer, leave Facilis to his fate and deal in the most strident of terms with anyone who threatened his own reputation. A little like the Boss' performance this morning, he thought, but having already invested a certain pride in showing solidarity with his team he really would prefer to do the right thing. He couldn't deny to himself it was daunting. O recurring doubt! O the fates, to land him with a problem like this. Why, when they could have sent Macula anywhere, from Gaul to Africa, Galicia to Cappadocia, did they have to send the man to him?

He wondered what his fellow tribune's ghost would have in store for him, to whisper in his ear now he was condemned to haunt the Antonine's gloomy portals for eternity, of his last days, of his villainous murder, of the duty of retribution. It was probably best he would never have the benefit of such advice. In the short time Macula had been in the garrison he'd been roundly hated, but that would hardly have been sufficient cause to silence him. Foul play and mayhem in a closed community on constant alert for its safety were unthinkable – a fleeting, errant image in his mind's eye that had to be expunged. The man had gone out into the city alone, which was a stupid and foolhardy thing to do, especially at a time like this; but he'd obviously been drunk, and very likely wenching. He would not have been the first in either respect. And then there was this other fool of a centurion, an officer for whom he had so recently entertained the highest regard but who, it now appeared, had lost all reason. And again at the worst possible time, when everyone was stretched to the limit and worried stiff the whole Province would go up in flames at any moment. Who was the real fool here – a religious head-case, or a commanding officer who could tolerate such nonsense? All this trouble for a few small words which meant very little, if anything at all. And what was the good of all his own mental meandering? But …

What if Macula's demise was linked to this oath business in some way? Surely not. But then …why not? Perhaps yes. In fact, quite plausibly yes! The coincidence was rather strong, after all. Yes, that was it! Why hadn't he thought of it before? Well they had been rather busy. But yes, it had to be. It was all too convenient for the accuser to be out of the picture so soon. It was the only explanation. Foul play then, without doubt …

Of course there had to be a perpetrator in the camp. And if so why not Facilis, for obvious reasons? But then he was in the Mess last night, a public place. Not that public. He could have done it. Though he'd probably have needed an accomplice or two. It just went to show how dangerous this new cult was, how it could take over a man's mind so completely. Did it mean there were other followers about, who'd also need winkling out and dealing with? Why hadn't he interrogated Facilis on that one, as the Governor had so insouciantly suggested? His apostate centurion, who always told nothing but the truth – was there so much more to this than he'd suspected? What would the Boss say if it turned out his cohort was already a veritable hotbed for this seditious creed? It looked like there was a long way to go yet before a line could be drawn under this investigation. Very well; it would be done. The Governor had of course been right: a little pragmatism, a touch of flexibility, a pinch of cynicism – that's what you needed; enlightened self-interest in harness with purpose. Good motto. He would definitely be speaking to the Senior Centurion immediately on his return.

*   *   *   *

The Governor was taking a break. He had left the wash-up meeting on the morning's events to continue the discussion whilst he went in search of quiet and refreshment. The Old Palace was useful for that: extensive personal apartments behind the Praetorium, right next to the job, and his wife close-by. It was fortunate that she usually well knew when to offer her thoughts and when not, though he suspected she wasn't going to be very loyal and loving now.

'You did it then', she said as soon as they were alone.

'Yes', he replied. 'I did it.'

'You knew that I followed Him, yet you still did it.' Tears were welling in her eyes.

'There's no point in upsetting yourself, My Dear.'

'Upset myself?! You condemn the innocent to death and tell me I'm upset! What about His friends and family, and all the people who had so much hope? And what about Him – the cruelty they're inflicting on Him, right now. How could you, oh how could you?'

He tried to embrace her but she shrugged him off. 'Do you realize what you've done? He was the only one who could bring salvation to this world. The only one who didn't see everything in terms of privilege and power and punishment, who cared for the poor and the weak and dispossessed. Oh, leave it to me, he'll be quite safe. That's what you said. And now you've gone and killed Him.'

'Claudia, *they* killed him, his own people. I had no choice. He had to come before me because the charge became one of treason. And it's just rotten luck that bar Abbas was waiting in the wings. If I'd thought of that then it might have been different.'

'Treason? What possible threat could he have posed to the might of Rome? Did He ever say He was against us, or you, or His own people – anyone? Where were His armies or the cunning plans to murder us in our beds?'

'I know. "Render to Caesar that which is Caesar's, and to god that which is god's". Adroit, I must say. Certainly threw the wise men.'

'You knew all that?! That expression? How did you know that?'

'Do you think I've sat through this last week like a dummy, My Dear?'

'Then you should have known they were out to get Him. Couldn't you see that?'

'Of course we did, but what could we do? From all the hysterical palm-waving and triumphal processions on donkeys, to trashing the money-changers' stalls in the Temple, prophesying the city's destruction, outwitting their leaders in public, talking about the son of man – what else was all that than deliberate provocation verging on suicide? He must have realized what the consequences would be.'

'You could have done something! Arrested Him on some pretext, got Him away for His own safety somehow. And don't talk of the royal "we". I don't want to know about your so-called advisors. It's you who are responsible and you who will take the blame, not them.'

'And do you think he would have listened, and not come back sooner or later with his preaching, here, or somewhere else in the Province? And what about Caiaphas – how do you think he would have reacted? Issued a statement thanking the government for undermining the Council's authority? How could it possibly have benefitted the outcome if I'd released him against that sort of pressure? We'd have needed to guard your prophet day and night to keep him alive, with very likely the whole of Judea in open rebellion. And how long do you expect my tenure of office would be after that? – you know how it would go down in Rome. My feet wouldn't touch this time, they'd be so quick to get rid of me.'

She turned away. 'So that's it', she said. It's about you and your career, as usual. How can that compare to such a good and special life as His? Do any of those calculations on state interests really add up to anything, when they could all change tomorrow on some other whim?'

'That's the nature of government. But we have no choice but try to use our best judgment given the known situation at the time. And, whilst in this case I agree my career interests seem to coincide with those of a wider nature, honestly I cannot say they were my chief motivation. I did it to keep the peace.'

He tried to approach her again. 'I am sorry, truly sorry My Dear. He was a good man, I'm sure. From all accounts a most unusual one, gifted with an intelligence and a presence far beyond anything one normally encounters. If I could have saved him I would. Even if you hadn't been to see him and I didn't have a clue how much he meant to you. Come on now, you're just over-wrought'.

She moved off, looking at him fiercely. 'You ... you knew that?'

'Yes.'

'Why didn't you say anything?'

'Why didn't you tell me? You could have told me any time. This morning, for instance.'

'There didn't seem any point. And you've just admitted it wouldn't have made any difference. According to you He sealed His own fate.'

'You shouldn't have dissimulated.'

There was a long silence before he resumed.

'We never lied to each other, Claudia – did we? We've always shared our secrets. I need you by my side now, as I always have. I need your good sense and humanity, I need your constancy. And your absolute and utter trustworthiness.'

'Yes. I did see Him. At the start of the week. You were out being important somewhere or other.'

'You really should have told me. We could have discussed it together, and found the best way.'

'How could I? You'd only have called me a silly woman. And how could you possibly have agreed anyway, in your position? You'd be the first to say it, there are some things you just can't talk about, you just have to go and do them.'

'I don't suppose I even have to ask about the towel.'

'It was the very least I could do.'

'And did he? Did he see you?'

'He said to have faith, only believe, hold fast to that which is good, and the kingdom of heaven would be yours to enter.'

'Did you say who you were? Did he ask?'

'He didn't need to. He knew perfectly well. Why were you spying on me?'

'Believe me, I wasn't My Dear. But naturally we had him under surveillance for some weeks. All his contacts were monitored as a matter of routine.'

'But you didn't tell me.'

'Claudia, the basis of intelligence work is need-to-know. It's not about trust, it's about management and limitation. Just be grateful there are people whose job it is to worry their heads about these things so you don't have to.'

'I'm your wife. You know how much Yeshua means to me.'

'And I'm the Prefect of Judea. As well as your husband. What's more important, would you say – duty or matrimonial devotion?'

'Please don't be cynical, Appius.'

'I know … I'm trying to understand, really. I wish I could believe in this, this new god of yours … that you clearly believe in so strongly. If I thought there was really something in it, don't you think I'd have been seeking your teacher out myself, if only from an academic interest? If only it were so easy.'

'But you don't understand. We have to have that initial hope. We have to be receptive to the possibility of faith, to let the match light the candle so the way is lit before us. And then we can truly believe. I had to go, go and see Him for myself. I had to reach out and discover for myself.'

'And keep it from me, your husband?'

'What's worse? That – or you knowing that I did so and letting me … dissimulate, as you put it – seeing how far I'd go to avoid coming clean? I couldn't tell you before because you wouldn't have let me do it. Oh, far too risky, whatever would the natives think? And I couldn't tell you afterwards because I thought you'd get angry and wouldn't understand, and wouldn't believe or even try, with all your cares and your politics and burdens of office, *et cetera, et cetera*.'

There was no answer for a while.

'Haven't you got a charity meeting today?'

'How can I possibly go in this state?'

'I know you're upset, My Dear. You've got a great deal of emotional capital bound up in all this. But getting out to something like that would help take your mind off it, wouldn't it?'

'Yes, I suppose so', she sniffed.

'And we must always think of our duty.'

'Yes, I know. Duty first.'

'And you've got the wife to speak to, remember?'

* * * *

The Adjutant came to take him to HQ. Everywhere seemed in normal routine, as though absolutely nothing untoward had happened and he hadn't just spent a day and a night under open arrest. His escort said nothing, and he didn't ask; what the CO was going to do now was anyone's guess. Of his own future he was almost past caring; weariness and despondency made for a feeling of helplessness only deepened by the overwhelming sadness of the news, the confirmation of his worst fears. The Saviour of the world was meeting His mortal end.

The short walk and sense of time running out brought brief and involuntary concentration. Grief and dejection mixed inchoately with resentment, then anger, of the kind driven by acceptance of inevitability, and finally clarity. He could see at once the scale, the scope, the compression of events in the trail of disaster, his own feeble flailing against the backdrop of this mighty act for all humanity which seemed – dare he for one terrifying moment countenance it? – as if it too might be meaningless. They might just as well be nailing him up on Golgotha too, behind his Lord and Saviour, who was suffering His death agony whilst his own unworthy feet still trod the earth in this parody of existence. Sweet Yeshua, whose sayings now made so much sense. He had come to the city to take them on. There could only have been one consequence, and now it was come to pass. This day they had meant to kill Him, and now sure enough as the sky was darkening so it was happening. The light of the world was being snuffed out by ignorance and brutality. And he couldn't do a thing to stop them, the agents of mindless cruelty, the silencers of the Word and slaughterers of the Holy Lamb of God – his own unknowing, careless, mindless compatriots and brothers-in-arms. He thought back, back to the cries and tumult, the darts and shot flying on that distant summit, the terror of the shield-wall, the creature stirring darkly within its net, whose defiance and rage he now understood too, the other Yeshua, son of Abbas so-called, robber, killer, slayer of the One who had come to bring peace and life. He remembered the sword sheathed and clean in its scabbard, the weakness, the pain. One simple thrust, that's all it would have taken. There would have been the severe reprimand, possibly worse, but what was that compared to saving the Prince of Peace? His own life did not matter now. But for his wife and children, he would gladly follow Him to torture and the cross.

His own impending fate might be little worse.

* * * *

Veranius received him coolly.

'I assume there's no change to your position.'

'No, Sir.'

'Then you are to be posted. As soon as I can arrange it. Somewhere you're unlikely to get yourself into trouble again, or at least where you won't bring this cohort into disrepute. Meanwhile, should you be required to swear the oath in public or on parade in front of troops, and refuse, you will give me no choice but have you court-martialed, with every chance of a penalty of death. Do you understand?'

'Yes, Sir', he said, dazed.

'Facilis.' The Prefect softened his voice. 'Think very carefully. Your record will count for nothing if you won't recant and demonstrate your innocence. You must realize that. If it happens again I won't be able to save you.'

'I do. I'm ...very grateful, Sir, thank you. In fact I don't know what to say.'

'Of course your career will now be on hold. Promotion is out of the question, unless there's a major war somewhere, and even then you'd be extremely lucky. I can't give you the ticket I'd have liked if you can't promise absolute loyalty – it would be dishonest of me. You can scarcely expect otherwise. Be grateful you're being kept in post until we can find you another somewhere, somewhere you can forget about all this and get it out of your system.'

'Sir, I don't know how to thank you.'

'Hadn't you better go and see that wife and family of yours? I want you back on duty in four hours. And for good measure you're confined to the fort until Century I is back in. Is that clear? The Senior Centurion won't need any help from you.'

'Yes Sir.'

'Just don't give me any more trouble. I've got quite enough of that right now. I expect you know about Macula?'

'I've heard, Sir. Bit of a shock.'

'Indeed. Not a problem for you, though – you've got a cast-iron alibi, eh?'

'Not really, Sir. Being confined to living-in rooms was hardly very secure.'

'Well it's more of an alibi than most of my officers will have. Not that you didn't have ample motive.'

'You think it could be an inside-job, Sir?'

'We can't rule it out. Who knows? I've opened an investigation but it might just be as obvious as it looks – the local Zealot cell got him. Don't worry, I think I know you better than to suspect you.'

'Thank you, Sir.'

'Well cheer up. They'll be waiting for you.'

'Yes Sir', he said, saluted, and took his leave.

*   *   *   *

His life was saved. He knew he ought to be grateful for such leniency, and indeed he was. Compared to the enormity of the day it seemed an unworthy sentiment. In this strange new life of faith and doubt, tension and relief, there were many times when he might have wished for the old simplicities. God had saved him who deserved so little, but overlying his confusion was the great over-shadowing guilt of survival, when like the ever-darkening billowing clouds which now seemed to have covered the sky in all directions the fate of the world was being decided in wrath. How could anyone be surprised at this sign from Almighty God who ruled heaven and earth, or be in any doubt about its meaning to all men when their Saviour was hanging in mortal agony in their very midst?

He sought some solitude and began to pray again, soon to find a strange comfort; and through all the anguish there came a kind of peace, a realization that this was how it was meant to be, how it had to be. For what had he heard not long before? Had He not said to the Twelve that He must go to Jerusalem so that all would be fulfilled, that He would be handed over to the Gentiles, who would mock Him, insult Him, spit on Him, scourge Him and put Him to death, and that on the third day He would rise again? It was all true then; it was come to pass. He with his own trials must steady himself therefore with a new resolve. His own little battle was over, and now he must carry on. His family needed him.

It wouldn't take long to get to Brutus and Vergilia's.

*   *   *   *

It had been an effort but the Governor's Lady had managed to retrieve her composure and re-make her face. It was important that appearances were maintained; she knew the ladies of the Soldiers' & Families' Welfare Fund would be awaiting their patroness for her annual visit with some expectation, and it was invariably a happy occasion, a good opportunity for the officers' and the few senior NCOs' wives to get together. The garrison paymaster would be there to report on the accounts, but quite properly it was the members who made the decisions, guided by Lavinia the Commandant's wife, and with she and the more senior of them naturally leading on proceedings. With no official welfare provision their charity work was important, an obligation to be taken seriously, the social side to be enjoyed as usual – particularly on this harrowing day.

They all stood politely for their guest, who accepted the welcome graciously, said a few words and cut a large cake, accepting a slice for herself though knowing she could barely manage a pretence at eating. Claudia listened to the talk on the finances and a welfare case or two and tried to look attentive, and when the formalities were over did her best to be sociable with them all, steered tactfully by Lavinia and Honoria, chatting with this one and that, renewing acquaintance, expressing interest, enquiring into health, almost verging on gossip, managing a smile here and there. But they all realized how shaken she must have felt, having been so close to the frightening scenes which had taken place under the palace windows only a few hours before. Conversation, always a little strained, started to become fitful, until slaves were summoned to fetch lamps to ward off the gloom, and that seemed to revive their conviviality. A little incommodiousness was an opportunity to show some spirit. The morning's episode was to be kept firmly out of mind; on no account was anything to be said to the Governor's Lady touching it. She was doing well; she, and they, had to keep going.

Sabena stood with her friends from the Cohort. Honoria felt obliged to make some remarks of re-acquaintance. Of course the Governor's Lady remembered the wives of the Regiment – how could she forget their recent hospitality, and wouldn't it be wonderful when the theatre troupe arrived from Damascus and they could have some real entertainment again? And she'd so much like to hear more from Sabena on how the family had coped with recuperating a wounded hero, which was what the Fund was all about. Not that officers' families were normally recipients, but it would be good to know what the problems were and how they could be overcome when there were so many deserving priorities to be met ... Could Sabena possibly call round this afternoon? It would be lovely to be able to take their minds off things for a little chat.

*   *   *   *

Sabena wasn't in when her husband returned. The servant ushered him in and the children came running. Their beautiful children, bright-eyed, adoring. He gathered them in his arms, kissed and hugged them. How he longed to take them back to their real home, away from this place and all its troubles.

'Where were you Daddy? Mummy says you haven't been well.'

'Oh, not far. I've been very busy.'

'Are you quite well now, Daddy?'

'Yes, I'm quite well now. And how are you, Little Squirrel?'

To be with them again after what seemed much longer than the reality seemed itself unreal. He was alive and back with his loved ones, and what could be more precious in that moment, when it could all have been so very different? They had been a mere walk away but it might just as well have been over the ocean. But how to relate joy to mourning, thanksgiving to the hard truth, for young minds so innocent and credulous? The children knew about Yeshua, about praying and being good. They had been told from the beginning, though also not to say anything to their young friends because some of them would not be able to understand. They should say a prayer now; but what should he say? That Yeshua the Son of God was dying for them this very afternoon to take on their sins, so they could follow Him and go to heaven? That He needed their prayers now and always, so that all might believe in Him and have everlasting life? That they should forgive the people who were doing this? And that the men who were doing it were Roman soldiers? From Daddy's cohort? He had to get a grip.

'Favonius.'

The woman's voice was quiet, unquerulous. He looked up to see Vergilia in the doorway.

'Sabena's gone to the Palace. You know, that wives' charity-do.'

'Oh yes, the Welfare Fund. Why haven't you gone too, Vergilia? Alright children, run along, we'll play a game in a moment.'

She sat down. 'How are you? I've been worried.'

'I'm fine. More to the point, how are you? Why aren't you there with Sabena?'

'I'm babysitting, of course.'

'You could have left them with your servant for the afternoon. They're quite old enough.'

She looked down, very pale, inordinately subdued even for her, he thought. 'It's not really my scene.'

'Are you alright?' he asked.

He hadn't known her well before their stay. His old self would have found her rather a mousy little woman, dutiful, obliging, pleasant enough, unremarkable. Their paths had crossed little until Brutus had offered their rooms at the previous Progress, and they'd repeated the offer this year. Sabena had been quite keen to accept, and he'd opted to be accompanied so they could all enjoy a break, though it had meant there wasn't much choice of suitable quartering, and it was desirable they shared with hosts of equal rank. The important thing was that the family was to be together, and that for a few relaxing days his wife could enjoy something of the life she was used to rather than the perpetual quiet of the country, even if he'd be fully engaged in increased security duties. And the children seemed to like Brutus, so he'd been happy to go along with the arrangement. He was glad when the last week had come around though, and now after all this unexpected trauma in the city he couldn't be away soon enough. They could return to their own place where things would sort themselves out, and now with a posting in the offing they could hope for a new start far away from this land with all its unhappy associations. Pray God he'd be getting the details soon, and that they'd be guided in every necessity.

That was for the future. The present however was before him in someone who had an air of integrity but also stoicism in her demeanour, someone he'd come to respect – and know well enough now to recognize the anguish in her face and all the troubles of the world.

'Oh Favonius', she said.

And with that his own long, slow crucifixion began.

* * * *

Publius Seneccio the Governor's Private Secretary folded his papers away neatly.

'Well, Camp Commandant. It looks as though we have some skullduggery on our hands.'

'Oh yes?'

'Tribune Macula dead for no obvious reason, treason apparently breaking out among regimental officers, near-rioting on the streets, and the Governor particularly reticent at the moment. All a bit coincidental, would you not say?'

'How well did you know our friend Macula? And why do you think anyone would have wanted to keep him quiet, which is what the implication of your remark is? Why not just accept the facts at face value? He got himself stupidly drunk, went whoring in the old quarter and got bumped off by the Zealots. Unfortunate, salutary and perfectly simple.'

'Yes, I did have a few dealings with him. A supercilious young man, undoubtedly, but with a lot more influence than you or me. Nothing happens without a reason, Camp Commandant. We have both been around too long to believe otherwise, and we should both be worried. Rome is not going to be happy.'

'Then we'll have to show some solidarity, won't we, Secretary?'

'It is all very well for you. You will be out of this in a few months.'

'To answer your question, I'm not aware of any burning animosities around our late tribune. But who knows what goes on behind the scenes? – what a man's character is really like, what he really thinks, how he behaves when no-one's watching. He seems to have had a weakness for the cup and a foray or two. Scarcely unusual for a red-bloodied young fellow, though from my own cursory enquiries I'm not sure he was particularly in that habit, despite what we hear from some quarters. But to go off in full uniform, by himself? – that was asking for trouble. As you say – let's look at the facts.'

'And if by the merest chance he did not happen to run into a bunch of back-street insurrectionists, but a person or persons unknown with the same murderous intent but for very different reasons – what then? All I can say is he must have had a serious enemy, with a commensurately serious motive.'

'Are you sure you're not reading too much into this?'

'Someone, or some people, of importance in their own right. At least senior enough to have had some sort of relationship with the deceased.'

'Not necessarily. Why bring rank into it? Why not some aggrieved squaddies, in revenge for something we'll never know of? The man was arrogant enough by all accounts.'

'Let us not fool ourselves here.'

'Well who, then?'

'Oh I think you might know, Camp Commandant. Why don't we consider for a moment one Centurion Favonius Facilis? A solid officer of *Secunda Italica* I believe. Good record, a war hero indeed, feted by the whole garrison not two days ago. Now why would his commanding officer place an officer like him under mess arrest, the very day after being awarded the second-highest gallantry medal the State has to bestow, and then request an interview with the Governor which goes on far longer than you or I would get? – and one-to-one, if you please.'

'A commanding officer has that right, especially for something in confidence, and particularly for something that's personnel-in-confidence.'

'Yes Camp Commandant, but you are responsible for all personnel matters in this garrison among your other duties, are you not? If you are unable to share a confidence with the Private Secretary in this case then that is quite understood, but you give the impression, if I may say so, that you are not party to it either. Might I venture to suggest it would be highly unusual for one so senior in the chain of command to be kept in the dark so, to say the least?'

'Career matters, Secretary, not all and sundry or I'd never get home at night. And stop angling.'

'I am but a lowly assistant, Camp Commandant. It is not my place to pry, even when the Governor is being more uncommunicative than his wont. But something, as they say, is clearly going on.'

'Nonsense, man. You're a nosey old cynic fully paid up to the well-known principle that knowledge is power – and put out when you haven't got it.'

'It is my job, Camp Commandant.'

'Well you always seem to know more than me. And quite a lot about Second Italians' affairs, that's for sure.'

'One would not have thought being confined to mess on one's word of honour terribly burdensome. All too easy to be tempted into a misdemeanor of some sort. Possibly even an abscondence.'

'Unlikely from what I hear of Facilis, to whom I imagine you're referring. How far do you think he'd have got, anyway, when he'd know the gate guard would have strict orders to stop him by all means necessary?'

'Let us suppose just for one moment our conscientious young tribune had something on him. Something so serious even a war hero felt obliged to take drastic action on; so important his commanding officer, who gets to know the substance, feels obliged to take it straight to the highest level. Now what might that possibly be, one wonders? And then there is so much alarmist talk at the moment about the inexplicable effect of the late-departing Nazarene – could it be that something untoward is abroad and deserving of serious attention?'

'What on earth are you talking about?'

'I am talking about the compromising of the officer corps, Camp Commandant. Or the whole garrison, if you prefer.'

'We're all about to sink in a sea of corruption and disaffection then?'

'Much more serious than that, Camp Commandant.   A sea of insidious religious mania.'

'What, more? If it's those Galileans you're referring to I don't think you need worry too much about them, Secretary. The Gods are safe with the Army. And the Security Committee doesn't need your advice. Anyway their leader's a gonner now, poor sod. For better or worse. Certainly made my job easier. One less problem to deal with in this hell-hole of a country. Rule'm with an iron fist, I say. That's the only way.'

'Guile is a lot more effective, Camp Commandant.'

'Guile? Against this lot?'

'Of course. You know that is what our employer the Governor would say, every time. Let the pot simmer for as long as it will, just make sure it never gets to the boil.'

'The Governor is not my employer, Secretary – he's my Commander-in-Chief. And I'd say sit on the lid and keep it in place with as much force as you need.'

'But easier if our troops maintain their full efficiency.'

'Meaning?'

'That they think as one. Act as one. Retain the ways of their ancestors. And that they worship the same Gods.'

'That's taken as read. Always was, always will be.'

'If I may presume to offer an opinion, Camp Commandant – I think you need to be vigilant. Keep your eyes on the Italian Regiment, that is all. And we have not even mentioned the questionable activity of the First Lady. Now if you will excuse me, I had better take this letter through.'

*　　*　　*　　*

'Thank you for coming, my dear. I couldn't say anything in front of the others.'

'No, My Lady.'

'Sabena, I had to speak to you. I heard the rumours, and thought –

can it be true? And then, well ... let's say I heard it from an authoritative source, and it all started to fall into place. How exciting! Do tell me all about it.'

She was completely thrown. What was she hearing? How could the woman have known anything? Blank confusion blotted out any instant attempt at comprehension. But wait. There could have been only two meanings to what Procula had just said – but which was the correct one, and what could she say without getting deeper into this unwelcome and sudden pitfall? She recovered herself, and anyone who did not know her well would not have detected any discomfiture – a slight hesitancy, the momentary loss of that trace of a half-smile of hers, that was all. But she would have to proceed with the utmost wariness, every sense alerted, every reflex coiled now as the initial panic abated enough to allow a cogent defence; of which to say nothing was the reactive and principal feature.

'Well, you know, it isn't very often such a man comes into our lives.'

'I ... I beg your pardon, Your Ladyship. I don't know what to say.'

It wasn't often she was held in suspense. Was this the moment of exposure, of denunciation from which there was no escape? How would the future beckon now the secret was out and official disapproval had to be faced, with opprobrium and disgrace awaiting their pleasure? Was this the price of true affection when cornered so cruelly by the guardians of rectitude?

'Oh I'm sorry my dear. Don't be alarmed. I should have been a little more forthcoming. For I too went to see the Master.'

Sabena breathed a silent breath of the deepest relief. The words drifted over her head like the scented air of a rose garden in which heavenly choirs sang songs of sweetness and her feet were tripping over cool petal-strewn grass.

'I got a message through to his friends and they met me in the city and took me to Bethany, on a donkey can you believe. I was in disguise of course – not a word to anyone, dear Sabena. I actually got to meet Him – such a short time but so lovely. They were all very, very good to me. I can honestly say they were the best moments of my life, more inspirational than I can tell you, riches beyond compare, which

I'll treasure always … and now He's … And He was so, well … you know of course, don't you?   I confess I was only drawn at first by His reputation, and fascination for His message, thought-provoking enough for any society – but I see it's so much more now, more wonderful than any human can describe.   And the … I don't know – the serenity, the quiet authority, the … love, pure unadulterated love, not the sweet and sickly sort but rugged and strong, so beautiful.   How could anyone have been in His presence for a few moments and not feel it?   Now I know how you and your dear Favonius must have felt.   And now all this.   On this day, at this very hour, and with the very heavens full of foreboding.'

It was almost too good to hear.   Instead of revelation and denunciation had come harmless candour and compassion.   Could it be true?   Had the Governor's wife really been spending time with these Galilean holy men?   Yes, apparently.   Could she have done so without the Governor's knowledge?   It didn't matter now.   All that mattered was that she herself was in the clear – for she was, wasn't she?   She had been caught off-guard, that's all, but her presence of mind had saved her. There were times when it was definitely better to say as little as possible. The real love, the love which must not speak its name, was bound to come out into the open sooner or later – though she'd rather it didn't just now, not face-to-face with the senior wife in province, not if she could help it.   But she wasn't out of the woods quite yet.

'Yes My Lady.   It's … terrible, more than anyone should have to bear', she said as Claudia came forward, tears welling, to embrace her. They stood together for some time, weeping, the one in inconsolable grief, the other with relief though not entirely without sympathy.   She did have a heart.

At length, with much sobbing and sniffling, they were able to carry on.

'But you met Him too.   Tell me all about it.'

'I never actually saw him.   It was just my husband, My Lady.'

'A hero, my dear, admired by everyone.   It was a delight to meet him at the dinner.'

'He did it for our servant, My Lady, as you may know.   It was a very moving experience.'

'And then? Did you … did your husband see the Master again?'

'No, My Lady, just that once. But he kept in touch with some of His followers until quite recently. He always said once was all anyone needed.'

'How wonderful! That must have been so exciting for you all. And to have your loving husband able to explain and discuss all those wonderful things with you.'

'It was, My Lady.'

'Have you … ever shared this wonderful experience yourself … told anyone else?'

'Oh no My Lady, we've always been very discreet.'

'Not even your children?'

'A little, My Lady, but they're too young to understand very much.'

'Of course they are. Of course you want them to be saved, but you must be prudent. Children are so innocent. You don't want them … saying things in the wrong company.'

'No, My Lady. It's very sad, but perhaps now it's all over it'll be safer, My Lady.'

'Safer, my dear? Over? But it isn't, dear Sabena! It isn't.'

She realized her mistake. 'I meant … they can't hurt him any more, not after this, My Lady. Nor those who followed him. No-one's going to expect anything to continue now, surely My Lady? That should make it safer for them, now he's no threat to anyone – My Lady?'

'Sabena, we must have faith. Out of this sorrow will come salvation. The Son of Man is taken from us this terrible day, but His glory will live on. I don't know how – I know so little, but that's what He said, and we who have been touched and live on must keep the light alive, for goodness and truth and everything that makes for a fuller life, for you and Favonius, for the Governor and me, for all of us. We must take strength from each other and confide like sisters. We must keep the Word alive and pass it on to those who will hear. Will you help me, Sabena – to learn more, to grow in faith and wisdom? We mustn't let all this be in vain. The Rabboni said we have only to believe, and that where two or three are gathered together then our prayers will be answered. Will you pray with me, now?'

And the two women knelt and prayed together, the elder leading, earnestly invoking the Father's mercy on his crucified Son and pleading for a speedy end to His mortal suffering; for strength and guidance at this terrible time of sorrow; for the forgiveness of their sins; for wisdom for themselves and all those in authority; for peace among men, and for themselves and their families. They had so much to be thankful for. Now they must remember His example, and go out bold and steadfast to live their lives as He would wish, not least among their countrywomen whose devotion and duty to their menfolk was so important in bringing up the next generation.

'Thank you my dear. Now we must bear with fortitude whatever will be. We must do what we can to bring good out of all this, Sabena, I'm sure. I thank God for you and Favonius, and I'm so pleased to have found you. Now I know how you must have been feeling these last months, to see everything in its proper light unobscured by the weakness and carnality all around us. We must stick together, you and I, Sabena. We must have courage, and live bravely and purely this new life to which we've been led. We must seek the true salvation of which He spoke. And we must do all we can to spread the Word, whilst taking every care to be on guard against those who would deny it and deny us. You will come and see me again, won't you? Not in this horrible place. In Caesarea. I'll arrange something somehow. Promise me?'

*　　*　　*　　*

In the outside world the Sabbath had almost begun. In theirs there was little sense of preparation, and none of celebration. Century I was back having done its duty, the garrison's routine for the close of day underway, guards mounted and relieved, aromas issuing from kitchens, lamps and braziers being lit. Once fallen out, most of the occupants of the two barracks could relax. For the more senior officers the work went on. Centurions reported to commanding officers, commanding officers to the garrison commander.

Longinus knew he faced some awkward questions, though not about the execution.

'That went well today, Senior Centurion. Now what about Tribune Macula? I understand you identified him personally.'

'Yes. The Samarians found him in the street of the shoemakers.'

'Strangled, it appears.'

'Looks like it.'

'Did he make a habit of slipping out of barracks after dark?'

'Not to my knowledge.'

'Was he a drinker?'

'Ever known a young single officer not like their wine? As long as they're capable of carrying out their duties next morning it does no harm. Probably quite a lot of good. Where would morale be without a bit of bonding?'

'But what about him?'

'I didn't know him well enough to say.'

'You're a liver-in!'

'He was only here ten days. I did see him worse for wear once, nothing out the ordinary. Mind you he did disappear of an evening a few times. We just assumed he was with the Governor or other of the great and good. Perhaps his predilections were elsewhere. He could have afforded all the best harlots in Jerusalem in one go. I might be the Mess senior but I'm not their nursemaid.'

Veranius came close to responding to that remark, but let it go. You took on Longinus at your peril, this imposing leader of the Cohort on the battlefield, held in the highest respect by every man in it though probably less generous with that quality in regard to his own superiors; adept at sailing close to the wind and operating in ways best not enquired into too closely; but, he had to admit, with an uncanny if annoying knack of invariably being right. It would be too easy to fall for the suspicion of an alternative agenda, too difficult to actually prove one of this individual, he had always been obliged to conclude. One had to be charitable: the Senior Centurion was simply a talented individual with a deserving ambition, who couldn't be faulted when it came to getting things done or sticking up for the unit and supporting its commander in every respect – especially where it would be conspicuous and noted. If there were any niggling doubt about what was really going on in his subordinate's head, that he might be up to something and not being entirely forthcoming, he'd learnt to accept it. It would have rankled with some, but Veranius convinced himself it was better to show the more easy-going side of one's nature in these situations, and to remember how useful it was to have such men on one's side when the going might get rough. Trust and confidence were inestimable commodities in any relationship such as this, where the two together determined the unit's style – and, more importantly, its success.

There were limits, however; and Longinus had reached them. No garrison commander worth his salt was likely to be appeased, and nor should he. Veterus rightly wanted his investigation, and he in turn would have to dig in.

'I want that guard report, Senior Centurion. I want every man who was on duty last night interviewed – all movements through the main gate, and the postern gate too for good measure. I've got to get to the Camp Commandant soonest or he'll want to know the reason why.'

'Right, Prefect. I'll get back to you as soon as possible.'

And with that Longinus returned to his company lines, fuming, short-of-sleep and wondering how he was going to conduct this charade – when he'd just spent the entire day witnessing something which made everything else utterly trivial. There was no getting out of it – he would have to carry the order out. It would take a while because most of his men were stood down. They'd need rousing and assembling and then receive the benefit of his advice. He would need to wield the rod of iron for which he was renowned, and then prepare himself for some creative thinking. He might just have gone through a most peculiar experience on that god-forsaken hillock which had made him think, but he was still the Senior Centurion. And no-one was going to get any reward for squealing on The Gripper.

But he'd addressed his superior properly, as 'Prefect', the first time for quite a while. And they'd both noticed.

*　*　*　*

Favonius had gone back to the Antonia shattered, wishing he'd been with his Lord on Golgotha instead of trying once again to act out a barracks routine that seemed devoid of any relevance. It had been no good; diversion had proved impossible. Barely aware of his movements, his surroundings or other people, at close of duty he returned to the family lodgings in the Old Palace as downcast and forlorn as ever. There was nowhere else to go, nothing to be done.

This is what betrayal felt like, then. It couldn't be true. But it was. By his darling wife. No, it couldn't be. This wasn't happening. But it was. Not after so much love and happiness and care and respect, and the gift of children, little ones who needed them both. But it was. Not after the Lord, who was truth and goodness itself, had entered their lives. It couldn't be. It was. Not with Bassus, please God. Not with that treacherous, scheming, callous man. Oh yes, it was. Unbelievable. But it was so. All of it. And how did he know his enemy hadn't also informed on him to that other viper Macula? – and that he could only have got that knowledge from Sabena, his dear Sabena. This must, must not be. What had he done to deserve this torment? How could God allow this to be happening? To his children? It could not be. But it was so. Then he must fight it. It could not be God's will. And he would hang on to that truth-of-all-truths through the whirling vortex which spun every attempt at rational thought into a jumble of empty nothingness.

He must pull himself together. He would suppress the emotional instincts and the anger that had superseded the initial numbness, and had to be controlled. The news about Macula didn't come into it. Macula had been as irrelevant as Bassus was now. He didn't want to know about the implications of the oath affair, or Macula, or anything else. They didn't matter a jot. All he could think of was the question: How could it possibly be this way? How had it reached this stage without any intimation of anything being wrong? Was it yet even true? Might she have a reasonable explanation of some kind – anything, no matter how slight, that would ameliorate this vile canker which had burst without warning in his face?

Was his lot really to be merely passive? He knew his other self wanted to kill Bassus of course, to tear him limb from limb. That was the manly option, the proper solution for a soldier, for any self-respecting man.

No. No! That was the instinct, and the sin. Vengeance was not, could not be, his. It would be a negation of all he had become, his new self which had been led gently on the path of understanding and salvation. Half-a-mile as the crow flew was his answer, on a cross of suffering, on a cross for Sabena and him, for their beloved children, for Matthias and his family, for Brutus and Vergilia, for all people if they would but know it. That was the way, the only way, the rugged road which would lead through trial and tribulation to the end that they and all believers might have eternal life, right for him, right for her, right for everyone, right for the whole world, so that all could be saved by the example of Him who was giving His life so they might have theirs eternal, and learn how to live their earthly lives in service to the Christ and one another. There had to be signposts like this which would instruct and encourage, and if the path were blocked with thorns until you couldn't see it, then you prayed harder, you asked what He would have done, what He would have said in His wisdom. To forgive seventy times seven, those had been His very words. So easy to hear and to nod in assent, so hard to imagine the difficulties, so very hard when the time came to put faith into practice; easy enough to accept the theory and out of context, but in real life, with real difficulties to confound you and fairness and justice nowhere to be seen, then so very hard to do. Yet only in the real world amid the knocks of life could the injunction have any meaning or value.

And Sabena? – yes, he could and would forgive her, he loved her more than he could think or say, and it was his duty to do so, just as it was his duty to follow God's will, and know this horrible reality was not God's will and would be beaten if he only followed the Father, sought His guidance, put himself and his own needs last, and believed. He would stick with her, protect her, cherish her, because his love was greater than this evil that had come between them. The children would justify everything, their welfare and their future the only priority on this earth now. They were not going to suffer in any way if he could possibly help it. He would keep the family together, no matter the cost to himself, his self-esteem, his career or even his life. And no, Bassus in this state couldn't, didn't matter. He was never, ever to become any sort of a consideration, but be shut out of mind in every way. And his own self didn't matter either. He had to keep going only to save the children, and spurn all thoughts of revenge. No, no revenge. The Lord would guide them both, husband and wife, and keep them from all vengeance. Wasn't he Sabena's loving husband, father of her children? She needed his help too, and his love, more than ever now, however hard it was for her to see it, however difficult it might be to live out, and however determined she might be to defy him. With God's good grace in time the wound might heal. Meanwhile his love was big enough for both of them, big enough to see them through this horror and find the best outcome for their little family, which had to stay together because it was right and because it was the Father's will. It would be done. His will be done who was giving His life as he himself must make his lesser sacrifice. As the Jews said, vengeance was the Lord's alone.

*   *   *   *

When she entered the room all latent anger was dissipated, his heart was melted. His love was there for her as it ever was, loyal and strong. He wanted to hold her, comfort her, touch her face, run his hand through her hair, be as one with her.

Though he knew it would be useless.

He had never seen her look so ashen before, so shaken and so hesitant.

'I have to tell you something.'

'It's good to see you, Darling.'

'I've been seeing Brutus. I want to leave you.'

'I know.'

It was all he could say. He didn't ask her how. He didn't ask why. It seemed to no purpose. The shock was out. But it still wasn't true. Not really. So there was no point in showing surprise, or anger, or enquiring, or complaining. It was all quite obvious and the details didn't matter. A week or two is all it had taken. The innocent start of it the previous year, no doubt. Living under someone else's roof. What had been impossible had become possible, then plausible, then inevitable. How blind could he have been? If it hadn't been for Vergilia he might never have known, although he could have lived with not knowing, forgiven her of course, not fully knowing, carried on loving her in the same old way. But know he now did. There must have been some sort of a confrontation between she and poor, hapless Vergilia, who must have found the courage to object. But for that the affair might have blown over. It wouldn't be blowing over now; too late for that. It was done, and he had to rise to the challenge. It would bring the best out in him. No recrimination, no retribution, no retaliation. He wanted to take her in his arms so much, even though she would reject him. This is what true love must mean then. To stand forsaken but true. The first time in his life. To love without love returned. To love, yet with consummate rejection.

'I want you to know that I love you and will do everything I can to keep us all together.'

'I can't. Don't fight. It'll just make it worse for you.'

'What do you mean?'

'I'll take the children.'

There was certainly nothing to say now. Her coldness should have angered him. He could have challenged her. He had offered magnanimity, no resistance, no animosity, but in return found only cold unyielding hostility. There was no sign on her part of any willingness to offer an explanation, or regret, or contrition, or sympathy. He'd long realized she was incapable of ever admitting blame or offering a word of apology, for anything, a characteristic he'd learned to accept. 'Sorry' was not in the vocabulary. Now when it was needed most it could not come; she could not say it. He must accept that, and then some more, accept everything, as though it were the natural order of things, and let the odds keep on stacking up against him. It would be beyond his own strength to beat this. Only his faith could help him now. All he could do was commend themselves to the One who could make all things well, and trust and believe in Him, so that somehow in ways which neither of them could foresee some good would come of this in the end.

Later he would recall the odd glance, the casual word, the unwonted

silence, which should have warned him if he hadn't been so blind. Of
how she had asked to visit a friend, last year in the city – the first time
she had ever left the house of an evening alone. Of how on a stroll
they had all made together one day, Bassus – he could scarcely bring
himself to form the man's name in his mind now – had seemed to go
on giving the children shoulder-rides rather too long than was proper
and normal; it seemed odd at the time, and now was all explained. Of
how only last night the man had clearly had his arm around her waist
a little too closely when he delivered her to his room in the Mess – the
brazen, hurtful nerve, showing him that it was he who was the new,
rightful and better protector, her ridiculous husband the one who was
side-lined and redundant. How many other signs should he have seen
in his blindness? How could he have allowed himself not to see what
was happening under his very nose? The memory would always jar
him now, his heart to be pierced and re-pierced incessantly for ever, and
he would be impotent, always impotent against the accomplished fact.
And what was all that about the she-wolf, striking to deliver him out of
his predicament? The flashing eyes, the male ego disconcerted? Yes,
but not for Veranius. As she'd said not so long ago, she would have done
anything for the children, abased herself in any menial way possible for
their welfare. Except when the test came she hadn't. So capable. So
beautiful. So loving. But in the end she'd put herself first. The she-
wolf had struck alright. Against him.

And then he thought he saw. The business over the oath was the
incidental calamity. There was also the faith. Her commitment to it had
seemed genuine if slow to begin with; she couldn't be blamed if it wasn't
as strong as his. She hadn't been there that day; she didn't actually
meet Him. Of course it was something highly personal, to which every
mortal soul came their different way. Nascent and fragile, her interest
hadn't been strong enough to resist the wiles of the great adversary; it
had been overcome before it had the chance to grow and flourish. The
stubborn streak in her nature had triumphed, and he wasn't to try and
put the blame on the Almighty. The Holy Spirit blew where it would,
but not always in time to stop the pollutant from seeping in to loving
relationships, to cause misery and mayhem to all that was good and

wholesome. Another man was taking that which was not his, and risking all to get it; and she had fallen. It was the way of the world: torture for him, joy and liberation for them. Partly down to his own failings, partly the working of the universal poison which sought out and struck with such unerring malice to bring its victims down. The how and the why, and all beslimed. But it wasn't God's fault, and it wasn't hers.

*   *   *   *

Veranius got his report in late, which was excusable after such a busy day. His senior centurion had been unambivalent: activity through the gates had been quite normal; and no-one had entered or left all night except for the routine patrols mounted by First Samarians and conducted without incident. Macula must have left before the main gate was closed, before last light, but he had not checked out with the guardroom, no-one remembered seeing him, and in any case everyone knew walking out by any rank during Passover Week was prohibited. How he got out was a mystery. The only possible explanation was that he'd passed a handsome tip to the gate guard and they, in time-honoured fashion, weren't owning up; or else – and this was so unlikely it was hardly worth considering – he'd somehow managed to get a copy for the key to the postern gate by similar means, in which case, by way of afterthought, they'd better change the lock as soon as possible. And yes, he had investigated every angle personally.

'We'll take it up again in the morning, Veranius. By the way, talking of bodies, did your man Longinus get my message about the Nazarene's – about handing it over to a councillor from the Sanhedrin?'

'Yes. All done, Commandant.' And then: 'Sorry, I meant to tell you. He subsequently had a similar request from some of the High Priest's men – Caiaphas himself also wanted the body, apparently. Claimed he had the right.'

'Really? He told them to get lost, I hope.'

'In no uncertain terms.'

'And explained about Councillor Joseph beating them to it? A member of some standing, apparently.'

'Yes, he mentioned another name to me, too. There's no way that other request from the priests could have come through your office, is there?'

'Of course not. The Boss handed the councillor on to me and I personally gave the order. That was the last of it.'

'Just checking, Commandant. You might get an official complaint.'

'They can complain all they like.' 'I'll see you tomorrow. Keep digging on Macula. If I were you I'd get the redoubtable Longinus to exercise a little more of that native cunning of his.'

'Yes. Till tomorrow then.'

*　*　*　*

The new dawn came in quietly, with everything in its rightful place after the alarum of its predecessor. The Passover could continue as it should, the city locked down in dutiful observance, Jew and Gentile in their allotted place.

Depressingly so. Could there be any beauty – any point – now the true light was gone? And who was this man, her husband of twenty years, lying at her side in peaceful repose, insensible to the momentous import of the event over which he'd presided? Did he have the first idea what he'd done, or how much it had hurt her, and was hurting her still? She couldn't let his callousness browbeat her into submission. In her nervous exhaustion Claudia Procula would surprise herself. She would determine it was time to make an effort and face the reality, while doing her very best to stay positive; which meant not only coming to terms with the immensity of this cruel and pointless tragedy, but also with her husband's attitude. Accommodation in this raw condition of hers would be going too far. She'd never be reconciled to the point of affirmation; but acceptance was different. Near-detestation had visited itself upon them before, and gone; and she knew better than to let those feelings return to get out of control. It was permissible to recognize he had a difficult job, and had enough to worry about without the burden of a neurotic woman – this man who could be so infuriating, with his worldly-wise detachment permanently hovering on cynicism, his refusal to engage in the emotions except for a residual temper reserved for slights against his person real or imagined, the wilfulness and obstinacy verging on pig-headedness, the lack of generosity of spirit which still disappointed after all these years.

Yet also whom she knew still loved her in his own way, and knew too his finer qualities. He was after all of his type, his pride and other traits no worse than the norm, his reaction to the continuing lack of support from the powers-that-be in Rome understandable, though he'd had ample time to get used to that. Perhaps that was why he'd mellowed over more recent time; and it was true – he hadn't seemed to have got too angry over the revelatory nature of their conversations yesterday. Quite the contrary – he'd been remarkably relaxed. Clearly her latest activities, topped by her visit to Bethany, had not been a surprise, although it would have been better if he hadn't withheld the fact of his knowledge, and no doubt of some of his staff too. She had to see his view on that; there would have been no point upsetting her unnecessarily, no sense in causing a rift between them whilst there was a chance the problem would go away; and it must have been no little embarrassment for the Commander-in-Chief to have his wife behaving, as he would say, so irresponsibly. Could it be that if everything in heaven and earth were for a purpose this included her husband's character? If this were part of the divine plan then perhaps she ought to see his part in a more benign light.

But this man whom she thought she loved had sent the Saviour of the world to His death! How could she share her bed with him after this? And yet – a thought more. He was the father of their dear child. A good father. And he had always loved her, and been constant. Must she not forgive, as she had now been taught? If in time she could accept that all things worked for the best, then was he too not God's agent, who had had no choice in what he had done? Would the same providence not work for them now and in their future? Was he beyond redemption? Or was the horror of her nightmare the previous night less of an instruction on the tragedy awaiting Yeshua, which on this reckoning was already long ordained, than the fate awaiting her husband? Good would prevail, He had taught, but how could that extend to one who had washed his hands not in mere water but the blood of the Blessed Saviour? The antithesis of good was evil. Was this man its instrument, to be held in infamy until the end of time?

It was too much. She had to calm down, reconcile herself to the prospect of continuing to stand by him with equanimity, and know that he would need her, increasingly. She knew too that she must hang on to the simple positives, and that she would be helped. It wasn't his fault if his nature was not receptive to the one thing that could save him. The Word could be revealed but it needed a willing mind, and in her husband it had encountered convention and scepticism. But there was always hope; he was capable of faith as well as reason, since the basis of faith was reason, and it was only a day since he'd met the Saviour face-to-face. Who could not be changed for ever who had received that great good fortune? It might take time, but the Holy Spirit would come upon them and show them the way. It was up to her now to be strong and, after the traumatic uncovering of her illicit liaison as though she had been a guilty lover, to embark on a more gentle sowing of the seeds and their nurturing into life, to allow his sense of enquiry to overcome his natural prejudices, to lead on to their seeking salvation together. She owed it him. For all his faults his affection for her was genuine, and she could never complain he hadn't always given her freedom to pursue her own interests and speak her mind. Together they would see it through, sinners to atone, with God's goodness penitents to be spared, disciples to evangelize in their turn. She would pray for patience, and courage when the right moments came. And now she must take heart again, and remember that beautiful time just a few evenings ago, and what Yeshua had said, and that however hard it might be, she must believe. And believe for her husband, too.

*　　*　　*　　*

He dismissed the slave, saying he would shave himself.

He looked deep into the mirror. Did he pass scrutiny? You did what you thought was best, knowing you, and others close to you, everyone in fact, had to live with the consequences. He had to be especially understanding of her, he thought. One day he would probably expound on the subject of divine intervention, or rather its implausibility, but with Claudia in such a fragile state this was not the best time to burden her with realities. Neither could he allow himself the indulgence of second thoughts, which would be of no use to anyone now. It was important that everyone pulled together and did what they were there for, and demonstrate the continuity of imperial power. The periodic reminder of a subject people's potential for open rebellion had to be matched by unruffled authority and the implicit and constant threat of superior force, of which his own calm presence was an essential component. Steadiness of nerve was the prescription for good government, plus several thousand well-armed men, whose efficiency was always to be expected as a matter of course. No time should have to be spent on distractions like matters of religious conscience in the officer corps. And no effort should have to be devoted to domestic concerns in the heart of his own household.

Yet here was this problem, a wife who was otherwise tolerably sensible if a little highly-strung, sharing his life, running the servants, running off to consult mystics in the night and clearly infatuated with this cult-like phenomenon which had threatened to destabilize everything – his province, his job, his existence – and still posed a residual threat now. In this strange state of over-dependence she could so easily go completely to pieces. Her moment with the Nazarene had clearly been an inspirational experience for her, but it could make no sense to anyone with their feet on the ground. It was vital no word of it got out or it would undermine the whole administration. There was no reason to doubt the discretion of the very few of his staff who were aware of her visit to Bethany and her interest in the cult, and it was unlikely it would be spread abroad by its native adherents either, since they were so few and wouldn't have much interest in trying to develop the connection. The main risk came from Claudia herself; she was quite capable of making a scene, spilling the beans in one of her lapses when salvational compulsion had to be shared. He would make an appeal to her sense of reason in due course, when the realities might have sunk in and the naivety diminished. Meanwhile he would do his uxorial duty, treat her as gently as he could, and get on with the important business of government.

*   *   *   *

'This is highly irregular. It won't do, you know.'

'Commandant, it is the fact. There is no record of that man leaving the fort that night. The back gate is the only possibility.'

'So you're trying to tell me young officers and senior ranks never grease the guard when they want to slip a curfew or two. Come on, Veranius. Don't tell me it never happens.'

'What do you want me to do – interrogate the entire Cohort? How about a quick bit of decimation whilst we're at it? – just so HQ can claim there's an explanation. The milk is spilt. Macula's dead. I've got quite enough trouble with my officers at the moment to start worrying about witch hunts.'

'You refer to Favonius Facilis, I assume.'

'The same. I might be needing a posting for him. He's got wife trouble.'

'Oh? Well, best time to kick a man's when he's down, I suppose. And by Jove, she is a looker. Who's the lucky man?'

'Brutus Bassus, Century IV. You're being a bit cavalier, aren't you? What's happened to standards?'

'Every man has his price, Veranius. Who wouldn't be tempted, with a prize like her?'

'Regrettable relapses resulting in unmanly manifestations must be rigidly suppressed at all times and in all places by the individual concerned, Commandant. Old school motto.'

'Or in the real world, managed. You can't fight human nature.'

'That's true.'

'Definitely when it comes to chasing women. And arguing about religion too, I'd say.'

Was the old sweat referring to the oath business? Probably yes. He mustn't rise. He wasn't having his unit's affairs bandied about by the staff any more than he could avoid. He should feign the assumption it was common knowledge, at least in the headquarters by now, and leave well alone.

'Well, we know the score.' Veterus went on. 'Bassus can have his cake or he can eat it, but he can't have both. If he wants her he'll have to go. And I don't mean posted and I don't mean an administrative discharge. It's out with no pension and no references. As for the other silly bugger, that's serious. Different matter altogether.'

There was no doubt then. Veterus knew about the oath, just as the Governor had, and both from the beginning. It had been worth a try. Never roll a die if you don't need to.

'Agreed. But the two things are related. It's not public yet. If Facilis shops him I think she'll desert. Take the children and go.'

'Unheard of. Wives don't desert – they put up with it.'

'Not this one.'

'Then we do the shopping. Sack Bassus for conduct unbecoming. He has to go.'

'And lose two officers. And she'll go anyway, and a good man loses his family for certain.'

'The priority is to keep Facilis in the Army, but only if he relents.'

'Quite, Commandant. He's not going to get the promotion leg-up he deserves now, that's obvious. But let's give him a chance back in the mainstream, not this backwater. He's done his bit here. I don't want scandal in my command – the sooner we can get him away the better. It won't save his marriage but it would solve the other problem.'

'So we are talking oaths, Veranius.'

'We are, Commandant.'

'And pass the baby conveniently on to somebody else? You do realize the brickbats that are going to come our way when his new unit discovers we didn't have the balls to sort the problem out ourselves? I may not have much time left but I'm not going to be responsible for something like that. It'd be a gross dereliction of duty.'

'He'd be a long way away – you'll be enjoying the rewards of a long and distinguished career by then. And what are they going to do about it?'

'It's very simple, Veranius. He needs to take the oath to Augustus. If he does, all well and good. If he doesn't that's his problem. The Army's not a welfare organization. And look on the bright side. If he won't save himself we've still got the option of retaining the services of one capable officer at least, in the form of officer Bassus. Any risk of disaffection from religious nutters is stopped outright, all other reputations survive intact and the Governor's estimation of CO Second Italians as a man to be relied upon knows no bounds.'

Should he admit here and now that he'd already as good as let Favonius Facilis off the hook? The idea of that quick posting, with the oath left tacitly to one side, didn't seem such an obvious option from this remove.

'I think the Governor would think I was forced into the last resort. I'd have failed to find the optimal practical solution.'

'I think the Governor would want you to do that which minimizes the damage from the strange death of Tribune Macula.' Veterus paused to stroke his chin. 'You know what they say about troubles coming in threes. I can understand your concern for your centurion. No-one wants to see a good man down, and we should do what we can for him – up to a point. Every man must follow his own conscience, but in doing so he must be prepared for the repercussions, both for himself, his family and everybody else. Yes he did well at Luz but he mustn't be allowed to forget he's a soldier of Rome, that as an officer there are additional obligations. He's got an example to set, and rules to follow, and enforce too – all the responsibilities that go with the job, in fact. He can't just pick and choose what he wants because he's taken up with some foreign god that he happens to believe in. What about the rest of us? No, this isn't just about him. He's the cause of the problem but he's no longer the main issue. Our concern is with bigger things – duty, discipline, morale, tradition – and every other soldier in this command. And the obeying of orders, Veranius. They all go together. You don't need me to tell you that.'

'He would say his personal beliefs are not prejudicial to good order and military discipline – to quote Caesar's Regulations for the Army.'

'And that's where he's wrong. You cannot have an army where anyone, let alone a field officer in command of troops, flouts convention with a lot of fancy foreign ideas – and specifically, if you please, refuses to take the loyal oath.'

'Correction. Loyal oath to a late-lamented emperor. Anyway

foreign cults are nothing new. Soldiers are always dabbling in them, especially out here.'

'Maybe. But they're not belittling our own Gods. They're complementing them, and they're not undermining discipline or subverting loyalty to the State. And they don't spout nonsense about treating your neighbour as yourself and turning the other cheek. What a load of rot!'

'Do old soldiers know much about that kind of thing then, Commandant?'

'That's why I know what's what. Take my advice, Veranius. Don't stick your neck out too far on this. You might have a friend in the Boss but you know the set-up. Don't give Seneccio the chance to make mischief.'

'He can't help being a politico.'

'He's as ambitious as the next one, and he's not exactly a friend of the Army. The Boss tolerates him because he's a good ferret and keeps him well-briefed, and supposedly has some political acumen. But if Seneccio thought he could gain more from his contacts in Rome I think we can guess where his loyalties might be in a crisis.'

'So he knows about all this too, I suppose.'

'Most of it, I expect. Though I've done my best to steer him clear. Anyway this can't be kept under wraps much longer, can it? Unless your centurion recants, of course.'

'He's been warned for this afternoon. He knows he'll be remanded for court-martial if he doesn't.'

He'd said it. On the spur of the moment. He must have thought it sensible to keep Veterus on-side, or at least try to dissuade him from taking too hostile a line. It wasn't exactly how he'd left it with Facilis a few hours before, but there'd been little choice now. In precipitately reversing the possibility of a quiet posting-out he had opted for prudence, and effectively abandoned his former position – all his efforts to do right for his centurion, gone, just like that. Not entirely, he said to himself; Facilis could still save himself. But in the loose moment he'd gone for the easy option, and given way; and he'd better not notice the bitter taste which threatened to spill up inside him and blunt what was left of his concentration.

'Good, Veranius. No witness available with Macula gone, but that's no longer relevant. If he won't take the oath in your presence that's all you need.'

'Yes, Commandant.'

'Speed's of the essence – I wouldn't hang about if I were you. It's only a detail compared to the main problem, but the concern, as you say, is that the two are related – I'm not bothered about the marital infidelity, I'm concerned with a murdered VIP officer, and treason against the State, and I doubt the Boss is going to send his report off without both matters being cleared up to his equal satisfaction. And there are bound to be some searching questions from Rome on their apprentice tribune, what with all those connections in high places. The Governor will need to be quite sure there's been nothing untoward in his demise. If there's any suspicion of any foul play, and we can't find a perpetrator, then we're all on the line. It'll be postings to the far-flung north, and not just for centurions – in double-quick time.'

'It should be a case for a formal in-province enquiry, surely. You can't do that overnight.'

'Oh yes, there'll have to be an enquiry all right, Veranius, but the one that matters is the one that should be in front of us now – your report as commanding officer, which could never be anything but comprehensive and factual, could it? You and I might think Macula was foolish enough and drunk enough to disobey standing orders during an especially sensitive local festival and get himself killed by some malcontent – it wouldn't be the first time a soldier has come to grief in the back streets of this city. But who's going to believe it in Rome when the Governor has so many enemies and a reputation for getting it wrong? Whatever the facts of the case they've got to be fully investigated and written up – if there's to be any credibility whatsoever.'

'Indeed.'

'Have you got the drift? We might have to consider a little creative evidence-making of our own, Veranius. Something purely on the commanding officer's authority, of course. Something as simple as the guard commander noting the egress at a certain time of the night of officer Macula of the First Augusta, despite a polite reminder on the curfew from a couple of overawed young soldiers. Regrettable, unfortunate, but convincing. And an explanation.'

'Yes, Commandant.'

'Let's hope it doesn't come to that. But sometimes things need to be chivvied along a bit, don't they? As to your other concern, it doesn't look like the lovely Sabena's going to stand by her husband, whatever we do.'

'I doubt it. He's given her the perfect excuse, hasn't he? I did arrange a little meeting but nothing came of it. And whom did she choose to escort her to the Mess? Not some reliable third party who wouldn't raise suspicion – but lover-boy. Takes some believing, but there we are. Couldn't do much about it, I'm afraid. I'll keep you posted.'

*   *   *   *

As soon as he was in a quiet place in the lines again, and with the prospect of another fraught day ahead, Favonius returned to his prayers. There could be no relief to be had in anything else; neglect of bodily needs and another sleepless night made it impossible to concentrate properly, but he had to keep trying. The immediate threat on the oath might have receded but he knew Veranius would be under enormous pressure, that anything could still happen – and probably would.

It was almost inconsequential now. Prayer made for a measure of pre-occupation and escape from chaos, the possibility of calm and rational dialogue; but there had been no real answers, just repetition beating around in his head until he must go mad. It was not a simple matter of asking for his marriage to be saved, in the way he had once asked for Matthias to be cured. Which is not to say exactly that he wasn't asking for that, since it was integral to everything else, but it begged the question of how far it was right to pray in effect for himself. Some would say there was nothing wrong with that; indeed, it was theologically justified. The issue came down to trying to distinguish between his own welfare and that of his family, and whether saving the marriage was really the most important consideration anyway, or rather how it could be saved, and whether drastic and immediate action was the only solution. He couldn't be sure. Back in Capernaum it had been straightforward, and Yeshua had been there with him in the flesh. Now everything seemed so complicated. Matthias' recovery had been truly miraculous. Were miracles to be sought and granted, not simply for their own sake, but only if they didn't directly benefit the self? Could pleas be valid which might in any way be subjective or even selfish? And why shouldn't her love be made whole again? Hadn't He said all things were possible, that if you asked for anything and only believed then it would be granted? Of course the object had to be intrinsically good and wholesome. Everyone's needs were known to the Father and would be met if they were right for them, and requested in faith. Wasn't it inconceivable that their marriage and their little family were not absolutely right and wholesome – in keeping therefore with the divine will? Their vows had been before pagan gods, though the Lord's blessing had surely been upon them then and surely held them in safety, though now it seemed the gates of hell had opened all around. Yet were the faithful not to forbear to concern themselves unduly, because the Father knew their every need and held them in His loving care, and they had His assurance everything would work out for the best according to His will? And how could that not be for the saving of this marriage, with the vows that had sealed it and the children it had succoured? He could understand if he had seriously transgressed in some way and was deserving of disfavour and chastisement. He had been a sinner, like everybody else. Perhaps it really was the case he was getting his just desserts, and if it seemed unfair compared to the fortunes of others then it was a cost of faith for which he should be glad. But for the children to be punished? – because punishment in whatever form would be the result. But then he had to face it – they might be better off without him …

He was only a man, who might have made some effort to live a good life though nevertheless was still capable of weakness and error. He had always loved his wife and she him, with scarcely a cross word all their life together, and they had been happy – so he'd thought. Maybe he'd put his work first too often, but no more than many of his peers, and it had never seemed to have any adverse effect – or so he'd thought. You often saw love dying in others' marriages, but not theirs, surely? She had clearly fallen under some kind of malign influence, and whatever she was saying now could not be the final outcome. This couldn't possibly be how it was meant to be – it might happen to others, but their union was special, their children, their dear children, innocent and unique. If his wife was now in trouble, there was an answer – he had enough love for them both, and they just had to see this thing through together, until by God's good grace it would all be put behind them. There must be no countenancing of any possibility of the children being affected in any way – which they surely would be if she left him. How could that possibly be God's will? It simply couldn't. So he had to fight, though forbidden to retaliate or seek any kind of revenge. Shopping the man was out. What good would that do? It wouldn't win her back, and the Army, normally keen to see honour upheld, wouldn't trouble to uphold it for him. He'd be a liability. They'd say 'you're a Nazarene now, sort it out with your superior conscience – your god will tell you what to do, won't he?' …

No, killing the culprit who was breaking up this marriage was not a solution. And killing himself was similarly out of the question, however his old self might once have been tempted. He had to get his priorities right and stick to his mantra. All that mattered was the children; everything else had to be around that citadel of certainty – what was best for them. His enemy was the least important consideration of all. Whatever happened he would go on loving his wife as he always had. He would not abandon her, though she was abandoning him. It was extremely unlikely that she would ever come back, yet while they both lived somehow there had to be hope, though he had no idea how it could be manifested. Only the Lord could resolve this trial; it was beyond his own strength and resources. And so he must commend everything to His wisdom, to be fulfilled in His own way and His own time, and he would be His agent in whatever way He ordained. He would be Yeshua's hands and lips. And he would suffer the pain and humiliation for as long as it took.

He would endure.

* * * *

'Have a date.'

'Thank you, Secretary. Oh good, they're honeyed.'

'The Governor received a large box this morning, from Antipas. Rosewater for her Ladyship.'

'How thoughtful.'

'A peace-offering. First contact since the shields affair. And a Thank You for the *de facto* recognition duly expressed in yesterday's legal proceedings, I'd surmise. The wheels of diplomacy turn strangely, do they not? Who would have thought? – the Nazarene seems to have brought them together at last. So did you seriously expect the Italians to come up with anything?'

'On Macula?'

'On Macula, Camp Commandant.'

'The Army's investigations continue, Secretary.'

'Far be it for me to suggest the Army's internal procedures to be anything but sound, Camp Commandant. Though one cannot help but observe it is all a bit odd.'

Seneccio sat himself down. 'First a very important individual is found at dawn by a routine patrol, stone dead and where he should not be. He appears to have been drinking, which might not be very remarkable, but no-one admits to have been long in his company that night, and the Officers' Mess staff say he was quite sober the last time he was seen. There is not a mark on him. But somehow he ends up garotted in a back-street with his body left to lie there for the riff-raff to gloat over come daylight. It could be a provocation by aggrieved elements in the populace, of course. Or simply an opportunistic armed robbery. A little careless on the part of the deceased, nonetheless, but all that is by-the-by. The real question is why he left a secure area when he must have known full well it is strictly forbidden and exceedingly dangerous. It makes one wonder whether there was not something about the company he was keeping that night after all. Would you not say?'

'Were you ever young, Secretary?'

'He spent the evening quietly in the Garrison Officers' Mess, one hears.'

'Did he?'

'So one is led to believe.'

'You seem to know quite a lot about mess life.'

'I am merely a humble secretary, Camp Commandant. But I would not be discharging my duties to my employer very conscientiously if I did not keep my ears to the ground.'

'I'm listening.'

'How do we know there was not something of interest going on in the Officers' Mess that night in the Antonine – no high-jinks, no arguments amongst the livers-in? That sort of thing.'

'What are you getting at?'

'We've already established Centurion Facilis was also in the Officers' Mess, have we not?'

'Yes yes, as we've discussed.'

'An inconclusive conversation, Camp Commandant, as I recall. Not only is our intriguing centurion detained under unusual and somewhat mysterious circumstances, precisely concurrent with the eve of a major civil incident and near-insurrection, which is, as I need hardly remind you, one's own particular area of responsibility, but we are now given to understand there are rumours of scandal concerning this officer's marriage. And that his wife is remarkably... exceptional.'

'And you want to jump to conclusions?'

'Not at all, Camp Commandant. Naturally one understands the call of outraged honour in such situations. One is gratified our soldiers traditionally display all the necessary qualities in that direction. Aristocratic status, or any other sort of consideration for that matter, might be of little consequence when the natural passions are aroused. And confining proximity only a spur to seek suitable redress... of a physical nature. But of course one merely speculates.'

'If you think Facilis killed Macula over his wife you could be barking up the wrong tree.'

'That is of course a matter for the Army, Camp Commandant. The civil interest remains totally... disinterested. I merely allude to the possibility should the military chain of command wish to ensure the right outcome to any judicial proceedings which might ensue. The system – Rome – will want certainty and satisfaction in such a high-profile case. What's the continuing existence of one middle-ranking officer against such pressing need?'

'And you'll remind us the certainty extends to maximum suppression of religious dissent too, I expect.'

'Which is, one trusts Camp Commandant, our common concern. The total elimination of this nefarious cult in or out the Army. But one only offers an alternative approach for the handling of a prime suspect for the Army's consideration – a suspect not content with one motive but apparently bent on two. Think of it as a supplement to the failsafe. We still have the Birthday of Eternal Rome next week – a good time for renewed oath-taking, one would have thought. And then, thank the Gods, some of us can get back to the sea air and leave your garrison in peace for another year. Now if you will excuse me, I must attend to my duties.'

*　*　*　*

'That's the truth, Prefect. I interviewed every member of the guard that night personally. No-one saw Macula leave – in fact they didn't see anyone at all. There were no movements outside the gates except the usual patrols. We're not completely sure about the keys though. It's possible the key to the back gate might have gone missing.'

'What?'

'The register isn't actually very clear.'

'Why not?'

'It looks like there were two keys once, but there's definitely only one now.'

'And when did it go missing?'

'Impossible to say. It's not my gate and not my barracks.'

'Don't try and be funny with me, Senior Centurion. It was your company on duty.'

'They'd had a hard day. These things happen. It might have gone ages ago.'

'Well somebody has to take the blame. Don't guard commanders sign for anything these days?'

'Not exactly. A bare guardroom's a bare guardroom. And if the only evidence consists of a smudged key register then there isn't much chance of any charges sticking.'

'Well you'd better get the lock changed, hadn't you?'

'Already in hand.'

'Damned sloppy, Senior Centurion!'

'Yes, Prefect.'

Veranius thought about a change of angle. Longinus had kept it short – too short.

'Let's go back a little in time, shall we? To the night before the mysterious case of the missing key that we can't be sure existed. What about the Mess that night – did you as the senior liver-in see anything of Macula that evening?'

'Yes, he was around, nothing unusual. He had dinner, drank too much, gave us the benefit of his sneering superiority and turned in when he realized he was embarrassing himself. Normal routine.'

'Tell me. What do you know about Facilis and Sabena?' Or is it Bassus and Sabena? Quite a problem – very much an in-barracks disciplinary matter of course, but you're his great comrade-in-arms. You must have an opinion.'

'Are you sure you want it?'

'Just tell me.'

'The whole garrison knows about it. Can't keep anything like that secret in a place like this. As you say, most unfortunate. Tragic, really.'

'And the background? How long's it been going on?'

'It's all rather sudden, though the seeds were probably sown a year ago when she and Bassus would have met for the first time. Facilis is the innocent party – totally. I'm afraid OC IV is behaving very badly.'

'It's not up to us to interfere in affairs of the heart. We can attempt a subtle effect or two from the margins but we can't stop her leaving him.'

'True, unfortunately. But you might know where my sympathies lie. You need to get rid of Bassus.'

'Coming from you, Senior Centurion, I could take that literally.'

Longinus did not react.

'If I get Bassus posted it could be a stop-gap, and might just save the marriage – but Facilis ought to be careful what he wishes for. There's nothing worse in a man's life than a woman at enmity, though that would be his problem and he'd have to live with it. Anyway it's a question of timing. Bassus has his promotion ticket, and there's nothing here for him now career-wise. And his departure could be expedited if necessary.'

'I wouldn't want him in my command.'

'You're not suggesting he loses his recommendation?'

'Oh I'd do more than that to the rotter. But you asked my advice.'

'And Facilis? Is there anything else about your friend you might suggest I need to take into account regarding his case? Apart from his marriage problems, I mean?'

'I don't think so, no.'

They looked each other in the eye, unblinking.

'Thank you. That will be all.'

Veranius arose, suspicion confirmed. The Senior Centurion had not come clean. It would have been better to have offered something, he thought – something on the lines of his friend's general difficulty with the Augustan oath, perhaps, as an indication of his *bona fides*, but he'd clearly gone for all-out defence against his own commanding officer. A mistake on Longinus' part, he also thought. Uncharacterisistc, if understandable; almost laudable. He might be their superior in camp, though not on the field of battle, and in that little exchange the brotherhood had clearly been in action. Why the dead pan reticence? Why the determination not to give an inch on any difficulty his friend might have with the oath, when a little obfuscation would have been the usual tactic? Because there was something else. There had to be. There always was with Longinus. Something which might lead on to even more hazardous territory, and there were few more hazardous territories than full-blown religion. Oaths in the religious context – and there were few not in that category – didn't exist in disconnected isolation; they were invested with meaning and principle, and had the potential to clash with other meanings and other principles. For the great majority, even the agnostics, this was never a problem – but it would be if you'd been changing your ideas sufficiently – and taken up with another religion. One in particular, on which he'd conspicuously failed to confront his apostate centurion and been obliged to admit that failure so embarrassingly to the Governor; which he'd known all along was going to be the root cause of all these unwelcome difficulties, but hadn't wanted to address face-to-face; which was the reason for all this stubbornness and intractable inconvenience: the cult from Galilee, with its pernicious effect on Army discipline now plain and undeniable. He'd wished it wasn't so, and he had tried to avoid the reality, but Facilis had gone more than native: he'd gone the whole hog, and taken up with the most controversial and inflammatory religious movement possible. And if we were in among such fundamental matters, why end there? Was there anything else, by any chance? And it occurred to him …

He allowed himself a wry smile. If Longinus was prepared to cover for his friend in this respect, why not another? Perhaps … ? Surely not. It was too far-fetched. But then again …

*   *   *   *

The Governor and his lady took luncheon in silence. She had eaten very little.

It was time to say something. 'My Dear, I'm afraid you ought to know …'

She looked pensive.

'Calm yourself, it's alright. It's nothing to do with the Nazarenes.'

Claudia gathered her frayed nerves. It would not take much to disturb the barely contrived dignity with which she had resolved to shield herself against present pain and future worry.

'You know that centurion I presented the medal to the other night? Favonius Facilis, with the good-looking wife.'

She froze. Her dear Favonius, completely unknown to her until so recently, now her fellow-disciple, true hero, bravely steadfast in the faith, with his lovely wife and family, sensibly lying low against this frightening tyranny bent on destroying all that was good and honest.

She mumbled a brief acknowledgement.

'She wants to leave him, My Dear. Just heard this morning. Most unfortunate.'

Her husband's words were as a battering ram against her heart. 'I know you've a high regard for her. You managed to see her yesterday, I imagine. It's all rather distasteful, I'm afraid. It's an affair, of course. What else? With an officer in the same cohort. Brutus Bassus, if you remember him. Wretched business.'

Claudia put a hand to her mouth but could not suppress a stifled cry.

The Governor continued, ignoring his wife's distress: 'Her husband is clearly the injured party. And another follower of your rabbi, by all accounts. They must have some interesting conversations over breakfast.'

She heard the words through a daze, stunned by the double shock, speechless.

'I'm not belittling anyone else's marital problems. Who knows what goes on behind closed doors in any house? But if one party strays, what does it say about them? – both parties, come to think of it. Particularly when the husband's in serious trouble already. And particularly when both husband and wife apparently had personal knowledge of the great seer himself, if not actual acquaintance – and presumably therefore tried to avoid that vulgar pitfall, adultery. Mind you, one learns even the holy man was known to mix with ladies of colourful repute from time to time.'

She wasn't capable of listening properly any longer, though the gist was plain enough. The tears wanted to come but she remembered her promise to herself. She would steady her feelings, keep her composure. She wasn't to let him domineer, with his matter-of-fact tones, his superficial interest in her opinions and what she'd come to hold so dear. And she wasn't to indulge in self-recrimination for not having thought more of the brave Favonius, who was risking everything for the faith while she had the protection of her status – that would be to take her eyes off the only subject deserving of her concern. Poor Favonius, betrayed by a lying and faithless wife. It was clear now. She had to fight. She would fight for him – and against her own cold, belittling husband.

'That's so unfair. And "nothing to do with the Nazarene", you said.

But it is, isn't it? As if there hasn't been enough suffering already. Why can't you just leave Him alone, now He's dead? Or his followers, who've never meant any harm.'

'I'm sorry, My Dear. Can't you see how disruptive a sect like this can be? We really can't have soldiers indulging in this sort of thing – where will it all end? But I notice you don't deny it.'

She wasn't going to admit it easily. 'I don't know what you mean.'

'Come, My Dear. You don't deny Facilis is a follower, do you?'

'I never met him before the other night. As you know. And I've never spoken to him on the subject.'

'Does the name Matthias mean anything to you?'

She looked at him, horrified.

'Really I'm surprised at such reticence from a religion claiming so much truth.'

There was still no answer. He could see she was on the verge of breaking down, and that he should desist.

'I'm sorry, Claudia. Sorry to press you.'

'How could you be so despicable? To try and trick your wife, who loves you, though heaven knows why.'

'Trick you?'

'Yes. To see how long it would take for your bullying to bring an admission.'

'It's only the truth one seeks, My Dear. And you don't appear to want to deny it.'

'I didn't know about his marriage problems, and I'm extremely sad to hear of them. Yes, I did talk to his wife yesterday. I ... I thought she was a good loyal wife and mother. It's all so sad.'

'And her husband?'

'What of him?'

'What of him? His desertion of the official religion and adherence to what looks remarkably like another, very foreign substitute. Isn't that enough?'

'Do you wish to have one of your officers condemned by your own wife?'

'It would have been better if you'd been completely honest with me, Claudia. You've presumably known all about Yeshua of Nazareth for some time. But couldn't content yourself with respectable, mild, academic interest from the comforts of the Palace, from which respectable distance your curiosity might have been satisfied. No, you have to take yourself off by night in your head-shawl to go and consult your preacher – the Governor's Lady, on a donkey! Do you realize the field-day Caiaphas & Co would have if this got out? Have you given any thought how Tiberius is likely to react when he finds out? This isn't about emotions. It's called affairs of state, for which I, your husband, am responsible.'

'I didn't do it to defy you, or make difficulties for anyone. I did it to hear the word of life direct from this man – whom they called their teacher, rabboni, whom you condemned yesterday. And I wasn't disappointed. What I found was goodness, and love, and wisdom, those novel ideas that have always been so alien to you and all you arrogant men. Yes, your wife is a follower, Appius. Now condemn me too.'

It was his turn to fail to reply.

*　*　*　*

Longinus strode into the room.

'Favonius it's time to bring you to your senses. You've got an hour before CO's Orders.'

'Thanks.'

'You're going to get in there and conduct yourself like a soldier.'

'Is that supposed to be a compliment or an insult?'

'In taking this stance you do more than dishonour yourself. You dishonour your family, the Army, your men, the chain of command, your friends, me, Caesar, the very Gods of Rome. You've got to shake out of this … this frame of mind, now. Wake up man, wake up, before it's too late.'

'You know where I am on this.'

'You do see, don't you? You're going to give Veranius no choice. He's leant over backwards to save you. But it's obvious he's been leant on, and there's a limit to what he can do. No-one in their right mind is going to jeopardize their own career over something as stupid as this. If you turn it into a confrontation with no way out then it can only end one way. And that's against you.'

'I know.'

'Look, Favonius. Is it right to risk your all because of these ... principles of yours? Because of what just so happens to have seized your mind these days, and might be gone the next? Whatever passes for thought in that head of yours, what you should be thinking about most is those you hold dearest. What do you think the future holds for them? You might get away with your life – just, if you're lucky, though I doubt it once they've thrown a charge of treason at you. But imagine the hardship they're going to suffer after you've gone, cast out of their class and polite society, near destitute and saddled with the stigma caused by your selfishness. Because that's what it is – downright utter selfishness. It's no good having a tender conscience if it means others have to suffer, especially your loved ones. Is it? And don't think Sabena and the children will have a halcyon future to look forward to once you've gone, not with all this baggage. Her looks aren't going to buy them happiness.'

'She's leaving me, Longinus.'

Longinus stopped abruptly. There was a long pause.

Then: 'Oh my friend. My dear, good friend. I'd hoped it wasn't true, that it wasn't irretrievable, that she'd stand by you, especially now you're in this other predicament. I'm so sorry. I should have spoken to you before. I should have expressed my fears and suspicions. Done something about it. Collared that bastard Bassus. There's always somebody else whenever anything like this happens. Had a heart-to-heart with Sabena. Anything. But I couldn't. I daredn't precipitate anything, in case it only made it worse. There wasn't enough to go on. If I'd gone blundering in and it turned out there was nothing really there – well, what good would that have done? Not with this other business as well. You'll need all your wits to get through that as it is. You don't need a broken marriage on top of everything else. You've had too much to bear.'

'It's alright.'

'Alright? You're about to be charged with treason. With any

normal kind of problem you could talk about rights and wrongs and help to see sense and find a way through step-by-step. But you're not in a normal kind of problem and you haven't got time. The enemy's in sight and you've got to make a battle appreciation and beat them, by taking the right decisions, quickly. And one thing's abundantly clear in this fog of war – don't expect anything from Sabena now, and don't base a thing on what she says or what she wants. You've got to look to yourself now. Do you understand me?'

'And my children? They should be the main consideration, shouldn't they? If that's the one certainty then everything has to be based on them.'

'Yes, they're your flesh and blood, they depend on you. But that means you've got to survive too.'

'They're too young to be without their mother. I can't do anything which would break that bond, and I can't do anything which puts the blame on her, for their sake and hers. I don't want them in disgrace.'

'For the sake of almighty Jove can't you get it into your thick skull? You've got to act like an officer now, in defence of your own honour. And do what's expected of you. Yes, as the Army expects. It's too complicated otherwise. Keep it simple. Think what the main objective is. Your survival. Do what's necessary to achieve it. Your children will then survive too, and in years to come they will understand. Maintain the honour. Be strong with Sabena. And with Bassus. Don't let them walk all over you. Give the Army what it wants – take the oath, help it to get rid of him. I know it's not what you want to hear, but they're both taking advantage of your ridiculous principles – of you. You have to see that. If you remove yourself from the scene through this obstinacy then she's won completely. Hasn't she? And so's he.'

'Honour, Longinus? And truth? Where does truth come into this? How can you have one without the other?'

'Is that all you can say? Blow the truth! Who knows what truth is anyway? What's the point in being right if you're dead?'

'Well I'm still capable of knowing truth and honour when I see them, Longinus. And until a few months ago I would have agreed with the old ways you're talking about. But not now. Everything's different now. Now I can see where before I was blind. That everything's for a reason, and the reason is goodness and decency, and you can't have goodness without truth, and that evil and wrong-doing bring misery to the world, and their main cause is the pursuit of self, and money, and advantage over our fellow men, and it has to be resisted wherever it raises its ugly head. We can only progress and break the cycle if we behave truthfully as well as honourably, not just to our neighbours but also to our enemies. Especially our enemies.'

'So what's to be done with the likes of Macula and Bassus then? Presumably they're to be left to your god's great plan for them to get their come-uppance in his own good time. Or not. More likely they'll prosper – in fact have their way vindicated, because all they can see is that putting self first pays, and the more ruthlessly and single-mindedly they do it then the more they succeed, and never mind the casualties left strewn behind them, or the ruin of good men like you. But then in your world where weakness is strength and strength weakness, everything can be left to a loving god who sees to it that everything works out for the best somehow. Well it isn't, and doesn't.'

'Sometimes you talk as though you have a special insight, Longinus. Which I respect. But it's not complete. We can't know what God's plan is for us. That's the point. We just have to put our trust in Him. That we'll be guided how to act when the time comes. That's what faith means.'

'Well that time's now, Favonius.'

'And God has already been at work.'

'Really? How?'

'Then why's Macula no more?'

'You tell me! By act of god, I expect.'

Their voices had been rising, faces set hard, stares unflinching.

Favonious broke the silence. 'Well? You tell me.'

'If you think a flight of angels whisked him up and dashed his body against the city wall, you need your head examining.'

'What?!'

They were stood nose-to-nose now.

'Yes, Favonius. I did it.'

'You killed him? Alright. It did occur to me that you might. In my weaker moments. Then I discounted it. Not even you would be so … but typical. For pity's sake. Why?'

'Because somebody had to, you idiot. Because for any scrap of justice in this world sometimes we have to take the law into our own hands. Because if we don't then bad men win and good men suffer. And because if there is a god, Favonius, loving or otherwise – you can be sure he's going to need a little helping hand from time to time.'

He backed off, not knowing what to say, a new and very sudden battery of doubt and disclosure to contend with. Macula, his accuser, done away with – murdered. By the Senior Centurion. By his best friend. Because of him. For him. To protect him. At unimaginable risk. And his commanding officer in an impossible position. Because of him. Who might still do all he could for him if he only gave way. His family torn apart, his wife leaving him and his children's whole future in peril. His Lord and Saviour crucified and life still going on and decisions having to be made. Longinus still before him, by him, with him, magnificent in his pagan strength and loyalty, demanding admiration – and solidarity. It might have been an act of madness on his friend's part, but how could he gainsay its intent or the lifeline it represented? And how could he know his friend, far from taking the law into his own hands, had not instead been doing the Lord's work, acting bravely when all he himself could do was wallow in despair? As the full import sank in, he knew he should feel only gratefulness to this tower of a man stood rock-bound against all disaster, this bastion of strength against chaos and calamity.

'Perhaps. Perhaps He does.'

* * * *

'I haven't told you about yesterday, have I?'

'I heard it was a long one.'

'It certainly was.'

'And of what you said at the end. I heard about that too.'

'It summed up the whole day. Then the next day comes and you wonder if it really could be the life-changing experience you thought. I don't know. You and me have seen too much, haven't we? Some poor blighter gets the cross though he's innocent as a lamb. He won't have been the first and he won't be the last. That's justice for you, and politics, and that thing they call diplomacy. It's a good job you weren't there to see Abbas brought out to the mob. You'd have probably lost it, and then really been in trouble. So there you are, Favonius – that's divine intervention for you. Be grateful. You could even have been OIC execution party, not me. How would you have coped with that?'

'If you say so.'

'I'll never forget it as long as I live. I've never seen soldiers so affected.'

'I can't think of a better man to have done it.'

'Two calls of duty in one day. A little onerous, even for the Senior Centurion. But this is all about you now. Get your thinking cap on. You have to keep the end-point in mind and work out what you have to do to get there. And now you've got me to worry about too – so you'll just have to add some creative dissembling to your other manifest failings, won't you, old man? Am I sorry, Favonius? Just shop Bassus, take the damned oath. And don't let me down.'

'If it were only so simple.'

'I must be going soft.'

'No-one could have gone through anything like that yesterday without it having a profound effect on them.'

'Even a cold-bloodied murderer?'

'Even a cold-bloodied murderer.'

'I'll live with it.'

And he was gone.

Courage, and God's providence, Favonius thought, took many forms.

*   *   *   *

The patch of sunlight lay at his feet, particles of dust floating in the column of light which made it, picked out in minute and haphazard detail against the dark interior. Its progress would be imperceptible, sure nevertheless. Would that his own darkness could be so illumined, the specks which constituted human affairs defined and identified. But you still couldn't catch them. They'd drift about, settling, which they eventually must, where they would; and unstoppable time would move continuously on.

For this was ignorant man, who might ordinarily expect a lifetime in which to find a little wisdom amid the complications of his existence, having to do so in an afternoon. The trap was as replete as any that could have been devised by the old immortals; he was a plaything for their amusement, a victim of doubt and indecision for the pleasure of their wagers. Yet this prison of the mind was of his own making, and reference to the capriciousness of old gods had to be nothing but foolishness. There were no other gods, just the Heavenly Father. And his predicament could not be God's will. It could not be right that his beloved wife was now with another, and his children about to be torn from him. But didn't the Word warn that everything might have to be given up, that a disciple should be prepared to give their all, to follow Him who had now given everything? In his own blundering striving to honour Christ's sacrifice on the cross, was his own true sacrifice not giving up the chance to get back at Sabena's suitor – but giving up Sabena? The thought of life without her was intolerable. Life without her would not be worth living. But have to be lived nonetheless. Was that to be his fate and penance?

He'd never win her back, not by his own efforts anyway. That was obvious. Friends might try and persuade her, but her antipathy toward him and her infatuation with his enemy were too strong. He could have him out the Army but would still lose the children. If by some fluke she were to stay then she was quite capable of remaining sour the rest of their lives, and probably would. Hadn't she said how much better it would be for the children if their mother were happy, in other words away from him? – and she was probably right. There was no doubting she herself would be happier with her beau. Whether that would always be the case wasn't the point – she would never, ever come back. Her pride would stop that, even if one day she might have half a mind to. And perhaps the right and generous thing would be to let her have her way to pursue her new happiness.

How could that be the right outcome when it would leave the children with another man as their father? If they were to be the centre of all considerations then the answer must be, as Longinus had said, to fight for them. She was not to get them. He should make the necessary arrangements, work things out with them as they got older. They weren't so young now they couldn't cope entirely; they'd adjust, get used to it. But no, again. They loved their mother, and it would break their little hearts. He couldn't do that. Wasn't recognizing that fundamental fact what putting them first actually meant? Of course young children needed their mother. It was natural. They'd never forgive him for taking them away. Parted now they might possibly be re-united one day; but more likely he would never see them again. At least they'd get an education – paid for by his enemy, if the man stayed in the Service. But how much would that man ever love them as his own? Could that even be possible – even if it could ever be right?

He didn't want to face these questions any more. They already ran cold in his veins, suffused throughout his body as silent, impotent rage.

Not enough to die for them, that was the very certain answer. The dying had to be done by him, and it was his enemy who wanted him dead. The one who had risked all, was winning and on course for total victory. He might hope that one day the children would come to understand that he'd done his best for them. But then they would never get told the truth, and he couldn't tell them their mother was behaving unconscionably badly, performing mental somersaults in justifying herself – and betraying them all. Somehow her paramour had to be stopped, but how could he accomplish that when before anything else it meant giving in on the oath? And holding out on the oath while his enemy triumphed wasn't brave. It was supine.

And how could this offering of himself, this inability to fight all-out for his marriage, be genuine, or have any real meaning when it was going to happen anyway, his loss and humiliation involuntary? What exactly was the self-sacrifice that he was being led to that was supposedly so noble, reasonable, almost unobjectionable, in which pain and loss had to be volunteered as though in some form of masochism? But faith wasn't faith unless you put it into practice, if need be to the ultimate test.

Perhaps for him there was to be no way out. The specks of dust, disturbed, would swirl about ineffectually, regardless. You made your stand and that's how it all ended. What would his death and disgrace solve? They wouldn't make him a hero, to his family, to his comrades, to anyone else who knew him. They would find it incomprehensible, a pointless gesture, a life needlessly thrown away. Though at least he'd be out of it.

But the call wasn't like that. It was about eternal life, not dying. There was the ideal, which the world would witness, quickly forget and move on in its ignorance. The essence though would have been fulfilled, glory found in courage, peace at the last obtained through faith. There was the inspiration to love God always, to love your neighbour as yourself, to forgive those who trespassed against you, to give and not to count the cost.

But oh what cost! He remembered the discussion with Longinus in the bathhouse – what use now the broken reed? Where were the safe pastures for those who fought the battle, and lost?

He was no nearer, the contradictions too many. And there was no hope.

*   *   *   *

In his torment he thought more of Longinus, and something Yeshua had reportedly said only a few days before: 'Greater love has no man than this, that he lay down his life for his friends.' The immensity of what his own friend had done in living example of this great adjuration had left him feeling more inadequate than grateful; he would have preferred not to be put in another's debt to such a degree, however well-intentioned. But it wasn't something they would ever have talked about. That wasn't Longinus' way. The man of action had acted, taking the most desperate of risks. For him. Longinus had done this for him. For better or for worse, his friend too was now part of the equation, as he'd flippantly acknowledged himself –

and he did have to be kept clear of the consequences somehow. But how? To hold out on the oath would be to keep all hostages held to fortune. To swear would help everything blow over; but then so would his own swift execution. And whatever happened he would never betray his friend. For that he would indeed have to lie and lie again. How easily the truth could be sullied, good intentions stifled in webs of deceit; if only the cause required. The reconciling god would understand, but what of God Almighty, God mighty in battle who could brook no compromise on his commandments? Execution was much the better option. It solved the problem of Longinus and his reckless intervention, and offered escape with some honour from the twin dilemma which had so comprehensively beset him. Oblivion seemed infinitely preferable to this living hell.

And then he imagined the penetrating gaze of Yeshua of Nazareth, and heard again those words spoken face-to-face: 'I will come and heal him. I tell you the truth, I have not found anyone in Israel with such faith. Go! It will be done just as you believed it would.'

And he sank to the hard stone again to pray.

The little patch of sunlight had moved noticeably further on its course.

*   *   *   *

She hadn't wanted to go. The new invitation had bothered her considerably. It was all getting out of hand. What Procula knew, so must the Governor. Instant dismissal could be so close. She'd stay with him. She'd decided that. Nothing they could do would hurt them now. For she loved Brutus. That was the main thing, the only thing to remember. The children would not be a problem. She would keep them, of course. Still, a summons by someone as powerful as the Governor's wife wasn't something you shrugged off with equanimity. Thankfully she'd had time to send word to Brutus, and he'd managed to get to her and reassure her. She wasn't to worry. He'd stay with her, whatever happened. Keep calm. Nothing mattered except their love. It was meant to be. It would work out. They'd be together, always.

*　*　*　*

The Governor's Lady had lost no time. She wasn't altogether sure her husband wouldn't see it as another act of defiance, or whether he would have approved, though he'd alluded to the possibility himself at one point and she would hold him to it. 'The woman might benefit from some pastoral support', he'd said, which might have been unnoteworthy as a well-meant statement devoid of ulterior motive – but where any adherence to the true faith was so beset with danger how could she be sure, either, this was the right thing to be doing? It was excusable to follow his assumption on the spousal connection through: if the husband why not the wife? It's what most married couples did, after all – to a great extent think alike. Not in her case, obviously; you weren't going to get a man like her own husband, arch-sceptic, to fall for anything as naive as the truth, especially if it emanated from a proselytizing mystic who'd none of the benefits of a proper education. She could do no other however but trust her husband and treat his remark as one of genuine concern for the centurion's family, or perhaps conciliation towards her own sensibilities, possibly even both. His own code of honour required protection of the fair sex; what a pity he couldn't show the same side to the Word of God. It was of little moment at present. Favonius Facilis was clearly a different sort to the one she'd married.

But religious conviction and marital familiarity did not always go hand-in-hand. There couldn't be anything too surprising if the centurion's wife had a lesser understanding and commitment to the new way. One had to hope the two of them had fully discussed the subject and what it meant for their lives, and that once the wife had come to see faith being lived out under the guidance of the Holy Spirit she would come to embrace the new way whole-heartedly, ensure her children were brought up in it, and support her husband with quiet devotion. All wives should be dutiful, though that was no bar to being an influential force in their own right; where opportunity arose in good cause there was also obligation to take it, foster it, rejoice in it; it was after all what wishing the best for your loved one entailed. She winced a little as she thought of her own situation, but was determined she

211

wasn't going to be stopped from reaching out. A woman much younger and less experienced than herself had fallen into temptation and needed help, had come into contact with the saving grace of the Word but needed encouragement – and was clearly an uncommitted believer in danger of being lost. Her own obligation was also clear. There had to be an attempt at a meeting of minds, and, with God's help, some gentle direction. The Governor's Lady would do her duty. She would be given strength for the challenge.

'Come in, Sabena. How nice to see you again.'

'Good afternoon, My Lady' said her guest.

'Thank you for coming at short notice. This is a difficult time, don't you agree? – with everyone trying to … get over the shock. We must all stay strong. Tell me – is it true?'

'Is what true, My Lady?'

'That you're having a … a liaison with a certain officer?'

There was no reply.

'Well my dear, don't you think you should desist?'

Sabena did not answer.

'Your silence must be taken as admission, and does you no credit, Sabena. You of all people should realize the full seriousness of what you're doing. Heaven knows, you have all the responsibility of a Roman matron – to your husband, to your children, to your friends and everyone around you, to your class, to your ancestors. And now to so much more – to Him who bids us faithfulness and constancy, who helps us through our travails with the promise of salvation. Think on it. Eternal fulfilment through the Father, by striving for what's right in this life, by seeking guidance and repenting our sins when we go wrong, by resolving to follow His way, whatever that might mean for us.'

Still there was no answer.

'Sabena, look at me. Yesterday we prayed together and asked for help at this terrible time. How can you profess to follow Our Lord and behave like this?'

Still there was silence.

'Do you know what happens to women caught in adultery in this country?'

She was met with a look of unmoved equanimity.

'Well? Then I'll tell you. They're stoned to death, Sabena.'

'And who would throw the first stone?' came the quick reply. 'He forgave that woman, as I recall the story, My Lady.'

'Yes, He did. But what did He then say to her?'

There was another pause.

'Have you lost your faculty of speech? Very well, I can see I'll have to tell you. "Go and sin no more." That's what He said.'

Sabena stood with head up and back straight, and did not answer.

'The adultery is not just yours. It's also your lover's, isn't it? Not your husband's, note. I dare say if it was his with some other woman you'd be taking a very different tone. But let's talk about Brutus Bassus for a moment. Your husband's brother officer. In charge of others, who are expected to place their trust in him, whose careers and even their lives in war depend on that trust. Do you have the faintest idea how disgraceful this is, Sabena? How serious a disciplinary matter it is – as if the Governor hasn't got enough problems? A senior officer behaving like a sewer rat and expecting to get away with it? This is not the way to behave, Sabena. How could you, with your poor husband still recuperating, your poor children, not to mention poor Vergilia. How do you think she feels? It's just too dreadful … Can't you see all the pain you're causing? God knows there's enough of that in the world already.'

'Your Ladyship. I'm not a girl. I'm a grown woman, with a heart of my own. And this is a matter of the heart.'

'Do you think married life is a bed of roses? Do you think it's all sweetness and light between any husband and wife? Between the Governor and me? That we don't have our disagreements and problems, more than I care to remember? Do you think you're the first to know temptation?'

'Of course not, My Lady. My husband is a good man, a fine one in many ways, but he's not always been easy to live with. I … I just don't love him any more. I can't help it. I love Brutus, and I've decided to spend the rest of my life with him.'

'And does your husband love you?'

'Yes, he does, My Lady.'

'Then that should be enough. You are lucky. Don't throw it away. And don't rob your children of their father. Their real father. Their loving father.'

'It's not that simple. I can't expect you to understand. It's not just that I don't love him any more – I can't bear him being with me. I can't bear being in the same room. You don't know what it's like.'

'Ough.' Claudia shivered. 'Yes, that's what the other man or woman does to a marriage, isn't it? It's rarely what goes on between husband and wife itself that's the problem. They can handle that. It's the interloper, the comer-in, the speculator, the chancer who wheedles their way in, who causes the damage, who sows the doubt, offers the possibility which becomes the great alternative, the promise of happiness, no matter the trail of misery and hurt to everybody else. That's how the common little problem gets out of proportion and insuperable in the mind, how mature love changes to indifference and then to hate, and it's all so horrible and stupid and very very unkind.'

Claudia checked herself. 'And what about your children? Have you thought about them?'

'Of course I have.'

'I suppose you think they'll quickly accept it, and that everything will always be fine in your nice new family.'

'Brutus is very good with them. They like him and I've no doubt they'll soon come to love him as their father.'

'That may be, Sabena. But do not deceive yourself. Children can appear happy enough, but there's no certainty what really goes on in their minds or what problems you're setting in store for them as they grow up, indeed throughout their lives. Children need their parents, both of them. Unless someone's an absolute monster, in which case separation may well be the only solution, our blood-ties must always come first. Children are a great responsibility and a great blessing. No-one with any decency would ever want to break into that, Sabena. It's unfair on the cheated spouse, and it's unfair on the poor children who have to put up with such an intrusion in their lives. You'll be depriving them of what should be every child's birthright, to be brought up by their mother and father in their family home, of whatever estate and in whatever circumstances. That's the sanctity of the family, Sabena. That's the sanctity of the home. That's the sanctity of marriage. And that's what you're now in the act of defiling. Two marriages ruined! I think it's cruel, and monstrous and ... unspeakable.

She pressed on. 'Then there are the practicalities. Have you really thought about the practicalities, Sabena? Well let me point a few out to you. You've convinced yourself you've got to run off with this man, into an uncertain future, possibly into penury though I dare say the likes of Bassus would find their feet soon enough, subjecting your children to unnecessary pain in their young lives and bringing all of you into disrepute in all but the lowest of society, whilst your husband, your true husband, who loves and needs you, you abandon. And you, who have had the singular privilege of encountering the Lord, in whom you have professed – you really are behaving shamefully.

'And on top of all this, do you realize your husband is in great danger? If he's ever discovered as a believer he'll be accused of dishonouring the gods. Any decent woman at a time like this would stand by her man – how can you desert him now? Well I can't say how this will end up, Sabena. You're giving the Army a real problem, you put your children's welfare at enormous risk, you betray the good man who is your husband, and you let our Lord Yeshua down badly. In His name, stop it now.'

Sabena too was angry. 'So personal happiness is to have no part in this? Do you think I haven't thought about this and very little else for months, tossing and turning and twizzling my hair all day like a nervous teenager? How can it be wrong for human beings to seek what little true happiness is to be found in this life, to recognize true love when you find it and let that love find its course? Nobody wants pain, either for others or themselves. But love is a matter of the heart, you can't stop it and nobody else can share it. It's between two people and them alone. Nobody can understand who hasn't experienced it themselves, and their children certainly can't, but neither should they be expected to. I don't deny it affects others in my case, but we get so few chances to find true happiness, and we only get one life. Don't we have to take them when we know it's right for ourselves, and in the long run for everyone else as well?'

'Your life, Sabena? What of the life eternal from which you're now excluding yourself? You talk of love and happiness yet what I hear is obstinacy and pride and foolishness. In the long run, as you call it, everything is vanity and shallowness and disillusion, unless we take positive steps to live our lives differently, in the way Our Lord offers. Our feelings are so easily misled. The human heart is fickle – only constancy and self-discipline and faith can help us at times like this, until we can look back and realize we were in grievous error, and that true love is the one that endures and wins in the end. You've been snared, Sabena, and you must start listening to those who would help you.'

'Will that be all, My Lady?'

'I cannot but tell you I'm very disappointed. And quite distressed. Only yesterday you and I prayed together for help and guidance as our Lord and Saviour died on the cross. Does that mean nothing to you? How could you? How could you?! How can you ever presume to our Father in heaven that you believe and trust in Him if you clearly have no intention of obeying His obvious will? You know that adultery is a mortal sin yet you are prepared to perjure your soul.'

Sabena stayed calm. 'I've never been able to believe like Marcus. And to be honest seeing him on his knees praying never made me very comfortable. From the beginning I tried so hard. I wasn't brought up that way. We kept the household traditions but nobody ever talked about religion. It was just what everyone did, without thinking, by custom. If others wanted to take it more seriously that was up to them, but I never could stand self-righteousness and hypocrisy. When we married I accepted that Marcus was more spiritual than me, and after his experience with the preacher I could see that he was deeply affected. So was I to begin with, until the doubts began to come.

'People do get over sickness sometimes, quite quickly, My Lady. Nobody will ever prove what happened to our servant wasn't just coincidence. So I don't know, and now the preacher's dead I think his ideas may have gone with him. I try to keep an open mind. If his message has lived on I don't see why that should be against Brutus and me. He didn't mean to hurt his wife either – they just grew apart, like we did.   Anyway we took our wedding vows under the Roman gods, and I don't suppose you approve very much of them now, do you?   And who has the right to say what's for the greater good?   And I include my children's future when I say that.   I have every right to follow my own judgment, as well as my heart.   It's a private matter, My Lady.   And I think you know that.'

Their exchange had reached its limit.

'Then you won't pray with me now, Sabena?'

'I don't think I can.   You would only want me to ask your god to find a way of staying in this broken marriage.'

'Not even just for help and guidance, so that the best may come about, whatever it might be?'

'There's really no point.'

'Then I shall pray for you Sabena, alone, and may God have mercy on you.   You may be excused.'

'You do know my husband's been arrested for refusing the oath to Augustus, don't you?'

'You'd ... you'd better go.'

'Thank you, My Lady.'

And as she left the room Sabena turned momentarily to see her interlocutor collapsed against a console table.

She did not stop.

*   *   *   *

It took a while for Claudia, alone and over-wrought, to recover.   She wasn't used to cool defiance, especially from a woman much junior in age and status.   A few weeks before, before her conversion, she would have castigated Sabena for her insolence;   now all she could do was rue her own failed powers of persuasion, even to seek the Lord's help together.   Nothing at that moment held any prospect of getting Sabena to listen, even less to offer any hope of a reconciliation with her husband.   It was too late now, a salutary lesson in the perils facing the seed, how some would fall on stony ground, set root a little only to wither away when temptation intervened – indeed, how this seemed to apply to most. Thus, but for the goodness of God, went the human race, for Sabena had been right about the heart and its wayward properties. Perhaps many years hence this headstrong young woman would look back with regret; perhaps not. Those for whom the seed had found more fertile ground were not to be disheartened but believe that all things would come well in the end, which included the welfare of those who would deny. She would live in hope. Meanwhile she would honour her promise and pray for her, and continue to do so as long as she was bidden.

The primary cause of her discomfiture however was not Sabena's steely resistance but her parting remark. Now this! Poor Favonius – isolated, deserted, and now without doubt in fear for his life. Why had she only found out like this? How long had this been going on? What oath to Augustus? When? That parade, that dinner. Why hadn't she been told by that devious, infuriating husband of hers, who would know of her immediate concern for a fellow-believer very well? How long had she got to front up to him?

Please Yeshua, save Favonius Facilis.

*   *   *   *

Veranius was pacing his office. The facts were as plain as they were going to get. The chances of Macula's death being entirely unconnected with Facilis' refusal to take the oath were almost nil, he reasoned, but with principal witness and accuser gone there was no imperative for a full-scale prosecution of the case unless and until ordered. On the other hand he couldn't be seen to be inactive; low-key enquiries would have to continue as a precaution against the likelihood of official proceedings being instigated, and any noted lack of initiative on his part in the interim. If there were high-level machinations going on behind the scenes, possibly going back all the way to power struggles in Rome, it was not at all certain how matters might develop. The whole thing might be quietly dropped, in which case perhaps the least of any significance actually done the better; or there'd be a full-scale investigation and the distinct possibility of wholesale recrimination – a potential career-stopper, or even worse. Important as all this was, it wasn't the most urgent thing on his mind.

The oath affair could not wait. He'd got face in it, his own reputation well and truly at stake now. If he was totally honest with himself he would acknowledge some regret in forcing the pace earlier; it had chiefly been an attempt to stamp his authority and impress the Governor rather than urgently to contain the risk of contagion; another day or two in that respect wouldn't have made any difference. He'd decreed the formal interview and ultimatum, though, and now had to see it through. With so much else going on a further adjournment might have been excusable, but a direct order was a direct order, and his own integrity, his own future the most important considerations of all. Nothing had been said to his knowledge about these events to link them or question his handling of the matter, but it couldn't be long before there was open speculation, and while attention in one's direction was usually to be courted this was definitely not such a moment. He can't have been the only one to have put two and two together. A connection between Macula's demise and another officer would surprise others as it had disappointed him, but speculation would become hard to resist, and when that officer was from his own cohort he'd better look sharp. The Officer Commanding Century V had no right to be causing all this trouble. Macula had been conscientiously doing his duty; he'd been silenced because of his revelations on the refusal to take the loyal oath to Augustus Caesar by this individual, who was a convert to the troublesome sect of Yeshuites. What more obvious connection did anyone need to find his guilt?

He'd been slow to realize it, but now the notion was in his head he was having difficulty dispelling it. Indeed, he had now reached the conclusion it must be incontrovertible. Few things were counter-intuitive: it was the most obvious explanation that was the likeliest, and this case was unlikely to be an exception. Of course OC V had the motive; so much couldn't be denied. All these claims about his new-found religion, how it was supposedly all about goodwill to men and eternal life in a place called heaven – people would go to any lengths to achieve their aims with such ideology. So long as extremists acted in the name of their god they could convince themselves of almost anything, including, incredibly, immunity from all harm, even on the battlefield. If that wasn't an indication of insanity to the point of self-destruction he didn't know what was, and the parallel with the centurion's single-minded protestations regarding his tender conscience and disregard for the consequences didn't seem unreasonable. Religious fervour and delusion went together rather closely.

And Facilis probably had more than sufficient opportunity to do the deed. How limp of his commanding officer to have merely confined him to the Mess like that, trusting an officer's honour when it was his sanity that was the real problem and the fact he wouldn't be capable of acting rationally. But no excuse – Facilis was responsible for his own behaviour. He'd have to confront him outright, then, and he mustn't shirk it. The original ultimatum would be enforced. In fact it would be quite interesting to see how the man's conscience coped with a charge of homicide to add to his other difficulties. And how remiss of that same commanding officer not to have been more robust in pursuing detailed enquiries of the livers-in, and every single individual in that part of the fort, right down to the humblest slave, on their whereabouts and recollections of that night. He'd have to get on to that one too, and insist the Senior Centurion conducted them personally. Meanwhile he must not delay proceedings; there was already plenty of rope to hang the fellow, who if he were the villain thoroughly deserved his fate, and anything concrete emerging from more official investigations would only be seen to reinforce CO Second Italians' prescience. Was that going too far? In the unlikely absence of further revelations emerging from wider enquiries then there might be a case for re-assessment, though that seemed inconceivable. There'd be no comfortable mess quarter next time, just a secure guardroom cell. He'd finally lost patience with Favonius Facilis. The Macula link had to be pursued. It was probably the only way of getting to the bottom of the whole tiresome and inconvenient business. And, he couldn't help but think, in disposing of Facilis his commanding officer would be credited with stopping religious sedition among the troops, and solving and avenging the heroic tribune's death, in one concurrent master-stroke. It was a tempting possibility.

To summon the Senior Centurion again, therefore – if he could be found. He did have a habit of disappearing just when you wanted him. As the senior liver-in he'd already have the best handle for the obvious line of enquiry. He'd surely see the priority here – to assure Garrison Headquarters that everything possible was being done behind the scenes, that no stone was being left unturned in the hunt for the killer. And no-one was better able to get to the truth than the mercurial Longinus, who always got results – providing he was properly managed.

It was put in hand forthwith.

So back to Facilis, who had to be dealt with as warned. Hadn't he told him fair and square, that he, his commanding officer, would not be responsible if he refused to desist from his stubbornness?

The doubts came crowding in again. Where were magnanimity, his loyalty to a competent and principled subordinate, his own sense of honour? Suspect or not, he owed it to Facilis to be as fair as summary military proceedings allowed, and he would have to be careful his own conduct could stand the light of a full-blown court-martial should it ever come to that. The centurion's record of service would stand him in good stead. He would take into account therefore the high regard in which he personally had habitually held him – but perhaps not too much; and put aside the obvious issues arising from this latest and rather alarming train of thought on his probable guilt – but not overlook them entirely. The oath was the immediate issue, notwithstanding other considerations. Benefit of the doubt was always to be respected, and to that had to be added the unfortunate difficulties of his marriage, though these couldn't be a mitigating factor in determining guilt – and wouldn't be either in the award of sentence, which was almost certain to be execution. It pained him to see a good man down, in dire trouble and now with his wife on the brink of final desertion. Running off with another of his officers – another problem he could do without. Two days ago the Cohort was riding high. Now all of a sudden it seemed as if all its unseen woes had been waiting to gang up on him. Very well. They would be mastered. Command would be exercised in the customary way. The important thing was to be decisive, always decisive, especially now the Cohort's affairs were bound to be the object of far too wide a public.

It was too bad if Facilis' loss would be Bassus' gain, but what more could he do to persuade him? Bassus would be out the Army if he had his way, and the Governor would probably agree, though the bounder would take the wife no doubt. It would be Facilis who would lose so much more, but what did career, gods, wife matter when life itself would be forfeit too? Not a bad haul for someone determined to destroy himself. At least he was doing it in style, with no half-measures. Ah well, you could take the horse to water, but you couldn't make it drink. All the fellow had to do was drop this absurd posturing and take the oath. It would be so easy. He might subsequently come unstuck over a murder accusation, but one thing at a time. But if he would not recant then his commanding officer would have done all he could; conscience would be clear. The centurion had to take the consequences of his refusal to be reasonable on his own head. Action had to be taken now, before HQ got any further involved. If it was taken out of his hands it wasn't going to be due to any failing of his own.

He had to do something.

Anything.

*　*　*　*

'That you, Veranius?'

The garrison commander was looking ebullient. 'The Secretary has some news for you. Tell him, Secretary.'

'It is what we suspected, Tribune. It looks as though Macula died in the Antonine. Murdered, to be precise.'

'Oh? Howso?'

'One of the guards has testified to that effect. For a suitable reward, you understand.'

'One of my soldiers, you mean. You had no right to go poking your nose in my command.'

'There was a cart that left in the early hours. He did not know with or by whom, just that it was out for less than half an hour and had one occupant, the driver. In and out, with no load that he could see.'

'That doesn't prove much.'

'Prove, Tribune? Regrettably it was not searched, either on exit or return. One understands that is not normal procedure. But it does indicate the likely turn of events, does it not? The murder takes place in the fort. The body is extricated in the dead of night and dumped in the city. The easiest way of disposal, if you come to think about it. Troublesome locals get the blame. All very convenient.'

'Certainly feasible, Secretary. I'm sure Veranius would agree.'

'Thank you, Camp Commandant. So we have to ask ourselves who would be in a position to take a cart from the stables and drive it through the main gate in the middle of the night without anybody paying any attention – except for our public-spirited sentry. And then coming back and reversing the procedure. It would have to be someone pretty senior to do that, one would think.'

'Not necessarily, Secretary. If the men got together on something it would be very difficult for anyone else to know. I do know my own men.'

'Even the guard commander, Tribune? Surely he'd know what was going on?'

'The corporal's not going to wake the duty sergeant just for one vehicle going through in the night, much less the duty officer.'

'But all movements in silent hours are supposed to be recorded.'

'No. Patrols are logged, but it's so rare for vehicles to be about after-hours that it hardly ever arises. But I did make enquiries, and no-one knew anything.'

'They do now, Tribune.'

'These are my men, Seneccio, and I demand to know this man's name and exactly who you've been speaking to.'

'Oh, you need not worry about that, Tribune. It has all been done officially, through the Camp Commandant here.'

Veterus shifted on his feet. 'Yes. It did have to be done, given the circumstances.'

'Well I'm not happy. And I don't suppose the Governor will approve of this sort of interference, either.'

'Your concern for the proprieties does you credit, Tribune Veranius. You may be prefect of your unit but you appear to wish to imply your soldiers were individually interrogated in a concerted effort to undermine your authority. Let me assure you there was nothing of the kind. I merely – in person, I might add – let it be known there might be a certain small inducement to duty and that the authorities should be informed accordingly – and surprise, surprise – a most welcome response was soon forthcoming. All it seemed to require was a little persuasion to jog the memory. And you are fully aware, I believe, of the Governor's subscription to that sound principle of leadership, of the means justifying the end?'

'And you believe this soldier, do you, Seneccio – with his recollections after inducement? What's his name? Is there a witness to his statement?'

'Let us say we have no reason not to. The man was not actually on gate guard at the time – he just happened to be stretching his legs when he saw the cart leave, and out of interest decided to stay awake and await its return.'

'And the rest of the guard? What did they all have to say about this claimed observation?

'Senior public servants should not have to concern themselves with minutiae, Tribune. Their word is sufficient.'

Veterus interjected. 'We're going to have to take it at face value, Veranius. It's all we've got to go on. Your men might have been up to something, but the most likely implication on this evidence is that it's your officers we've got to look to. Someone with enough clout to demand silence. And one in particular – Favonius Facilis. With the obvious motive of silencing his accuser – because he did have an accuser, didn't he? The man's clearly unhinged. His wife's as good as left him, he's lost his marbles to a lot of foreign gobbledegook, decided to chuck his career in and generally behave like a madman. Seems an open-and-shut case to me.'

The secretary's self-satisfaction was bad enough; this was the last straw. The old dotard had reached the right conclusion too soon, and it was almost enough to bring out the defensive. The pair of them were encroaching on his space, his officers, his authority. There was no point in arguing though. To take them on he would need to immediately escalate the matter again to the Governor, with the significant risk this time that he'd take their side – after the Macula incident and all the discussions which must have been going on in this building since then he was probably firmly on it already. An alternative would be to throw himself into the demeaning business of finding out personally what really went on at the main gate that night, but with the chances of getting to the truth almost nil. Neither prospect was attractive. Damn it. Damn them all. Damn these two interfering old time-servers in particular. The Cohort was being dragged through the mud, and him with it. But all wasn't quite lost. On their own admission there hadn't been an actual identification of the cart driver, or an assertion there was anything visible in the bottom of the cart that could have been taken for a body, so with luck the vital lead wouldn't materialize. The price of fish hadn't changed, whatever they might claim. Anyway hadn't he beaten them to it? Hadn't he already decided Facilis was expendable? At least the damage would be minimized, with no loose ends. As for these impudent old upstarts it was best his tongue stayed held firmly in mouth for the time being. He'd have his revenge later.

'Good day, gentlemen. I've an appointment back at the Antonia.' And with that he left, as coolly as he could.

* * * *

'So what do you think, Camp Commandant?'

'I reckon we let him put his centurion back in order as he thinks best, and carry on.'

'Ah the military mind! So straightforward. So admirably simple, one might say. Our duty, Camp Commandant, is to support the Governor, in every way necessary and by every means necessary. We cannot just, as you put it, carry on, as though nothing has happened. The most pressing imperative, if we know what is good for us, is getting an objective and timely report to Rome and Damascus on how our most distinguished military tribune, albeit a decidedly high-handed one, has ended up dead on the Governor's watch. Yesterday it might have been how a Jewish revolt threatened to sweep us all away, but thanks to some good statecraft that threat has dissipated, at least for now. Today it is one very deceased young wearer of the purple that is the problem. Our job is to find out who did it, and if we cannot do that then we have to offer the most plausible explanation, the one that is most likely to satisfy the inevitable outcry and renewed questioning of the Governor's competence – and ours with it. Facilis and his cult are the obvious culprits. And we cannot just lamely report we might have a suspect – we will have to report the facts without exception and say what we intend to do about them. We cannot prevaricate. Personally I would have thought summary execution a reasonable option. It would show decisiveness, put an end to further contamination from that particular source, and encourage any other likely defaulters to remember their priorities. And it is within the Governor's powers.'

'We're doing our best, Secretary. Meanwhile Veranius has to carry on, doesn't he? He's got a unit to run. Are you suggesting he goes for a death sentence immediately? Because if so you'd better start running after the Boss now. We'd need top-cover on that, and before everyone's committed.'

'Private secretaries do not run anywhere, Camp Commandant. But you do not deny a certain utility in my suggestion – a timely solution, plus an end to the Yeshua nonsense.'

'Which seems to be what you're most concerned with, Secretary.'

'As a matter of fact, Camp Commandant – no. Oh yes, the cult needs crushing, and any servant of the State foolish enough to associate with it must be eradicated equally expeditiously. Macula was on to it, discovered too much and paid the price. But here is the point, Camp Commandant. Even if Facilis is not the guilty party – which one reiterates seems most unlikely – he provides a felicitous answer to our little problem. Rome is to be assuaged with remarkable economy if we merely join the dots. Very well. There is no need to bother them with any philandering – that dog can lie sleeping. Among his other duties their agent stumbles upon gross disloyalty in the officer corps directly attributable to a dangerous revolutionary movement, bravely reports his findings and is brutally murdered for his pains. The suspect – the only suspect – is a follower of said sect whose guilt is proven from his own mouth. Guilty as charged, one has to say. How could Rome not fail to accept such a plausible explanation? And we could all get back to some much-needed normality. That must be our clear priority. What more do you want?'

'You make it sound too easy, Secretary.'

'As I say, Camp Commandant – soldiers like simple solutions, do they not? Is that one not simple enough?'

* * * *

'May I interrupt you for a moment.'

'Of course, My Dear. I need a break anyway.'

They sat on the couch looking through to the garden courtyard, now all in shade. 'You've been crying again.'

'I know. Feeble woman.'

'Don't be silly. It's a difficult time for all of us, but you … well, you have troubles of your own, I know.'

'Yes. I suppose I do. I can't pretend to be immune. It is, I suppose … all to do with Yeshua.'

'Define "all", My Dear.'

'I saw Sabena again. You know, Favonius Facilis' wife.'

'Good. How did it go?'

'Not very well. It's so difficult when people won't believe... I, I didn't mean to say it quite like that. Sorry.'

He avoided looking reproachful. 'It's alright, I understand. I did assume she was another … devotee. Given the marital situation there had to be complications.'

'I thought she was too. And I think she truly was, once.'

'You know how very personal religion can be for many people – difficult, even. We can't expect everyone to see things as we ourselves. Especially with something that's new and strange. How is she coping with the family upheavals? That's rather more important, I would suggest.'

'All too well, I should think. That's the problem. She's stubborn. I couldn't get through to her, so all I can do is pray. But she's not the concern. It's her husband and the children I'm worried about. He's …

he's stayed strong in the faith. I know that's not what you want to hear, but I can say it now, now there are no secrets between us. Appius, I'm so worried for him.'

'It's hard not to feel some sympathy, I'll admit.'

'Do you really mean that?'

'In some ways he's to be admired, My Dear. As well as pitied.'

'I can't tell you how much you saying that means to me.'

'It doesn't do to identify too closely with people who bring their own problems upon themselves.'

'How can I not?   It's my duty, as you have yours.   His life is in danger, isn't it?   And she's not helping – she might have done once, but not now this horrible Bassus is out in the open.   And I can't see Veranius sticking his neck out either – weak, silly man.'

'Not the sharpest, I agree.'

'I feel so useless.   I've prayed so hard but there seems no hope. Unless ... unless you can do something to save him, Appius.'

'And how do you propose I do that, My Dear?'

'There must be something you can do.'

'I can't interfere in the military justice system any more than the civil, even if I was so minded. You know the law has to take its course.'

'Like it did yesterday, you mean?   And a good man gets done away with?   Put to death by cruel and wicked men?   I don't mean you, of course – but, you know ... And for what?'

'Don't let's go into all that again, Claudia.'

'Don't make the same mistake, Appius.   Hasn't there been enough killing? Show some clemency. Choose life. Please.'

'The commanding officer has to exercise summary justice within his powers or forward the case for court-martial.'

'Why can't he just dismiss it?'

'He could, but he'd be very brave to do so in the circumstances of this case. It's a capital offence. We can't have the Army full of officers and men who won't swear allegiance.'

'To a dead emperor, not the live one! I can understand your difficulty if it came to confirming the sentence – which would be death as a matter of course, wouldn't it – what else for standing up for what you believe in? But why can't you just give the word to Veranius to quietly drop it, or go on leave or something? It would soon be all forgotten.'

'I suspect not, My Dear.'

'Or is it Rome again, and what they want?'

'Claudia, if his wife won't tell Facilis to withdraw, why don't you go and tell him yourself? I'll make the arrangements for you to meet. See if you can work your powers of persuasion on him.'

'You didn't have to say it like that.'

There was silence.

'Not so easy, is it?'

'But you're the Governor! You could order Veranius to back off. Just tell him what he's got to do, what you require. And don't worry about your career.'

'I don't think I have much of that left to worry about. People in positions of responsibility must be left to their best judgment and conscience.'

'So they're all quite ready to have another innocent man's blood on their hands. I bet if anything cropped up which affected *them* deeply enough they'd soon adjust their precious consciences.'

'I think you do the Army a disservice, My Dear. I know you're distraught. Veterus is in a quandary, Veranius is in a quandary, I'm sure Facilis is in a quandary – we all are. But we have to let the law take its course.'

'I think Favonius Facilis knows exactly what he must do. It's all you others who won't put natural justice first. Take the easy way out and get rid of him, then. Let Bassus take his wife and children. And let this good man, one of your officers, be silenced once and for all.'

'Oh dear.'

'Doesn't it mean anything to you that I try to be my Teacher's follower too?!'

'Yes My Dear, it does. It also means a great deal of concern to me. You still don't seem to realize how this new-found interest of yours impacts on my position here. How I have to pretend not to notice the reactions of my staff, all too plain despite their efforts to save me embarrassment. I am Caesar's representative and servant. I try to do my job, which includes upholding our state religion. I try to maintain the standards expected by my superiors and the people we govern. I try to keep the peace. I try to promote prosperity. I endeavour to be fair to all men. I didn't persecute these Nazarenes, because to me the Jews' attempts to paint them as challenging the Emperor's authority were clearly wrong. But I cannot be held responsible for anyone who in following their leader creates difficulties for themselves with their own people. Don't you see how your behaviour puts me in an impossible position? The Prefect's own wife! Not only that, you're asking me to show favouritism to an officer who's got himself in a mess of his own making, and for the very same reason. In fact in an even bigger one now. Licinius Macula's body was discovered in the city yesterday, before the disturbances. So who do you take to be the obvious chief suspect? And I am expected, quite rightly, to get a report to Rome on the demise of their wonder-boy in the fastest possible time, on top of my latest little contretemps with Caiaphas. You do see how it's all related, don't you? And you think I might be able to seek guidance on this Gordian knot of a centurion from this god of yours – who seems to have quite a lot of explaining to do already?'

She said quietly: 'That's terrible about Macula. I don't know about him. I do know about Favonius Facilis, though I've barely met him. I can understand what he must be going through. A man of conscience, something most of his detractors wouldn't have the first idea about. And yes, I do. I do think guidance is there to be requested. God's mercy and guidance is available to all, but there has to be some humility. There has to be some belief.'

'Your teacher's dead, Claudia. There's nothing there now, if ever there was. It's all over.'

'It isn't for the highest and mightiest of all though, is it? – the rulers of the whole civilized world, who think they deserve to be gods themselves?'

'If you mean Augustus – he was unique. Is, I should say.'

'He'll just be the start of it. Where else does megalomania end but deification?'

'You know it's all pretty meaningless to me.'

'Perhaps one day you too will come to see. If only you'd let me talk about the Lord to you, and pass on what I've learned. You might be surprised.'

'I think you might be surprised too, My Dear.

'Save him, Appius. You didn't Yeshua. Perhaps you couldn't. But don't let them stop you doing what's right now. Save him.'

*　　*　　*　　*

The Adjutant was in attendance and marched him in.

Fastened to the wall behind the Commanding Officer was the Standard, redolent of so much noble memory and sentiment now made painful, the olive wreath from the parade still draped over the burnished eagle, its leaves showing signs of desiccation, the new gold-bound Victory roundel lustrous in the interior light.

He was not to dwell on pain and difficulty – but resolution.

Tribune Veranius was seated behind his desk wearing his helm and full field uniform. 'Centurion Favonius Facilis, are you ready to take the oath to Augustus Deified?'

He stood silently at attention.

Veranius got to his feet, motioned to the Adjutant who moved around to the front and handed him the Standard. Veranius took it by the staff and presented it as though on the parade ground.

'Centurion Facilis, it is my direct order that you now salute the Cohort Standard and take the oath of allegiance to the Divine Augustus. These are the words you are to use – "I pledge my undying loyalty to Augustus Caesar, Imperator, The Deified One".'

After all his agonies of indecision there was one thought only in his head. It was not of any god. It was not of conflicted loyalty to the Army. It was not even of his family. It was how to protect his friend, who had risked his life to save his. He no longer had to ask himself how to do it. To recant and take the oath would save his own life on one count and give himself a chance of surviving a murder charge on another; it would also divert attention and give his friend some cover to remaining unsuspected. To hold out and refuse would mean near-certain safety for his friend but near-certain death for himself. He hadn't asked his friend to do what he had done. Nor was he to let himself question his friend's motives for what he had done, or its consequences. That would be a betrayal. His friend had done what any good friend would believe was for the best. That was all he needed to know.

There was nothing more to think, or say, or do.

'I will say this one more time. If you still refuse you will be charged with disobeying a direct order, namely failing to take the loyal oath when legally ordered to do so, and placed under immediate close arrest pending court-martial.'

Favonius, drained, near-oblivious, remained tightlipped.

So help him any god that would, or could.

*　　*　　*　　*

There was a knock at the door.

'What is it? I'm taking orders.'

A voice came from without. 'It's urgent from HQ, Sir.'

'Then wait, damn you!'

The door was knocked again, louder.

'I'm not to wait, Sir. Those were my orders.'

'By Jupiter! Very well.'

The door opened. A scared soldier cast a puzzled look, recovered quickly.

'Well man, what is it that's so bloody urgent?'

'It's from the Camp Commandant, Sir. He said you're to stop whatever you're doing, Sir, and report to the Praetorium immediately, Sir. The Governor wishes to see you immediately, Sir. And he said I was to tell you again: "Whatever you're doing", Sir!'

The Prefect scowled darkly at the Adjutant and then at Favonius; passed the Standard back to the Adjutant without a word; and stormed out. The Adjutant, turning to him blankly before gathering his wits, said: 'Commanding Officer's Orders adjourned, Sir.'

*　　*　　*　　*

Veterus stood waiting at the top of the stairway, great hairy forearms folded firmly across barrel chest.

'The Governor's called for you, Veranius.'

'I suppose you know what it's about?'

'Of course I bloody do. I'm the garrison commander, which you seem to forget sometimes. And in case you're wondering, Seneccio is fully in the picture too. We do work as a team in this HQ, you know.'

'Then perhaps you can tell me what this is all about?' he asked in his best mock-polite manner.

'It's nothing you haven't been acquainted with already.'

'I was just taking orders, Veterus. That's a serious breach of military etiquette which I'm sure the Governor would not have contemplated for one moment.'

'Well you'd better raise your concern with him, hadn't you?'

'Give me a clue.'

'I don't suppose you've had many centurions to charge this afternoon. For some strange reason the Governor seems to place a lot of value on your advice. That's all I'm telling you. Now I suggest you get yourself to him tootsweet. You know where to find him.'

And as an afterthought: 'Well, did he?'

'Did he what?'

'What do you think?'

'No. Your runner came at the very moment of truth.'

If that was the way the old fool wanted it then he'd get the same treatment back, he muttered to himself as he found the familiar corridor. Trying to show off like an old passed-over ape, indeed. Demob-happy and pleased to think he might get one over a knight of the Roman Empire, that's what Veterus' problem was. It mattered not – class should never stoop to inferior levels and coarseness. He was now on immeasurably more important business with a fellow member of the honourable equestrian order, who understood the bond of gentlemen and how things should be done. It was urgent; he was angry; and he wasn't going to have his style cramped by anybody. Not even the Governor. But he'd better have a response ready this time, just in case what he was feeling now was all bravado. It didn't matter to what, exactly. Flexibility was the name of the game. He had a career to pursue. He was alive to every possibility. And it was good to be in the thick of it.

* * * *

The Governor rose for him, as was his habit. 'Veranius Pulcher! How good to see you. I've got an idea I'd like to tell you about.'

THE DELIBERATION – I

They'd supped well. The servants were gone, the lamps topped up and the flagons well charged.

They were the select. Not Petronius, who was on duty at the tomb. Not Cogitus, who was ill and anyway too dull. And certainly not Brutus, for obvious reasons. The chosen ones would do nicely – the right balance, the right mix, they all knew each other as well as brothers, and with a bit of luck would be suitably argumentative when it came to the substance. A modicum of self-congratulation might be in order. He'd managed to assemble the best of his team for the task in hand, the intellectual challenge of which might prove best not under-estimated. If it could be done they were the ones to do it. They were his officers, under his leadership, which gratifyingly seemed to have a measure of the Governor's confidence after all; and here they were, his quorum of three, apparently relaxed and behaving as professional colleagues should, in friendly if competitive cooperation, almost as though nothing out of the ordinary had been happening around them these last few days. Even Facilis. Surprisingly so, he thought, given his situation. He must have realized his reprieve was permanent, though nothing had been said on that score. After such a lucky escape it would be excusable if a little elation didn't find its way into the average psyche, nevertheless who was the man in that position who wouldn't want to think very carefully about what he had to say next, particularly one already carrying a burden of introspection, when what was needed now was engagement and exchange? Hadn't the Governor said: 'I specifically want Facilis there. I want him there because his experience will be unique. Without him we may as well not bother'? An extraordinary decision, he'd thought, and no way to treat a commanding officer of his standing so arbitrarily, but he'd been in no position to protest, and, he had to admit, could now see the point. He'd better get on with it.

'Gentlemen, you may be wondering why I've called you together like this. Well now I can now tell you. We're not just here to enjoy a little get-together after a few trying days, though may I just say how much I appreciate your personal contribution to the Cohort's conduct of late – and how pleasing it is to have your company this evening.'

There was a quiet 'hear, hear.'

'No, we have some work to do. I've invited you because we have a small matter to decide. I say small, but actually it's rather pressing.'

He looked round at their politely expectant faces. Under the mask there would be steely alertness, quiet confidence not easily fazed, self-belief undaunted. There was nothing new under the sun.

'The Governor wants our advice.'

If such an unusual statement excited much interest it didn't show. The wine had passed agreeably. The threshold for the breaching of phlegmatic self-assurance was not yet crossed.

'He wants to know whether we should relieve the tomb of its occupant.'

*　　*　　*　　*

He now had their full attention.

'Should we secrete the body of Yeshua of Nazareth away from its resting place? Tonight?'

*　　*　　*　　*

That's what the Governor had said to him, word for word. Stunned silence had been his reaction too. What could possibly have motivated the Commander-in-Chief to consider such a thing?

'Let me explain, Veranius.' And the Governor had followed on from their previous conversation, and explained.

And he'd concluded: 'We haven't got very long. The prophecy was three days. Call on me any time of the night if you need me. I mean that. Any time. And in any case as soon as you've come to a decision.'

And he'd said 'Yes, Your Excellency. I understand.'

And he'd thought, as they all did now, there was after all something very new under the sun.

THE DELIBERATION – II

Someone whistled under their breath.

Longinus was the first to speak, as befitted his rank. 'There's rather more to this question than meets the eye, isn't there? If I've got it right, Prefect, we've got to go into every aspect of the last few days – weeks – in some depth.'

'Yes, we have.'

'Of all those things one doesn't talk about in the mess – politics, religion, women – well, not them. Oh, sorry. That was careless of me.' He glanced in his friend's direction.

'Yes, Senior Centurion. But there's nothing frivolous about this. We're not here for a discussion in the abstract. We're here to reach a conclusion based on the facts and sound argument in relation to the practical courses open, and keep it as objective as we can. Personal belief might underpin our outlook and inclinations, insofar as we have any freedom in these things, especially in such a matter as this where politics, religion and ethics meet – but we might find ourselves having to adjust our preconceptions, or put them aside altogether. The order of the day is open-minded perspicacity tempered with shrewd discernment, for which I know you're more than qualified. What's to be done, and why? Those are the questions we must address. And why we may be here some time.'

'Nothing frivolous, Prefect? This is a joke, isn't it? Some sort of jape to break the tension the garrison's been under.'

'It's no joke, Festus.'

'Then why are we even discussing this? The Governor doesn't need our opinions – whoever heard the like? What's going on here?'

'This subject has to be resolved and the Governor wants our views precisely because of who we are – practical men of some experience but unburdened by great riches or undue responsibility, raised to a life of discipline but able to think for ourselves – and untainted by politics, always a worthy qualification. He'd simply like to hear our advice before making a decision, for which I think we should consider ourselves rather flattered. We also know about the elemental power of religion as evidenced yesterday, how it can drive men to extremes from fury to self-sacrifice, how it affects the good government of this Province and so much of human affairs everywhere, but also how it needs to be managed if optimal outcomes are to be achieved. It's our common sense the Governor wants, our best judgment on the proposition, because he knows he can count on us to be rational and objective.'

'And presumably the Governor supports his own idea?'

'The Governor wishes his idea to be debated. It's something he's recently given a lot of thought to. But he claims no monopoly of wisdom on the subject. To help reach a final decision he prefers to put his trust in his soldiers. And he can think of none more representative than the officers of this cohort.'

"And what about you, Prefect? Where do you fit into this? You're not without responsibility yourself.'

'In the hierarchy of the Army even my rank doesn't count for much, as well you know, Festus. I'm to be the impartial chairman for this exercise, as much as I can be anyway, and my vote carries no more weight than yours. My role is to find a consensus, so we can reach the most sensible conclusion we can. Should we be unable to come to a view one way or the other then the Governor will make the final call. Oh yes – and we are to voice our opinions candidly, without fear or favour. I don't want anyone holding back out of deference – we've got to thrash this out in as much detail as necessary, and wherever the discussion takes us, though I'd stress that where there are opposing ideas on religion we must make every effort to keep the more subjective tendencies under control, at least sufficiently to allow all sides of the argument to be explored.'

'And all off the record, Prefect?'

'Off the record and unattributable, but prepare to hear the other side and suspend any deeply-held personal views until we find some agreement. That might be a lot to ask, but the emphasis must be on finding a common line on the logic, like we would with any group decision, though this one's against the widest backcloth we could ever imagine. We don't need to be practised in the wiles of statecraft, just apply some straightforward thinking on both the immediate implications and the bigger picture. In military terms this is all about selection and maintenance of the aim – bold, innovative, achievable and appropriate in relation to the situation. It's brains that win battles, gentlemen, not brawn. We're here to think.'

'By the Gods!'

'Indeed, Festus. But that's the Governor's order and therefore our duty. And nothing is to be said outside this meeting tonight, not a word to anyone that it's even taken place. Is that understood?

'Well if there are no more questions, perhaps it would be useful if we remind ourselves of exactly where we're at. Yesterday morning's commotion, when the entire garrison was stood-up, resulted in the execution of an itinerant preacher called Yeshua of Nazareth. We needn't detain ourselves now with the background or the precise reasons, though you may wish to make reference to them in any arguments which might arise. The upshot is that he dies at the usual place of public execution with a couple of other prisoners. The duty company is Century I, which has to provide a significant security presence due to the size and fervour of the crowds, and also find an execution party. The Senior Centurion takes personal command of the execution due to its high-profile nature and the continuing risk to public order. In the event there's no more trouble and the crowd soon disperses once the excitement's over, except for friends and relatives and a few hard-liners waiting to see justice meted out to the very end.

'OC 1 and every soldier there, so I'm told, is impressed by the Nazarene's dignity. Mercifully he doesn't last very long – not surprising considering the severe flogging he's received before the start. We all know the afternoon is unusually dark and overcast, which becomes quite a talking point, but that's neither here nor there. What's more relevant is the care and custody of the body after it's taken down from the cross. A couple of well-to-do locals, one Joseph who's known to the Governor, and another Council elder named Nicodemus, approach OC I with written authority from the Camp Commandant authorizing them to take possession. All seems in order, and the body's moved by these two gentlemen and presumably at least some of the mourners to a rock-tomb beyond the north wall owned by the said Joseph, and given the traditional Jewish preparation as though for a person of substance. Century I returns to barracks.

'And then first thing this morning the High Priest turns up in person again at the Old Palace, almost in a repeat of yesterday but without the theatricals, and asks the Governor to mount a guard at the tomb. In case you're not entirely familiar with the Nazarene's teachings, this is to prevent any possibility of his followers stealing the body from its resting place in order to try and give some credence to the prophecy he'd made about rising from the dead on the third day. The Governor accedes to the request because it seems reasonable and there's no point in antagonizing the hierarchy any further after what's happened. They want our soldiers involved of course to ensure credibility is maximized. So the new duty company sends a couple of sections down there sharpish, which will have to stay till tomorrow, time of withdrawal to be decided. And Petronius being a conscientious officer is down there with them now, and intends to stay all night himself.'

Veranius looked about him. 'So let's take that as our starting point, shall we? Why exactly was the High Priest so keen to want this body guarded – and presumably still is?'

*   *   *   *

'That's easy enough. As you've just said, and as the priests quite openly claimed in their request, if the followers have effective control of the body they could remove it under cover of dark and proclaim their risen lord. If Caiaphas had effective control then he'd be able to forestall any attempt on those lines. But imagine the consequences if control was in place and it still went missing – the news would spread like wildfire, the priests' authority would be completely overturned, the whole Jewish establishment in turmoil. You can understand their concern.'

'We can, Festus, and we can agree on the potential for destabilization, though it would depend on how successful the Council were in suppressing any popular unrest which might occur – if they ever needed to, since in practice the great majority of those who got to hear about this ... this apparent miracle, would probably still dismiss it as totally implausible. Before taking to the streets people would want much stronger evidence that the man many had wanted dead so recently was in fact their long-awaited messiah, rather than mere hearsay about his body purportedly rising from a sealed tomb – wouldn't they? A mass rising of the people against their priests, who have always commanded allegiance through strict custom and tradition, seems very unlikely.'

'But we can't be sure of that.'

'No, and we do have to be ready for all eventualities, Festus. We can be sure anything with potential to really challenge the native establishment would be fiercely resisted and cause ructions on the way – which aren't likely to be in our interests either. That's why we need to keep a watch on any developments and assess their implications for the stability of the Province. We can agree, however, on the main point whatever the subsequent likely effect of a disappearance – Caiaphas is out to reduce risks, and get control of tomb and contents if he can.'

'The security briefings have given us quite a lot on this Galilean cult, Prefect. It's incumbent on all of us to know what's going on and take an interest, and to do that we have to understand a little about religious attitudes in this country and what makes the religious mind work.'

'We appreciate your insight in this field, Festus.'

'The significance of a risen body is fundamental – noteworthy even for the most disinterested. A dead person, a corpse – whose soul departs for the after-life? Nothing new in that, it's the universal hope. But departing complete with mortal frame, never to be seen by mortal eye again? How likely is that, in any religion? Yet some of the Jews, some of the Pharisees especially, believe in physical resurrection – that's what they all mockingly accused Yeshua of yesterday, his saying that he would rise from the dead. As far as most of them were concerned, I suggest, he'd made the claim in order to gain the maximum attention he'd need for his self-publicizing mission – to spectacularly succeed, or fizzle out as just another mystic's fantasy, because as we know, this man wasn't the first to claim he was the messiah, even in our own time. For a people acquainted with the idea of bodily resurrection it would be the great test – although there's scant reference in the Hebrew scriptures, I understand – which accounts for much of the rivalry between the Sadducees and the Pharisees. They seem to be at odds over a subject for which there's very little scriptural authority.

'Nicodemus is a Pharisee, a member of the High Council – pretty rich, influential, used to getting his own way, and clearly his friend the Arimathean is too. We know they had contact with the controversial rabbi – Joseph was definitely a closet disciple of sorts, while Nicodemus, though perhaps not so convinced, is known to have had at least one discussion with him, and to have publicly stuck up for him on one occasion, which must have been quite a brave thing to do. It's possible both these sympathizers in their respective degrees are interested in bodily resurrection, perhaps in Nicodemus' case more than in Yeshua's other claims, and have thus taken every care to help it come about. We know they took official possession of the body, courtesy of the Governor and with the implied approval of the relatives, one providing expensive spices, the other a new tomb which he had bought for himself and would have cost a considerable sum – fulfilling another piece of old scripture about a man of poverty ending up in a rich man's grave. And we know every good Jew knows his scripture backwards – these details are significant. So these men probably believe in bodily resurrection and think Yeshua, son of Joseph of the royal line of David, could well be the long-promised messiah, or at any rate has sufficient claim to make their investment of time, expense and reputation justified.

'Corpses however also have their uses in popular movements, Prefect. Preserved relics can be used as a rallying point, for resistance against us perhaps, a flashpoint for the uprising of a subject people, sweeping the collaborators away and kicking Rome out of their country. Except this isn't a violent movement. It might be an insurgency of a kind but it's not an insurrection. In fact it's entirely peaceable and no threat to the occupying power, which by all accounts it seems to respect. It's said one of Yeshua's followers did inflict a minor injury at the time of his arrest by the Temple Guard, but that seems to have been very much the exception. An armed revolt is not going to come from them, therefore, and I wouldn't have thought the Zealots would wish to be associated either, since they tend to despise these turn-the-other-cheek characters as weak or unpatriotic or both.

'But a man's complete body that disappears never to be seen again, at least by authenticated sources, which has supposedly risen into thin air – and this man's in particular, who said he would rise again on the third day? That's an infinitely more powerful idea, if it could ever be proved – vindication and encouragement for the followers, disaster for the Sadducees and the Sanhedrin as a whole, and stupendously arresting for everybody else. After yesterday's outcome I wouldn't have thought there's anything for Caiaphas to worry about, though. Thanks to the Governor agreeing his request for a guard on the tomb, he's got what he wanted – in fact better, in that it's us guarding it rather than his own men.'

'So long as the tomb's secure long enough to cover the three days, you mean?'

'Yes, Prefect – though we may need to come back to that in a moment. After three days Caiaphas can begin to relax. Of course, if we're still *in situ* and the body were to disappear, it really would strengthen the claim for a miracle, wouldn't it? As opposed to it just disappearing from an unguarded tomb with perhaps only a mourner or two around – in which case who'd believe it? And come to think of it, we ought to think through what would happen if it were Caiaphas' men guarding the place and not us – just in case posterity gets confused about who actually did what.

'Because if the body were to disappear with the Temple Guard doing the guarding – what then? You might say it would be even more powerful, because the people would expect their own guards to be more hostile to Yeshua's claim, both to the idea of such a thing and to anyone foolish enough to try and effect it. The Council wouldn't want to be complicit in any plot to remove the body covertly, unless they were to do so directly themselves in a situation of guaranteed secrecy and control, perhaps intending to be able to display it later to counteract any resurrection claims, at least before physical decomposition made that problematic. But would anyone trust them in any case? It's far better for Caiaphas's credibility that the tomb is safely guarded by us, who don't have a dog in this fight and would most likely be seen as impartial if it came to a dispute between one faction or another. Which, by the way, is an argument to keep our own reputation intact and not get further involved with any such business.

'But this is all by way of diversion, Prefect, since we know it's our soldiers who are there, and at the High Priest's express request. Posterity might erroneously get the impression that Caiaphas was asking permission to post his own men for the task, which he'd need to obtain since the site is well away from the Temple precinct, but we know the actuality and the reason for it. The perception will be that we're simply responding to the security requirement and providing the most reliable means of doing so, at the request of a High Priest with his own agenda. There's no reason why any motive should be imputed to us other than a wish to help restore good relations with the Council, in support of our strategic aim of maintaining public order and keeping out of Jewish religious affairs – consistent, we could say, with yesterday's trial. In practice that means continuing to deny the body to all comers – including Caiaphas, wealthy individuals with an academic interest in bodily resurrection, or the Nazarene's close followers. The priests have got all they're going to get, the academics are honest men and unlikely to be tempted to try and move bodies about in the dead of night, and his close followers would not want to disturb their leader's resting place now. With security thus guaranteed, the only people we're likely to see return to the tomb are from among that last group, the genuine mourners, because that's the natural thing to do, and we have no desire to make it difficult for them. As far as they're concerned we're neutral and simply doing our job.'

'Fact can be stranger than fiction, Festus. Unless there were a reliable vigil for the whole duration how could anyone be absolutely certain of anything?'

'We can only go on probabilities, Prefect. I suppose you could consider some extreme possibilities if only to rule them out – such as the guard indulging in horseplay or being bribed, though we know that's a near-impossibility, and I can't imagine anyone in the future thinking it likely either.'

'I should hope not, Festus. Thank you for that assessment. I agree we do have to take into account what anyone who might be interested in this in the future might make of it all. But just suppose persons unknown, malcontents of some kind, have realized they've got to act tonight if the prophecy is to be fulfilled, and somehow manage to drug, bribe, bamboozle or otherwise overcome the guard without physically attacking them, move the seal and take the body – or else the guard's all asleep and simply allows this to happen. How could people in the future be sure that wasn't actually what happened?'

'With us in position now we can safely rule out anything like that. It would take a major effort to overcome even a small guard or render it otherwise non-effective, and the chance of its success without news of such an event spreading would be remote. And never mind horseplay, the standing sentence for any Roman soldier caught sleeping on watch is capital punishment. Have we ever heard of any soldier risking that, be he ever so tired?'

'In which case, Festus, any disappearance really would be a miracle and Yeshua of Galilee will have risen from the dead without help of human hand – which is of course impossible.'

'Exactly, Prefect. That's the point – the impossibility of any normal explanation for a vanishing body. What else could effect such a thing but the hand of god? – which is what we must assume the Governor has in mind – and what worries me. The problem is motive. Whilst I agree it's important to take cognizance of what the Jewish authorities fear most, it's our own motives that we're concerned with now, not theirs, and it just so happens we've ended up with control of the tomb. The opportunity is ours – but that doesn't mean we should take it.'

'Indeed not, Festus.'

'And we mustn't forget the first night, when there was no guard and no control. What was to stop anything untoward happening then?'

'The prophecy was to rise on the third day, not the second.'

'But anyone minded to move the body isn't going to be put off by that, are they? They're going to hope no-one would check until the third day, and they'd probably be right. And who witnessed the actual entombment? – no-one we'd ordinarily call reliable. We don't even know with absolute certainty the body was buried in a particular tomb, do we – one that couldn't be later confused with another nearby?'

'You'd think the family would have something to say about that.'

'Maybe they didn't stay long enough for the interment, Prefect. Maybe they didn't know anything about a real final alternative resting place – because no-one ever told them.'

'But they'd get to find out later.'

'How? And if they did, who in all the confusion of claim and counter-claim would get to know the real truth, or be able to disseminate it? But we come back to the question, Prefect. Who would have the motive as well as means and opportunity to take the matter into their own hands, considering also there might be mourners about till quite late the first day despite the impending Sabbath, and there's presumably the physical problem of a seal-stone to contend with too?'

'Senior Centurion? – you were on the ground. Can you confirm that last point?'

'I didn't see the location, Prefect, but I was assured by the man of Arimathea that the tomb did have a large seal-stone – because I asked him. We've all seen them – two-man job at least, plus crowbar and a timber or two, and then not quick. It's there for a purpose – it's got to stay in place for several years, until the bones can be removed to an ossuary. Sounded pretty secure to me. But ...

'... I do have to ... confess. In hindsight I should have accompanied the funeral procession to see the site for myself, and posted a guard there straightaway, just to be absolutely certain Caiaphas' men, or anybody else, didn't get up to any tricks.'

'Bit unlike you, Senior Centurion – in more ways than one. But hey-ho, hindsight's a wonderful thing, and I'm sure as far as you were concerned it was all over and the possibility of interference didn't arise. Why would it, any normal person might ask? Not to worry – if our concern with posterity is to cover all eventualities across the board, what happened that first night won't get much scrutiny either – and they won't be sure you didn't post a guard anyway.'

'Couldn't have been feeling myself, Prefect.'

'Perhaps the stone's not relevant, Prefect. Why would it have to be rolled aside for the son of god to rise anyway? Does god need clear egress? Seems to me the only purpose in removing it would be for dramatic effect – or enable men to do his bidding, so to speak.'

'Thank you Festus, noted. Let's move on. The present reality is that while there might have been some opportunity to remove the body last night, with all its implications, it's safe to say it's highly unlikely. The priests would be the likeliest culprits, had it been the case, but unless they manage to display a body as and when required in the not-too-distant future we can effectively discount them. If there doesn't turn out to be a mass Yeshua-inspired protest movement they'd have no pressing reason to produce it, so it might never be seen again in any case, and there would always be the risk for them that the disputed identity of a corpse would have to vie with rumour of an empty tomb in convincing a confused populace. Better lie low.'

'True, Prefect, though on the question of motive we might need to consider some other parties in a little more detail before we rule them out too.'

'Yes, yes, Festus – the Zealots. We know some of Yeshua's followers have connections with them – who knows what political use could be made of such a disappearance?'

'Very little, I'd surmise, Prefect. If they've been thinking otherwise they'd be making a major miscalculation, though I suppose we can't rule out the cock-up theory of history – decision-makers often just make mistakes, or decisions may be sound but the unforeseen ensues, or things simply go wrong. Unlikely with canny operators living so long on their wits, however. The Zealots have long been disappointed that the Nazarene was not to be their deliverer from the Roman yoke. The putative messiah come to save Israel proved untrue, so would be no help for their cause – in fact, in preaching peace and recognizing secular authority, he would be a decided hindrance. That was plain to everyone.   On a list of possibles the Zealots have to be ruled out too.'

'But Festus, while they couldn't claim Yeshua as a figurehead or be associated with his preaching, they'll certainly have been on the lookout for any chance to destabilize the authorities.'

'Yes Prefect, but what would be their precise motive in effecting a disappearance? How would that help the cause of armed resistance when its subject, Yeshua of Nazareth, was the accepted symbol of peaceful co-existence, not of nationalist resistance? And it remains to be seen whether there'll be any attempt at serious destabilization now – my money's against, in the immediate future anyway. The people haven't risen against either their priests, or us, yet, and they aren't going to be shaken out of their quiescence by unsubstantiated rumour easily.   Yeshua's supposed resurrection might indeed be stupendously arresting for many, but among his own people, with all their history and attachment to their religion? – I doubt it.'

'Then who? We're running out of candidates. I've got it! What about Nicodemus – with his rather shadowy role and likely belief in resurrection, eh?'

'With his friend the Arimathean, since it's hard to think they're not to some extent like-minded. Possibly, but you'd think pulling off a stunt like that could only be predicated on a belief that Yeshua was who he said he was, in which case the logic would be there'd be no need of help from living hands.   It doesn't make sense.'

'As you said, Nicodemus in particular might be less interested in full acceptance of the rabbi's divinity than in winning his argument with his opponents over the idea of resurrection.   And we all know how far some people will go to win an argument.'

'It doesn't sound like he's a dishonest man to me, Prefect – far from it.   Like many others, I expect, he's curious, torn, undecided, but fair-minded, and he's already shown some identification with the rabbi.   If he were intent on taking the matter into his own hands he'd know he'd be taking the same risk as the priests, of being found out, and he'd need some help carrying out the plan, which might be forthcoming from his friend Joseph or it might not.   I don't think we should see them as devious individuals intent on intervention.'

'Anyone else you want to rule out?'

'Only the Nazarene's own followers, Prefect. In any group of people who are initially at one on the big idea which draws them together you're going to find different views, differing emphases, gradually increasing divergence. There'll be disparate backgrounds, and there's even a Zealot connection. We've talked about the Zealots and all but ruled them out, but there could be some among the Nazarene's following, perhaps in the wider circle, thinking along lines little different in terms of publicity and impact, and fully prepared to put that well-known motto into effect – that the end justifies the means. Aren't we touching on the same conclusion the Governor seems to have reached – that a beneficial purpose may be achieved through methods which would otherwise be very dubious, that Yeshua's self-sacrifice will not have been in vain, that man will after all be reformed and the kingdom of heaven descend upon earth?'

'Is that likely, Festus – that such thinking about an intervention could exist among his followers? It wouldn't be much of a basis for any claim to be doing the lord's work, would it?'

'One thing we can all agree on is the power of religious conviction, Prefect. Once the convolutions of the over-religious mind are settled on a conclusion then it so easily becomes a tenet of the faith, irrevocably justified. It goes with the territory. With the necessary adjustments, what might otherwise be seen as questionable or even heinous becomes transformed into god's will, revealed to those willing to obey it and impose it on others if they possibly can. Yeshua, they might say, is indeed a mighty prophet and deserving of justification on his third day – but we're not going to take any chances. God's work is done through men on earth, and they must act if they wish to see it come to fruition. The mindset of false certainty applies to all mistaken religion, if we think about it. A body risen corporeally to heaven would be a mighty powerful event in anyone's language, a claim of such stark simplicity which, if it could only be accepted as true, would out-do any amount of persuasion from numberless sermons. Proponents wouldn't call man-assisted occurrence false. They'd say it was all part of god's plan for the redemption of mankind and that everything falls into place around this one all-embracing event – the resurrection of Yeshua of Nazareth.'

'They'd be few then, Festus. This sect's unlike any other we know, its sincerity impressive. I suppose on the law of averages there could be a bad apple among its adherents, prepared to take matters into their own hands – perhaps we should be looking there, though the loyal ones would want to prevent anything of the kind. With crisis and panic in the camp all sorts of strange things could be going on, but no matter how effective direct action might be in gaining some advantage, one thing we can't accuse his genuine followers of is any lack of integrity. There's no reason to question the sincerity with which they've followed their master, including the one former known Zealot in his closest circle. Specifically we're not aware of any serious faction among them which might want to consider an attempt at a staged resurrection. It'd be anathema to the spirit of the movement, which isn't very numerous, and if there were a breakaway movement of some kind it's hard to see it being strong enough to pull it off.'

'A fair assessment, Prefect.'

'So it looks as though we're back at the beginning. Gentlemen, we're going to have to make some assumptions about the sum of the known facts, the various possibilities and the way people in the future will view them. That it's we the Roman Army who are guarding the tomb now and will do so until tomorrow morning. That the tomb was reasonably secure until we got there this morning, and that the lack of a security presence until then isn't of great relevance, since it's the second night – tonight – which is the critical one. That the only other party with a significant motive to steal the body has not yet done so, and now won't be able to. And that no-one will have any reason to suspect that we, the Roman Army, might be planning to do just that.'

*   *   *   *

'And we talk of misguided people who think the end justifies the means, Prefect.'

'That might be one way of looking at it, Festus. We'll come to our own motives shortly.'

'Are any of these details going to make the slightest difference to how people come to see things anyway, when all they're going to know is that the tomb was guarded and found empty on the third day? – because that's what they'll be told. Something so attention-grabbing is bound to get written down, and the next you know half the known world believes it, because people set store on the written word and want so much to believe such a remarkable story could be true.'

'Hence the Governor's proposition, Festus.'

'It's right in that respect, Prefect – this would have enormous potential to survive and grow as an idea. What might seem only a remote possibility to us in our time – one small event in a small province with its own self-identifying and all-dominating religion, but from which springs a movement which might one day conquer far and wide in its own name.'

'Even though turning the other cheek doesn't seem much in keeping with human nature, Festus?'

'Maybe not, Prefect, but human nature is contradictory. The message will appeal to many, especially the underdog, the less fortunate, in fact to the great mass of humanity everywhere which sees life as desperately hard and unfair and would welcome the idea of heavenly rest after its labours – plus the idealists who yearn for goodwill, peace and justice between men. Don't underestimate it.'

'You mean the feeble-minded and the fantasists.'

'You and I might think so, Prefect. We could be greatly outnumbered one day.'

'Very well. Let's explore further, bearing in mind the immediate practicalities. What precisely would be the point of the Roman Army secreting the body away, as our exam question has it?'

'To get back at the Jews, of course.'

'Really?'

'The Governor does have a certain reputation.'

'Meaning?'

'Am I to spell it out, Prefect? He's no time for them all. He finds their religious culture objectionable and their unreasoning adherence to it irksome. Unfortunately his whole attitude to the trial yesterday was to challenge their predictable reaction to the Nazarene's activities, knowing they found it offensive and would take full opportunity to show their outrage, and then to compound the error by letting them play the loyalty-to-Rome tactic, the one thing they knew he couldn't fight on – and ended up giving them their Zealot favourite, or at least the crowd's. He might just as well have condemned the man in the first place and done something for our public relations.'

'You could say the Governor's reputation with the locals was past saving in any case, that he was managing the political reality. But he couldn't condemn the man for breaking Roman law when he hadn't. The Governor is not without principle, Festus, as I'm sure you'd like to acknowledge.'

'Yes of course, Prefect. But this man did call himself king of the Jews.'

'Not quite, as I understand. That came from others.'

'But he didn't deny it.'

'No, I don't believe he did. But he did make it clear his kingdom was not an earthly one.'

'To avoid any opprobrium for Yeshua's death on their own heads, the priests may well have sought to direct it to the Governor's. But when they threw in *amicus Caesaris* they knew they'd got him, didn't they? Was he Caesar's friend, or not? You can't run a province on behalf of the Emperor by walking into a trap like that.'

'He wasn't going to be forced into admitting Yeshua was an enemy of the State when he wasn't. He didn't give way on that, Festus.'

'The Nazarene's movement might be the opposite of a conventional insurgency, but that's what made it all the more intolerable to the priests, and the mass of the population has been behind them. Blasphemy was the last straw. Yet the Governor goes and exacerbates everything by letting our soldiers put that notice on the cross, and refuses to have it altered to make it clear it was only referring to the claim, not the fact. Perhaps he should have thought twice on that one too, before allowing himself to be put in such a position. It's almost as though he was allowing his temperament to rule his head, if I may say so.'

'The Governor wouldn't deny his long record in dealing with these people on matters of principle.'

'As I say, you can't blame the Jews for defending their religion, because it's what we'd do too. No doubt the Governor anticipated their reaction, though whether he was ready for the Passover-release custom isn't so clear. Perhaps all-in-all he had no alternative in doing what he did, but it looks to me like the predictable culmination of the Sejanan misappreciation of this Province – disdain, disrespect and despoliation. Refusing to change the superscription on that cross was the finishing touch.'

'We're not here to question the Governor's decisions, Festus – career-ending recklessness on your part at any other time, if *I* may say so, though we appreciate your forthrightness. The Governor had to show impartiality, and that due legal process was being observed. He found the Nazarene was not in rebellion, but with the crowd in uproar, and acutely conscious of his first duty being to peace and good order he reluctantly gave way – but in a way which minimized any damage to the State's authority.'

'By washing his hands.'

'It's history, Festus. The question we're directed to consider is about the future.'

'You asked what the reasoning might be, Prefect, and I'm saying it's obvious. The Governor's seen a way to get back at the Jews far more potently than anything about washing hands or superscriptions. The whole idea of *us* taking the body! Whatever moral machinations and supposed benefits we might be being asked to engineer, the first and immediate practical effect would be to discredit the Jewish establishment and get one back on Caiaphas.'

'Aren't you being a little parochial, Festus?'

'You tell us, Prefect. I expect you've discussed it with him.'

'Look, inevitably there's an element of province power politics here, I'm sure he'd admit. You can't blame him after eight years of nothing but obstructionism, surely? It would be asking quite a lot of anyone in his position, when the king of the Jews comes before him and he's forced to condemn him against his better judgment, not to derive a tiny crumb of satisfaction from the general outrage over the superscription and his refusal to change it. To that extent you could say he was playing them at their own game.'

'But you're about to tell us there's a lot more behind it than that, I suspect. The Governor can't be going to all this trouble just over his ego.'

'Correct, Festus. I think we have to credit him with rather more than that. Of course he wants peace and stability, like anybody else entrusted with a commission like his. He also has to show everyone who's in charge – not him personally so much as the imperial power, of which he is the chief embodiment in this Province.'

'May we enquire how this peace and stability are to be translated into his proposition, Prefect?'

'The decision on guarding the tomb was simply the result of a quick assessment this morning when Caiaphas made the request. It set the sequence in train, and I'm at liberty to say that he's since taken it to a further conclusion – that it fortuitously opens the way to this momentous possibility before us now, this biggest responsibility anyone could ever be given. And we've only just begun to explore it.'

'What, bigger than running an empire of fifty million people?'

'Infinitely, Festus. This is for all people for all time.'

'And the granting of permission for the man of Arimathea to take the body? Was that another quick appreciation? Caiaphas was bound to see it as a gratuitous provocation, a challenge to his authority. We'll have gained nothing from the gesture except more animosity. So why do it?'

'The Governor had no reason to refuse a humanitarian request with a humanitarian response of his own. He's aware that behind Joseph of Arimathea's generosity there could have been an interest in providing proof for a resurrection, but regarded it then and now as being essentially harmless, and as far as the relatives would have been concerned, only beneficial. It might have annoyed the High Priest but it's also important to try and keep both factions of the Council happy. The Governor's accession to Caiaphas' demand this morning was a convenient balancing gesture.'

'The fact remains, Prefect. Any unexplained disappearance now would seriously undermine the Jewish establishment, wouldn't it? But the Governor doesn't want to rock the boat.'

'We've been into that, Festus.'

'For the life of me, Prefect, I can't see how upsetting the Jews could be compatible with a policy of stability and respecting the *status quo*. Widening the split in the Sanhedrin on the question of resurrection, and antagonizing the Chief Priest beyond his endurance, would be child's play compared to the risk of this scheme ever getting out. Judea would be up in flames overnight and the damage to our prestige and credibility irreparable.'

'The Jewish establishment's far too strong to be rocked that much, Festus. There might be some repercussions if the disappearance could be attributed to us, and the risk of that does have to be taken into account, but the Governor's view is that it's really quite slight. How is anyone going to find out? Caiaphas might have his suspicions but he's not going to want any talk of resurrection in any context whatsoever. In the end it's what your posterity will make of it all that matters – and the benefits of that would be beyond calculation.'

'Why should posterity care a fig about a little discrediting of the local authorities of Tiberian Judea, Prefect?'

'We've got to think bigger than that, Festus.'

'So that's it then. We're guarding the tomb so we can snatch the body so his followers can proclaim their messiah so the Jews can get blamed for killing him by everyone else for centuries to come.'

'That would be an extreme interpretation.'

'I think I'm coming to the conclusion this is madness, Prefect. We're sitting on a perpetual tinder box as it is – we should stick to proven policy and keep out of all local religious matters as much as possible, yet here we are proposing to risk starting a conflagration, and by very devious means indeed.'

'A small residual risk. Imperial policy hasn't exactly been a roaring success so far, has it? We contain, just, but we don't win over, we don't convince, we don't expand. Think about it, Festus – the greatest risk in this proposal isn't to the Province, it's to the Governor's own reputation, and he knows it. In fact it's a certainty already set in concrete. If we do nothing then these events, so fresh in the mind to us but obscure to the wide world out there, will soon be forgotten, almost entirely so if not absolutely entirely – like the Governor himself. But if we act and it comes off – which it will – then his name will go down in calumny for all time as the man who executed Yeshua the son of god, and for no other reason in some people's books than the personal expediency of trying to save his own tarnished reputation.'

'As if there hasn't been enough pointless gesturing already, Prefect. If it's all about the Governor's conscience why is he playing this silly discussion game with us? We can't be his keeper.'

'You think we should refuse his request for some support on such a trifling concern, Festus?'

'I'm sure we're all flattered, Prefect.'

'And why your pre-occupation with how the Jews might react?'

'Because they're a proud nation which has given Rome nothing but trouble, and will probably go on doing so until we have to destroy its heartland and scatter its people to the four winds. It can't be long before there is a hideous slaughter in this place. And the Governor wouldn't be averse to seeing it happen.'

'That's a strong charge, Festus. If it does it won't be anything to do with what we're talking about now. The Governor isn't bellicose by nature and no less alive to the need to justify our actions than the rest of us, insofar as the world may judge Roman arms. The years ahead here might well see problems, but having held the ring so far they're unlikely to become catastrophic in his time. The garrison's nowhere near strong enough for major repressive action, he's not going to run off to Flaccus for his Syrian legions if he can avoid it, and anyway his stock with Rome isn't high enough to guarantee the support we'd need. He wouldn't deny the frustrations of dealing with the local establishment – of course not. It's their claim to ancient authority, the unbending enforcement of petty rules of observance, their hold on the people through the covenant with their god, all too resolutely adhered to in defiance of superior force and civilizing power, that's always been the problem. He's long ceased to find the enigma very intriguing.'

'He'd have our sympathies there, I'm sure.'

'There's never been any attempt by them to spread their faith to others, which every conqueror since the world began has done. It just stays with this one god's people, as they call themselves, who've always rejected all other gods and stuck to their own through thick and thin, and insist their identity and their religion and their land are all one and the same. Which is admirable – unless you're trying to administer the imperial destiny to a people determined to resist it. Our influence stretches to barbarians at every edge of the known world, but not here. The Jews have their own accomplishments, which we bend over backwards to recognize. But there's no reciprocity, no grateful acceptance in return, just barely-concealed hostility.'

'The Governor's frustrations all seem to be coming to a head with this little incident.'

'I'm sure he'd prefer to leave a better legacy here, Festus, but what happens in Judea isn't the issue. Nor what becomes of the Governor's reputation, whatever others will think. I asked you all to think big, and you're the one who claims to know a bit about religion.'

It was the centurion's turn to be silent.

* * * *

'You've touched on the answer already. Look at the cause of why we're having this discussion at all. It's not the Jews whom we should be concentrating on – but the central fact behind these events and the man at the very centre of them, one of their own but who fell foul of them. And his message – that's where we must look.'

'Yeshua of Nazareth.'

'Yeshua of Nazareth, Festus. What is it about the man's teachings that could be of interest to us? We've already looked at some of the implications of his claim that he'd rise from the dead, but there's more – much more.'

'Other than the absurdity of rising from the dead? It's difficult to see anything more revolutionary than that.'

'Revolution's the word, Festus. Resurrection, ascension – the ultimate attention-getters, the foundation of faith and the means of hope. But forget applying it to the dead and the dream of eternal life. Think of the living, whom some call the quick – a prescription for them.'

'A prescription for life?'

'And what's our understanding of this prescription, Festus, especially its comparison with the old Mosaic precepts? What's new about what the Nazarene was saying? What is it between the god of Elijah and the god of this rabbi that might give us a pointer?'

'The Nazarene taught on the prophets, Prefect. Nothing he said contradicted them, and indeed he was always widely quoting from them in the synagogues, where people were astonished by the erudition of a poor carpenter. His criticism of the religious establishment was largely of its neglect of the right way to follow god, in the way god really wants, as a personal god, with personal mercy and justice, and of its hypocrisy in the over-observance of the trappings of religious law – "whited sepulchres" was a particularly stinging phrase. The priests had gone astray in over-emphasizing the letter of the law at the expense of its spirit, and the final imputation, if not his direct claim according to some reports, that he was indeed the long-awaited messiah, the very son of god, was too much for the guardians of the faith, who were already infuriated by the challenge to their authority. That anyone of flesh and blood could be the actual incarnation of the scriptures, and have the gall to call himself the son of man, was neither credible nor acceptable. To accuse the elders of being hypocrites to their faces and challenge their control of revenues to the Temple was to set in train a sequence of events which was entirely predictable. Other self-proclaimed messiahs do appear from time to time, but none that we know of have been quite so foolhardy as this one – or effective, if getting people to take notice is how success is measured.'

'Yes, you could say that describes the restrictions of the law and the "don'ts" of personal behaviour. But what about more on the "do's", Festus? Prescription has to be about the positive, doesn't it?'

'Facilis will tell us more about them, I'm sure, Prefect. You mean all those things like the absolute primacy of loving god, loving your neighbour as yourself, the need for genuine repentance for sins, and infinite forgiveness?'

'Agree with that sentiment or not, I'd say that's pretty revolutionary, wouldn't you?'

'Undoubtedly, both to supporter and detractor, Prefect. Penitence comes easy at the time. If someone – or something – has total power over you, and you transgress, especially knowingly, against their will – you'd be well advised to show some remorse if you know what's good for you. The test comes with the next time – how genuine was your penitence in the first place? And, to round off that question, how ready are you to forgive those who transgress against you? The Jews have much to say about repentance, particularly as a collective act for collective failings, but therein lies a possible difference for a people steeped in the concept – Yeshua was talking about individual responsibility, individual repentance and sincerity before a personal god.'

'This personal god you keep referring to, Festus? Aren't all gods personal? Or else how can we have any relationship with any of them?'

'In the broadest sense, perhaps, but we're now told individual responsibility only comes from a closer relationship, of opening up to this god and allowing ourselves to be drawn closer, naturally like a child to its father. We are already known, but our fulfilment comes with our own understanding, which we can only attain by acknowledging our poverty and wretchedness and seeking to walk with god, until in his service we find perfect freedom. We don't need to go into the difference between loving and fearing the gods too much, Prefect. The underlying basis for all religion is that the gods are there to be obeyed, or else they are meaningless and don't exist. Whether it's love or fear the greater motivation is largely immaterial – it's the outcome and the action which matter. We want the gods' forgiveness, because we're weak and foolish and go astray and fear retribution, so we make an issue of seeking that forgiveness – in public, a big show. Depends on whether you're a cup half-full or cup half-empty sort of person, or whole people, I suppose. In practice, as the power and benevolence of the gods go together, so love and fear of them are complementary. You can't have one without the other, however much you try. Anyway, man does what he's told, or at least makes an attempt to do so.'

'Depending on the status of the gods in question, Festus. A minor deity deserves respect, but no-one messes with Jupiter Best and Greatest.'

'The god of the Hebrews is even more awesome to them by

the very nature of his solitary splendour. He's all-powerful in his creation because he made it and presides over it alone, and guides his chosen people through his covenant with them. Then along comes the Nazarene and suddenly the emphasis is more on the individual creature, who should relate to the creator individually before collectively and in so doing recognize their true place in the universal. The chosen people is the whole of humanity, not just Israel, and individual men and women the essential vessels of creation. That's why his Samaritan story is so important, that we should all love one another, including our neighbour and even our enemy, even to the extent of forgiving their failings against us endlessly, as we ourselves are endlessly forgiven despite our unworthiness. This turning-of-the-cheek comes from another particularly vivid episode, what they called his sermon on the mount, which supplements the Jews' ten commandments on rules of behaviour with what we might call the great consolation – that the meek shall inherit the earth and find their reward in heaven. No matter how beastly life might be there is a better one ahead where there is no suffering or hardship, no hatred or animosity, no injury or injustice, and man's true vocation in loving god is to institute these heavenly ways on earth. That's the revolutionary bit, if you like, Prefect. The only trouble is it's hopelessly idealistic, because it flies in the face of human nature, doesn't it? Great in theory but in the messy reality it's just a flight of fancy. Well, we could argue about that.'

'There has to be some element of forgiveness in everyone's make-up and personal relationships, Festus, since we know it's part of the give-and-take of everyday life. And treating your neighbour as yourself is only enlightened self-interest.'

'True, Prefect. Doing to others as you would have done to yourself, or, more commonly though less radically, not doing to them as you would not have done to you, is supposed to be widespread among mankind's creeds. The Egyptians had it long ago, the Greek philosophers also, and the books of Moses too talk of loving your neighbour as yourself. We Romans tend not to write these things down explicitly, though it's implicit in our ethics as the principle of reciprocity. Of course it's one of the better things about all men – nobody gets very far without some regard to those around them, unless they're in some kind of privileged position, and then not without damage to their reputation. It's often said you should always be prepared to meet people half-way – some would say more than half-way – and that the secret of happiness is to think of others before yourself. But yes, you're right, Prefect. Here with the Nazarene we have a specific injunction to extend such altruism to those we might normally regard as our enemy, or at least to those we could reasonably expect wouldn't do the same for us. As if that weren't enough, we are even enjoined to suppose that loving your own life means you'll lose it, and that being prepared to lose it for these principles leads the believer to eternal life. And that's certainly the stuff of revolution. To him it meant the way of the cross. To others who might follow it will provide the inspiration for messianic mission, which might be based genuinely on self-sacrifice but also at times on rather less noble convictions. Men may have frequently invoked the gods for success in their wars and disputes, though it is only in these lands around us that they have killed in their name to our knowledge. When gods become singular and exclusive what can we expect but more of the same? War becomes total, necessary and justified. We should be terrified for such a monotheistic future.'

'To my simple mind the Gods remain our protectors, Festus, and need to be assuaged in order to keep them powerful in order to better do so. Apart from needing no other divine company, what's essentially different with this great god of the Hebrews?'

'Because instead of our many and varied supplications to the Immortals, Prefect, in this case there's one arbiter, and one only. In place of men placating a host of capricious deities, they must prostrate themselves before one all-powerful, omniscient being. Singularity or plurality, brooding or ethereal, however – in terms of man's essential relationship with the force that created him, does it matter? It's the same general idea, isn't it? Man proposes, god disposes. There isn't much that's very positive about it if we're looking to stand on our own feet. We do what we think we're told, or face the consequences of being cut off from the source of life, and incur disfavour, abandonment, even comprehensive retribution. But now with the son of god everything changes, we're told.   God is not about retribution, nor his mercy conditional.   In fact his love and mercy are so great that he sends his only son to save us from our sins, and show us the way to eternal life through personal redemption and service to others.   Both to Jew and to Gentile, the Nazarene's teaching on all this compassion, and the potential for man to grow in love and peace with his fellow-man, is almost grotesque. It's so eccentric, Prefect, that in practice it's completely unworkable.   It'll never catch on because man can't change his nature any more than the leopard can change its spots.   That might be regrettable but it's true. And it doesn't mean we all have to go to Hades in a handcart.   Most people might stray from the right path occasionally, put themselves first a little too often, do others down more than they should, but the great majority are fundamentally honest and well-meaning, want harmony in their dealings with others, and don't go out of their way to cause trouble with their neighbour or make enemies lightly.   They've got their gods and their customary ways of serving them with as much sincerity as they choose, and it will take a great deal more than one mystic, however charismatic, to make them change.   No, I can't see how such nonsensical ideas could be of use to our purposes – or how any of this is relevant to the Governor's problems in running Judea.'

'We realists can agree on that, Festus.   My only concern is of any sanguine view of human nature whatsoever.   The proportion of people prepared to break the rules if they think they can get away with it is a remarkably high one, gods or no gods.'

'Depends on what rules you're talking about, Prefect.   If it's the system, authority, the government, paying taxes, then yes.   If it's more of a social context we're concerned with, especially where people can relate to those who might be personally disadvantaged by their actions or behaviour, then less so.   As you implied yourself, no-one wants to be thought of badly, or do someone down whom they know, at least without good reason.   Self-interest, selfishness, simple thoughtlessness – these things are all in the eye of the beholder and bound to have fluid boundaries of acceptability, and context is everything.   Devise what you think is an unbreakable rule and it won't be long before even the most principled finds pressing reasons for an exception.   At least if we're under divine observation some will curb their excesses. Isn't that the best we can reasonably expect?'

'It's always difficult to imagine change. No-one can predict the future, however many auguries they consult, and human affairs are inherently unstable. All we can be certain of is that everything changes over time, that change is a constant. The question for us, Festus, is whether we – and I mean we in this room now – are to be agents of transformation in the hope it can lead to some good. Are we to act, or sit on our hands and let everything go on in the same old way?'

'In Judea, where one thing never changes, Prefect? Where the constant is the god of timelessness?'

'It's precisely here that the rock of ages gives forth new life-giving waters, Festus, with interesting results. The religious hierarchy couldn't abide being called hypocrites by someone who claimed to be the long-awaited messiah, the saviour who would rescue his people. They were confounded by the Nazarene's humble origin, his open lack of respect for their show of devoutness, ultimately the alleged blasphemy that would seal his fate. But there's no doubt his ideas would resonate, especially if they can break out from the rigid society which seeks to contain them. We've seen that with the crowds who flocked to hear him. What can we deduce from their reception, other than a widespread conviction that life must be about more than struggle and dog-eat-dog? Salvation comes not from strict observance of religious custom and ostentatious good works but genuine repentance, forgiveness of others and charity to all, god's good grace freely given to all that seek it. Instead of an eye-for-an-eye and a tooth-for-a-tooth, which everyone understands, we now genuinely have to love our neighbour as ourselves, without end.'

'You astound me, Prefect.'

'Whether that makes any sense or not doesn't matter. Whether this personal god could ever really exist or have a son who was walking the earth until yesterday is impossible to really be sure about. It's what people believe that counts. Think of the powerful effect that could have – eternal life for those who look beyond the god of vengeance and his enforcers on earth. What a slogan! What a problem to set loose on the High Priest!'

'So you admit it then, Prefect – the aim is really the undermining of the Jewish establishment.'

'An incidental detail, Festus.   We'll come back to the bigger picture in a moment. To stick to your politics, let's perhaps consider the Governor's proposal as an expedient which he might well believe in his interests as far as his relationship with the Jewish establishment is concerned, but is also unlikely to meet any opposition from the other powerbase we haven't mentioned yet – Herod Antipas. The Tetrarchy has no formal powers in Judea but it does have influence, as we saw over the votive shields affair. With the possibility of a significant Yeshua-based movement we might find a more emollient and pre-occupied Council diminished in authority and status, which both we and Antipas could only welcome. The Nazarene's given us a golden opportunity to open a rift between the religious and the secular by undermining the hold of the priests over the people, which is how the Sanhedrin derives its power – from the current inseparability of religion and politics, two sides of the same coin. It's fine to have a state religion, so long as religion is in support of the state. Put the priests in charge and it's the other way round. At present they win because their hold on the people is unchallengeable.'

'Divide and rule, Prefect, that's the thing!'

'Give the people something else to think about.   "Render to Caesar what is Caesar's" becomes easier to accept, and the profanity of our presence here is first tempered and finally begins to recede, until it becomes a thing of the past and we can govern the place properly. We've stamped out barbarian religions elsewhere where they threaten the *pax Romana* – why not here? We can and do tolerate native gods where they don't pose a threat, but where they can't be assimilated we have no choice but destroy them. How else does civilization advance? And here we have a chance to do it without resorting to force, with good government and none of your Sejanan extortion. What is there to object to?'

'Nice theory, Prefect. A people more amenable to Roman rule might in time reduce their support for their more nationalistic elements, which would then be easier to neutralize. But don't rule out the possibility of the opposite happening, of the theocracy being driven into the radicals' camp and the greater part of the country with them. Next thing you know you've got a real war on your hands, and not of limited aims but annihilation.'

'True enough, Festus. But those risks might accrue whatever we do, whereas if we do nothing there is no chance of assimilation or long-term peace whatsoever.'

'Unfortunately it's not going to work, Prefect. I don't really see any rift between priests and people getting very far. To achieve that you'd need widespread popular support for any dissenting movement, and judging from yesterday there isn't going to be enough of that to make a difference. A faint underground stirring in the margins, perhaps, but nothing to trouble the establishment very much, no widespread protests and certainly no armed uprising.'

'Business as usual then.'

'I think we're looking at two extremes here. Either the Jews somehow recognize their true messiah after all and undergo a wholesale conversion, which let's face it isn't very likely – or eventually, as I say, the whole Province blows. A future emperor loses patience, marches in and wipes every trace of these people from their ancestral land. And the Governor knows it. He's torn between encouraging them to be more amenable and thus more receptive to our rule – or letting them hang themselves. He can't make his mind up, because he knows whatever he does has incalculable long-term consequences.'

'That's right as far as it goes, Festus. The prospect of eventual Armageddon in the land of Israel is very real. We all know the colossal effort required to deal with fanaticism in an enemy prepared to fight to the death. The ruthlessness needed for victory wouldn't endear us to that posterity we seem to be so concerned about here, either. But what's the problem with turning this hard-hearted people into a more emollient one – the imperial design achieved through a bit of guile, not a bloodbath – beyond expediency to real progress, and on a grand scale?'

'We've gone around expunging native religions quite successfully, Prefect, and will no doubt go on doing so as the Empire expands, and naturally the real Gods take over as civilization spreads. But it's different here. Can you see these people exchanging Yahweh for Jupiter? – it's never been in the offing away from the Hellenistic coast, and they're not going to start now just because that's what we want. The unstated proposition seems to be to replace their mysterious and singular god with the son, whose underlying message was one of harmony and co-existence. That might make our rule here more acceptable, but is that ever really likely anyway – and why does it have to be Yeshua's version? Why not Jupiter's? We might end up creating a new god at the expense of the rightful one.'

'Festus, Yeshua is one of their own. His god and their god are still the same, but his at least brings some prospect of local acceptability, however slight. That's a reasonable start, I'd have thought.'

'What concerns me most, Prefect, isn't the futility of trying to change this ancient people – it's the potential for the success of his message far beyond, due to its beguiling if facile attraction. It'll never shift the Jews, but who knows the havoc it might wreak among people with a less monolithic god controlling their lives – including even ourselves? You know – people more inclined to listen, who let sentiment cloud their judgment.'

'Congratulations! Festus, I do believe you have it at last. As I tried to tell you, our local concerns are of passing interest, but that's all. Yeshua's missionaries will shake the dust off their feet and look to the world, as we must now. Others will accept where the Jews cannot.'

*   *   *   *

'I have to say, the Governor's state of mind also worries me – one man with the power for good or ill, and struggling apparently to know the difference. He can't have been seriously considering all this without being obliged to take some interest in the cult's intellectual appeal. That's got to be the case because he's obviously discussed it with you, Prefect, and it's coming out in this debate. How do we know some of these ridiculous ideas haven't been rubbing off on him? Look at us – one of us here has been deeply affected already, so why not the Governor too? When does state pragmatism become personal conviction? How much of this stuff does he actually believe himself?'

'You're trying to evade the issue, Festus. Yes, the Governor and I have conversed, but I don't claim to know the whole of his mind. A brand new religion, always a matter of some interest, fascination for some – that's what we're talking about! There's the novelty, the superficial, the emotional, and where there's intellectual coherence, the attraction. The Nazarene's appeal was intensely personal, so how much any of it might stick is anyone's guess. We can all have private thoughts on that, whatever our official obligations and duties. Or simply be well informed – like you.'

'Needless to say, we should strongly disapprove, Prefect. If one of our number here can be sympathetic, should we be surprised if the Governor himself starts to take more interest than he really ought? Far be it for us to give him advice on religion, but he does by virtue of his office have duties and obligations. If news of this got back to Rome he'd be finished. And worst of all, to follow your line – if this cult ever spread beyond these shores and took hold, in Italia itself let's say, he'd be undermining the true Gods and the very State itself. How do we know it won't spread and spread and even become the official religion one day? How long do we think Rome, bereft of its manliness and senses, would last then?'

'Yes. What seems impossible might one day prove the reality. The world's turned upside down and in doing so becomes normal. That is itself the lesson of history – the Eternal City born from the ashes of Troy, the Empire sprung from the ruined certainties of the old Republic. But now perhaps you begin to see the enormity of our charge, Festus. Why stop with Judea? – which may not offer much scope, I agree. If the formula offers better prospects elsewhere, why not try it? Having an exotic origin shouldn't be a bar to a movement if it brings a better order and a higher morality to other peoples prepared to listen.'

'Order, Prefect? Order comes from firm government, discipline, tradition. And higher morality? You increasingly sound as though you think the Nazarene's message has a merit of its own.'

'That, Festus, may be our inescapable conclusion.'

'This is outrageous! It's a conspiracy to subvert the Gods and the very State. And we're being asked to participate in it. To become co-conspirators!'

'The Governor accepts there will be different views here tonight, but would remind us that it's not just what we handful think that counts – but what we think others will think, not in handfuls but millions. We need to assess the likelihood of a new religion with the memory of the Nazarene as its basis growing exponentially, perhaps even becoming dominant. Your fears may well be valid, Festus, but fortuitously so, I'd suggest – Yeshua's mission to his own people fails in Judea, but failure here encourages his disciples to set forth with spectacular success beyond, though it's bound to take time, long after we're all gone. That will be the true legacy – peace and stability, based on the highest morality likely to have the greatest appeal to the greatest number, if not in Judea but the world far beyond.'

'And within a few generations our own Gods will have vanished.'

'And we have to face the likely fact, Festus – that no-one will miss them.'

*   *   *   *

'The Governor's been got at. Let's be honest, Prefect – what about Procula? There're rumours she's been in contact with these people very recently. And we know she's an impulsive, impressionable woman.'

'You mean, can the Nazarene have got through not just to the Governor's wife but her husband too?'

'Through her first and foremost, Prefect. It's the sort of thing that appeals to women. And like most of us she'd have known all about Facilis and his servant – ask him – and when the Nazarene's circus eventually hits the city she couldn't resist the opportunity to make contact. The nonsense is eminently catchable, so naturally she catches it. And naturally she speaks to her husband. Man and wife may not always agree, but it's a rare marriage where there's no mutual influence – one holding a view is alone sufficient to affect the other, if only subconsciously. So I ask you – what assurance do we have the

Governor himself hasn't been tainted? Because if he has, it wouldn't just egg him on with this hare-brained scheme to confound the Jews – far worse, it makes him open to accusations of apostasy himself. He's supposed to set an example, not renounce everything's that's fit and proper and betray those he's supposed to be leading.'

'Hold on, Festus! It's not for us to pry into the Governor's conscience or his conversations with his wife. You don't honestly think a man in his position would abandon the Gods so easily, do you? Anyway, by your reckoning, if he'd thought there was really something in these new teachings he'd have wanted to save the Nazarene, not kill him.'

'He could have been toying with just that, and you could say he did actually come quite close to saving him. That he didn't in the end merely reflected the political imperative, manifest in the pressing form of a howling mob. If events had transpired differently it's quite possible to see a very different outcome. It's because it was all so public and spontaneous there was no choice, and the man ended up condemned. You could also argue that anyone in the Governor's position who'd been turned might actually believe the man had to die in order to fulfill the prophecy. Is that far-fetched? As we agreed, I think – once people get a fixed idea of their god's will, or, perhaps in this case, simply the desirable outcome, there are no limits to what they'll do to justify it. It's patently what the Nazarene himself did, isn't it? At any rate, it's clear the Governor did have some degree of sympathy – and something must have been going on in his head, Prefect, or else we wouldn't be sitting here arguing about it.'

'Just because he wasn't enthusiastic about the condemnation doesn't indicate anything about his own thoughts on the religious aspects one way or the other, Festus. I could equally well say that if it hadn't been for the threat of real disorder he might have quietly acceded to an execution anyway – a lower-profile case of the public relations gambit you were talking of. The Governor, as we know however, does have a temper, and he doesn't take kindly to hostile crowds, which could well have influenced his actions. I don't think it's up to us to speculate on these lines.'

'But the likelier possibility is the sympathy one, isn't it? And once you admit that then you admit everything. The cult's message is insidious. It puts the worm of conscience in a man and leads we know not where. This is now extremely serious. We have our own leader contemplating a gross subterfuge and apparently in need of advice and moral support from his own subordinates. Just the sort of weakness you'd expect in someone enamoured with a cult like this – loss of reason and mental faculty. Well it won't just be him in serious trouble – it'll be us too. In fact if we were really concerned to do our duty we'd be considering relieving him of command in the name of Caesar, right now.'

'Don't be ridiculous. Look Festus, our invitation to candour doesn't give free rein to start bandying outrageous accusations about. The way to approach this whole question is to respect the trust being shown in us, and do our best to respond with a calm examination of all the factors and possibilities.'

'And it just so happens I seem to be the only one here standing up for sense and reason and the old Roman ways – yet I can't imagine it's not a view shared by every true servant of Caesar. We can't have a proper discussion of this subject if certain aspects are out-of-bounds, Prefect. How else do you expect us to be able to offer the right advice? The Governor's state of mind regarding this cult must be germane to this debate. Does he have any sympathy with it, or not? And I must say – if there's any doubt you should ask him to clear it up, though it all seems pretty clear to me.'

'We are not here to countenance impertinence to the Commander-in-Chief, Festus. And neither is your concern important to the outcome. Not compared to other things he might wish to say to us.'

'Such as?'

'Not the proposition's intellectual merit but it's potential for influence, as I've tried to explain. That's what he wants to hear our views on, and what we should be addressing.'

'Well you know mine. Influence yes, but it's the wrong sort. I want to know exactly what underlies the Governor's question, because if it's some sort of manoeuvering to spread a subversive cult then you can count me out. No idea which doesn't have a sound footing in the real Gods is going to stand much scrutiny. Has this been thought through dispassionately? Has the right conclusion been reached at the top? Obviously not.'

'I'm trying to be patient here, Festus. That's precisely what we're trying to do, isn't it? And your view is much valued – it goes into the mix. Very well. You reject the idea on both theological and political grounds, a conventional response and very possibly quite valid. I don't know what the others are going to say – they might well agree with you.'

'Prefect, I think you well know there's no compromise here. Our entire Roman religion is being undermined around this table as we speak. Do we really understand what we're doing with this? If we lose our wits over this wonderful new-look god, straightaway the Immortals become enraged. The two beliefs cannot be compatible. Jupiter and Juno, Mars and Minerva, Venus and Vesta, who succour and protect us, guide us now in all our thoughts and actions as they did our forefathers, probably long before the Jews found their Yahweh. They brought Aeneas to the founding of the Eternal City and made us the greatest power on earth, inspiring us to succeed through our *genius* and endeavour under their protection. The Gods of Rome are the very embodiment of the State. They are Rome. We were nurtured on them from our earliest days. We consult them, we offer libations, we thank them for their munificence. We preserve their honour through public festivals and special societies charged with passing their secrets to new generations. And if we ever so much as think of deserting them, they will abandon us and Rome will one day fall to barbarians. Never again will we deserve to aspire to greatness. Instead there will only be chaos and bloodshed and uncertainty and mediocrity and weakness and misery without end. How can we sit here and contemplate our leader doing this?'

'We're not, Festus. You can take it from me the Governor is far too sensible to let himself be carried away along the lines you're suggesting.'

'Are you sure, Prefect? That it's only about – what did you call it – influence? The Governor doesn't personally agree with the Nazarene's message but nevertheless wants it spread to all people everywhere – never mind whether it's false or not. And by trickery! Because it will somehow make men better, and somehow easier to govern.'

'Almost.'

'What do you mean?'

'Because I can't answer for another man's soul.'

'Because you don't know, Prefect. The Governor thinks it should be spread to all and sundry though you don't know whether he thinks it's true or false. Or whether it'll end up destroying our own religion. You just can't be sure about the Governor and this Yeshua, can you?'

'Alright Festus. No, I can't. Perhaps he doesn't know either. But as I've told you, it's not relevant.'

'Some men take their devotions more seriously than others, Prefect. How do we know what the Governor really thinks about anything? The last time I saw him sacrifice last year, I couldn't help thinking how he seemed to be approaching the sacred ceremony with ill-disguised distaste.'

'It's a solemn duty, not an occasion for levity. Perhaps he's had to do too many.'

'Very likely. But those with the privilege of power have obligations to uphold the beliefs of the State. They speak and act on our behalf. And I'm merely thinking out loud, Prefect, as you enjoined us.'

'Which has to include the unthinkable, I agree.'

'The Gods of Rome are a fact. They're as real as you or me. All our experience tells us so.'

'We're trying to suspend the thinking habits of a lifetime here, Festus – as I said at the beginning. It's good to have your view so eloquently before us but we can't keep going round in circles.'

'Well I'm confused. Perhaps we should ask Facilis. He evidently knows more about these things.'

'I'm sure OC V will answer for himself when he's ready.'

'Fine, but if I may say so it's stretching things a bit to have him in this discussion at all. Nothing personal, Facilis. I know you've been through a lot the last few days, but the more I think about this the more questionable it becomes. I don't mean you personally, old man, I mean about the rumours, and even stranger talk I'm hearing about oaths, which has to be bordering on ... Sorry, I may have had too much to drink. The truth of the wine cup and all that. You know what I mean. If you ask me ...'

'Before we ask OC V – Senior Centurion, you've said nothing all evening, other than remind us of an essential fact or two. Why don't you continue on that theme? We can then hear Centurion Facilis' considered view. He might have some interesting things to tell us, but we'd all benefit from re-visiting the factual basis first, I think.'

* * * *

Longinus kept his eyes on the table-top which seemed to have been occupying his attention most of the evening. 'Thank you, Prefect. What do I think?

'I think the man I crucified yesterday was the Son of God.'

THE DELIBERATION – III

'I can't take any more of this.'

'Sit down, Festus.'

'This is beyond stupid now. I'm going to have to be excused.'

'Denied. You will stay and listen and continue to participate, as ordered. You have made a valuable contribution so far. You've given us a very cogent account of this new sect and reminded us of the *status quo* and our own obligations. It's for good reason that discussion about religion is normally frowned upon, but the situation we're in here is anything but normal. Let's remember above all that we're brothers-in-arms – the least we can do is hear each other speak. Continue, Senior Centurion.'

'Maybe I'm just short of sleep, Prefect. I'm not sure I can find the words I need. Reckon it started at the trial. I could hear everything.'

'And you were there when they first brought him to the Praetorium?'

'Yes, I was there with my men from the start. I was close to the Governor and the Camp Commandant, ready for orders. And the second time you were present yourself, Prefect. You heard it too.'

'I did.'

'Which of us could have stood there like He did, answering so coolly? He had an impressive calm about Him. I've seen it in others going through condemnation and pronouncement of sentence, as though resignation and detachment have already taken over and the soul starts to prepare for its journey. But this was different. There was a strength and dignity here which were almost tangible. And against the tumult outside His few words to the Governor had an authority like no other I've heard before, His words on the cross the most moving any of us could ever imagine.'

'Stuff and nonsense. This country's crawling with wandering vagrants pretending to be the anointed one. Are we losing our wits entirely?'

'You weren't there, Festus. I didn't set out to be impressed. Go and ask my soldiers – how many of them felt the same. I doubt you'll find a more hard-bitten bunch anywhere. I can't express it adequately.'

'Might I suggest you were a little taken-in by the pathos of the occasion, Chief? No-one actually likes a crucifixion, unless he's a total sadist.'

'I tell you, the sky which hung dark over the city yesterday was like no other. Yes the whole thing was moving. It might even have moved you, Festus. You don't get the families going to executions, but there they were. It was absolutely pitiful. We heard him tell a follower to take his mother as his own, and also "forgive them Father for they know not what they do". What sort of criminal – or anyone – does that? Would any of us be big enough to have borne it so well? – I doubt it. If you must know, his mother actually came up to me afterwards. She didn't say anything. She didn't need to. She just wanted to let me know she didn't hold it against me.'

'Perhaps she was just thanking you for granting them the body. It would have been a natural instinct for some people.'

'Possibly, Prefect. But I think it was more than that. It was a gracious gesture, and I was touched. At the end, as we were packing up and they were getting ready to go round to the cemetery, it was almost as though we were all one body – them and us together versus the rest, versus the whole uncaring world which had done this thing to them and then departed, back to its banality, job done. And we were the instrument. We were the ones who'd just done it, though we had nothing against Him, far more in fact against his accusers. We had killed these good people's beloved, their hope. They say life is full of irony. So, it seems, is death.'

'Then what?'

'We made our way back to the fort, escorting the cart this time – those timbers are heavy. It was almost dark by the time everything was sorted away, and there was quite a lot to do.'

'Ah yes, the Macula affair. You'd have a few enquiries to be making, eh?'

'I couldn't concentrate. I'll admit I was fairly shattered, but also acutely aware I'd never be the same again after that day. I slept lightly and woke early, but full of absolute certainty that something very real had changed in my life, with the sort of dynamic energy you get when a personal crisis hits you and makes you reach for the highest levels of readiness, and everything else seems of no consequence and falls away. Before the fatigue sets in.'

'Have you discussed this with anyone?'

'Of course not, Prefect.'

'Not even Facilis? We know what great pals you are. Can you enlighten us now?'

'It's all very new, Prefect, but some things are crystal clear which before wouldn't have occurred to me. Call it revelation, if you like. I can talk about them if you think it'd be helpful.'

'Please continue, Senior Centurion. We need to know.'

'I can see that true moral courage requires us to stand up for the things we really believe to be right, no matter what others might say. Men pass this truth off lightly, vaguely thinking they too would be up to it if the test ever came to them, but rarely ever having to experience it in earnest themselves. When you see it first-hand like that, and what it means in the price to be paid, you notice alright.'

'The Senior Centurion talks of truth, Prefect, but his experience seems to have had a peculiar effect on his perception of reality. We can't let duty become emotional involvement, or allow a single episode in the course of that duty to convince us everything's the precise opposite of what it really is. Where's the judgment in that?'

'I'm still Longinus Sdapeze, your Senior Centurion, Festus – still a soldier, still The Gripper. I hope no-one's going to try and equate acknowledging the Son of God with going soft.'

'Not at all, Chief.'

'This isn't about empty rhetoric, or military efficiency, or a theoretical exercise in neology. We're discussing the relevance of Yeshua of Nazareth, to every man, woman and child alive and countless millions yet to be born. That is, if we're going to answer the Governor's question – which to my mind comes down to "What is the greatest good?" And if you saw what I saw yesterday and the revelation of His truth – what I believe to be the truth – I don't think you'd have the slightest doubt where the greatest good lies. Any of you.'

'We have our truth, Chief, given to us by our own Gods.'

'Men should use their intelligence and what they see with their own eyes to determine the truth for themselves, Festus, from which derives their conscience. Conscience is not to be relegated by resort to false gods.'

'More heresy, Prefect! The Senior Centurion's spouting heresy. Not to mention treason, if he includes the late Emperor in that statement.'

'Festus, I've explained the rules of this discussion.'

'But we cannot proceed on any basis which isn't totally truthful. Is truth now to be a relative concept?'

'Senior Centurion?'

'Some will deny that, and hold their own version sacrosanct. The argument will then be between absolutes and their merits. Others will openly admit relativity, though they won't call it that, and attempt to obfuscate the issues. They will say no-one has a monopoly of truth, that one man's truth is not the same as another's, that both have a right to interpret facts in their rightful context, that everything, including what we call truth, is thereby relative. And it's almost true – appearances can change according to the angle of view, or like light being cast on something partly in shadow. It's understandable that not everyone sees everything the same way, but that's usually because they don't trouble to look around the object properly, or only see what they want to, or won't let what they do see overcome their predisposition or prejudice and draw appropriate conclusions. The relativity applies to the protagonist, not the fact. Often things are said or perceived which are partly true, or true in specified contexts, but one thing ought to be very clear – the truth can't be anything you want it to mean. You have to make sure you allow for any deception of the angle or light, and challenge your own pre-conceived ideas, and then you might arrive at the truth you seek or recognize it when it finds you. There have to be some absolutes –

ask any mathematician. We cannot allow those who aren't prepared to acknowledge the totality of the truth to claim only those parts they prefer. Where the totality cannot be known there will often have to be some selective weighting or approximations made to arrive at a balanced understanding, which we have to do all the time as a matter of practicality in reaching conclusions, but that's where the discernment and judgment you mentioned come in. Keeping a sense of proportion does not exempt us from facing binary realities – in so many of the fundamentals, and especially in matters of faith, there has to be either truth or falsehood, right or wrong, yes or no. In a sea of grey some things remain black or white. We eat, we drink, we are alive, we know God. Yahweh and Jupiter can't co-exist. This isn't academic. It's life – and death.'

'So when the Governor asked Yeshua: "What is truth?" – what was the answer?'

'He didn't, Prefect. As you know, He didn't reply.'

'Because he couldn't, Chief! Yes, there can only be one truth, one set of beliefs, and that's the one that exists already and which everyone from our superior Greco-Roman heritage acknowledges. It's absolute and eternal, not something to be picked about for convenience. You can't make it into something it isn't, and you can't compromise with it.'

'We can agree on that last statement, Festus. The problem is realizing it when you're face-to-face with it. For me yesterday, confronted in the most graphic way possible, there was no difficulty – but on the contrary, outright compulsion, and though I know so little, I hope to learn. You're right, though it's not what you want to hear – there can only be one true God. And the purpose of Yeshua's ministry was to reveal him in all his glory. Men however who won't have had my own life-changing experience will have to accept it for themselves. Some never will, because they won't look or listen, or acknowledge it when they see it, either because of their temperament or because the society in which they live discourages it, and all the while they will be beset by the false prophets of which He warned. But those who seek will find, and in time all men may do so though it take many generations.'

'He had the chance to say something like that yesterday, and didn't.'

'He said it before, as I'm sure you know. Yesterday He knew His time had come, Festus, that His mission was achieved and the time for speaking over. And I think the Governor realized that too. We can assume he too already knew something of the Word, and that Yeshua knew he knew. There was nothing more to be said or gained, no hope of a sensible discussion in such fraught proceedings. And there was no point – nobody was going to listen or be converted in a cauldron of hate and emotion like that. To believe in Him is to believe in quiet goodness, not in the implacable unbelief of an angry crowd. The truth was there in the dignified figure of Yeshua Himself, and needed no elaboration.'

'And you're going to tell us the Governor made a mistake in condemning him, that he showed weakness in the face of the mob.'

'I ...'

'That will be all on that subject, Festus. Ours is not to criticize.'

'Correct, Prefect. The Governor got it entirely right. You're not going to censure me for supporting him on that one, are you?'

'We don't know exactly why the Governor acted as he did yesterday, Festus. It's just possible he planned everything from the start. It's common knowledge he's no stranger to the vehemence of the people here concerning their religion, or the likely consequences of defying the Sanhedrin, so he must have had a good idea of what he was in for. I can't imagine after so long in office he'd have forgotten about the annual pardon, even if the precise timing might have caught him unawares, and he did seem a little taken aback when the chanting for bar Abbas started. But I think any degree of premeditation on the precise outcome is unlikely. His main consideration would have been to uphold the law, and on that basis, seeing that Yeshua was clearly innocent, exoneration might have been expected. But as we've discussed – things happen in the heat of the moment, events take on a momentum of their own, and there was no going back once the decision was made, however regrettable.'

'He did uphold the law, keep the peace and leave the Jews to their own business, Prefect.'

'That is so, Festus. Our concern now is what happens next. I can't tell you about the Governor's personal view of Yeshua of Nazareth – but I can tell you something of what's on his mind now we're in the aftermath. If Yeshua's prophecy should really come to pass then it will have been due to his decision yesterday, and his alone, to abandon him to the Jews – which would be a daunting prospect for anyone. But there's something even more important – that having instigated what he thinks could have the potential to be the most significant event in the history of mankind, the best should now be made of it. The promise should be made real, for a great force has been stirred but not yet released. You can take the possibility of a resurrection as seriously or with as large a pinch of salt as you wish – the vital thing is for the message to be spread and received.'

'Sounds like hedging bets to me.'

'Not quite how I'd put it, Festus.'

'You're saying the Governor's not quite sure he didn't make a mistake, Prefect? He wants to limit the damage to his reputation in putting Yeshua to death just in case the holy man turns out to have been who he said he was? Except he wasn't – but we'll have a resurrection just in case?'

'Festus, let us suppose for argument's sake the Governor did indeed think he might have executed the son of god. If this were to be proven by the resurrection prophecy there wouldn't be any point in ... in additional measures. This god will be known by that fact to all, his rule affirmed through his crucified son, and whatever the Governor does now, his reputation among his critics would be sealed for all time and there'd be nothing he could do about it. He'd have to reconcile himself to eternal ignominy. If however he didn't think he'd made a mistake, as you put it, and the prophecy wasn't going to come true, then again there wouldn't be any point in further action – just let everything die down and be forgotten in the detritus of man's time on earth. But that's not what he wants. He's suggesting there might be a better outcome, one which has real good come of it, and he's asking for our view on whether we should go ahead and make it happen. More than that – he's actually putting it in our hands. It's too momentous for one man, but you can't seem to accept that.'

'But Prefect, if these so-called additional measures are implemented – well, he still goes down in history as the villain.'

'He knows that.'

'Don't worry about the Sanhedrin and the god of the Hebrews, though. They'll survive, having managed so far. It'll be the Olympians who are swept away, the Gods of Rome whose roots are false and shallow – according to my brother officers here.'

'Who can say, Festus? Perhaps the Olympians should take their chances.'

'Then this truly is treasonous, Prefect. All because of a self-publicist radical preacher and the unaccountable effect he seems to have had on the Governor and his wife. I can't believe we're even discussing this. Changing the course of human history in a paragraph. Four of us gathered around one table and pretending to decide the future of mankind as … as casually as preparing an invitation list.'

'Not a bad analogy, Festus, and we'll overlook the unfortunate reference to treason. Let me as your Senior Centurion enlighten you. You object to Favonius' presence because you think he's been turned, compromised – well now you've got me to balance things up a little. It is appropriate the Prefect invited you too, though, since you never experienced Yeshua's physical presence yourself, so we might say you represent the many who haven't and never will, not in the flesh anyway. If you had then you might be singing a very different tune. You too might have known the power drawing you towards Him, almost against your will. The Governor must have felt it too yesterday morning. I certainly did – even my soldiers, in their usual stolid way, but then only we were at Golgotha. If something like that doesn't shake you to the core and make you see and believe, then nothing will. Yes, this is one of those matters of fact we were talking about, where there can be no half-measures, which is either true or it isn't, and I believe with all my heart and mind that Yeshua truly is the Son of God. I don't fully understand what that might mean, nor do I know what it might hold for me in my life, but I believe it to be the truth.'

'That's right, Chief, I never saw him. Probably that's an advantage. I'm free of the madness which seems to be afflicting everyone tonight.

Wherever the truth lies, surely it's with enlightened peoples who find it through long experience and custom. The Gods of Rome have been since time began. It is in them that our people have always put their trust, and through them that our trust has been rewarded with greatness. It is thus our duty – and our right – to stand by them in the face of would-be usurpers of the truth who surround us in foreign lands, of strange ideas which spring up in the desert, the voices of Babel all clamouring for attention – and which can't themselves be true because they have no pedigree, no plausibility and no association with the greatest power on earth. If they have no history, how can the truth they proclaim suddenly materialize out of nowhere? If they were really true then civilized men would have known about them from the beginning, as our ancestors did the Immortals.'

'Could there be some truth in all the gods, Festus? What about the Egyptians, Medes and Hittites, the Celts, Scythians, the Germanic peoples, and no doubt many others we don't know about? They've been worshipping their gods possibly as long as we have ours. Are they insane too, or just wrong? Could it be there's wisdom in all religions, that different peoples approach belief in their own way but all have one thing in common – the need to worship something, some body, some entity greater than themselves, that can explain why they are alive and why things are as they are? It seems all men have to believe in something.'

'In which case not mad, Prefect, just wrong – and contrary to everything the Chief was saying about relative and absolute truth. They can't all be right, can they?'

'In that case a greater question might be whether all the various gods are in fact one – one entity but seen from those different angles the Senior Centurion also talked of, interpreted from different cultural perspectives and in differing social environments, and venerated in different ways accordingly – the absolute truth indeed but obscured by appearances, and it is these that men squabble over? When men across the earth pray and invoke the divine, are they appealing to a multiplicity of powers, or the same power manifest in many outward expressions? You can see the attraction, can't you? Forget the animistic forms, which are frankly too primitive to concern us here. Our subject is the creative force which governs all life, a unity on which all religions draw, a presence to which all men feel connected – one all-embracing god, or perhaps one all-encompassing presence most would think as god for want of a better word. How would you answer that, Festus?'

'Some describe that as spirituality, Prefect, which underlies all religion though the two are not the same. Spirituality isn't formalized, though if you ask people who claim they're not religious but nevertheless spiritual you don't get much sense back, more mystical notions of awareness of something they can't describe but without the obligations – a vague idea there's something there which ought to be given its due but no-one's sure quite what or how. People whom you'd think otherwise quite sensible give credence to all sorts of mystical nonsense without reference to any gods, and taken to excess it can so easily end in witchcraft, which is the negation of all religion, and, even more worryingly, in witch-finding hysteria. And is it surprising that the one-god mentality seems to give rise to an associated if embarrassed recognition of the collective forces of darkness, as though one can't exist without the other? Plural gods co-exist with plural and often undefined negative beings, although the Immortals, being prone to take sides and capable of malice, themselves have no such need. The mono-god however begets his own concentrated antithesis, from which no good can ever come.'

'You would condemn most of the human race then, Festus? You can't blame people for thinking we must be more than animal bodies, that the mystery of life requires there to be something beyond our understanding.'

'We have our own Gods for that, Prefect, and what use is mere spirituality to anyone? The only spirits we know are the ancestors and those of the household and all of nature, which can be mischievous so have to be given their due, but the unnamed spirits of the mind are for those of infirm and inchoate thought, which does lead to madness. Our deities have identities, which is why they're real and to be venerated. The Gods reside in earth and sky, ocean and underworld, the spirits in every hearth and home, in glade and spring and stream, and all men who call themselves civilized give them their rightful place.'

'What does the Senior Centurion have to say about that?'

'Perhaps my imagination's a bit lacking, Prefect. I've never seen or heard a sylvan spirit, or any other sort, despite taking them for granted until now. Nor, far more importantly, have I ever known of Jovian intervention, in my own life or the lives of those around me or who've gone before. And I don't know much about the god of the Hebrews, other than what Yeshua is known to have said of the First Commandment, to love God above all else. To me he's the God of justice, austere and remote – perhaps that's how a stern but loving father should mostly be. But the Son is different and attracts through His humility and humanity, but also His divine strength. Above all He is the personification of the truth, borne out to me while He hung there on the cross. I was just doing my job, doing what had to be done, when it took me like a tingling flood through my veins, as though I too were transfixed, rooted to the spot, oblivious to all other sensation.'

'You let it get to you, Chief.'

'He didn't have to be there, Festus. He didn't have to die. He could have chosen life, mortal life. His friends and family didn't have to witness the most appalling death we can imagine, which, we need scarcely remind ourselves, we alone now seem to inflict on the condemned. Why do we think this was? What made this man go through that agony and suffering, voluntarily? If you think He was a miscreant like the other two, then I respectfully suggest you're sorely mistaken. Criminals and charlatans don't behave like that. They can be brave, yes. But magnanimous, considerate, forgiving to the last? Is it likely He would have subjected Himself to that terrible ordeal if He didn't think He was doing it for something infinitely more noble and worthy – for the will of the Father, to save us from our sins by taking them on His own head – for the truth?'

'You mean his version of it, Chief.'

'I saw, and I believed, Festus. My interest was caught at the Pavement. My curiosity was aroused at the Praetorium. My concern was secured on the Way of Tears. My whole being was taken over at Golgotha, the Hill of Calvary. In that moment I experienced understanding and overwhelming gratefulness, despite the horror, and that rarest of feelings you get when you know something extremely unusual and important is happening and that you're part of it. It wasn't that anybody else was excluded – it felt as though the whole of heaven were looking on in awe and sorrow. But it was also personal. Very personal. He was dying for my sins, taking on the agony to save me, unworthy as I am.'

'The man wanted martyrdom, that's plain. It was all in the plan. Not just his but his god's.'

'By all accounts, it was. "The Son of Man will be betrayed to the chief priests and the teachers of the law, who will condemn Him to death and hand Him over to the Gentiles to be mocked and flogged and crucified, and on the third day He will be raised to life and seated at the right hand of God." That's what He'd said Himself. And as the prophet foretold of the Messiah, "He was oppressed and afflicted, yet did not open His mouth. He was led like a lamb to the slaughter, and as a sheep is silent before her shearers, so He did not open his mouth." He knew His duty. And we can relate to that, can't we?'

'Then you too have been keeping your ear to the ground on the Nazarene and his sayings, Senior Centurion.'

'How else could I argue with Favonius about such things far beyond my own abilities, Prefect? He also said "I am the light of the world. Whoever follows me will never walk in darkness, but have the light of life."'

'He was also quite open in claiming to be a king, if only in indirect terms I believe, which seems a strange claim and quite at odds with the rest of his call for humility.'

'Yes, Prefect. And, "if Abraham was your father you would do as Abraham did". If you wanted to antagonize the Jews you could scarcely find a surer way of doing it. He knew full well what He was doing in saying things like that, that it would end in His death, but that it had to be so if the scriptures were to be fulfilled. "For God so loved the world that he gave his one and only Son, that whoever believes in Him shall not perish but have eternal life." That's the key. Eternal life with the Son of God as our advocate, who as His cousin the Baptist said "takes away the sins of the world". A call to live our lives in a new way, hearing God's word with new ears and truly believing, turning the other cheek, forgiving those who trespass against us as often as it takes, until they too see the light and man's life on earth is transformed.'

'But we have eternal life too in the Elysian Fields, do we not, as long as we pay for our passage and aren't dispatched to the torture of the Furies?'

'So Festus would say, Prefect, though according to him we can escape them in time if our debts are paid. To enter the new heaven I'm talking about we need to repent our sins, forsake the temptations of the world and follow Yeshua's example. Hell is being cut off from God, having turned away from his Son. Think about it. They're going to say in years to come that He died for our sins, that He's taken the punishment that should rightly be reserved for ourselves as sinners. Are we to spurn His offer of eternal life?'

'And they're going to say he rose from the dead.'

'Yes, Festus.'

'When everyone talks of the afterlife, most Jews included, they mean the soul. If you're talking metaphorically that's fine. But the body too? As the Sadducees would say, that's preposterous.'

'That's reserved for the Son of God, not us, Festus. We're mortal beings, not divine.'

'But the Nazarene was mortal too. A carpenter from somewhere no-one's ever heard of. You saw him die, for pity's sake. The Immortals take human form at will, but can never die. How can this man rise from the dead who was obviously mortal, not a god but flesh and blood like us?'

'He was – He is – the Son of God, Festus. That's all I know.'

'I see. So where do you think all this will take you?'

'I wish I knew. There's a lot to think about. If it hadn't been me there yesterday I wouldn't be talking like this. But I was, and I am. And now in this deliberation it strikes me the Governor shouldn't be asking his question, though I can see why he believes it's extremely important. God will not be mocked.'

'If the Nazarene really is the son of god, Chief, then it wouldn't matter what question any of us asked, would it? He'd be a god himself, and man would have no say in this or anything else.'

*　　*　　*　　*

'Well come on Chief, don't go like the shearing sheep on us, like your god yesterday, all silent and enigmatic.'

'I've told you what I think, Festus.'

'And I suppose he must therefore rise some time before midnight tomorrow. Except it isn't going to be in the light of day, is it? That would be asking too much. No, by dawn, then. Like a new moon amid the constellations.'

'We have to believe, or else there is no power. Your gods require that too, Festus.'

'You really do believe this – this tosh, Chief?'

'All I know is I witnessed something yesterday completely beyond my experience and understanding. You press me, Festus, and I answer that I believe, because I have to. Yeshua will rise from the dead.'

'We'll know soon enough. It's a good job we're sworn to secrecy or even your reputation would be a thing of the past. But there's a problem for you here, isn't there, Chief? Whatever we might like to think about man having no say in your god's existence, if we do take the body it follows you're not going to be sure whether this god really exists or not, are you? If we don't, it'll be the end of it and your theory too. Unless of course it happens to vanish into thin air all by itself, in which case the most astounding event in the history of mankind will have occurred, except no-one with any sense will believe it – they'll just refuse to, or blame human hand, if they ever stop to think. You'll never know the real truth, however much you might wish it. Quite a dilemma.'

'That's not just my problem, Festus. It's yours too. Everyone's. And what would you say if we did resolve to take the body and get there to find it gone? That would shut you up, wouldn't it?'

'It would just mean there's been an intervention along any of the lines we've discussed, and the Governor's object gets implemented one way or the other. If your miracle did take place you'd never be able to prove it or convince anyone, so it wouldn't get you very far. Bit of another paradox there, Chief. God agrees to vanish, but only a few culprits – hated Romans, no doubt – know anything about it. But miracles don't happen anyway.'

'It would be up to us then, wouldn't it? – to follow the risen Lord wherever and however we are called. It might not impress you, Festus, but personally I'd have no doubt. I saw how He conducted Himself in His hour of need. I relate that with what I've heard about His preaching. If I was satisfied the scripture had been fulfilled then all doubt would be gone, and that's how people far distant from us in time will come to see it, because such a miracle can never be suppressed. Why, it'd be a pretty compelling case even for you, Festus. Meanwhile those of us not quite so sceptical have to learn the meaning of faith.'

'But real, actual, proven miracles don't happen.'

'They don't in your world of mythic mountain-dwellers, except in poetical imagination, that's certain. What have the gods of Rome ever actually done for you, Festus? You talk correctly of evidence – where is it for the ancient gods? Your attachment to them is all about tradition and sentiment and a large dollop of superstition – however much you try to defend them. And I dare say the Governor would agree, were he to tell us what he really thinks.'

'And Favonius Facilis? What's this great god done for him in his hour of need?'

'There has to be so much more to life than cynicism, Festus. You've got to leave some room for things we can't comprehend, for God to work His will, for possibilities to become reality. Don't call it spirituality. Call it the divine mystery, the foundation of which isn't folklore but divine truth, the blessed reality that the personal God only ever wishes good for us, unlike yours who treat men so lightly. You argue your case well but for this crucial omission, Festus. Do you think I'd be telling you this if I didn't believe it? Do you imagine Favonius would have been struck with the new faith if he too hadn't had his encounter with the living God? Oh yes, I freely admit my old self would share the incredulity and derision that one of us could have weakened so, like a virile man reduced to feebleness by woman. But now I think I begin to see. Strength isn't always to be found where we expect it. It comes in many different ways. Now I understand what Favonius has been going through, and I can only express my appreciation and admiration.'

'It'll be interesting to get his views on that, Chief.'

'How did you know about his problems anyway?'

'There's no need to respond to that, Festus. It's time we heard from the Centurion of the Fifth himself.'

* * * *

'I've listened patiently, Prefect.'

'You have.'

Favonius hesitated, gathering his thoughts.

'There is no god. There are no gods. It's all an illusion.'

THE DELIBERATION – IV

'Favonius, you're not being serious.'

'I most certainly am.'

'Only yesterday you were ready to give everything up for the faith. Even your life. What's happened, my friend?'

'Nothing, Longinus. Except that I took your very good advice after all. I've got myself in order. I'm free. Too late to be any possible help for my marriage. It's only an arrogant fool who has no regrets.'

'First your life. Now your soul. Don't throw it away.'

'It's not just the Nazarene. It's the whole lot of them, so-called gods – every one of them false, a manifestation of man's ignorance and infinite capacity for deceiving himself.'

'Strong stuff, Facilis. But aren't you going from one extreme to the other?'

'Prefect, the human race has so many failings. It's not just its propensity for conflict, in every situation and on every scale, but the everyday behaviour – its cruelties and stupidities, its ambitions and enmities, its rapaciousness and wastefulness and criminality, its obsession with celebrity and fads and trivia, its endless idiocies, its lurchings from one collective madness to another. We scurry about like ants on a great mountain, but with half their wisdom. We claim over-lordship of the earth, but everything we do ends up in difficulties and disputation. They say all living things carry the seeds of their own destruction one way or another. And we must be the prime example.'

'Come on man, don't let your troubles spoil you. You're bound to feel a little jaundiced after what you've been through. You'll get over it and come to see the good side of human nature again. Festus is right –most people are pretty decent, eh?'

'Oh I know about the redeeming features, Prefect. About altruism and generosity and the nobility of self-sacrifice, and how people generally try to rub along with their neighbour. And we soldiers especially appreciate team-work and genuine comradeship. Healthy self-interest is natural and commendable, but even when the good isn't outdone by the bad there's always the underlying ooze waiting to seep out – the petty jealousies, the disloyalties, the backbiting, the smug superiority, the satisfaction at the failings and misfortunes of others which all but the most virtuous can't help feel at some time or other, and are almost synonymous with what it is to be human.'

'There's good and bad in all of us, Facilis. We've got to be positive, be grateful for the good and encourage it.'

'I agree entirely, Prefect, but we're considering the role of religion, which like men themselves can be a force for good or bad, but chiefly the latter. You can pray to be delivered from the power of all those failings and any manner of temptation, but does it make any difference in the bigger scheme of things? The human race keeps rolling along, but does it have to go on treating itself so inhumanely until the end of time? I've come to the conclusion religiosity is an inherent characteristic of *homo non sapiens*, fully in keeping with the paradox of our underlying traits – over-estimation of our cleverness and importance, under-estimation of our own responsibility and limitations. How can that be anything but dangerous, given our record of destruction and discord, when any good that might come from religion is based on a false premise, and any bad seen as collateral, relative, acceptable, inevitable? How can thinking man, who thinks he knows so much, convince himself of something so essentially unlikely, unnecessary and unproven?'

'I take exception to your charge of ignorance. Intelligence manifestly varies from man to man, and probably from people to people if the relative states of their civilization are any yardstick, but there'd be no civilization at all if we were that stupid.'

'The purpose of thinking, Prefect, ought to be to learn, solve, improve – and question. And questioning has to be radical. We progress only minutely incrementally, which is why it's so painfully slow, when what we need is to get to the bottom of our problems and discontents and put them properly right, instead of having to look back and wonder why it took so long to make any advance at all, and why our forefathers had to endure as they did. The answer to that of course is because they weren't radical enough either, the proportion of people prepared to break out of the received wisdom of any age so small they're stifled by a morass of indifference and acceptance.'

'There's obviously a religious instinct, Facilis, which admittedly hasn't given us much peace yet – but patience! We're not going to change the world overnight. We live in our own times and have to accept things as they are, as they've been bequeathed to us, even though they're not always as we might wish. But bit by bit man does progress, and we should be grateful and not over-rush. Religion is eternal, and gives safety and stability, a foundation on which to build solidity and prosperity, a fortress from which to defend our morals and take the truth to those who would oppose it.'

'Prefect, we accept the ordering of men as though it were ordained by god, or gods if you like, sparing little thought for how life in this great master-plan has to be endured by its less fortunate subjects. Get close up to anyone for any length of time and it's not difficult to identify with them, even to take their side in whatever situation they're in, but it's collective mass behaviour we should be more concerned with. We all belong in our parts within a bigger whole, and yes, that's how it all is – one class or group or whole people against another in constant struggle for their own interests and their own versions of the truth, in which our better qualities will too often fail against baser instincts to aggression and general unreason. And the greatest manifestation of that is religion, which marks mankind's divisions like none other. It's not the only cause of friction of course, but there is no hope for the long-term peace of the world if we can't release ourselves from its shackles, which restrict every man and woman and whole societies from conducting their affairs more rationally, and they are shackles which are self-imposed. And I'm only too well aware it will upset people to challenge their deeply-held beliefs, here in this room and outside it. They should be questioning themselves on those beliefs, beyond the normal level of tentative self-doubt which many will experience but suppress out-of-hand. Our own State religion might be at a mature stage, capable in time of accommodation, but others will be less so, less able to tolerate questioning, more ready to punish heresy, blasphemy, apostasy, dissent of any kind. In the end all religion, however benign, has to be taken on trust, and the norm will be for no serious discussion among adherents on the fundamentals whatsoever.'

'I'd have thought the Nazarene was your solution, Facilis. He aimed his preaching to the poor and dispossessed, and seemed to upset the establishment every way he could. He wanted to end deference to custom and the rigidity of the past, didn't he? Wasn't that radical enough for you?'

'I've alluded to the divisiveness of religions, Festus, but that's not the immediate issue here. I'm more concerned with what they all have in common, which is the universal tyranny of irrationality.'

'How you can turn yourself about so abruptly, when we all know you've been dallying with this Galilean business? How you can now use it to deny the true Gods is beyond me. It's unforgiveable, Facilis, and you're courting the wrath of men and Gods.'

'I seem to have earned that opprobrium already, Festus. But we've been granted immunity from the wrath of men by this discussion, thanks to the Governor, and if I'm right about the gods there is nothing to fear, nothing to lose but those shackles of superstition.'

'And if you're wrong?'

'Then I'll stand as a man and call your gods out for the impostors they are, and if I'm cast into the underworld without trace they can take their hollow triumph. None of us can be absolutely certain of any of this until we die, but no believer has ever passed on and managed to warn us yet, because of course they can't, they're dead, as we will be too. So we come back to the start – we'll never know, but I'm not going to stop using my faculties in my living years to come to the inescapable truth – you know, that elusive commodity you were all talking about earlier.'

'You seem very sure of yourself.'

'As sure as I can be.'

'And may we ask why you're so certain? What has brought you to this sudden revelation, when every man and woman alive in every clime seems to think it right, seemly and dutiful to believe in some god or other? Set aside your unfortunate personal situation, Facilis – which by the Chief's convoluted logic ought almost to be some kind of privilege through suffering, no less. I mean the weighing of the evidence in your head. Let's hear the case for this rationalism of yours.'

*   *   *   *

'Because, Festus, contrary to your assertion that religion explains the world, it's the precise opposite. Can't you see? – everything's random, and randomness is so much easier to explain once we dare to admit there are no gods. The only thing you could say isn't completely random is man's continuing fitful progress by means of his own intellect, as we've already discussed, though that itself is subject to random influences. There's a clue there – because using our heads is our only hope for a more reason-based future in which the ill-effects of randomness can be better mitigated. You seek for meaning, but there isn't any. There's no such thing as the meaning of life. We're 'ere because we're 'ere, like all other lifeforms on earth, having our little day and being succeeded in our turn. You can pray all you like, keep all the observances, examine all the innards, consult all the auguries you want, it doesn't make any difference. Our lives turn out the way they do because of the decisions we make and actions we take, but against a plethora of events and situations outside our control, and amid the forces of nature which bring their own inevitabilities and random distributions. This is why bad things happen to good people, and, more tellingly perhaps, why good things happen to bad, not because of any arcane theology but very simply because of the much likelier explanation – that there are no gods. Oh, sometimes things go well, and you get the outcome you wanted and thought yourself deserving – the gods are with you after all. But the other times, when it doesn't – when you get the wrong outcomes, the wrong people suffering, the wrong people rewarded? What about them? And please don't tell me the failures don't exist, because that's just wishful thinking, the first cousin of intellectual dishonesty and self-delusion. There can't be any problem in the affairs of mankind not made worse by irrational misplaced certainties on the existence of god.'

'But Facilis, don't the just get their reward in the afterlife? And we know if we give the Gods their due they do listen and do favour the observant, though it has to be done sincerely and the interpretation of their response has to be correct. Sometimes the answer will be "wait", or "think again". But to ignore the response altogether, or, which is unthinkable, to fail to consult them in the first place, that would be to court disaster for any enterprise, big or small. And how can anyone take that risk on behalf of those for whom they may be responsible, who expect the proper observances to be made on their behalf – be it emperor or head of a humble household?'

'It's more of the same, Prefect. We hear what we want to hear, and since the ideal of rational man may never come to full fruition then the enlightened leader will have to make allowances accordingly. But let me try and get to that which we all seem ready to neglect – explanation. When our forefathers lived in the mists of time and there was no higher knowledge, since we know this came later, they must have been primitive, impressionable creatures struggling to survive against hunger and the elements. How can we begin to imagine the awe with which they viewed the world before we had any understanding – the turning of the seasons, the sun which gives light and warmth, the swelling of the seed, the plenty of the forests and the seas, skies of lightning and thunder, weird phenomena like rainbows, eclipses of the sun and moon, volcanoes, monstrous sea-waves which can submerge whole lands? And when they looked up at night and saw the great array of the heavens, the planets and comets and stars shooting across the sky – of course they wondered, and were in awe. How could these things be explained except by divine power, and how could they themselves not be completely at its mercy?

'It was natural therefore to attribute them to the gods who must rule the firmaments and brought us night and day and wind and rain, above all the warming of the land through the returning sun upon which all life depends, and then to make obeisance that their favour might not be withdrawn but continue, so man might live. Then came learning, so that now we have algebra and geometry, and medicine, and architecture and engineering, literature, drama and poetry, history and geography and philosophy, all to temper our ignorance, and the heavens are charted to enable navigation and exploration and trade with foreign lands, and thus the laws of nature start to be understood – which helps us, if not to master nature, then to live with it to our great benefit. And knowledge begets knowledge, above all in the field of natural philosophy, so that one day many mysteries will be revealed and men will understand why these things are as they are, and not have to live in ignorance.'

'Such a time is beyond our imagination. We can only live in our own and as the wisdom of the age dictates, Facilis.'

'But it's poor wisdom if there's no questioning but only acceptance of existing belief, Prefect. Who will strive to find greater knowledge if not we ourselves? We are the inheritors of all who have gone before. We came to know the gods at our mother's knee, and saw our fathers perform the offices day in, day out. Ask yourself – would we still have the great panoply of the gods of Olympus if our ancestors had not handed it on to us in full array, but stopped to question the rationality? Would we ourselves have created such an artifice if we'd been forced to consider from the start how our private conduct and public affairs could be governed without reference to the immanent? No, we've been conditioned to accept religion through habit, each generation inculcating the next since time immemorial, not through religion's intrinsic intellectual merits but through custom derived of little more than fireside yarns and mythic verse. The ignorance of our ancestors is excusable, but it's time we came of age and brought our intellect to bear. Yet religious people are determined their beliefs must be right, so questioning is not to be countenanced. They cite evidence in defence which wouldn't get very far in a court of law, and no amount of attempting to reason with them is likely to make them think again.'

'Which also could be said of you, Facilis.'

'Yes, Festus, but I have deviated, and been forced to consider, and consider again. And the onus of proof should be on the positive assertion, not the negative. Some progress does get made, I agree. The gods don't demand human sacrifice any more this side of the brute periphery – though yesterday's events might give some food for thought on that. When enlightenment does dare challenge engrained religion, however – who then has to be silenced in order to stave off ruin and disaster for the people but Socrates, the personification of reason, and, we might add, courage? For a surfeit of ignorance and stupidity look no further than the execution of that truly enlightened and innocent man, for the responsibility of breaking the never-ending cycle look to our own generation. All we need to do to liberate ourselves from this oppression is take the first really questioning step, yet we are afraid to do so in case we're punished by man and god, the whole edifice comes tumbling down and civilization is left bereft of its false certainties – so on we go, heads down, determined, justified. Without that first bold move in allowing ourselves to question all religion, intellectual and thus social and political progress will continue as before, slow and fitful, and their opposite, stagnation and backwardness, reign supreme without end. Religious people will always claim the higher moral position derived of their truths, which they will hold with sincerity and passion, but reality is dispassionate, and no-one can do this questioning for us but we ourselves. There can be no validity in any claim to reason or morality where the claim is itself based on an erroneous concept.'

'But religion gives us an explanation, doesn't it? Of who we are, where we've come from, why the world is as it is. It gives us our beginning, it takes us to our end and on to immortality.'

'It fulfills a need, Prefect, in answer to our primitive quest for understanding. But that's mostly about our self-imposed craving for reassurance and sense of purpose – typical of impressionable man in all his insecurity. Who are we? Why are we here? How did we get here? We yearn for answers, but what's the point of constructs which aren't based on proper evidence but speculation at best and self-deception at worst, with lazy mental comfort somewhere in between? Our state of knowledge can't explain how men came to populate the earth, but that's no reason to suppose we were made by some sort of omniscient force. Far from Jupiter Best and Greatest fathering the Immortals and ordaining the lives of men through caprice, or Yahweh guiding his chosen people through unbending dominion, I suggest a rather more prosaic explanation – our forefathers in their primeval state invented them both. Man invented god, not god invented man. Shocking, I know.'

'But without the Gods men would be mere animals, Facilis. Men were created to be elevated above the animal state and equipped for such dominion as the Gods have decreed.'

'And do we behave any better than animals, for all our sentience and conscience? Don't they too procreate and guard their young, show courage and cooperate for the common good of their kind? I've already spoken of the time before history began, when men were truly ignorant and life precarious in the extreme. It isn't hard to see how they tried to make sense of their existence and recruited deities to help them survive in a hostile environment. These they anthropomorphized to make them identifiable and to share the human experience, but also to rise above it with superhuman ease, so that great things could be achieved in deeds of imagination to release earth-bound mortals from the stark reality. From a time when all lived in goatskins, and gods emerged from elemental myth, is it any surprise Jupiter is the god of thunder? Or is it Zeus?'

'Then how do you account for the nature of the god of the Hebrews, Facilis? Not a king of gods, but god alone, jealous and austere? The question's relevant because of the Nazarene's teachings, which seem to be a further progression from Yahweh being the one-and-only god while also, it is claimed, being the basis for this new, softer interpretation.'

'Sects and heresies come into the picture all the time because of man's restless nature, Prefect – possibly more so in a monotheistic religion since there is less scope for recognized variation from the standard, no pantheon of existing alternatives from which to pick and choose. Our societies are not static. Within the generalization that they must have their gods, the details of their form and worship will vary considerably over time. New orthodoxies become accepted, new armies of adherents become convinced only they have exclusive access to the correct interpretation of the eternal truths. But none are right. None can see that our understanding from when time began should be evolving more radically than that, that there is an alternative explanation for our existence, that their own certainties could be flawed. Who knows how the god of the Hebrews came upon his people as they first wandered with their flocks? They would say they were god's chosen people from the beginning and were given their law and their promised land through his covenant with them, and although to our knowledge this idea is precisely replicated nowhere else, the fundamentals are the same as any other religion. The covenant is drawn, following which divine protection and guidance have to be invoked by conscientious observance. A powerful authority figure rules over the fate of men because they have to believe they are not alone in this uncertain world, that someone or something is on their side. If in addition you have a holy book and believe it really is the word of god, that every word is literally god-given and the prophets his mouthpieces, and try and act on those precepts, then you will be doing good and keeping the law, firm in the assurance that you abide in the land given your people by the one true god.'

'And the proof of this one true god, Facilis?'

'There we could agree, Festus, though that question applies equally to the myriad myths of Mount Olympus, which even the devout among us don't take too literally these days. We know our own Olympians are essentially the same as Homer's and our Trojan founder's, though they've taken on a more business-like demeanour to reflect the Roman character – more down-to-earth, you might say. Compare them with the god of the Jews and a neutral observer might be more impressed with the idea of solitary splendour and indivisibility, but these different religions all serve the same purpose and share one convenient characteristic – they can't actually be proved.'

'We hear what you say about absence of hard proof and the closing of minds, Facilis, and there must be many who harbour doubt from time to time. But that is the nub of faith. We doubt because we are frail, we overcome because we are given strength. There would be no higher calling, nothing to which men can aspire – no religion – without faith. We need it to give power to the ideal, even though we can't prove it by what you would call an objective process. Yes we are taught the first steps as children so that we might grow in this faith – what else do you expect one's parents to do? As long as we hang on to it somehow in later life then we can weather the times of doubt and backsliding, and always come home.'

'To the safety of the teat, Prefect.'

'But the profession of faith alone is sufficient to sustain both the individual soul and the religion itself, even though for some it may only be going through the motions of observance. Inconstancy and laziness are common failings, and a measure of doubt does occur to the more thoughtful, more than you suggest, Facilis. But doubt purifies faith, justifies it, spurs it on, making the religion a live force because enough people believe in it to make it real, and thus carry it on to their descendants. It helps take them out of themselves, raise them above the Prefect's animals, give them an identity, bind them together as a society. Everyone benefits because the Gods watch over each new generation and the future is thereby secured.'

'So long as the people remain faithful, you mean, Festus.'

'But you say it's all in vain, Facilis, that everything happens by chance and therefore the Gods are careless, or impotent, or non-existent – in any case quite useless. Well, you might have been through a life-changing experience, and so apparently has the Senior Centurion, but what about the rest of us who lack your insight? What are we supposed to believe in other than the Gods of our ancestors?'

'How about pure reason, Festus? Observation – or rather, in searching for the divine, its fruitless result? And thus deduction. Shouldn't that be enough? As I said, the burden of proof should be on believers, not on those who can't see anything of gods however hard they look. You talk, rightly, about the very act of belief which underpins and almost in itself justifies the whole system to its adherents, but that's asking a bit much of irony, don't you think? Religion is right because its believers believe it and practise it, not wrong because you can't prove a negative? Or should religion therefore be recognized only – or even because – its authenticity can't be demonstrated? Is that really what you're saying?'

'That doesn't follow at all.'

'Maybe not, but it's a measure of the absurdity you expect me to believe in, Festus.   Simply accepting and reciting something doesn't make it intrinsically true, whatever adherents may profess.   And for those who might have second thoughts, who wouldn't instinctively accept anything else at face value, why should acceptance of any claim to truth – in this case, of religious belief – seem to be made so very difficult?   If something is true and admirable and essential, why can't it be demonstrated indisputably by these powerful gods for all to see? Why shouldn't the gods operate openly in such a manner, if they want us to believe and believing is so important?   Or are they hiding behind this opaque thing we call faith in order to perpetuate their existence – or, as a more rational observer would argue, their non-existence?'

'Go on Facilis, say it. Their non-existence as concealed by men, you mean.'

'We venerate the gods and ask them to bring us health and fortune, but when did anyone see them appear before their eyes, or do anything to actually prove their presence?   If something succeeds and we've being doing our religious duty, then our faithfulness is rewarded and reinforced. If we've been doing that duty and things haven't turned out so well, then we tell ourselves we can't have been doing it quite well enough, or the object of our entreaties has decreed it's not in our interests to have our request granted, or not to worry, it clearly wasn't meant to be, or there'll be a silver lining somehow.   Does it never occur to us that the reason we haven't had the answer we would have liked might be for a very simple reason – there's nothing there? The question doesn't get asked because the habit is so engrained in us that we cannot, dare not, whatever quiet doubts we may have, allow them free rein to pursue this obvious possibility. Reason is stifled at birth by the warm blanket of habit, which descends to block all enquiry and suppress any rebellion of free thought. And the religious establishment continues on its way rejoicing.'

'But those demonstrations of proof were clearly made to previous generations, or else they wouldn't have handed them on.   Or are you calling our ancestors liars?'

'I don't suppose anyone ever set out to systematically set up any religion to mislead, Festus – although, irony of ironies, that does indeed seem to be what the Governor's proposition amounts to.

Religion is best described as an involuntary attempt at an explanation for our existence by minds collectively too immature and ill-equipped for rational understanding. Creation myths and ever-more elaborate folk-tales metamorphosed and formalized over time, resulting in rigid doctrines and forms of worship requiring conformity from whole peoples – that's what religion has been throughout the ages, and still is now. The origin of our religious inheritance is mere primitive assumption, yet its continued acceptance is now so embedded it drives some to think they have a duty in its name to save souls, even, *in extremis*, to kill their living owners in order to do so. And suppressing those who believe in other gods in the name of your own seems commonplace. If you think about that for a moment then religion isn't benign at all – it's utterly terrifying. And I worry that any tendency to monotheism will only make things worse. It will only be a matter of time before monotheistic belief-systems clash, and don't expect much harmony within either. Men will always make war. Far from stopping it, religion, the claimant to peace and order, will only exacerbate. Within the same religion the invocation of god in war will double and re-double the struggle. Without, the ultimate resort will be savage suppression and even complete extermination.'

'Your definition is unfounded, Facilis, your speculation on the future wild. No-one's saying the Gods are anything but a mystery. If we concede that religion by its nature is objectively incapable of proof, it's going to be too easy to have doubts. I agree with Festus on doubt, it's an integral part of faith. In fact it's essential and to be welcomed. It shows we're all human, lest that was ever in question, and, with all our faults and weaknesses, in need of divine correction. It's a spur to discipline, because it has to be resisted. It forces us to think what we're doing, and why. And it's a strength, because it's there to be faced and grappled with, a process to be gone through, to emerge from clearer and justified. But proof comes from long experience in one's own life and the lives of others, seeing the Gods at work in them, and the trust which that brings – and not by tempting the Gods. There has to be a limit to doubt, a bed-rock of belief which man by his nature seems fitted to live by, indeed needs.'

'I'm tempted, Prefect, to think that would weigh more heavily for the followers of what we might call a god of conscience like the god of the Hebrews, but not for the stage-directors of Olympus with their plots and posturings. There can be no real faith if it's the sort invested in mythical characters dreamt up in the imagination of Achaean shepherds thousands of years ago, in she-wolves suckling human infants – or in dead emperors. Just think what's the more likely – that these imaginings are actually real, or are all simply products of folklore and superstition, which we accept because, we're told, we have to believe in something.'

'That's treasonous talk again, Facilis. Think yourself lucky the Prefect hasn't warned you for court-martial.'

'That's enough, Festus. Facilis, I have to say as your commanding officer, the obvious course for anyone with doubts is simply to do as everyone else does. Go with the flow. Accept the conventions, accept that society needs some sort of religious habit to keep functioning. How else could rites of passage for example be marked, without people coming together in common and convenient affirmation of their identity, or an organization like the Army maintain its corporate spirit without official religious observance? It's chiefly a matter of practicality. Whether anyone actually believes all the incantations and pronouncements in detail is completely immaterial. The man of principle shouldn't have to torture himself over a dead emperor, eh?'

Favonius did not respond.

'If I may, Prefect. We shouldn't be talking about hypothetical situations. It's clear OC V has had a catharsis, a crisis of faith, possibly a nervous breakdown. We shouldn't be hounding him in this state.'

'I've never felt so certain about anything in my life, Longinus.'

*　　*　　*　　*

'Nor I, Favonius. Nor I. I'm just so sorry you've had to endure so much and that you're now in this unsettled frame of mind. I can only hope and pray that time will heal and that you'll be led gently to see things aright again. Because it's staring us in the face, present and

revealed, offered freely to all in our blindness – the living Word of God.
I say it reluctantly – I'd almost wish it wasn't so, since you and this new-
found freedom of yours are almost to be envied. You're nearly right –
why lumber yourself with the burden of prayer and the still small voice
of conscience, when life is too short and there are so many other things
to be done? But in your repudiation of the false you miss the truth, by
a mile. The reality is not to be denied. For the lone and jealous God,
all-powerful, all-conquering, all-seeing, all-saving, terrible in vengeance,
stern in his lasting justice, the embodiment of his people, their history
and identity, their hopes and certainties, is also Lord of the whole of
mankind, our Father of love and compassion and hope, and the only
way to Him is through his Son, who together with the Holy Spirit is the
means of our salvation. The Son's body lies broken now but will rise in
glory, and shall be called the anointed one, the Christ.'

'Have you lost your right mind too, Chief?'

'No, Festus. Nor have I had too much to drink. Like Favonius I've
found this conversation very useful. But I haven't lost my mind – I've
found it. I am this day a prisoner to Christ, and in so doing I've found
perfect freedom.'

'Just about as clear as that stuff about three-in-one!'

'Now that's a good phrase, Festus. No doubt learned men will
make much of triune unity in years to come. For a simple man like me it
seems simple enough. Yeshua the Son is the Almighty's representative
on earth, mortal yet now immortal, man from God, while the Spirit of
which He talked comes to any who will listen, to unify and to fold into
the mystery of faith. A Holy Trinity for the saving grace of the world.'

'And you claim you don't understand everything about your sudden
conversion! I can see why – how do you expect anyone to believe all
that?'

'Because for people who don't think man created himself and that
there must be something else – which includes you Festus, if I heard
you right – it offers a new way of seeing things. Eternal life through
the forgiveness of sins. Salvation through humility, not the unremitting
self-righteousness of those who call themselves godly, or the selfishness
and greed and cruelty of the ungodly we see everywhere around us.'

'Well it doesn't sound simple to me, Chief. Give me the good old Gods any day. And strength, and manliness. I can't be doing with all this self-abasement.'

'And credulity, Festus.'

'That's insolent, Facilis. It's a good job you have your immunity tonight. You may not always have it. There are some who would strike you dead for an insult like that.'

'I don't mean to belittle your faith, Festus. All men's beliefs should be respected, particularly in the matter of religion. And I don't agree with the Senior Centurion's implication that conscience is better for belief in god. The one thing's that not in dispute is that genuine belief is founded on deep conviction, but if we here can't be frank and honest with each other, when can we ever be? What exactly is it about religion that makes its adherents unable to hear a word against their own interpretation of it, this code for life which people in polite company don't want to talk about, as if all reason and transparency must be abandoned? You and I both are critical of Longinus and his attraction to the Yeshua phenomenon, which I was so convinced by too. He's not taken offence to your sort of attitude – yet – but if he stays with it and comes to live his life by it then he might well, and with rather more intellectual rigour than proponents of the old gods will muster. You've heard what I now think about all religion, but I think we have to be even-handed, don't you? Whether we think we understand or agree with everything about particular religions is not the issue. All religions have more than a sense of the numinous and mysterious about them, or, as we were saying, they could hardly be religions. They're all about things unseen, which is why I personally can't accept any of them. We're not going to change minds easily, in any direction. If there's no visual proof then what chance reason? But as the Prefect has been getting at – the issue before us is not so academic. It's how to make men behave best.'

'How can you say that, Favonius? You who saw and spoke with Him, and witnessed your servant healed? How can you, having set your hand to the plough, look back so soon and forsake the way of truth Yeshua has shown us? We know you're going through a difficult time, but you need His strength more than ever now. Yeshua's Resurrection would be the proof you need, but it must be fulfilled for all. For all that's good, not just in men's behaviour but in their recognition of His eternal truth, this miracle must be allowed to come to pass.'

'I'm sorry Longinus, if there's one good thing to come out of my problems it's my freedom to cast the whole works off. I'm no longer in thrall to the incredible. I shall go and read the Stoics and the Cynics, and find beauty where I can. I shall take our Prefect's advice and do whatever meaningless acts I'm required to comply with in public, but there it will end. It was my wishful thinking in the beginning, against your own good advice, that got me into this mess. It didn't do my marriage any good – far from helping, it very likely just added to my wife's alienation. The loving god, the divine plan to keep us all together – that's all over and done with now. I prayed so hard for its saving, for my children's sake, but I tried not to be selfish, and left it to this loving god to resolve, knowing it was too big a problem for me alone. "Your will be done" means to a believer what it says, but it's hard, very hard, when there's no sign of any response consistent with such a god, and you ask yourself what the will of god really is – which in my own unremarkable and insignificant little case isn't a lot, I can only conclude. If it takes two to break a marriage, with three the outcome is a foregone conclusion, and when the third party seems so out-of-keeping with anything that might be expected to correspond to the divine will – then it all gets too much. But my misfortune is a miniscule perturbation in the sea of human unhappiness. There are many far worse things in life, and whatever we believe about any religion it's important to appreciate what we do have.'

'Can't you only wait a day more?'

'I wish we all could, Longinus, but we're required by circumstance and explicit order to decide now, and we must all do according to our conscience. My other problem also forced me to a timely decision. Yes Festus, the matter of the oath – entirely of my own making and willing gullibility. But looking back I don't think I'd have done anything different in responding in the way I did to the Galilean and his friends, since I knew no better. I was led, and followed in good faith, you might say. People so want to hear a message of good news, to have a reason to carry on, to hope. And I believed. I took it seriously. I tried to live my life accordingly, and encouraged my family to do the same. "Anyone who does not take up his cross and follow me is not worthy of me." That's a powerful call – and an even more powerful indictment for a waverer.'

'Don't give up, Favonius. Our earthly life is never over till the final call. None of us can tell what good things may yet await those who believe, and at the last your reward will be in heaven. Ask yourself honestly why you can't summon back the same faith for which you prepared my own way. Yes, Favonius Facilis – don't you realize it was your witness that set me on my path, for the moment when I too came to stand before our Saviour? Come on, you can do this.'

'I have, Longinus. I've asked myself a thousand times. But I can't.'

'Why not, for the sake of heaven?

'For the best and only reason. It's no good wishing for all these good things about the kingdom of heaven on earth if they're not true.'

'We can talk about the truth all night.'

'This isn't about any other gods now, Longinus. It's between your new-found god of Yeshua on one hand and rationalism on the other – the only debate that matters. The supreme omniscient being re-interpreted, versus the laws of nature and the intelligence of its principal and most dangerous inhabitant, man.'

* * * *

'God's creation and God's creature, you mean, created to acknowledge his Creator and thus find eternal life through the Son.'

'If Yeshua is the son then I am lost, deservedly. I have sought to know the reason for things – *rerum cognescere causas* – but everywhere I see only the hubris of man. I've come to my conclusion the hard way.'

'And I haven't? There's an arrogance in atheism too, but while you draw breath it will never be too late, Favonius.'

'What's the first question, the common sense check, you should ask yourself whether something is true or not? I'd suggest, "Is it likely?" Is it plausible that a man could be born to a virgin mother, or rise from the dead, or that the lion could ever lie down with the lamb? Why would we expect anything to happen which breaks the normal laws of existence? Doesn't that immediately make you want to be suspicious?'

'But that's the whole point. For the true God nothing is impossible.'

'So long as we have faith, I know. A response remarkably common to every other religion as well. Religion is true, truth is to be believed because it's palpably true and without it there'd be no religion, so you'd better believe it.'

'So many have seen His wondrous doings, Favonius. You can't gainsay that.'

'We've already discussed the problem of proof. I'm afraid not much seems to have got done in the presence of the sceptical.'

'Because there was no faith on those occasions, either in His own country or Judea. The power comes when people are ready to believe, and the evidence is in changed lives and testimonies, to be borne out countlessly whilst man lives.'

'More likely as a source of comfort and consolation for all his suffering.'

'No, as an aid to making suffering bearable, in the name of the Christ and in certain hope of the Resurrection.'

'In a world where everything eats everything else, what is the suffering of man, Longinus? Where his refuge from what he calls acts of god? Where his defence from self-destructive wars in god's name? With so much disease and imperfection seeming to come from within our own bodies, so much pestilence from we know not where, how can a benevolent intelligent creator allow this? And how can anyone seriously argue one of the most insufferable things of all – that a loving god lets us suffer to make us get the message, to ensure we stay believers? Suffering is necessary to man to make him listen, pain to make him obedient, so they say. We go wrong, even if it's merely failing to pay obeisance, so we have to be punished, and never mind the innocent. Pain is necessary and is good for us, because it's a reminder of our frailty and mortality and a summons to listen. It's almost as though god required it. Well if such a disgusting theory is a requisite for believing in any god then count me out.'

'God suffers with us, Favonious. Through his Son he suffered the sins of the world for us, nailed near-naked to the tree by us, fallen men.'

'Such self-sacrifice is only justifiable in extreme situations and for the strongest of ethical reasons, of which the physical saving of others or their substantial other benefit will invariably be the paramount concern. The very idea of sacrifice of any life whatsoever as any sort of propitiation is repugnant, and in the name of any god delusional. Where there is no self-evident proof where is the justification? It might have success in drawing attention, but as an attempt at some kind of intrinsic proof of its own it's pointless, adding only to the pain of the world. Pain and suffering are regrettably part of life, but unless they're deliberately self-imposed aren't they more likely to reflect its random nature than the design and dispensation of any god – particularly one which doesn't exist? We recognize life's precariousness so we need a comforter to help us get through it – the perils of infancy, the carefree days of youth before we begin to know what infirmity and pain and loss are in all their hard reality, and in time to contemplate our own mortality. Then in our vulnerability we take comfort that we're not alone, that there is a very present help if we will but turn to it, which will be with us to the end. It's understandable. But the whole basis is false. To love truth is to reject falsehood in all its forms.'

'Christ is truth, Favonius, and only with that truth revealed can we escape from the sin we were all born into.'

'You mean a baby born of carnal desire is guilty the moment it appears in the world – even from conception? So man is born in sin and must be saved in order to save him from himself?'

'It's not to condemn the child, it's to recognize the essential first step on the path to personal salvation. We are all marked with the broken innocence of Adam, the first man – and our necessary duty, though far from sufficient on the journey, is to avoid the mark of Cain, who murdered his brother. We have it on the highest authority that none can come to the kingdom unless they are born again, Favonius.'

'And accept it with the innocence of children, though it condemns all men to chains.'

'Man's troubles and rebellion come from his free will. Only when he learns to walk humbly with God will he reap the blessings of the kingdom on earth. You know that, Favonius.'

'The kingdom might discourage Cain from murdering his brother, but it's not going to stop people dying at the hands of nature, or suffering from so many cruel afflictions in their time, is it? Is that consistent with the loving god?'

'We can't stop that suffering, but faith makes it bearable. Yeshua has shown us the way. He's taken on the pain that we may follow with courage.'

'Your patient re-iteration would persuade many, especially those in weakness or the shadow of death, but it doesn't win the argument, least of all when people are vulnerable. We'd do better to accept the real truth, and still reach for that courage and true morality – bare of props which can only give false comfort and mislead. There is a case for mass self-delusion if it brings comfort, but it's a very poor one, and only reinforces the case for secular rationalism.'

'Christ is that truth, Favonius.'

'I'm sorry Longinus, simply repeating that doesn't make it so, any more than the sceptic counter-view is capable of proof. People want to believe what they're told about desirable ends, and will the more so when this story comes to be recorded, as Festus said, and if there are differences in the various accounts then they'll be taken as incidental proof of authenticity – whether it's actually true or not.'

'The Jews take strength from their holy book, undoubtedly. I imagine the new followers will want to emulate it.'

'A holy testament for a chosen people, Longinus, but I wonder how the new chroniclers will manage to reconcile the teachings of Yeshua with those of the jealous god of judgment and an eye-for-an-eye, a tooth-for-a-tooth.'

'He made it very clear – Father, Son and Holy Spirit.'

'If he was saying the Jews misinterpret their god then he might have been clearer about it. He said several things which stressed the need for continuity and giving Yahweh his proper due – but taking the totality of his message, what he was advocating was effectively and in practice a new religion, a second monotheistic creed to rival Judaism, based on the ten commandments and some prophesies about the messiah, but little else of real relevance from the old faith.   His message was too revolutionary for that, his vision for mankind based on ideas we've been talking about, and far more inspiring – love of god through forgiveness of sins, brotherly engagement with all men, in place of constant admonition and threat of retribution from on high.   There had to be a new beginning for the word to have appeal, though it still has the same root in scripture as before – so how therefore can something so meek come from something so uncompromising, without them being plain different things, and without there being, for all intents and purposes, two separate gods?   And Yeshua himself doesn't claim to be god in his own right, though some might have him do.   Isn't all this essentially nonsensical?'

'You and Festus may think so, others won't see it that way.   As you rightly say, a whole new following will come forth before long.   Many will struggle with these things, but it won't negate their belief.   They'll be looking for the positive and the fundamentals – and there'll be more than enough of both to contemplate, and turn into action to make the world a better place.'

'One thing they'll never give up is the Hebrew idea of being made in the likeness of their god.   As with the make-believe inhabitants of Olympus, so even with this great god now deemed father.   If we ever needed an indication of man's hubris, that we are made in god's image, this is it.   It's a claim better seen as a reflection of our own self-absorption and overweening self-aggrandizement, our delusion that man will live for ever, than any claim to reality.'

'How else do you suppose mortal men can relate to the supreme being of the universe, Favonius?   There'll be those who'd prefer to think more in terms of spirit rather than an old man with a white beard, but one step at a time.   Of course men are only mortal and have limitations when it comes to understanding and imagination – which is one reason why we all need God.'

'We can take a more realistic view of the creator when we've become a little less primitive, you mean, Longinus.   We can always fall back on the purely spiritual if the challenge of life lived in freedom becomes too much – can we? When precisely on man's journey from his primitive state did he decide god and he looked the same – or when, more pertinently from your viewpoint, did god decide? And there's a limit to how much the symbolic claim of god's image can be adhered to without losing credibility altogether, isn't there? Either this elusive god has a white beard or he hasn't. And if not, the basis of the old religion is in question again, though as an aside we know to our cost the Jews forbid any sort of image whatsoever, for their own reasons. And if the basis of the old is false, where does that leave the new? Does god's physical nature mean anything at all for those determined to take up this new faith, or doesn't he actually have one – and is nothing else about him therefore substantive either?'

'I know little of this, Favonius. Festus will probably tell us that Yeshua isn't known to have ever mentioned the subject of God's image – that all comes from the old scriptures. We shouldn't be making so much of it, neither of my understanding that they contain no mention of God as Father in the personal sense, though Yeshua makes frequent reference to him as such – as we'd expect. What are you trying to say?'

'It's just a further indication of inconsistency between the Hebrew god and Yeshua's interpretation of the godhead. Followers of the latter will find themselves having to believe in the bearded image when, as you say, there might be a more spiritual understanding, and there'll probably be other significant differences between the two approaches than the emphases we've covered. In effect we'll have not just two religions but, as I say, two gods. Or are we to relegate Yeshua's revolution to a social movement for the tender-hearted?'

'It's a new interpretation of the divine, Favonius, a glimpse into how things could and should be on earth – a new Jerusalem.'

'And it's very moving. Blessed are the poor, those that mourn, the meek, those who hunger and thirst for righteousness, the merciful, the pure in heart, the persecuted, the insulted and falsely accused in his name – the long queue of the downtrodden through the ages, hope and dignity for suffering humanity. And I too in my time wanted to hear more. Every word brought a fresh insight to what I thought was my true understanding. I saw people around me in a new light, people to whom I'd paid little notice before. We were all equal in the sight of god, all on a journey to the same heavenly destination, on which we had to help each other and try to put his words into effect, to live out the new life of fullness and fulfilment. And I came to know the true meaning of prayer, not as the means to procuring our desires but for ascertaining and doing the will of the father in heaven.'

'And now I'm in your footsteps, Favonius. You should take that as a compliment.'

'But it's too good to be true, Longinus. For one, it's asking too much of human nature for it to fundamentally change, whatever progress we might appear to make in the outward norms of our behaviour over time. Our inherent characteristics will probably go on blighting our own existence and despoiling this beautiful world as long as we inhabit it. For another it's all so simplistic. Providing we've been good on our journey there'll be a welcome in heaven, where we'll spend eternity praising the father, free of all the pain and misfortune of mortal life. And if we're not, or even if we've tried to be decent moral people but still don't believe – then we'll be judged not as faithful sheep but wayward goats anyway, and face the consequences of our unbelief. Heaven and hell are the means to attract and frighten people, to get their attention and keep them a captive audience. Worse, once you have power over people's imagination, you invite corruption among those who wield it, and phonies and fanatics who will confuse and lead the faithful astray still further. If something sounds too good to be true, Longinus, it probably is. The real answers on how to live a good life are already in our midst – the philosophers have shown that rationality is within man's capability. For any good it does, religion doesn't seem to have changed men for the better yet. The most we can say is that the evidence is mixed, certainly debatable. If we're ever to improve then it's at least equally arguable that religion is a hindrance, not a help, part of our problem, not our solution. Being good to your neighbour does not require the intervention of any god.'

'We need Yeshua's truth more than ever, Favonius. Fear of god is a positive thing, not negative. To take something from your own argument, it's about realism. True, the old gods, even Yahweh, I agree, don't speak much of charity, and we shouldn't in turn expect much altruism from people inured to the remoteness or the displeasure. But they do provide some restraint on our excesses, and on balance I believe religion does indeed make men better, with results of which you should approve. Without it we'd revert to worse ignorance and barbarism, with every man and every people for themselves, and no limit to cruelty in all its forms. But I'm not interested in anything that's gone before. I'm not here to defend any and all religion, even that of the Hebrews. I'm here to advocate the new and the true. Where there is doubt Yeshua the Teacher dispels it, because everything's different now – for now we have hope, a new way to see God and do his will.'

'Everything, Longinus? You may see your new version in that light, others will see theirs in a light of their own. Religion can be a great unifying force, especially in times of trouble when we turn to god, but it can also separate people and nations. Who shall win the favour of heaven when both sides are certain heaven is on their side? Within religions and society we see ubiquitous schisms and alienation. Look at us now, arguing like this. How easy it would be to tear us apart, unless we had other ties to keep us together. Look at Yeshua too, with a conviction so strong he was prepared to die for it. If people are prepared to die for their faith, if that's the way people think they should spread the word of their god or defend it from others with the same in mind, or, heaven forfend, punish what they claim is error by force, then it's not hard to envisage a future which isn't benign at all but truly frightening. Yes, religion might have the power to influence men's minds in some ways for the better, but it also has the potential to take them over completely, and very much for the worse. Oh yes, they'll think they're doing god's work, but there's nothing more dangerous on this earth. Wars will be waged, atrocities committed, whole peoples massacred – all in the name of some god or other. Including yours. Is this what we really want?'

'You don't know that, Favonius, and anyone who did such a thing would not be a true believer. And you're ignoring religion's great potential for good in promoting goodwill among people and peace between nations.'

'All religions claim to be peace-loving, but they'll want the peace and co-existence on their terms. Your new religion will claim the high moral ground, but so will all the others. In fact when it suits, you and they will find common cause, since people who acknowledge any great god are clearly more moral, they'll claim, and to be called godless axiomatically pejorative. One could retort that, on the contrary, morality which isn't dependent on trepidation and submission, but on man's own virtue alone and free from any self-interest in the welfare of his supposed soul, ought to be on the higher plane – and that's without taking any account of the courage which might be involved either way. The simple question then might be whether the sum of the greater goodness of virtuous believers outweighs that of virtuous non-believers. The more practicable comparison is with their respective effects – not are we better or worse people for religion, but are we better or worse off because of it.'

'Religion brings morality and order and is the foundation of society, Favonius. Not everyone does the right thing, as we see around us all the time. We all need guidance, and so many want something better in our time on earth, and a hereafter they can understand and relate to. The great crowds Yeshua attracted show there's an immense need to channel all that hope into something expressed and organized, to make the world better and offer the prospect of eternal life to those who seek it. Yeshua is the Prince of Peace as foretold by prophecy, but it's not a social movement we're discussing, Favonius. It's God's call to arms, and we must respond.'

'There will always be the apathetic, Longinus, for whom religion is to be endured but of no consequence, the insincere who will never reform, the hypocrites who make a show of it and still won't soften their hearts – we can agree with Yeshua there. A better world, however? I'd call it a form of control, another means of keeping people compliant, the poor and voiceless in their place, in unwitting support of their superiors through their labour and their blood. Love of country should not be confused with any religion, which will often try to identify itself with country but so easily become an aggravating factor in national animosities, its power to moderate outdone by self-righteous excess.

Perhaps one day mankind will be chastened and wiser, but until then religion will continue to be a baleful presence in many of its difficulties and disputes. To err is certainly human, but if it entails making allowances for god, that's not good enough.'

* * * *

'Favonius, do you, or do you not, think Yeshua was a good man? Because if you do, you have to accept also that he wasn't misleading us, he was telling the absolute truth. And if he was telling the truth then you've got it seriously wrong.'

'Patently he was a good man, Longinus. No-one of any decency could deny that, but that doesn't make him the son of god. I'm sure he thought he was telling the absolute truth, yes, but I also think it's very simple – he was deluded. Quite simply he was mistaken.'

'How can someone so obviously sincere and with a wisdom so far beyond our own be deluded?'

'Because self-deception is a widespread human trait, Longinus, and it can take time, acuity and reflection to judge claims to wisdom. No-one can deny Yeshua's existence or the prodigious feat of his ministry, or its sincerity. He impressed many, many people, and you and I both. But we're not doctors. Irregularities in a man's mind come in many forms, and he was a man, and fallible. Clearly he believed in his god-given path, and none of us is accusing him of being a fraud – though many Jews would subscribe to that view, if chiefly as a misguided innocent, though remember, they're used to false messiahs. He was certainly highly charismatic, with a magnetism about him which made people listen, and they liked what they heard. Here was a new message, of new hope and new life. When people have so little they will respond, they will be optimistic. Only in this case optimism exceeded all bounds, almost to the point of hysteria, and everything got out of hand. When he decided to make his triumphal entry into the city to take the hierarchy on directly, it could only end one way, and when he needed them most the crowds deserted him – though that's more a comment on human nature, since he must have known they would.'

'If not the Son of God then, a false prophet?'

'No more false than any others who have laid claim to that description, Longinus. The Jews have numerous prophecies in their holy book and some of them foresee the coming of a messiah, which is bound to generate some interest when a new claimant appears. Yeshua was exceptional – the prophet of our lifetime, greater even than his harbinger and cousin whom they called the Baptist. His unshakeable self-belief and ability to impress we have seen for ourselves, but he's nevertheless been rejected by the great majority of his people. You do hear of individuals who are so fixated on something and so determined they're right that they'll keep on and on to the point of self-destruction. They might seem of sound mind but really their mental health must be questionable. I guess I know something of that only too well.'

'You're saying He deliberately sought His own death, and was mad into the bargain?'

'He thought he had to fulfil his destiny. So yes, deliberately. If you're going to be his follower you need to believe that too.'

'And I do, Favonius. The will of God has to be done if we are to be saved. It was – it is – His divine mission. As we agreed an hour ago.'

'As the scriptures would be fulfilled.'

'As the scriptures would be fulfilled. And Favonius, you're going to have to face something too. When the new scriptures come to be written which give the whole story of His deeds and sayings and the sheer wisdom and humanity contained therein, far above those of mortal men, far beyond anything the priests could have said to silence Him, and all from a humble carpenter with no education, which is what so many found truly astounding – what will you say? If they weren't from God, then where? Will you still say he was deluded?'

'I've told you how I was impressed from the beginning, astounded in fact from the moment of my servant's recovery. But I should have hesitated and asked myself the questions which I've finally had to face. Could there have been another explanation for what happened? Could it have been sheer coincidence that Yeshua the wandering preacher came to Capernaum that day, and might Matthias have got better anyway? There was no direct contact between them for me to witness – was my response just the natural reaction to a very unusual person coming into my life to dazzle it briefly with an unforgettable memory, one which was bound to affect my judgment? Was my subsequent experience compatible with those heady days? Or had I allowed myself to get carried away by Yeshua's charisma and the other accounts of his mission? You've got to be more than a remarkable man to be the son of god – a bit of an under-statement, we might think. I still need real evidence if I'm to believe again. Incontrovertible, this time. Is that so much to ask?'

'And this from you, who had the great good fortune to come into His presence and witness His power. Think of those who will believe yet will never have that privilege. But we have evidence, and lots of it. There are hundreds of people – thousands – who heard Him speak, and many who saw Him perform his miracles. Or are you saying they're all suffering from self-delusion too?'

'Many did hear him speak, Longinus. At those events where miracles are supposed to have occurred, however? – rather fewer. When you consider how close you've got to be to something to be really sure of what you're seeing – fewer still, I'd say. Thinking you've seen something and actually doing so aren't necessarily the same thing, but if you thought you'd really seen water turned into wine, or a multitude fed with a basket of food, or a deceased man alive and walking and you were convinced it wasn't an illusion, I think you'd want to do something about it. You'd spread the word. You'd seriously consider changing your long-held views on religion in favour of what the source of these miracles was saying. You'd want to write it down, if you could. You'd protest to the authorities, I hope, if they tried to arrest him. Only six days ago those crowds were out waving their palm fronds – where did they all get to on the day of reckoning? How feckless did they prove when their countrymen were out screaming for blood? How much had they really been convinced, to the point of serious cost to themselves? And that's probably what we'll see in the next few years – a trickle of people coming forward claiming to have been there and seen it, whilst everyone else will have to take it on trust.'

'And you'll discount them when they do come forward, I suppose. But what if two or three do so and leave cogent accounts, with no exaggeration or embellishment, just a recording of all the facts as known to honest men? What then? Would you say they're all delusional too?'

'I'd say credulous, Longinus. I'd want to know how far the writers were in time between their accounts and the events they describe. I'd want to know all about them as individuals – their background, their personal proximity to the characters and events they relate, what became of them. I'd want to know the extent to which they might have known, influenced or copied each other, or used oral traditions. Unless I could be very sure that they were direct eye-witnesses, or had access to reliable, close-up, eye-witness reports, then I'd have to be sceptical, because of the high standard of proof required. This isn't trivial. The question we're addressing couldn't be more important for the whole of humanity. Is there a god, and is this the Son of God?'

'And the answer, Favonius?'

'We shouldn't expect such a titanic issue to be decided for future generations on evidence which isn't of the very highest order. And if in some future beyond our imagination, people ask why this god could not reveal himself in their own time too, when they might have wondrous machines which could show his truth once and for all, and wonder why it had taken so long after centuries of confusion and strife – would you then hold their unbelief against them? Or would they have to carry on taking it all on faith about the last days and the coming of the son of man to judge the living and the dead, as though fate was cast for all time in the eighteenth year of Tiberius and no-one was ever allowed to move on?'

'Favonius, your unbelief is understandable but it does you no credit. You don't know what Yeshua's friends are going to do. They will proselytize and they're going to have a hard time, that's certain. The details are for conjecture, but when they start to record these events you can be quite sure they'll seek to do it faithfully. Their evidence will be crucial, I agree. Many who hear will be sceptical, but those with open minds and hearts will take it at face value – and why shouldn't they? In a sinful world we should welcome the gift which lights the way and leads on to the kingdom. It may take a long time but gradually more and more will come to believe. It will entail struggle, and sacrifice, and commitment, by men and women and whole nations together, like that for any other great prize, but now for the living God. Yes they will know doubt, which they will overcome because they will realize faith is the only lifeline to salvation. The pathway has to be rugged, as it was for our Saviour. Where there is rejection it will be because of men's obstinacy and failure, but that's what the Prince of Peace has come to overcome. The word of God is here to save us sinners, and the men who write it will record the truth as best they know. To ascribe any other motive ill becomes you.'

'I'm sure they'll be honourable men, Longinus, but they'll be selective because they'll have a story to impart and it's going to be from their viewpoint, while other accounts may not fit the narrative so well and won't make the main record. This will tell of what they will think was a series of miraculous events, from which nothing will be allowed to detract, but rather the contrary – creative embellishment will be justified, because the cause is so good, and if the central miracle of the resurrection occurred then the other stories must be plausible too, and can and should be woven in to support the theme. It would be interesting for example to see how they explain the story of the annunciation and virgin birth, any account of which can only be as tenuous as the myths of Olympus. Or the temptation in the wilderness, for which there seems no witness other, apparently, than Yeshua himself, the account of whose presumed relation we'll be expected to accept completely on trust. That might be unremarkable if we're happy to do so – but are we? Recorders of history can only do their best with the information available to them. It's excusable of them to write what they think they know rather than make no attempt at all, but it's also excusable of us to be sceptical if reliable corroboration of extraordinary claims is missing. I'd go further. If their accounts are to be the lynchpin for the faith of countless people in the future, I don't see why they should be exempt from questions like these – or even charges that somewhere in all this there won't be some sort of conspiracy, however well-intentioned. Because that's exactly what we're talking about here and now, by us, isn't it? But the best conspiracies don't try and break new ground entirely. They feed on existing expectation, however unlikely, involve very few people, and don't invite awkward questions.'

*　　*　　*　　*

'Favonius, when they write about the new faith they'll be faithfully recording the event, complete with witnesses.'

'No doubt they will, though it'd still be a lot more convincing if there were some real objective proof. I doubt we'll get it, because close and disinterested observation is unlikely to be available. Just as important it won't be necessary, because it will all be so miraculous, so irresistible for millions who so want it to be that way. They'll accept a low standard of proof, saying, if they were ever required to articulate their reasoning, that it convinced those who were there and met the standards of the day, when the ideas of divine deeds and a universal creator were universally accepted. There'll be eye-witnesses to the empty tomb, which we'd expect – we ourselves, if this proposal goes ahead, could hardly succeed without them – and probably to encounters with the risen Yeshua too. But to a body actually in the act of disappearing before people's eyes, in full view? Like the other professed miracles, reliable evidence will be in very short supply, and there's always the old problem of hearsay, which tends to distort and exaggerate. Yet the resurrection will become the irrefutable crux of faith, and lack of real proof won't really matter. Nor in a sense will it matter who or what is behind the acclaimed miracle, since it will be readily taken for granted that such a truly stupendous event could only be by act of god, and only serve to make the other claimed miracles credible too. In reality something rather more prosaic will have had to initiate it, something we decide on this very night – but there'll still be no doubt for the narrators or their readers. It will have come to pass, and they will block their ears to alternative explanations.'

*　　*　　*　　*

'If I can come in here, gentlemen. Not everyone's as – shall we say, imaginative – as the Governor, but perhaps Facilis has a point. Quite how anyone in the future would conclusively prove there's no plot by any party, I don't know. Save for Festus, I imagine, we've accepted the chroniclers of Yeshua's story will be men of good faith – we have to take that as a given, though they'll probably err on the credulous side – and that their work will be remembered for many a year. As for us Romans, the Governor might well be remembered for his decision yesterday, and perhaps the Senior Centurion, but that's all – the rest of us will be completely forgotten. Few out there will ever suspect the truth of our involvement – and that's how it should stay. There might be some intermittent debate in the margins about whether we or the High Priest provided the guard, but we've been into that. Leaving aside the question of its integrity, on the importance of the claim itself there will be little dispute. The Nazarene's rising will take its place as one of the great watersheds of history for believers and non-believers alike, and the Roman Army, already indelibly stained with the crucifixion, will now also be linked to the resurrection and its inevitable consequences. For the Governor's assumption must be correct. With such an extraordinary and apparently incontrovertible vindication of the self-proclaimed son of god, how could a new faith in his name fail to succeed?'

'So the blood will be on our hands, Prefect. Not just the holy blood of the Saviour already shed but of the martyrs who will follow, the ones who will die on the orders of the Sanhedrin and the many in other lands who will follow down the ages for professing their faith. To act now is to condemn them as surely as any tyrant.'

'That'll be the case whatever we do now, Senior Centurion. It's the divine destiny, remember?'

'Prefect, it comes down to accepting God's will. We cannot tell his plan. All we can do is trust in his love for all men, and believe. Some people will always have difficulty, like my friend here in his present state, but we can't let their unbelief stand in the way. They'll always be suspicious, but lack of witness testimony to the absolute standards they'd like doesn't make believers' acceptance unfounded. Right from the beginning Yeshua's humble birth may have been loosely recorded, but what do we expect when so few people were able to make records of any kind, or have any inkling how His destiny was to be made manifest? That won't be the case for His ministry now, or His death and Resurrection. We can be very sure of that.'

'That won't satisfy the credibility problem.'

'What we should be more concerned about right now, Prefect, is what's going to happen next. Let me tell you. Yes, people are going to be put to death, because no government, no established religion, will tolerate a rival movement in its midst. The close followers, the proselytizers, the writers who profess the new teaching and refuse to renounce it – they'll be seen as subversives putting the existing order at risk. Wherever it's taken the new faith will meet the same reaction of violent repression. But the missionaries and the adherents will persevere bravely. In time people will get used to it, begin to accept it, and then as so often happens throughout history, what starts as strange and unwelcome becomes the norm, and then behold! – it becomes our very own, celebrated in Rome itself, and irony will once more have had its way. You're right, Prefect. Eventually it holds sway across the earth, in places of which presently we have no knowledge, because people of goodwill will be attracted to these ideas in great numbers. I truly believe that.

'And Favonius, you might be right. Some may be drawn because they're irrational or weak or tender-hearted, in your view at any rate. But it's better than anything else that's ever come before – God's grace and providence, bestowed freely on mankind for all time. All because of the early martyrs, inspired by Yeshua himself, who dies on the cross to make it all possible, to take away our sins and be our advocate in heaven, and for all who follow too, purely for their faith in the risen Lord. Now, you tell me, Favonius. If we agree their own self-sacrifice is now unavoidable whatever we do, why would those saints suffer unto death, often in the most brutal of ways, if they didn't believe what He'd said with every ounce of moral and physical strength human beings can muster?'

'For the same reasons the chroniclers will write what they will write, Longinus. The martyrs will be doing god's work, and their inspiration will be the glorious resurrection of their lord. It is much to be regretted that their deaths would be the direct results of our actions tonight, but we can console ourselves. It's like accepting casualties in war, and accepting you might be one yourself. Any self-sacrifice of one's life in a truly proven cause is to be endued with greatness. We of all men can subscribe to that.'

'You would have them die for a lie.'

'For their good cause. Not for any conspiracy to which they weren't party, Longinus, but for your truth. It's harsh, I know, but the only thing that sacrificial gestures prove is that people are prepared to die for what they believe in. We can't help that. Man in his folly is capable of every sort of error conceivable, by individuals and whole peoples, so we shouldn't be surprised. We convince ourselves but make mistakes, and the so-called wisdom of the crowd becomes collective insanity. But that's not justification, it's just more folly.'

'And the Governor's idea isn't?'

'We've gone into that. I wish it wasn't necessary, but I'm afraid it looks as though it is. This is about the greatest good, nothing else.'

'This new belief isn't just wishful thinking, Favonius, however much you try and link it to human weakness. It's taking on trust the words and deeds of Yeshua of Nazareth.'

'But that doesn't just apply to home-spun words of wisdom, Longinus. It's also acceptance of miracles which we can only describe as dubious, news of which had to be spread from the beginning if the movement was to gain traction. Do we have to go through this again?'

'And to deny those is to take those who were there for fools? You wouldn't expect anyone who was there to keep quiet about things like that, would you? Are people going to make up stories about walking on water, or the recent dead walking out of tombs among astonished relatives, if they weren't true? People aren't stupid – nobody wants to be ridiculed.'

'And because they were good and honest people, like their lord, they must be right, and have to be believed? They could have been mistaken. I don't know how – it's for them to prove, not me to disprove. Let's face it – rumour and speculation, not to say disinformation, are facts of life in any society and get muddled up with many a cause, good and not-so-good.'

'So He was disingenuous, as well as deluded? In fact by all accounts His deeds were invariably accomplished with the utmost modesty. He would command the sick He had just healed not to tell anyone, though of course they did. He never courted crowds – they came to Him, and in Galilee He sometimes had to escape them. Where the people lacked faith He would move on, because it was faith that was needed for His power to work. He was driven out of His home town because the inhabitants couldn't see why He should have the privilege or capacity to preach to them. Others were drawn by His reputation, just like you were, Favonius, because they wanted to hear, and recognized He was addressing their needs, especially those of the common people in all their poverty. As soon as He was able He would withdraw and find a quiet place to pray. Does that strike you as the behaviour of a rabble-rouser?'

'I never said he was a rabble-rouser. Though he probably knew very well if you restore sight to the blind and tell them to keep quiet about it, the news will travel even quicker. I've already said – the only question is whether the proclaimed miracle really happened. What was the blind man's precise condition? What did Yeshua actually do to cure it? Was it anything that a good doctor couldn't have done? Was it a coincidence of some sort? Was it witnessed by a reliable witness, and preferably more than one? Within a very short time of something like that supposedly happening, we can be sure the facts get lost in the telling. I'm not saying something didn't take place. With Matthias I was that witness, indeed I played my own role in the spreading of the news, which went like wildfire. But I can't swear now his recovery was a miracle. It looked like one at the time, and you know how it affected me, but I just can't be absolutely certain – not enough anyway to stake my life on it, or devote the rest of it to a god which now I don't believe exists. And you know my later troubles. I didn't need a miracle. I just needed to use my own judgment, determine my own resolution, and perhaps have a bit of luck and a helping hand for my family.'

'Which is why we have to have faith, Favonius. That things will somehow be better in the end, though what we may think an obvious good is denied us now. I'm afraid you have to face the fact that the break-up with Sabena could be the best thing for the children, and for you too, even if it means they will have a step-father in their lives from now on. You don't know how staying together would have worked out. God will provide you happiness elsewhere and keep you close to your children somehow. You mustn't allow this to cloud your judgment and turn you away from the best invitation any of us will ever have. Think of the good things in all this. That Yeshua – the Christ – knows your sorrow and travail and has taken the burden from you, that He came into the world to save sinners like us and has shown us the way to live. Don't throw it away. Don't be sceptical. Let the Holy Spirit come upon you so you may believe again.'

'I can't hear you without tenderness, my dear Longinus. This is the point of decision, I know, which no man should take lightly. The prospect of a lonely life, without the comfort of this faith, and at the last the terror of the unknown – I'll grant that's daunting for every person who ever lived. Of course it is, and yes, I'm still impressed by Yeshua. But my faith is in the truth I am most sure of. If I'm wrong then may your god forgive me. If I'm right then I must remember the goodness Yeshua personified and do my best to live up to it in my own way, for I do realize that his was the greatest possible example of how we should try to live our lives. And that none of us will ever be quite the same again.'

'Can't you at least say you don't know? We've talked of the many who only go through the outward motions of faith. They get by. Agnostics get by. They reserve their position, even if it means keeping their thoughts to themselves. They don't cut themselves off from all hope of salvation.'

'I think we need to be braver, Longinus. To say that nothing can be known or is likely to be known about any god might be strictly correct, but it ducks the issue. Until there's any convincing proof we should base our thinking on the balance of probabilities, and thus acknowledge their great preponderance against theism in all its forms. We should step out free of fear, being grateful we're not to be put, we hope, in quite the same position as Socrates in ancient times. I've said I will do of our official religion what's expected in public. Our more enlightened descendants may find freedom to make their views more fully known, and be able to withdraw from the tyranny of religion altogether – or they may not. I sincerely hope they can. If we ever get a properly free and enlightened society the choice would be available as a matter of course, and there is no question what it should be. When men look up at the stars they should wonder but not be frightened, and have the courage to face the truth – that we are alone.'

'Gentlemen, gentlemen. We must move on.'

* * * *

And they talked on, tired now, into the night.

* * * *

'We were saying. Evidence.'

'Yes. The parables. His many sayings – their sheer power. And the wisdom and logic of His replies to the scribes, and to the Governor yesterday. Unanswerable by the learned of the land, beyond the power of mortal man to devise. How do you account for that?'

'I can't, Longinus. Other than to repeat my admission, that he was a very gifted and unusual individual, with great presence and composure, who affected all who met him. But that doesn't make him the son of god.'

'So what would convince you now, who have come so far but are still so far off?'

'An empty tomb, Longinus. Which I could see for myself. That I knew for certain had been well guarded throughout and hadn't been interfered with. But it's not going to happen, any more than a virgin birth. Is it, Prefect?'

'Well, you two. You're never going to agree, that's obvious. But it's been good to hear you put your cases. It's been … most interesting. And now you seem to have returned us to the point of this discussion. We need to draw things together and decide what we're doing.'

THE DELIBERATION – V

'Your final word, Senior Centurion.'

'The tomb will be empty alright, but not by our hand, or any other living one.'

'Just god's.'

'Yes, Prefect. God's alone. The last thing we should be is so brazenly presumptuous as to interfere with God's plan.'

'Even though, after this, the fact can't be known with any certainty?'

'It will be for me, and many others too. Any meddling by us won't make the slightest difference – we'll be irrelevant whatever we do. The Son of God will have risen.'

'Which is rather the Governor's aim, isn't it?'

'Don't you want to know the truth?'

'Perhaps the almighty will just have to find another way to prove himself, eh?'

'Prefect, this is the time. This is the place. I ask again. Do you want to know the truth?'

'Festus, what do you think?'

'I think we've heard everything there is to know about the Nazarene and his message. To me it's all nonsensical conjecture, a passing little tale from a forgotten corner of the Empire – an empire built on faith in the true Gods and the *genius* of Rome. If the tomb's left long enough before the dawn, opened and found to be empty, then I guess we'd have to think again – but it's entirely fanciful since that could never be possible. If it's still occupied, which will certainly be the case, well, then we'll prove it's all nonsense and we can give thanks to Mighty Jove. After that anyone can do what they like, but I'm not going to lose any sleep over it. Nothing important will have changed. The god of the Nazarene, whoever he is, will have failed, and in a year or so someone will look in again and find a decomposing body in its shroud. Which is how it should be.'

'Yes, we've got to move before first-light if we're going to do this – to be caught in broad daylight would cause mayhem with the Jews. But on the central issue, to leave the matter to this new-look god, or to his non-existence according to preference, when there's so much at stake? Are we any nearer? Favonius?'

'Neither of the others wants to do this, Prefect, that's clear. The old is indefensible but, for Festus, still trumps everything – look but don't touch, don't act other than display a body for the Jews' delight, carry on. But then the Senior Centurion can't countenance anything which could be construed as challenging the new, and I don't want to deny him the chance to find it. It does at least have the merit of novelty, though it is, I believe, equally baseless. And I don't like the idea of attempting to alter human behaviour on a lie, which is what this whole proposition amounts to. I worry it could become a Pandora's box of unintended consequences which can only add to the confusion and troubles of the world, and compete with reason and concord in the affairs of men. I would far rather no religion at all, in the hope that men might quicker find true enlightenment.

'But I also acknowledge that without some radical new thinking based on self-denial and really trying to love our neighbour, mankind could well destroy itself. It might do that anyway, in ways we can't possibly conceive, but if religion does persist into a more rational and knowledgeable age it's nevertheless likely to remain a contributory factor in the frictions to which the human race seems indefinitely fated. Religion long ago cast its grip and seems set to keep it. We have to accept that the universal need to believe is part of our make-up, will be a very long time a-going, and that we'd have to become very different creatures before we are mature enough to cast it off. Our slow and erratic progress amid countless wars and struggles of all kinds might allow a kindlier and freer existence for us one day, but that will be so far in the future it will be of little comfort to us now or the generations which follow. The city mob with its bread and circuses already frightens me, and we hear of far-off lands where men live in great profusion, with strange beliefs and customs of their own. Is all this god-worship ever likely to bring harmony to fractious mankind? Is this the future – with our numbers like sand-grains on the seashore and the incessant clash of so many different truths?

'All I can say in the end, having had some brush with this thing called faith, is that as long as people are determined to hang on to notions of religion, if any call to god is to temper the human race, then this is the one to do it – the way of Yeshua of Nazareth, for all the good reasons we've heard about from the Senior Centurion, though you've heard me regret I personally cannot hold them true. In war we soldiers would have no hesitation engaging in deception, its justification simple – the achievement of victory, the bringing of peace, the ending of man-made suffering. Outside a state of war deception is never attractive, but it's the elemental nature of the human mind and the unique and limitless scale of the possibilities before us in this proposal which force the issue. If it takes a lie to save mankind from itself – the greatest deception in human history – so be it. This is, I believe, the only resurrection on offer. I'm sorry, my friend.'

'Does it matter, Facilis – any of this?'

'Of course it matters, Prefect. If men can't accept the truth then the next-best thing is its judicious re-fashioning to give the next-best outcome.'

'Seems clear enough to me. I take it that doesn't change your position, Senior Centurion?'

'No, Prefect. I want to see the glory of the living God, proved beyond all doubt.'

'Festus?'

'I can see the Governor's point. Difficult. It would completely go against everything I believe in.'

'We're trying to wind up here, Festus. Are we to remove the body or not?'

'No. We must stand with our inheritance, or face the wrath of Jupiter Maximus for daring to undermine His power with any impostor, real or imaginary.'

'Which leaves me, I suppose. Well I won't beat about the bush. It may not entirely surprise you I'm with Facilis, less perhaps some of his philosophizing – and of course the Governor, though we have yet to get his confirmation. And I can be more candid about the Governor's own view now. I believe he's a man acutely conscious of his place in history, trapped by a vision of perpetual disgrace whatever he does after this, but determined to try and make something good of it too. He didn't start out with this intention, but the fates have brought him to it. He believes that the opportunity outlined tonight is here, for mortal men to reach for the power of heaven themselves. An extraordinary claim of course, and ironically only possible because it is so very extraordinary. He won't deny a small satisfaction in unsettling the native establishment of this Province with which he's had so many disputes, and has asked me to convey his thanks for your forbearance in that regard – we were not to allow any such feelings to detract from the greater consideration, and I don't think we have. However, we were enjoined to enter this discussion with mature and equal voice, and he thanks you, as do I, for doing so –to reach a decision on something infinitely more important. Fittingly perhaps we are split equally at its end.

'Wait here gentlemen whilst I fetch the Governor. I won't be long.'

THE DELIBERATION – VI

'What will you do now, Favonius?'

'I think I'll ask to go back to the Twentieth. It'll be good to get some fresh northern air again. And you?'

'Looks like I'll have to keep an eye on Centurion Facilis, doesn't it? But after all you tiresome Romans it'll be the quiet life for me now. I'll make my way again as a trooper in the cavalry, my first love. They tell me First Thracians are still attached to the Twentieth. That is if Veranius can see his way to fixing it.'

'I dare say the Commanding Officer will be able to arrange something, Centurion Longinus.'

*   *   *   *

The sentry let him through. The house slave was stood by the doorway, and disappeared for a moment before returning to admit him. Pontius Pilatus was stirring from the chair in which he had been dozing.

'Well, Veranius?'

'We're evenly divided, Your Excellency.'

'I'll get my cloak. It's a cold night.'

As they made their way through the colonnades Tribune Veranius attempted the briefest of summaries. Racking his wits for any glimmer of coherence after such a long discussion, wishing the Governor would only stop and let him explain properly, he rather disconcerted himself, rambling on how it could not have been a more thorough or far-reaching debate, to which everyone had contributed positively and there could be no aspect which hadn't been considered in some depth. His efforts were of little avail: there was no time, and Pilatus wasn't stopping. Attribution of opinion was proving difficult, balanced summary unattainable, the finer points impossible. Dear Jove, was mankind's future to be decided so precipitately?

'The only problem now, Veranius, is whether I have to use the authority of office, as well as my casting vote', said the Governor as he paused a few steps short. 'I'd rather not, but needs must.'

Veranius wanted to say he was sure that wouldn't be necessary, or yes, he didn't intend to mean that applied to the aforementioned vote, he meant … 'Indeed, Your Excellency.'

It was after all extremely late. And he could take some pride. He'd held it all together. And, he admitted to himself, even he had learned something.

'We'll see', the Governor said.

*   *   *   *

They got to their feet as one.

'Good evening. Or is it "good morning?"'

'Good morning, Your Excellency!'

'Do resume your seats.'

'Well gentlemen, your Prefect tells me you've had a very full and interesting discussion, but that Second Italian are split fifty / fifty. Let me guess. The Senior Centurion is keen to let the prophecy be proved – *id est* in the proper manner, so to speak. Quite understandable, given his recent experience. He is joined by Centurion III, who as a traditionalist has commendable reservations about the possible effect on our Roman religion. Opposing you both are Centurion V, who has misgivings about being over-creative but has reluctantly come round to the argument. And finally your Prefect, who very wisely favours the view of the senior officer present, who just happens to be me, your Commander-in-Chief. An analysis not entirely due to prescience, you'll be pleased to hear – he did manage to brief me quite thoroughly. Is there anything anyone wishes to add?

'No? Very well. It appears I am to have the casting vote. Before we draw these proceedings to a close, let me say thank you for your invaluable assistance in this matter. I know you have pondered the issues to the best of your considerable abilities. You will have weighed the arguments and gone into many of the more pertinent aspects of the religious and wider issues, searching your consciences and endeavouring to identify the merits and possible consequences of the two options open.

'For my part, that process is complete, to my satisfaction at least. We may take some comfort that, with very few exceptions, we share the company of the whole human race in our individual and ultimate insignificance in the great story of its time on earth. We are creatures of time and space, not knowing what life holds for us – fortuitously, no doubt – and allotted only the shortest of spans in which to have our being and leave our little mark. Powers and kingdoms come and go, great events as well as the numberless humdrum ones, all alike turning so much on chance, whatever the designs of puny man. But tonight there is that rarest of things – one of those very few exceptions. For we few find ourselves with the opportunity to make not only man's history but also his distant future – a sequel to what happened in this city yesterday, though which for its success must of necessity remain totally hidden and unknown. A score of lifetimes might pass before that peculiar conjunction of circumstance arise whereby one small single act might truly be said to change our destiny. The question is whether we gathered here should recognize this moment, and thus our great responsibility. To be bold, or let the moment slip from our grasp. This deliberation has given us the answer. It's been close, very close, but it is now my duty to decide the final outcome.'

'Are there any questions?'

'Very well. Tribune Veranius, it must be well into the second watch. You'd better be quick.'

EPILOGUE

The September light flooded through the magnificent Early Perpendicular east window, the heads of the apostles and great stories of the New Testament brought to life in a rich blaze of colour, strong but subtle and very beautiful, a credit to Victorian craftsmanship. A sepia wash flooded the interior, accentuating memorials to the ancient dead, glinting on silver candlestick and brass eagle-head, lightening the crossed Union Flags atop the faded roll of honour, the near-empty pews of burnished pine, the flaking whitewash and the rough-hewn ashlar of the nave columns with their primitive carvings, the uneven and off-centre chancel arch built by country masons, the high timbered ceiling defying the ages and the elements, the weathered door, still open because it was no-one's job to shut and because it was good to let the warm air into the hymn-book must of this cool and hallowed space. Through it came the lowing of cattle, the cawing of crows in the great beeches, the tchacks of jackdaws around the red sandstone-quoined tower. Distraction might have vied with concentration. The lay-reader was saying something that caught the ear, his distinctive colonial accent adding clarity and precision to what he was saying.

'... there can only have been three explanations. His family and friends could have taken the body, but if so then why did the gospel writers give us the accounts they did, and why did so many go on to die terrible deaths steadfast in their belief in the risen Lord? They would hardly have done so if they had not believed. Or the Jewish authorities stole the body away in order to forestall any claim from his followers that Jesus had risen from the dead. If they had the body they would be able to refute any such claim. We know from Matthew they were very alert to the possibility of a resurrection cult, and that they were keen on the tomb being properly sealed and guarded.   But again we know from the gospel accounts there was no body on that first Easter Morning, so is that a plausible explanation either?   We are left therefore with the only option that makes any sense, that it is indeed the truth that Jesus Christ rose from the dead, that He is the Son of God, the Truth and the Way, that the Lord of Life died for us and wants us so much to come to Him and try, however feebly, to follow Him in everything we do and say.'

*   *   *   *

And they all said 'Amen,' as they had done on that spot where the Anglo-Saxons had buried their pagan dead and first started to worship this new god under roofs of thatch and oak fifteen hundred years before, not many a day's march from the mortal remains in the rich soil of Britannia of two soldiers of the Roman Army, who in their own ways brought the Word to the new land and thereby to the whole wide world.

The tombstones of
Marcus Favonius Facilis, Twentieth Legion
and
Longinus Sdapeze, First Thracian Cavalry
were discovered in 1868 and 1928/1996 respectively
and are on display in Castle Museum Colchester, Essex

Both were found damaged, probably from
the Boudican Revolt of AD 60 or 61

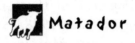 Matador

For exclusive discounts on Matador titles,
sign up to our occasional newsletter at
troubador.co.uk/bookshop